Lord Angle Theta and his men seemed unstoppable. Unbeatable. No matter the odds against them.
But when they met their match in the swamps of storied Jutenheim, Lomerian blood ran like rivers.

Ector and Malcolm Eotrus had a simple duty. Keep safe their family's mighty fortress, as had their ancestors for untold centuries.
They failed.
Trolls loped out of the northern mists, a hunger for man-flesh in their bellies.
The trolls took what they wanted.
They didn't even leave the bones behind.

Karktan of Malvegil knew that the Black Hand assassins had hunted his beloved lord for years.
They finally caught him. Murdered him, along with Karktan's brother, and Lomion's troubled king.
Now Kartkan is hunting them.

Frem Sorlons and his Pointmen could fight their way out of anything. Until they found themselves trapped between an army of bloodthirsty Ettins and the relentless legions of Svartleheim.

Time and again, Lomerian wizards conquered challenges that brawn and brain alone could not master.

But magic has a weighty price.

Even the greatest sorcerers cannot escape the Wizard's Toll.

BOOKS BY GLENN G. THATER

THE HARBINGER OF DOOM SAGA

GATEWAY TO NIFLEHEIM
THE FALLEN ANGLE
KNIGHT ETERNAL
DWELLERS OF THE DEEP
BLOOD, FIRE, AND THORN
GODS OF THE SWORD
THE SHAMBLING DEAD
MASTER OF THE DEAD
SHADOW OF DOOM
WIZARD'S TOLL
VOLUME 11+ (FORTHCOMING)

HARBINGER OF DOOM
(COMBINES *GATEWAY TO NIFLEHEIM* AND *THE FALLEN ANGLE* INTO A SINGLE VOLUME)

THE HERO AND THE FIEND
(A NOVELETTE SET IN THE HARBINGER OF DOOM UNIVERSE)

THE GATEWAY
(A NOVELLA LENGTH VERSION OF *GATEWAY TO NIFLEHEIM*)

THE DEMON KING OF BERGHER
(A SHORT STORY SET IN THE HARBINGER OF DOOM UNIVERSE)

To be notified about my new book releases and any special offers or discounts regarding my books, please join my mailing list here: http://eepurl.com/vwubH

GLENN G. THATER

WIZARD'S TOLL

A TALE FROM THE
HARBINGER OF DOOM SAGA

This book is a work of fiction. Names, characters, places, and incidents herein are either the product of the author's imagination or are used fictitiously. Any resemblance to actual persons, living or dead, events, or locales is entirely coincidental.

Copyright © 2015 by Glenn G. Thater.

All rights reserved.

WIZARD'S TOLL © 2015 by Glenn G. Thater

ISBN-13: 978-0692592168
ISBN-10: 0692592164

Visit Glenn G. Thater's website at
http://www.glenngthater.com

December 2015 Print Edition
Published by Lomion Press

1

LOTHMARGEN PLAINS

THE AGE OF HEROES

MILTON DEBOORS

DeBoors rushed through the camp to the command tent. He hated being late.

The cordon around the tent was tight. Men from List, Tyre, and Myrr were on one side. On the other, Miskelstrans from the Dragoth Peaks lined up shoulder to shoulder, their golden helmets gleaming in the early-morning sun. A contingent of wild men from The Horn were there, unable to quiet themselves. A group of heavy foot from Drogan Bay. Horsemen from Dingel.

The men of Tyre knew DeBoors' face, so he passed unmolested to the command tent's entrance. The stooped wizard at the flap eyed him up and down with milky eyes, and spat some cantrip his way. The old mage pondered him for several moments and then, satisfied, stepped aside without a word.

The great men sat in big chairs about a round table, all their battle gear donned and ready, save for their helmets, which hung with their shields from the backs of their chairs. Azrael the Wise was speaking, his plate armor, emerald green, urging caution about something. Mithron was there at the table, of course, his armor and cape black as obsidian. Thetan sat across from him, armor of midnight blue, shield to match. Gabriel was there. So was Master Rascatlan, Uriel the Bold, Blazren, Steriel, Hogar, Dekkar, and Bose. So too was Hoenir the Swift, Vidar the Silent, Magni the Strong, and Njord of the Sea, all in their places. Emperor Gladsol sat the table with them, as did King Melkar of Ulek Morn. Lesser men: generals, dukes, princes, and assorted kings, sat in rows about the tent's perimeter.

"Only by bold maneuver have we achieved our greatest victories," said Gabriel. "If we embrace caution now, as Azrael counsels, we weaken our position and lengthen this conflict for who knows how many more years."

"Bold maneuvers were fine when we tracked individual creatures," said Azrael. "But now we face an entire city of fiends. We know not their numbers, their defenses. They could have anything in there."

"I have counseled for weeks that we should plan for a long siege," said King Melkar.

"They may have creatures that fly," said Gabriel.

"What do you mean, creatures that fly?" said the emperor.

"Wyvern, Roc, Dragon, or Wyrm," said Rascatlan.

"You jest?" said the emperor.

"The enemy commands such beasts," said Gabriel. "Though we know not if Malik-Morn yet harbors any."

"What is your counsel, Lord Thetan?" said Mithron.

"A rapid assault from all sides," said Thetan. "We hit them with everything we have, all at once. If we catch them off guard, they'll panic. And in that panic we'll find victory."

"What losses can we expect?" said the emperor.

"The cost will be great," said Thetan. "But this deed must be done. And if we are victorious, onward we must go to R'yleh. This age of monsters must end."

2

DOR EOTRUS THE FIRST UNDERHALL

YEAR 1267, 4TH AGE
LAST YEAR OF KING TENZIVEL'S RULE

SERGEANT BARET

Sir Sarbek du Martegran, Dor Eotrus's acting castellan, held court in the temporary command center in the First Underhall, below Dor Eotrus's Odinhome. It was a large room by any standard, yet that day it felt cramped and close; being a basement, the ceiling was lower than elsewhere in the Dor, the decor was spartan, and the place was crowded with men and stacks of supplies. The lighting was better than you might expect considering it had no natural light, but the air tended toward stale, musty, and damp.

Sarbek stood at the room's center and leaned over the wood and stone model of Dor Eotrus that dominated the place. The Dor's named men gathered around that model. Sir Ector Eotrus was at Sarbek's right hand, Sir Indigo Eldswroth at his left. The captains of this battalion and that troop lined the table two rows deep. Captain Pellan, the Beardless Dwarf, was there, as were all the ranking officers except those few that couldn't be spared from the walls or other critical locations.

The model, Brother Donnelin's work, depicted

the central tower, the Odinhome, all the outbuildings, the walls, the Outer Dor and all its myriad buildings and winding ways, the moat — everything, and all constructed of wood and stone to an accurate scale and intricate detail that made it not only a practical tool, but a work of art. Many years back, Donnelin added ingenious winch systems to the model, which raised the buildings, bringing the underground levels up to the surface for easy viewing (when not so raised, they hung below the table — a hole in the table beneath the base of each building with a basement). The roofs of the buildings came off, and the backs opened up, to allow access to every level, every room. Sarbek had the whole thing hauled down from the central tower's war room and hastily reset. It wasn't set up quite right but it was close enough; the best they could do on short notice, considering.

The officers debated strategy in grim and serious tones as they repositioned wooden figures, carved in the likenesses of soldiers, around the tabletop – resetting them based on recent troop movements and the latest observations of the enemy. Many of the figures that populated the model were meticulously sculpted, and painted in accurate hues, as finely wrought as those from the prize *Mages and Monsters* game sets the wealthy purchased on Merchant's Way in Lomion City. Each of the friendly pieces represented a key squadron, or a company, a full battalion, or a named man or officer of import. Some of the figures were so exquisitely crafted that one could tell at a glance who they represented; the relative heights were right, the body shapes, hair color, the cut and color of the uniforms, the sigils, stripes, and flourishes, even the characteristic expressions on their faces. Sarbek's figure was there, as was one for Ector, Indigo, Leren Sverdes, Captain Pellan, and all the rest.

Sarbek held Malcolm Eotrus's wooden figure in his hand; the figure's left arm missing below the elbow. Sarbek didn't know where about the model to place that figure. And that was the problem.

Sergeant Baret, his heavy gray mustache turned down that day instead of up, entered the chamber in full-dress uniform — all polished brass, deep blues, brick reds, and bleached whites. Baret approached the war council, no doubt wondering how best to get Sarbek's attention, steeped as he was in the heady debate. Baret's shorter, corpulent shadow, Corporal Graham, was a step behind him, padding silently along despite his bulk and the arsenal he carried everywhere.

There wasn't a man at the war council, Sarbek included, that intimidated Baret, old-school veteran that he was, but still, he didn't like interrupting officers. Too often that led to some sharp retort or unwarranted insult directed his way. He never had much stomach or patience for that sort of behavior, and less so nowadays, age coming on apace. In times past, his reaction to the blue bloods' barbs had gotten him into more trouble than was good for him. No doubt, that was what kept him from a major command of his own — though that was fine with him. He preferred to work for a living. Even so, he came to learn that it was best to avoid officers, except when they couldn't be avoided. He gave respect to them, where and when it was due, not because he had to, but because it was right and proper, and he expected the same in return. When it wasn't due, he didn't give it, come what may. He'd shed his blood for the Eotrus over the previous forty years, and he figured that that should buy him respect, if nothing else. All things considered, he was honored to serve them. They were good folk, the Eotrus. Mayhap the best of all the Lomerian nobles.

Sarbek saw Baret coming. The old castellan didn't miss much. Hell, he didn't miss anything.

"It's not parade day, Mister," said Sarbek before his eyes flicked from Baret to Graham, and then searched around behind them. The gathered officers took notice and stopped talking. The room went silent. All eyes turned to Baret.

"If I'm to meet the All-father this day, castellan," said Baret, "I aim to be properly dressed."

Sarbek's face drew into a scowl, his eyebrows arching up the way they did. He opened his mouth to speak again, but before he did, Baret interrupted.

"He wouldn't come," said Baret, his voice strong, confident, and serious. "I told him you wanted him back here straightaway. Told him it wasn't optional. But he said no. Said it was his duty to stay on the wall. Said an Eotrus had to be there with the men, come what may. Said he was gonna stay and that was that."

Sarbek's voice went low and slow. "I will not lose another Eotrus under my watch, Mister. I will not. Not today. Not tomorrow. Not ever again."

"The boy is a cripple," Sarbek continued. "He can't fight. He's got no business on the wall. Fetch Malcolm back here, Mister Baret. If he doesn't come willingly, pick him the hell up, and carry him. Do you understand me?"

"Aye," said Baret. His eyes studied the gathered officers for a moment, looking quickly from man to man. There were no snickers hovering in the corners, no snide remarks nipping at his ears. And that was good. He wouldn't suffer that. Not that day.

What he did see was concern. Grave concern on the officers' faces. Most of their eyes were already fixed back on the model and the troops depicted therein.

They were worried. Smart men were they. Experienced officers. Not some uniformed dandies out on tourney day.

They knew what was out there.

And they knew the walls weren't going to stop them.

It was going to be a hard day. A red day. A day awash of blood, sorrow, and tears. The Eotrus had weathered many such days. Too many in recent times. Baret figured they'd weather that one too, one way or another.

"Tell Malcolm that I need him here," said Ector. "That I need his counsel."

Baret nodded, turned, and began to march away, Graham beside him.

"Ten minutes," said Sarbek.

"Here it comes," muttered Baret shaking his head and then gritting his teeth.

"You have that boy here within ten minutes,

or I will feed your sorry behinds to the trolls."

3

DOR EOTRUS ON THE BATTLEMENTS

***YEAR 1267, 4TH AGE
LAST YEAR OF KING TENZIVEL'S RULE***

MALCOLM EOTRUS

Sir Malcolm Eotrus heaved up another rock and made ready to toss it over Dor Eotrus's battlements. It was a big stone. One hundred pounds at the least. Before that day, the Eotrus troopers wouldn't have guessed that Malcolm could handle such a load, skinny and crippled as he was. He hadn't been the same since the day a solitary messenger called on the Dor, asking after the Eotrus brothers. The cowled and fetid envoy carried a missive – a ransom demand for the safe return of Malcolm's father, Lord Aradon (who Malcolm and his brothers believed to have been recently killed in the Vermion Forest).

The missive was a ruse. A fraud designed to draw the Eotrus brothers away from the safety of their castle. Away from their tall walls and stalwart guardsmen.

Malcolm, who was little more than a boy, the youngest, and most hotheaded of Aradon's brood, had no interest in hearing what the messenger had to say. Once he knew that the messenger was in league with those who ambushed his father,

Malcolm's sword — still sharp from his knighting — sprang to action. He skewered the messenger through the chest before anyone could stop him.

Unfortunately for Malcolm and the folk of the Dor, the messenger was no living man. He . . . no — it, was a creature, a thing conjured up from the Nether Realms by the wizards of the League of Shadows. By what dark and evil magic they found that thing and brought it forth to Midgaard, no goodly man could say, for conjurings were unknown in the North, save for in song and story.

The messenger wreaked havoc at Dor Eotrus that day, for it could not be killed by sword or axe, arrow or bolt, hammer or club, or by any force of arms that the Eotrus could muster against it. Worse, its merest touch was death. Anything that its bony fingers so much as brushed: skin, cloth, wood, or metal, fell victim to its evil magic.

Many men died.

Good men. Brave men. Men that deserved a better fate.

The messenger's dark work was a terrible thing to behold. For it instantly burned whatever it touched to ash. Malcolm's sword went that way; the withering traveling from tip to hilt in seconds. Not comprehending what was happening, Malcolm froze for a moment after he stabbed the thing. If he had been thinking straight, if he had not panicked for that brief instant, he could've thrown down the hilt and been left unscathed.

But to his everlasting regret, that's not what happened. As his sword blackened and turned to ash, the wasting roaring toward him, Malcolm stood rigid and openmouthed, shock and disbelief filling his face. That hesitation lasted but a moment, but that moment was too long. It was only the actions of Sir Marzdan, the watch captain of the gate, that saved his life. Malcolm would've died there that day, were it not for the good captain. He would've died right there, at the gates of the Outer Dor, his home, in the heart of Eotrus demesne. At the center of Eotrus power. A place that should've been safe for him; for all his family.

It was no longer.

The world had changed.

It changed the day the wizards from the League of Shadows wrenched open that godforsaken gateway to Nifleheim in the Vermion Forest; the day the Lords of Nifleheim infiltrated Midgaard and put into motion their evil schemes.

There was no going back. Not to the way things were. Nothing would ever be again the way that it had been. That was a frightful thought. But it was the truth. A truth that Malcolm and all the Eotrus had to face. The same truth that had to be faced by all who knew of the Nifleheim Lords and their dark plans to bring back their long-lost god, Azathoth, to the world of man.

If not for Captain Marzdan, Malcolm's part to play in that great struggle would've ended that day. He would've been burned to ash, just like his sword. Perhaps he should have been. Perhaps he deserved it for his brash foolishness in attacking the messenger; for his stupidity.

Instead, a good man died in his place. Marzdan died in his place. A named man that had served the Eotrus faithfully, heroically, for decades, in campaign after campaign with Lord Aradon and his fellows. The good captain was rewarded for his heroism with a horrific, albeit swift, death. He was burned to ash, helm to boot, when he fell atop Malcolm's sword in the act of knocking it away from the young nobleman's hand.

In seconds, nothing of Marzdan remained but the dust from which he sprang. And even those sorry remnants, little more than soot, scattered and blew away with the breeze, leaving nothing to bury. Nothing to honor. Nothing to mourn over, to say words over. Nothing but memories of a hero.

Despite the captain's sacrifice, Malcolm did not get away clean. The curse was too swift for that. Too hungry. Rabid. It raced down the sword's blade and leaped from the hilt to Malcolm's fingers; onto his living flesh, before Marzdan knocked it away.

And when that magic touched him, nearly invisible though it was, his fingers burned. The horror of that white-hot burning pain was unlike anything Malcolm had experienced before or since, but despite it, he kept his eyes open as the sorcery assailed his arm.

He witnessed it all.

He saw his fingers burn, char, disintegrate. It all happened nearly instantly. Yet to Malcolm's eyes, to his awareness, it occurred in slow motion; it took forever.

He saw the white of his finger bones become exposed to the air as the flesh fell away. Then it was the same for his wrist. The dark fire stalked unrelentingly up his arm, toward his elbow. Hungry. Ravenous. All the flesh burned away, dissolved.

Malcolm thought he was dead. He thought

that the magic would travel up his arm to his shoulder, to his head, to his heart. That it would burn him alive, leaving him nothing but dust. And in those seconds, he knew despair.

But then, as quick as it came, the evil magic fled of its own accord or else fizzled out; the burning stopped just shy of Malcolm's elbow.

Nothing remained below that joint but bones. Malcolm watched as even the bones charred — turned gray, then black, and crumbled to ash. He saw the ash fall and scatter with the breeze. All in but a handful of heartbeats.

Malcolm hadn't been the same since that day. None of the men that encountered the messenger and lived were the same after that day. Malcolm had spent months recovering, but he still felt weak, drained, his youthful vitality not nearly what it once was.

But months later, atop Dor Eotrus's battlements, Sir Malcolm Eotrus showed the men his quality. Showed them that he wasn't weak. He wasn't a useless cripple. He wasn't a burden to be coddled or protected. He was a knight of the Dor. A man, a warrior, to be reckoned with.

4

ABOARD THE WHITE ROSE

YEAR 1267, 4TH AGE
LAST YEAR OF KING TENZIVEL'S RULE

MILTON DEBOORS

DeBoors marveled that when he saw Thetan in Tragoss Mor, he looked the same as he had the day that they assaulted Malik-Morn, far back in olden days, during the *Age of Heroes*. Then again, DeBoors looked the same too. It felt odd to see another like him. It had been so long. He wondered whether they were the last, save for Rascatlan and Sendarth.

DeBoors didn't know how many years ago that that assault took place. Dates were not uniformly recorded back in the *Age of Heroes*. Few writings yet survived. And with the Fourth Age came a new calendar. A new "year one". His guess, *ten thousand years*.

An odd thing to live so long that you forget so much. He never thought he'd find himself opposed to Thetan. He never thought he'd cross swords with him. Yet he did.

Albeit, unknowingly. Back in Tragoss Mor, when he sought to bring Claradon Eotrus to justice, two warriors stepped in to defend the wolf's-head. A hulking brute, seven feet tall, traded blow for blow with DeBoors in a battle that raged on and on. Mayhap that giant was the toughest man DeBoors had faced in his long life. In the end, DeBoors got the better of him.

And then Thetan stepped in.

DeBoors didn't recognize him at first. He moved with speed and skill unmatched by any. Tired and battered as he was after facing the giant, DeBoors was overmatched. To have lived so many thousands of years, a warrior's life the entire time, and yet to have faced one's two greatest opponents, one after another, in the same battle — what were the odds? This time, things would be different. DeBoors was at his best — at least the best one could be after weeks aboard a ship sailing the southern Azure Sea. At times a difficult voyage, fraught with dangers and death. *The Gray Talon* had a skilled crew and an even better captain, that had seen them through storm and stagnant sea. And the Alder marines, and the Knights of Kalathan that DeBoors commanded, saw them through dangers unexpected.

But now, what to do? Thetan was not his enemy. In days past, he might even have considered him a friend. At the very least, a man that held his respect and his loyalty. But now they stood at odds. And all for the sake of a contract with the Alders. Chancellor Barusa had been wronged by Claradon Eotrus — a man accused of murdering his own father. And young Edwin of Alder claimed that Claradon and his associates had waylaid him and his fellows on the streets of Lomion City, killing several of Edwin's friends, and maiming Edwin — a terrible, jagged scar forever lined his face to harken back to that night.

The Alders wanted revenge. But they also wanted justice. They hired DeBoors and his men — the Knights of Kalathan — to track Claradon and bring him to heel. The warrant also required DeBoors to capture the tall, foreign knight that traveled with the young Eotrus. The Alders apparently didn't even know Thetan's name. Who he was. Or his reputation.

If DeBoors had known it was Thetan that they were after, he would never have taken on the contract. Though since he had, he was honor bound to fulfill it, come what may.

Or was he?

The Alders mentioned that there were other soldiers with Claradon — but they were men of so little consequence they need not be named. They conveniently failed to mention an Archwizard was amongst them — a man capable of throwing devastating incendiary magic that would put a fire drake to shame.

Perhaps they didn't know about the wizard.

So too did they forget the giant, whoever he was, and the other uncommon knights amongst them?

His charge was clear — capture these men if at all possible and bring them back to Lomion City to face justice. Kill them if necessary.

DeBoors was no assassin. He was a bounty hunter. The best in the business. He hunted men for money. He didn't kill them for it. For that you want *The Black Hand* or *The Brotherhood of Blood*. Assassins always had laughable names for their guilds and for themselves. He never understood them.

DeBoors had spent many hours thinking about what Thetan had said to him at Tragoss Mor's docks. Thetan claimed that the League of Shadows was hell-bent on opening a portal to Nifleheim and bringing Azathoth back over to Midgaard.

That sounded like madness.

DeBoors had no idea whether Azathoth ever really existed or whether he was naught but a product of myth and legend.

But DeBoors knew about monsters. Creatures. Demons. Beasts. He had hunted them with Thetan and the others many a time.

For years.

Decades.

How long exactly, he could not recall. Thetan and his Eternals always claimed the monsters came over from Nifleheim at the time that Azathoth was banished there. They were unwavering in their hold to that story. But it always sounded like a fable. A tale to convince goodly men that the assorted creatures that they hunted were aliens.

Invaders.

Creatures of another realm come to prey on them.

It made the creatures feel foreign. Instilled in the men the idea that by hunting them, they were protecting all Midgaard from unnatural monsters. A clever tactic is what DeBoors always believed that to be.

The truth being much simpler.

Some of the creatures were but dangerous and rare animals; others were intelligent creatures of bloodlines long in decline and dying out, that nature had forsaken. There was no denying that some of them posed a threat to human folk that they encountered and some few of the creatures threatened whole countries from time to time. It made sense to deal with them. To make Midgaard safe for humanity. DeBoors went along. He thought the story of Nifleheim a useful fiction. Something the common soldier needed to hear, to believe, to spur them to action.

And now Thetan claimed that another portal to Nifleheim was about to be opened. That a flood of otherworldly creatures would follow. It couldn't be true. There were no other worlds. Not really. Only myths, stories, nothing more.

But what if it were true? What if such a place really did exist? What if that's where some or all the monsters of legend came from? The ones that he helped hunt down long ago during the *Age of Heroes*? If that portal stayed open long enough, if enough creatures came through, there would be no end of death and suffering. Truly, all Midgaard could be threatened.

DeBoors would have to stand with Thetan, wouldn't he? Wasn't that fight infinitely more important than making good on his contract? Than keeping his word?

Honor was everything to DeBoors. More important than anything he ever owned. It was the one thing that always traveled with him down through the long years. He could not set it aside. Not for anything. He wrestled with those thoughts every day since Tragoss Mor. He could find no resolution that satisfied him, save to speak to Thetan again. To hear his words. To listen to his evidence. Perhaps that would sway him one way or another.

   The decision was large. Bigger than him. If Thetan spoke true, the fate of all Midgaard may well hang in the balance. If the Alders canceled their contract, then he'd be free of it. The path was clear. Discuss with the Alders. Convince them.

5

DOR EOTRUS ON THE BATTLEMENTS

YEAR 1267, 4TH AGE
LAST YEAR OF KING TENZIVEL'S RULE

MALCOLM EOTRUS

Malcolm stood shoulder to shoulder with the other soldiers on Dor Eotrus's wall — a stalwart line of plate-armored men, bedecked in burnished steel, navy-blue capes trimmed in gold, and steel helms; the Eotrus sigil proudly inscribed on their breastplates and white tunics; the House colors of blue and red on a field of white accented their uniforms at shoulder, collar, waist, and boot. Their weapons were their own – each man held close his favorite. That line of honest steel stretched unbroken all the way around the fortress, through each fortified tower and turret, around every twist and turn, and past each corner and crevice. So tightly were they packed that not even a mouse could pass them unseen or unchallenged. A grim line of metal and muscle, grit and determination, youth and veteran alike.

The smell of oil was heady in the air; the outside face of the walls drowned in it; barrel upon barrel poured down their faces in preparation to repel the troll. But that smell was nothing compared to the musky stink of the trolls that filled the air, a noxious cloud that set more than a few men to retching over the crenels.

Though he'd been on the wall since sunup, Malcolm barely processed what he saw. A vast horde sieging Dor Eotrus! A thing unheard of in modern times.

And it was not a horde of men. Not even of Lugron.

It was an army of trolls.

Trolls!

Mythical things right out of legend.

The Outer Dor was already overrun. It happened in no time at all. But that was no surprise to Malcolm, for they had left only a skeleton force behind to man the Outer Dor's bulwarks. They just didn't have enough men to man all the walls. Not against opponents as fearsome as the trolls. Opponents known to climb as swiftly and skillfully as squirrels, despite their bulk and generally man-like appearance. For such as them, the Eotrus needed men aligned shoulder to shoulder on the walls, and better yet, two rows deep.

If all the Eotrus bannermen had come in, the walls would've been crowded, many men still left in reserve.

Many.

But the trolls had caught them off guard. They came on too quickly. And in such force. Resourceful as they were, the Eotrus were woefully unprepared for this siege of trolls.

But the Eotrus were no fools. They hadn't delayed calling for aid hoping the trolls would wander away. As soon as Sarbek returned from the northern woods and raised the alarm about the trolls, messages were sent. More messages than they had ever sent at one time in living memory. Missives to every Eotrus bannerman: to every fortress, castle, and keep in Eotrus demesne; to all the grand manors, the towns, the villages, the large farms and the freeholds. So too did messages fly to the great cities: to Lomion City, of course, to Kern, to Sarnack, to Dyvers, and even to distant Dover. The Eotrus warned all of the kingdom of what was happening, as best they could, though they knew it unlikely that most outside their demesne would believe the tale. One missive to the cities and the other Dors would surely not suffice. But to the Eotrus bannermen, no more need be done than raise the call-to-arms. They would come in — to the Dor. All of them. And with speed.

The ravens flew tirelessly for three days and three nights, no respite or reprieve. More than a few birds, far more than chance could claim, failed to return.

That meant only one thing. That somehow the ravens were being intercepted. Not all of them, mind you. Not even many. But a troubling number of them. And that made the Eotrus wonder if the trolls were able to shoot them down. If not that, then was there someone else out there in the woods? Some other force acting against them? Acting in league with the trolls?

Three days had passed since the first warnings went out, the first calls for aid. But that wasn't enough time. Not nearly. The allies of the Eotrus were spread far and wide around the Northlands. The message that the ravens bore was clear: Dor Eotrus was under siege. The bannermen, many shrewd and able warriors, would not trickle toward the Dor a few at a time, stumbling into an ambush. There were pre-made plans in place, contingencies and such, for just such circumstances. Plans in place for generations. The bannermen would marshal their forces in select locations around Eotrus demesne, and then advance on the Dor in force.

All that took time.

Too much time.

More time than Dor Eotrus had.

Truth be told, by the time the messages were sent out, it was already too late. The trolls were already on the approach. Youth and inexperience notwithstanding, Malcolm saw that. He saw that it was too late. Far too late.

6

ABOARD THE WHITE ROSE

YEAR 1267, 4TH AGE
LAST YEAR OF KING TENZIVEL'S RULE

MILTON DEBOORS

"The captain says we should reach Jutenheim in one or two days," said Bartol Alder as he sat in the officers' mess.

"I can't believe we've chased the Eotrus bastard halfway across the world," said Edwin Alder. "I'll be happy to get this over with and get off home."

"We have to catch them first," said Blain Alder, father to Edwin, brother to Bartol. "And defeat them. You think that will be easy?"

"Easy or not, we'll do it," said Edwin. "That's what we're here for. That's our mission."

"Is it?" said Blain.

Bartol leaned forward. "What are you spewing?"

"There's more to this than getting revenge on the Eotrus for their slights," said Blain. "They're not running from us, you know. They're on a mission of their own." He looked to DeBoors.

DeBoors took the opening. "The foreign knight with the Eotrus is called Thetan. He is known to me from years back. A man of honor."

"He killed our men," said Edwin. "Cut them down in the streets. He's just as bad as the Eotrus."

"I've heard that you attacked them," said DeBoors. "Jumped them in an alley in Southeast."

"Are you questioning me?" said Edwin. "They attacked me. Anyone that says different is a liar."

DeBoors looked to Bartol and then to Blain. "When Thetan spoke to me on the docks of Tragoss Mor, he claimed that he's chasing a cabal of wizards that seek to open a pathway to the Nether Realms. A magical portal through which creatures from there can come here."

"Is that a jest?" said Edwin.

"Thetan believes it to be true," said DeBoors, "and he is not a man to believe in fairy stories."

"What of it?" said Bartol.

"If the passage that opens is wide enough and stays open long enough," said DeBoors, "then a horde of creatures of the Nether Realms may well come through."

"A madman's ravings, it sounds like," said Bartol.

"Thetan is no madman," said DeBoors.

"This doesn't change our mission," said Bartol. "If those wizards even exist, let them do as they will. We're so far from home, who cares?"

"What if a flight of dragons came through?" said DeBoors. "Or the great demons of legend, from the tales of the *Age of Heroes*?"

"Ridiculous," said Bartol.

"But what if it were true?" said DeBoors.

"Still I say, we are too far from home to care," said Bartol. Bartol narrowed his eyes. "DeBoors, I need to know where your loyalties lie. Do you intend to fulfill your contract with us or not?"

"Will you release me from it?" said DeBoors. "All monies paid to be returned in full. A good deal, given I've done my share so far."

"I saw that man fight in Tragoss," said Bartol. "I saw how those with him fought. We need you and your Kalathans to beat them. Our numbers and our skills won't be enough, at least not without incurring terrible casualties. I'll not slink back to House Alder with half my men dead. Thus, I will not withdraw the contract. So I put it to you, will you fulfill it or not?"

"I am honor bound to do so," said DeBoors, his jaw clenched, his eyes downcast.

7

DOR EOTRUS ON THE BATTLEMENTS

***YEAR 1267, 4TH AGE
LAST YEAR OF KING TENZIVEL'S RULE***

MALCOLM EOTRUS

The Outer Dor was aflame.

Every door of every building was broken in. Most every window too.

The trolls were thorough.

They searched every building, every stable, every shed, cellar, and shack. They didn't even spare the rooftops. The things crawled over the pitched and peaked roofs; their heavy tread cracked and dislodged hordes of clay and stone tiles that rained down onto the streets below.

The trolls searched every penthouse, rookery, and chimney, so determined were they that not a single soul would elude them.

And they were out for blood.

They showed no mercy and gave no quarter. Perhaps, they had no concept of those things. No understanding of civilization or of civilized behavior. No respect or appreciation of the common rules of warfare.

How could they, living in the mountains, isolated from all intelligent folk? Living in caves like animals. Maybe that's all they were.

The screaming from the Outer Dor had stopped almost an hour before the trolls launched their first assault on the keep's wall and the main gate. It seemed they wanted to make certain that the Outer Dor was firmly in hand before they moved on to the keep.

Luckily, there weren't many citizens left in the Outer Dor when the trolls rampaged through. The evacuation had been swift, but thorough. Only a few holdouts remained: people that refused to abandon their homes; refused to take shelter inside the keep. There were always some like that, in every storm, blizzard, plague, famine, or flood. Some few that put all sense and reason aside, assuming that they had any to begin with. Maybe it was a driving need to be free to choose, to control one's destiny — or at least, to pretend that they were in control. Probably though, it was just thickheaded stubbornness. Or else stupidity. Or both. Wherever men gathered, there was seldom a shortage of either. And for some of the holdouts, Malcolm figured, it was just craziness that kept them out there. Whatever their reasons, it didn't matter any longer. Because the trolls hounded them out. They found the holdouts wherever they hid. And from the sound of it, they killed them slowly. The trolls even dragged a few poor souls down the streets, and put them on display before the main gate. They made a grand show of it. Tied them to poles, they did. Made sport of them. And then they pulled them apart with their bare hands. No mercy. No conscience on display. They tore those poor folk to shreds as they screamed and wriggled, begged and gibbered.

And then the fiends ate them.

They ate those sorry folk that they murdered. Ate them raw for all to see.

The trolls passed around bits; bits that they tore off their victims, the way a man would tear apart and pass around crusts of bread. They did it with ease. All casual like. As if they'd done the same a hundred times before. As if it didn't bother them at all. And that made the scene, unbelievably horrific as it was, all the more disturbing.

Perhaps the Eotrus shouldn't have been surprised by the trolls' actions, for what they did that day, the slaughter, and the feasting — it's what trolls do. It's what they've always done. Just as in all the old stories — now undeniably more fact than fiction.

And the trolls did what they did to those poor folk under a hail of arrows, bolts, ballistae fire, and catapult shot. To put on that gruesome show, the trolls took casualties that they need not have taken.

But Malcolm knew why they did it.

It was to put the fear in the Eotrus.

To put the fear in the men on the walls. To make certain that they understood that when the trolls came over the walls and got a hold of them, they'd kill them slowly too. And when they were done with their fun, they'd eat them. Dead or alive, they'd eat them.

Fear.

It's a powerful weapon. And the trolls knew how to wield it. When Malcolm realized that, he knew that the trolls were no animals. They were smart. Shifty. Cunning. And that made them infinitely more dangerous than did their brutish strength and uncanny agility.

Madness, that's what the whole thing was.

A few days prior, nearly all Malcolm knew of trolls came from children's tales. Bogeymen to frighten the whelps. More myth than living creature were they, or so he had thought. That and whispered rumors that his grandfather had killed a real one sometime way back when. Malcolm hadn't believed those tales, though his father insisted that they were true. He figured that the story was made up. Everyone thought so much of his grandfather, old Lord Nardon, and his many accomplishments on and off the battlefield, that someone had likely embellished a much more pedestrian tale and made it tall indeed.

But now he knew trolls weren't fiction or fable. They were real. And they were there. And at his doorstep. Destroying everything in their path.

The horror of it was overwhelming.

The fear.

His head was spinning. The whole thing didn't feel real.

Where did the trolls come from? Down from the northern mountains? Out of some cave that stretched down deep into the bowels of Midgaard? The Eotrus knew the Kronar Range better than any civilized men alive. Better even than some of the Lugron. Yet they never before came across the trolls. Not in Malcolm's lifetime at least. Knew nothing of them. Where did they hail from? And how could there be so many? It made no sense.

8

MONASTERY OF IVALD ISLE OF JUTENHEIM

YEAR 1267, 4TH AGE
LAST YEAR OF KING TENZIVEL'S RULE

OB

Ob felt like a fool. He walked into an ambush and dropped his comrades into it too. The stinking Alders had them surrounded, the whole expedition. Crossbows leveled, at near point blank range. The Alder marines outnumbered them at least three to one. Bartol and Blain Alder were there. So was Blain's son, Edwin, that rat bastard. If that weren't enough, they had the Knights of Kalathan with them — some of the toughest fighters amongst the militant orders. And their leader — Milton DeBoors, the Duelist of Dyvers, was the man that nearly killed Claradon, stabbed him through the chest. DeBoors even bested Artol in a straight up fight. Nobody ever did that before. And beside DeBoors was the Wild Pict, Kaladon of the Gray Waste. Nine lives that man had, just like Claradon.

"Throw your weapons down, Thetan, and surrender," shouted DeBoors the moment that he and his jumped out of hiding, "and order your men to do the same, or mine will open fire. Your armor may well be bolt proof, but I'd wager that theirs are not. On three we fire. One. Two. Three!"

9

DOR EOTRUS ON THE BATTLEMENTS

***YEAR 1267, 4TH AGE
LAST YEAR OF KING TENZIVEL'S RULE***

MALCOLM EOTRUS

Malcolm hefted another large rock, foot to shoulder — no easy feat with but one good arm. He dropped it over the wall, down onto his enemies. His opponents, those things that were out there, they weren't just the enemies of the Eotrus, of his House, his family. They were the enemies of all mankind. The very thought was ridiculous. They were fighting fairy tales. But he could not deny what he saw, what he heard, what he smelled. They were there. They were real. Threatening the walls. Climbing halfway up despite the smooth, slick surface. Getting closer every moment. He prayed it was all a nightmare. But he knew that it wasn't.

That's when the order came. Malcolm wasn't certain who gave it. Probably Sarbek, but maybe not.

"Light the wall!" went the cry, which was repeated by the officer-in-charge of every section of the wall, one after another, all the way around the Dor.

Men from every squadron grabbed torches,

held ready for just that purpose, and pressed the fire to the outside faces of the walls. The oil ignited, not as quick as one might expect, but it ignited all the same. And once it did, the fires roared down and across the walls. Within a minute, the entire outside face of Dor Eotrus's grand wall was fully engulfed in flame.

Smoke rose up in black and gray clouds. The heat soared and pushed the soldiers back from the crenels. In some spots they had to temporarily abandon whole swaths of the wall altogether.

Malcolm wanted to look over the parapet. He wanted to see whether the trolls fled back from the wall, as anyone with any sense would do. Or did they keep trying to climb up — right through the flames? Dead gods, what if the flames did them no harm?

But he couldn't look. None of the men could. Not with that fire blazing. They'd have to wait it out. Wait for the fires to die down or go out, and then look over to see what was left of the trolls.

He knew that some of them burned. The screams were terrible. But they were few.

Minutes passed. The flames died. The men inched toward the crenels, the stone still hot all around.

Malcolm looked over and there they were, massed at the base of the wall and the plaza beyond. A sea of trolls. Some had already started to climb up. Determined bastards.

Malcolm lifted a rock and dropped it over.
And then another.
And another.
And in doing so, Malcolm did his duty, or such

was his mind. He did everything that could be expected of him. More than should be expected, considering his condition.

Too bad that he had to do it against his brother's orders. But Ector was wrong to tell him to stay out of the fight; to stay off the wall. He was a Northman; an Eotrus; a knight. He would fight beside the others. Fight for his land, his House, his people. That was his duty and he did it no matter the consequences; no matter the risks. He would not sit back while other men took all the risks, while he was safe and sound behind the lines, huddling with the women, the children, the sick, and the old folk. He wouldn't do that. He couldn't. The shame of it. What would his father say? Just the thought of the look on his father's face if he saw him cowering with the noncombatants — it was too much for him to bear. And he knew with just as much certainty as he knew anything, that his father was watching him at that very moment. Looking down on him from Valhalla. Judging him — as worthy or wanting.

He would not let his father down. He would make him proud.

The trolls moved up the wall faster, much faster than before. With the oil burned off, the walls were not so slippery. The difference that made in the trolls' pace was astounding.

After a few more big rocks, Malcolm went arm weary. His muscles, rubbery, burning, and quivering. He felt as if only half his normal strength remained. And that was despite the adrenaline that coursed through his body: the battle surge was what the men called it. He wouldn't give up. He wouldn't abandon his position. He'd stand there and fight as long as any strength remained in his limbs. He'd make his father proud.

10

HOUSE ALDER LOMION CITY

YEAR 1267, 4TH AGE
LAST YEAR OF KING TENZIVEL'S RULE

MOTHER ALDER

Chancellor Barusa stood by the fireplace, a tumbler of Trackan Brandy in hand. Mother Alder lounged on the divan, her feet up, a smug smile on her angular face.

"Rom should be here for this," said Mother Alder. "I wish I could see the look on his face when he hears this news."

"Tenzivel dead," said Barusa. "Malvegil dead. Harringgold out of action. Captain Korvalan dead. The Dramadeens decimated. It's more than we could have hoped for."

"But not more than what's right and just," said Mother Alder. "Tenzivel was a disgrace to the throne. Malvegil, a corrupt, evil bastard. They got what they long deserved."

"But who put the contract out on them?" said Barusa. "The cost for the king alone would have been extraordinary."

"We must find out," said Mother Alder.

"A powerful ally they may make," said Barusa.

"Or a powerful enemy," said Mother Alder. "Let's not be too quick to embrace them."

"I'm more concerned with the succession," said Barusa. "Cartegian is unpredictable. Hard to control."

"In the long term it will be easy," said Mother Alder. "We'll marry him to one of ours. Once he has produced an heir, Cartegian will join his father in the afterlife. You will take over as regent until the child is of age."

"You aim to kill him?" said Barusa.

"We can't have a madman on the Granite Throne," said Mother Alder. "We must protect the realm. It's our duty. He would lead us into ruin."

"I cannot argue with that," said Barusa. "Lomion would not fare well under his leadership. The Vizier will block us at every turn. So will Jhensezil. And Harringgold."

"Then we must tip the balance," said Mother Alder. "Who in Lomion City has the wealth and power to eliminate the king?"

"More than a few if truth be told," said Barusa.

"One of them is Harringgold," said Mother Alder. "And who is Harringgold's close associate?"

"Jhensezil," said Barusa.

"We can eliminate them both in one stroke by pinning the murder on Harringgold," said Mother Alder. "Who would dare oppose you then?"

"A dangerous gambit," said Barusa.

"One can't attain great power without risk, firstborn," said Mother Alder. "It's for the good of the realm. Cartegian is unfit. Harringgold is corrupt. So is most of the council and half the lords. You are the right man for the throne, even if only as regent. It's your time, Barusa. We've waited long years for such an opportunity. Now that it lies before us, we must act. Decisively.

Swiftly."

Sirnick Butler knocked and entered.

He looked flustered and at a loss for words.

"Spit it out, Sirnick," said Mother Alder, "before your head pops off."

"A caller, Mother Alder," he said stammering.

"Who is it?"

"The Grandmistress of the Black Hand," said Sirnick.

Barusa's tumbler slipped from his hand and shattered when it hit the floor.

Mother Alder bounced up from her seat.

"How do we know it's really her?" said Barusa.

"Who would dare?" said Mother Alder.

"She carries the sigil of her office," said Sirnick.

"Is she alone?" said Mother Alder.

"Only her did I see," said Sirnick, "but no doubt, more of her brethren lurk about the lane. They say *The Hand* always travels in packs, like wolves."

"What do we do?" said Barusa.

Mother Alder retook her seat. "Show the bitch in," she said.

11

MONASTERY OF IVALD ISLE OF JUTENHEIM

YEAR 1267, 4TH AGE
LAST YEAR OF KING TENZIVEL'S RULE

As DeBoors shouted his count, cueing his men to open fire, there was a flurry of movement amongst the Eotrus.

Several things happened at once.

The Eotrus men crouched. Raised their shields.

Dolan shot an arrow at DeBoors.

Claradon and Glimador spoke mystic words.

Tanch thumped the base of his staff to the floor with tremendous force.

And Theta charged DeBoors.

A mystic shield of translucent white appeared in front of Claradon. Expanded in an instant — a magical barrier. A veritable wall of energy. It floated between Claradon and the Alders and protected several men to either side. Glimador spat a similar spell in but a word or two. His magical barrier, translucent blue, protected an even larger swath of their troop.

From the base of Tanch's staff erupted a shock wave of thunderous power; his Ring of Talidousen aglow with sorcery. Tendrils of yellow and orange fire sprang from that staff. Shot toward the Alders. It had no effect on Tanch or any of his comrades. Passed by them as if nothing but a breeze. No heat. No odor. No pain. But the crossbow bolts that the Alders fired had no such immunity. Tanch's sorcery plucked them from the air, mid-flight; sent them spinning back whence they came, as if a hurricane wind had greeted them. Some few bolts outpaced the sorcery, but were repelled by Eotrus shields, or by Claradon's or Glimador's magic. The shock wave continued. Just before the magical blast hit DeBoors, Dolan's arrow struck his head.

Blain Alder had dropped to the floor, pulled Edwin down with him.

The shock wave struck the Alder men like a tornado. It flung them backward. Lifted them into the air like a child would toss a rag doll. But the maelstrom was short-lived. All its strength dissipated after but a brief moment.

Five heartbeats later it was the Alders that were entrapped. They lay strewn about the edges of the room. Battered. Dazed. Eotrus men stood amongst them. Disarmed them. Threatened them with death if they dared resist. Theta shouted three times to the men not to kill the Alders. The Eotrus obeyed him. DeBoors was on his feet by the time that Theta reached him, though that was barely three seconds after the shock wave hit him and flung him into the far wall. He'd lost his sword in the impact, but held a long dagger. His helmet was badly dented. He was unsteady, obviously dazed. The only Alders on their feet were Blain and Edwin. They stood back to back, swords at the ready. Claradon marched up to them. Seran Harringgold and four soldiers backed him.

"Stand down," said Claradon.

"Let's go," hissed Edwin to Blain.

Blain grabbed Edwin's sword arm even as he lowered his own sword and let it fall to the floor.

"We're undone and outmatched, son," said Blain. "Put down your sword and we may yet live to see the morrow."

"What?" said Edwin, spittle flying from his mouth. "After what they did to me? You won't even fight them? You coward. Coward!"

Blain punched his son in the jaw. Edwin went down. Claradon stepped on the tip of his sword.

And quick as that, it was over.

Ob rushed over to Par Tanch who lay sprawled on the ground. Glimador poured water on him. Smoke rose from the wizard's body. The bandages around his hands were blackened. Blisters ran up his arms. His eyes were closed. His breathing shallow.

"How bad is it?" said Ob.

"I don't know," said Glimador. "I've never see anyone throw magic like he does. It's more than his body can handle."

"Saved our butts again, he did," said Ob. "I'll never call him a hedge again, I'll tell you. He's a stinking archwizard if I ever saw one. Goes to show you, it don't take brains. Or a work ethic, since he's still a lazy bugger what complains nonstop. And crazy too. But he saved our butts. Again. We're not going to forget that. Let's wrap up his arms best we can. Keep pouring water on him. I'm afraid he's going to burst into flame, the crazy bugger."

12

DOR EOTRUS ON THE BATTLEMENTS

***YEAR 1267, 4TH AGE
LAST YEAR OF KING TENZIVEL'S RULE***

MALCOLM EOTRUS

Hundreds of trolls climbed the walls. Their claws dug into the hard stone, and found purchase where no man could have. In truth, there was no need for Malcolm to aim with the rocks. Packed so tightly were the trolls, he couldn't miss if he tried. Not that it mattered.

The stones didn't kill them.

The best that he could hope for, was for a stone to knock a troll or two off the wall. Even that didn't do much. When they hit the ground, however far their fall, they got up straightaway, and began to climb up again. Mostly, all the stones did was make them angry.

A few trolls what got pounded directly atop their heads didn't get up again. How could you, with a crushed skull and splattered brains? But short of that, they kept coming.

Malcolm kept trying. They all did. Trooper Bront on his left. Krint on his right. The battlements were lined with some of the best-trained fighting men of the North. Eotrus men, born and bred. Men trained since they were lads to fight: sword and spear, hammer and bow, axe and dagger. They wore their armor like a second skin. Their shields, extensions of their arms. These were real soldiers. Not fat merchants or unemployable peasants doled up in pretty uniforms like those the Southerners from Lomion city sent to the field.

Malcolm felt good to stand beside them, those Eotrus men. To fight with them. To be one of them. It made him feel strong. It made him feel whole again.

Trouble was, too many of the Eotrus men were no older than Malcolm was. Despite all their training, all their skills, many were inexperienced in real combat. Sparring, practicing — was one thing. A bar brawl another. But a battle. A real life-and-death struggle between large groups of men, well, that was something different. That was wild. Chaos. Hell. Most of the men that stood the wall with Malcolm had not seen that kind of action.

Most of Dor Eotrus's best and most experienced soldiers died with Malcolm's father some months back. More died when the messenger attacked the Dor. Still more soldiers died when Malcolm's brother, Jude, rode out with a troop of men and got ambushed on the road — presumably, by the same scum that were responsible for Malcolm's father's death. And more of the best named men had gone off with Claradon, Malcolm's oldest brother (and with his father's passing, the new Lord of the House). Claradon was away in far-off lands to avenge their father and destroy the enemies of House Eotrus.

So the core of Eotrus strength was away or

dead. Mostly the young ones were left. But there were some veterans still at their posts. Sarbek – the acting castellan — led the keep in Claradon's absence. He prepared the men for battle. A great leader and soldier was Sarbek. A great mentor to Malcolm and all his brothers, was he.

And Captain Pellan was back — the beardless dwarf. The trolls apparently enticed her out of retirement. The men say she fought the trolls in the northern woods, and that she gave them what for even by her lonesome. Malcolm didn't doubt it. He'd heard many stories about her and her battle skills. Before her retirement, she'd served with the Eotrus for years, participating in several storied campaigns. Tough as nails and twice as sharp was Pellan.

And there were others. Veterans. Named men. Many, sprinkled amongst the troops of greenhorns. But Malcolm didn't think that there were enough. Not when he looked at that horde that stood poised to overrun the walls.

Walls never breached before in living memory.

It had only been a few hours since the attack began. Who could believe it? The Outer Dor sacked. The walls of the citadel threatened with breach. In so short a time. Who could believe it? It was beyond imagination.

But it was happening. It was real. And Malcolm wondered, would he live through it? Would he live to tell the tale?

Malcolm leaned through the crenel and looked out. He wanted to drop his last rock on the nearest troll. Hopefully, splatter its brains. Then he'd wait until one made it up close enough. It would be knife-work from then on. Every moment that they kept the trolls from reaching the battlements helped. Or so they hoped. Or at least, that's what Sarbek's orders said: *keep them off the battlements; hold them back; and hold your positions until ordered to move*.

The din of battle was so loud, so frantic, as to make a man's head spin. The shouting. The roaring. The screaming. Malcolm had never experienced anything quite like it.

When Malcolm looked over the battlement, a troll stared back at him from less than three feet down. It bared its teeth and lunged.

13

DORIATH HALL LOMION CITY

YEAR 1267, 4TH AGE
LAST YEAR OF KING TENZIVEL'S RULE

LANDOLYN MALVEGIL

Lady Landolyn entered the room. No energy to her step. She looked dazed. Her cheeks were red. Her eyes were wet. She was barely able to breathe, her throat constricted with fear, grief, and anger. She tried to hold it back. She didn't want to reveal her emotions. To appear weak. She couldn't afford that, especially not now.

To her credit, she didn't break down, lose her composure. But the tears came; rolled down her face. She couldn't hold them back. There would be time enough for proper grieving when she was alone.

Her husband. The finest man in all Lomion.

Dead.

Murdered.

There he lay. His bright eyes forever closed. His face battered, bruised.

The moment that she saw him, a groan escaped her mouth of its own will. She could deny the truth of his death no longer.

Odd that they had him in a bed, as if he were sleeping. For her benefit, she concluded.

Lord Sluug closed the door behind her. They were three levels down in the subbasement of Doriath Hall, the Rangers Guild. She didn't understand why they had to hide his body down there. Karktan was with her, of course. So was McDuff. No others. There was another man already in the room. A Leren by his garb. Probably waiting to prepare the body.

Lord Sluug took her gently by the arm and they shuffled toward Torbin. She inched along like an old crone, stooped over, hands against her gut, thinking of retching.

"I'm truly sorry that it had to be this way," said Sluug.

What?

"Your grief had to be seen," said Sluug. "Had to be genuine."

"What are you saying?" She pulled away from him.

"He's alive," said Sluug.

"What?" Landolyn turned toward her husband. "Torbin! Torbin!"

He stirred. His head moved. A grunt. He lived!

The Leren spoke up. "I have him sedated for the pain. He should wake up soon. If the pain is less, I can cut back on the medicines so that he'll be able to remain awake."

Her mind raced. Alive. Torbin is alive. She turned back to Sluug. Her hand whipped out to strike him across the face. The bastard had lied to her. Told her that her husband was dead along with the king. The whole city chattered about the king's assassination. It's all she heard when she, Karktan, and McDuff approached and entered the city.

Sluug caught her hand in his. He squeezed it firmly and held it for several moments. The message clear. Don't try that again. The bastard.

"Release her," said Karktan. Menace in his voice.

"How bad is he?" said McDuff, already at Torbin's side, searching for a pulse at his wrist.

"A nasty bump on the head knocked him out, but likely saved his life, as the killers thought him dead," said the Leren. "He may have a concussion, but it will heal. The worse injury was an arrow he took to the back. It hit his spine. May well have broken it."

"What does that mean?" said Landolyn.

"It means if it is broken, he'll be off his feet for a long time," said the Leren. "Months. Maybe longer."

Torbin made a sound. He opened his eyes. Blinked and took some breaths.

"Torbin! Torbin," said Landolyn. "I'm here. I'm with you."

He smiled half a smile at her. "The king?"

"Dead," said Sluug.

"How do you feel?" said the Leren.

He turned his head from side to side and moved his arms. Then his voice went grim indeed. "I cannot feel my legs."

14

MONASTERY OF IVALD ISLE OF JUTENHEIM

YEAR 1267, 4TH AGE
LAST YEAR OF KING TENZIVEL'S RULE

MILTON DEBOORS

"**W**hy did you not strike from ambush?" said Theta to DeBoors after he'd pulled the mercenary out of earshot of the others. "You had us dead to rights. Why step out and announce yourself?"

"You already know why," said DeBoors. "You just want to hear me say it."

"So say it," said Theta.

"To give your wizards time to act," said DeBoors.

"Why?"

"If not, it would have been a fight to the death," said DeBoors. "Regardless of who was left at the end, both sides would have lost. More importantly, your quest would've been broken. The League's maneuvers would go unchecked."

"Are you telling me that I convinced you," said Theta, "when we spoke on the docks of Tragoss Mor about the gateway to Nifleheim?"

"You did," said DeBoors. "Though it took a good deal of thinking. I'm a bit dense — old age and all. I couldn't convince the Alders. Save mayhap Blain."

Theta looked back at the Alder men. "They seem sturdy enough," said Theta. "Will they fight for me?"

"My Kalathans will follow me," said DeBoors. "But that's only twenty men. Most are still on the ship or about the town. The Alders are a different story. Do we need them?"

"Korrgonn has several archwizards with him," said Theta. "And who knows what he's capable of himself. Every competent man we have will help."

"Then we've some convincing to do," said DeBoors. "But first, tell me how the Eotrus boy is still alive. I took him through the heart. No man could survive that."

"No mortal man," said Theta.

DeBoors nodded. "So he's an Eternal?"

"Aye, though he doesn't know it, so keep it to yourself."

15

DOR EOTRUS ON THE BATTLEMENTS

YEAR 1267, 4TH AGE
LAST YEAR OF KING TENZIVEL'S RULE

MALCOLM EOTRUS

A few more seconds and the troll would reach the top of the battlement and vault over the wall. Then it would be at Malcolm's throat.

Malcolm had no time to lift the stone and throw it down, so he shoved it over the edge. Only gravity to carry on its way. One hundred pounds falling three feet right onto the troll's head as it dangled from a wall. That should have knocked it from its perch, if not cracked its skull.

The troll dodged its head to the side, but couldn't escape the stone entirely. The falling rock caught it. Its head took a glancing blow, but the main weight of the stone hit the troll's shoulder before bouncing off and plummeting into the climbing trolls farther down the wall. The troll let out a roar, which Malcolm barely heard over the general din, but somehow, the thing didn't lose its grip on the wall. It didn't fall.

How those things climbed the walls at all, Malcolm couldn't understand. The walls of the Dor were straight and tall, well-kept and solid. They had few if any handholds to make use of. Yet the trolls, human in shape as they were, climbed them with nearly as much ease as a spider or an ant.

Malcolm, ever the swordsman, by training and temperament, went for his sword, forgetting the array of spears that lay ready behind him. Just as he drew the blade from its sheath, the troll's clawed hands wrapped about the top of the crenelation and its head appeared. Close up, how big that thing was! The teeth. The evil look to it. Unsavory. Foul.

Out of nowhere, Sergeant Baret lunged forward and sunk the tip of his spear through the thing's right eye; it blasted out the back of its head.

Then it fell; Baret's spear with it.

"We've got to go boy," said Baret. "We've got to run."

"We have orders to hold the wall," said Malcolm as he looked about. He couldn't believe what he saw. The trolls were over the walls all around. Not many of them. Not yet. In some spots, the men held them at bay. Squads of spearmen pincushioned them and pinned them to the ground. At other spots, the fighting was desperate and grim. The trolls wreaked havoc, battering, tearing, and biting at the men. Malcolm's position was one of the last that still held firm.

16

BLACK HALL LOMION CITY

YEAR 1267, 4TH AGE
LAST YEAR OF KING TENZIVEL'S RULE

WEATER THE MOUSE

Weater the Mouse knocked on the Grandmistress's door. Instantly, he knew he hadn't knocked loud enough; she'd never hear it. He took a deep breath and knocked again, louder this time, but not much louder.

No response.

Had she heard him? Was she just making him wait? Or was the knock not loud enough? Was she indisposed? He wanted to turn about and walk away. But he knew that she'd want to hear the news, immediately. He'd suffer her wrath if she heard it late or from another source. Best to avoid that.

He knocked again. This time louder.

"Come," said the Grandmistress.

She lay on the couch, scantily clad as always, three of her favorite girls around her. The usual female guards just inside the door. The place smelled vaguely of puke covered over with perfume. What the heck were they up to now?

"Have you found me a true seer that can use the stone?" said the Grandmistress, not bothering to look up at him. The heavily lined box containing the Seer Stone that her agents had stolen from Torbin Malvegil lay on the floor nearby the divan.

"I advised against opening the box," said Weater. He tried not to look at her. It was too distracting. The girls made a game of trying to catch his eyes. They liked to watch him squirm.

"I had to," she said. "Curiosity kills the cat and such. Mila spent half an hour puking her guts up after she took it out of the box. We had a heck of a time putting it back in. I had to throw out the carpet and most of our clothes."

"I'm still working on finding that seer," said Weater. "There are a hundred of them in the bazaar, but they're all frauds, as best we can tell."

The grandmistress's angular face grew serious, which made her high cheekbones stand out all the more. "I need a true seer."

"And you'll have one," said Weater.

"You haven't come by only to stand and gawk at me again, have you?"

Weater felt his face go red. He wondered if at some point his face might explode or catch fire. "A raven tells of Dor Eotrus under attack by trolls."

"Is that a joke?"

"We've heard it from three sources. One unconfirmed report says the Eotrus have fallen."

The Grandmistress shoved one girl off her, knocking her to the floor. The others scrambled back. "You're telling me that there's an army of trolls up in the northlands? An entire army?"

"That's what the ravens report."

"What of Rom Alder?"

"His brigade reached Dor Eotrus, but then went silent. It appears the trolls didn't care for the Alders any more than they did the Eotrus."

"You think him dead?"

"More than likely, but not for certain."

"How in Helheim are we going to get paid if he's dead?" said the Grandmistress.

Weater's lips moved but no words managed to tumble out.

"We just pulled off the biggest hit in modern history and one of our clients is dead by trolls. Is that what you're telling me? Is it Weater?" she said as she marched up to him.

"Rom may not be dead. He's tough as—"

"If they wiped out an entire Dor, what difference does tough make, you moron? We lost twenty brethren on that hit. Twenty! Our biggest loss in memory. How much did those Southron mercs cost us?"

"Twenty-five thousand silver stars," said Weater, his voice weak and monotone. She knew the cost as well as he did.

"How are we going to get paid if Rom Alder is dead? Tell me, Weater? Do you have that answer for me?"

"Did we get payment for the king?" said Weater.

"Coburn collected what was due," said the Grandmistress, "but that's besides the point. We had two contracts and fulfilled them both. We will collect on both of them. Every last copper. How do you plan to get me that payment?"

"I don't—" started Weater.

"Mother Alder," said the Grandmistress.

Weater nodded because it seemed like the

right response and he didn't know what else to do.

"What are the chances that Rom put out this contract without telling her? The Alders don't pee without asking permission from the old hag. She'd have to know. Besides, she controls the family purse. The money would be coming from her anyway."

Weater nodded again. He figured she was onto something. "What if she doesn't know?" said Weater.

"Then we'll tell her. She'll make good on the debt."

"And if she doesn't?"

The Grandmistress smiled. "The Alders will pay one way or another. They're smart enough to know that. They'll cover the debt."

"You want me to pay Mother Alder a visit?" said Weater.

"She's no ordinary client," said the Grandmistress. "I think she warrants special attention."

"What do you have in mind?" said Weater, confused. The Grandmistress knew that he could handle Mother Alder and her brood. He didn't know where she was going with this.

"I think it's time that I meet the old girl myself," said the Grandmistress. "Maybe we'll have a meeting of the minds. Or maybe more," she said, smiling. "I'll get that debt paid in full, one way or another."

17

MONASTERY OF IVALD ISLE OF JUTENHEIM

YEAR 1267, 4TH AGE
LAST YEAR OF KING TENZIVEL'S RULE

Bartol and Blain Alder sat side by side at a conference table off the Abbot's chambers. Their hands were bound before them. DeBoors sat next to them, similarly bound. Most men would have looked afraid. These looked angry.

Across from them sat Theta, Claradon, and Ob. Glimador, Artol, and Dolan stood about the room. Artol blocked the door, which was closed and guarded on the outside as well. The prisoners weren't getting out. No chance of it. Everyone in the room knew that.

"I've no interest in being tortured," said Bartol as soon as his captors took their seats. "So ask us your questions and we'll give you our answers and be done with this. You've won."

"There is no information that I want from you," said Claradon. "Save to know whether the Alders are allied with the League of Shadows."

Bartol rolled his eyes. Blain shook his head. "We're a noble House," said Bartol. "We're not a cult of crazies, nor would we ever have anything to do with such folk. You people imagine us having a hand in every evil in the kingdom just because we're rivals. That paranoia has been the source of many of the problems between our Houses."

"Falsely accusing me of murdering my father so that you could steal my lands is the source of our current problems," said Claradon sharply.

"The Council accused you of that," said Bartol. "Not House Alder. We're merely carrying out Council orders."

"Your brother controls the Council," said Claradon. "It's his doing. Let's not play games here."

"Does Barusa control Duke Harringgold? Does he control Lord Jhensezil? Lady Aramere? Bishop Tobin? He's merely the head of the Council. That's his job. Is this to be about revenge then? Kill us for the feud between our Houses?"

"If the aim was to kill you," said Theta, "you'd already be dead."

"Then it's to be the torture for torture's sake?" said Bartol. "You bastards. I'm a Myrdonian Knight. You've no honor. Let me die like a soldier. Don't deny me Valhalla."

Blain leaned forward, his eyes fixed on Theta. "What do you want from us?"

"For now, I want you to listen," said Theta. "Listen to every word." He told them what happened in the Vermion Forest. About the League opening a mystical gateway to Nifleheim, with the aim to return Azathoth to Midgaard. He told them that instead, Korrgonn came through, along with a host of demonic creatures. He told of how they barely managed to close the gateway before untold numbers of their kind entered Midgaard. He told how the League of Shadows was behind it. How they worshipped Azathoth and would stop at nothing to bring him back. How this entire journey was about finding another mystical place, an ancient temple of power, where another such gateway could be opened. And he explained, how if left unchecked, Korrgonn and the League would likely succeed. And if they did, and the hordes of Nifleheim came over to Midgaard, the entire world would be lost.

"He's asking for our help," said Blain as he looked to his brother and DeBoors. "He needs more men to stop the Leaguers. Even more to close to gateway if they get it opened. Am I right?"

"That is why we are talking," said Claradon.

"And if we refuse?" said Bartol.

"Then our men will hold you until we're well away into the interior," said Claradon. "After we're beyond your reach, they'll let you and your ship go. With no arms. Only food and water to see you back across the Azure Sea."

"Why not slit our throats and be done with it?" said Bartol. "Not that I'm suggesting you do that."

"That's not the Eotrus way," said Claradon. "I'm no murderer. At this point, you're no threat, so I'll let you go. But understand this, after this mercy that I gift you, if you act in violence against the Eotrus again, I will burn House Alder to the ground and leave your heads on spikes for all the world to see."

There was a pause of some moments as everyone in the room took that in. The looks on the Eotrus men were more shocked than that of the Alders.

"And if we help you?" said Blain.

"Then give your solemn pledge to help us stop

the League," said Ob.

"But you must do so willingly," said Claradon. "We'll not force you into it. As I said, we'll let you go if you don't believe us, or just won't help. But if you're with us, you need to be committed to the end. All disputes between us on hold until we return to Lomion City. A complete truce until then. There must be no trickery or backstabbing while we're about this business. It's too important."

"Why do you need us so badly?" said Blain.

"We don't," said Claradon. "But every good sword we have adds to our chances of success. And we must succeed. It's more important than anything. The fate of the world is at stake. Putting aside our issues with you is a small price to pay to save the world."

"What say you?" said Theta.

"I'll not have my men used as fodder," said Bartol. "You'll treat us the same as your own."

"Agreed," said Claradon. "But they'll take my orders, same as everyone else."

"Agreed," said Bartol.

"And you?" said Claradon to Blain.

"I believe you," said Blain. "Though the tale sounds like a fireside story rather than truth. I will lend you my sword in this quest."

"And you?" said Claradon to DeBoors.

"If the Alders will release me from my contract, I will aid your quest," said DeBoors.

"You're so released," said Bartol.

"Your word of honor that you will not betray us in word or deed," said Theta. They all agreed.

***

DeBoors approached Claradon as they prepared to leave the Ivald Monastery.

"You've healed well," said DeBoors.

"I was lucky, I suppose," said Claradon.

"The man you were fighting," said DeBoors. "Kaladon. He's my closest friend. I thought you'd killed him."

"I'd have done the same in your position," said Claradon. "Though I'd never hunt a man for money. Especially not for the wrong side. Does he live, this Kaladon?"

"He's on *The Talon*," said Deboors. "He will join us in our quest."

"Best you keep him clear of me," said Claradon.

***

"**B**artol says they've near as many fighting men on *The Talon* as they have here," said Ob. "If we take them along, we'll be outnumbered five to one. That's a terrible risk. A terrible temptation for them to break their oaths."

"How can we leave them behind?" said Claradon. "We may well need every sword they have and more to see this through."

"There won't be any seeing it through if they jump us in the night and slit our throats."

"They gave their words of honor," said Claradon.

"What honor do the Alders have?" said Ob.

"DeBoors is with us," said Theta. "And his Kalathans will follow him, not the Alders. With them on our side, the Alders will fear to betray us."

"They will still outnumber us nearly four to one," said Ob.

"A calculated risk," said Theta. "I think Blain was truly convinced. Convinced by DeBoors before we encountered them here. It's Bartol that we have to watch."

"We'll put three good men on him," said Ob. "They'll watch his every move. And if he steps out of line. . ."

"Slit his throat and all the rest turn on us," said Theta. "Blain included. They're family. We must move carefully in this. And we've spent too much time here. We need to get over these cliffs and back on Korrgonn's trail."

18

ANGLOTOR THE OLDEN DOME JUTENHEIM

***YEAR 1267, 4TH AGE
LAST YEAR OF KING TENZIVEL'S RULE***

URIEL THE BOLD

"**W**hat do you see?" said Uriel the Bold, his voice calm but loud enough that it reverberated off the cylindrical room's stark walls and ceiling — a ponderous stone dome that loomed high overhead, its upper reaches lost in the gloom. Uriel's breath steamed as he spoke; the hairs stood up on his arms and on the back of his neck, and his feet felt like an army of tiny ants manically crawled over them, intent on driving him mad. Those strange manifestations were nothing new or unexpected. To varying extents, such symptoms, and more, afflicted everyone that entered that eerie, antediluvian chamber that they called the Olden Dome. Those symptoms derived in small part from the unnatural cold that plagued the place regardless of the weather outside, but in the main, by the unwholesome atmosphere that abided within the chamber's confines. A morbid gloom that sucked the joy from one's heart and the vitality from one's soul. Even light shrank from the vapors of that melancholy chamber. A dozen lanterns hung about the place burned dimly and gave off no warmth, the shadows ever encroaching, threatening to prematurely extinguish them.

To Uriel, the Olden Dome felt unnatural. Otherworldly. Alien. No matter how much time he spent there, which was no more than needs be, it made him dizzy. Discomforted. On edge. Exactly how that was, he didn't know, except that it was a real phenomenon, and not some figment born of olden superstition, dark and sullen atmosphere, or maldigested meat. What bothered him most though, was that he was no more immune to the effects than was anyone else. That spoke to ancient and mystical forces that predated the Eternals. Things that harkened back to those depths of time were best avoided. And that's what he did. Avoided the Olden Dome and its weirdness. Left it to Malth'Urn to haunt, for its preternatural energies enlivened her Seer skills beyond their normal ken and gifted her with curious powers that she possessed nowhere and nowhen else. And so she suffered the room's affects without complaint. The stoicism of the Svart did her good service in that respect.

That day, however, Uriel needed to hear firsthand what secrets the seer stone deigned to tell, so he braved its vapors.

That lonely domed chamber, along with the temple, were the only two structures on the stony site on Jutenheim's southernmost tip when Uriel first arrived there untold ages ago. He built his fortress around those two structures and named it Anglotor after a weathered inscription he found on a stone plinth within the temple's confines. That inscription was in a language long dead and forgotten, but similar enough to old Negish that he was able to translate the letters. What the word meant, whether it be a name, a place, or a thing, he knew not, but deemed it a fitting name for his fortress and dubbed it so. The temple was at his keep's core, for it was the reason that he was there. The isolation of the place had its advantages — in the main, permitting Uriel to do as he will without governmental entanglements or the vagaries of societal mores. But truth be told, if not for the temple, and the grave need to protect it, he'd not have settled within two thousand leagues of the place.

How old the temple was, or the Olden Dome, he knew not. Who could possibly have built them remained a mystery unsolved, perhaps, unsolvable. That irked him. He liked to know things. Define them. And use that knowledge to best advantage. Begrudgingly he conceded, the truth of certain ancient things is sometimes best left unknown.

At the very center of the Olden Dome chamber, Malth'Urn of Svartleheim sat unclothed atop a ten-foot tall single-legged stool, a match to the glass-topped table upon which the seer stone sat on a curved glass base.

Uriel stood below, out of range of the stone's deleterious effects. But the stone was visible to him through the glass tabletop. Glass that was of uncommon make. Thick. Clear. Devoid of defects. At first glance it appeared as if the stone floated in midair. Uriel's Svartish minions created that glass long ago at his behest. Useful in many ways were the Svarts, despite their limitations.

Uriel's apprentice, Mysinious — tall, blonde, and scantily clad, stood close to Uriel, hand discretely resting against his leg, and gazed up at the stone. She and Malth'Urn were about as different from each other as two females could be. Both, however, served well his purposes.

Another apprentice, Kapte, strolled in. Younger, shorter, and even more scantily clad than Mysinious. "Any word from Starkbarrow?" she whispered as she took her place by Uriel's side. She noted the position of Mysinious's hand, and she mirrored it on Uriel's opposite leg.

"Fighting in the caverns was the last we heard," said Mysinious. "There's been nothing further for hours. Malth'Urn is trying again."

"Could it be the ones that you sensed, Master? From that ship?" said Kapte.

"Undoubtedly," said Uriel.

"Do you really think they're Azathothians?" said Kapte. "After all this time?"

"There are two or three amongst them not born of Midgaard," said Uriel. "I am certain now that they destroyed the Ivaldis. If not, we would have heard from them. Now Starkbarrow's tunnels are invaded. This is an assault. They have a mission. They're coming here. To Anglotor. To the temple. There can be no other explanation."

"You think they mean to open a portal to the Nether Realms?" said Kapte. "For real?"

"To Nifleheim," said Uriel. "That is their purpose. It's what we're here to prevent." Uriel stared off in a different direction and paused a moment before he spoke again. "They are not the first to come. A group of adventurers ventured here long ago — named men, famous in their lands, heroes to some — treasure hunters and tomb raiders, in truth. Over the years, three different cults of demon worshippers have schemed to open the portal. One time, way back, a mercenary army raised by the Monks of Trilkmaktor assaulted us. A hundred years ago, a famed archwizard of Lomion came here with evil intent. Twenty years ago it was a group of smallfolk — sneak thieves and illusionists. I have stopped them all. Of them all, not one left Jutenheim alive."

"Not even some of that army you mentioned?" said Kapte.

"Not even one of them," said Uriel.

Kapte nodded, wide eyed. "But how do you know that some of the ones coming are not Midgaardians, Master? And where else could they have come from?"

"He knows," said Mysinious. "Were you asleep during your lessons? Have you forgotten the nine worlds. And the great tree, Yggdrasil, that connects them and supports them all?"

Kapte narrowed her eyes. "Those are just fables. Myths. Aren't they?"

They both looked to Uriel. "We've no time now for cosmology or metaphysics lessons. If we survive what's coming, I'll gift you all I know on the subject, half at least you've heard already."

"Anything?" said Uriel, calling up to Malth'Urn.

She raised her hand, giving sign she was concentrating.

"If they've passed the Svarts," said Uriel, "it is only a matter of days before they will be at our doorstep."

"We are well prepared," said Mysinious.

"We're prepared for soldiers," said Uriel. "A wizard or two. Even one of great power. We're not prepared for a Nifleheim Lord and worse. The mystical aura that that group gives off speaks of magics beyond me. Either a god walks amongst them, or a dozen archwizards, or both. We're not prepared for that. No one could be."

The color drained from the faces of both apprentices. They had not expected this. Were not prepared for it. Uriel was confidence personified. Strength. Energy. Wisdom. Immortal. Unbeatable. Eternal. But if he thought that they weren't prepared for what was coming — if it was beyond him —what did that mean? Were they doomed?

"I cannot find Karakta," said Malth'Urn. "Dead she be. Or cloaked of magic beyond my sight."

"We must make ready," said Uriel as he turned and made for the exit, his apprentices alongside, fearful looks on the women's faces. "They will be coming all too soon."

"Master," said Malth'Urn as she turned from the stone and looked down at Uriel. "There is more. Eyes are upon us. The enemy watches us even as we attempt to watch them."

Uriel's brow furrowed. He turned to the apprentices. "Mys, send word to our allies. Call them in. All of them. Kapte — gather all my consorts in my chambers. Go now, I must stay and hear more of this."

Looking dazed, the apprentices nodded and made for the exit. Mysinious opened the door. A tall figure stood before her. Cloaked in shadow. Shimmering. Indistinct. A grey fog hung all about it and the corridor beyond. Mysinious's mouth dropped open in surprise even as a long black blade plunged through her abdomen and exited her back. Blood sprayed across the room.

19

DOR EOTRUS ON THE BATTLEMENTS

YEAR 1267, 4TH AGE
LAST YEAR OF KING TENZIVEL'S RULE

MALCOLM EOTRUS

"Let's go boys," said Baret as he pulled Malcolm by the arm.

"We're supposed to wait for the horn," said Malcolm. He sounded dazed; looked it too. He peeked over the battlements. The view, surreal. The Outer Dor, a seething mass of angry trolls. So densely packed were they, he couldn't see the smallest patch of pavement. Some crowded the rooftops, others clung to the walls. All were hell-bent on getting into the keep. On feasting on Eotrus flesh.

"Make for the underhalls, you fools," shouted Baret to whoever was listening.

A troll pulled itself up over the crenel.

Malcolm felt himself moving toward it, but he didn't know how or for what purpose. His sword took the top half of the troll's head off. Its blood spurted onto his tabard and face. For some reason, that snapped him out of his daze. His cut surely must have killed the creature, but Malcolm didn't pause to find out.

He turned and rushed down the steps with

Baret, several veterans following on their heels.

When they reached the courtyard far below, they ran. The horns were blasting by then. They called for the retreat. Malcolm was in shock. The battle had barely begun — and yet the trolls were over the wall. The fighting, hand-to-hand and bloody. The keep on the verge of falling.

Already, there were trolls on the courtyard. Malcolm saw more leap down from the battlements across the way. Fifty feet that drop was, if an inch. Most of the trolls got up straightaway, seemingly unharmed. Others rolled about, howling, some bone or other broken.

A mass of men stood in formation before the Odinhome, guarding that hallowed building and its entry to the Dor's Underhalls below. They were hard pressed already, that brave company, though they outnumbered the trolls that came at them, ten to one at the least. That's where Malcolm needed to go. The Underhalls. Everyone was to retreat there if the withdrawal sounded. That's where Ector would be. And Sarbek. And all the civilians.

If the trolls breached the walls, the plan was to barricade themselves down in the Underhalls. To hold out until help arrived from the Eotrus bannermen or from Lomion City. However long that took. The problem was, Malcolm couldn't get there. A dozen trolls barred his path. Thank the gods, their attention was not on him, for other men ran all about.

More trolls surged over the walls every moment.

Malcolm sensed something behind him and spun about.

A troll!

A huge one — two strides away, bearing down on him.

There was no escape.

Malcolm raised his sword, to block or swing, but before he did either, Baret's blade slashed the troll's neck. It cut deep.

The troll staggered back. Baret's kick drove it to the ground. His foot pinned it down.

But the troll was not done.

Its arm swiped out, knocked Baret from his feet.

Malcolm looked for an opening. To jump in. To help. They moved so fast. He couldn't risk hitting Baret.

Baret and the troll made their feet in an instant. Blood sprayed from the troll's neck. Droplets landed across Malcolm's tabard. A few struck his cheek.

The terrible wound didn't even slow the troll.

Baret sidestepped. His sword flashed by again. And the troll's head flew from its neck.

Malcolm didn't even have time to get in position to help, little less take a swing. He was out of his league in that fight. And he knew it. He was no storied knight. No weapons master. He was little more than a boy, his rank and pedigree notwithstanding. He wasn't ready to fight trolls, if ever a mortal man could be.

Baret grabbed his arm and pulled him along without a word. The fighting surged all around them. Thicker by the moment. Eotrus men ran this way and that — some toward the Odinhome; others made for the citadel. The trolls leaped and pounced. They howled and slavered. They pulled the men down, one after another. Kicking. Screaming. Fighting to the last. Tooth and nail. Dagger and foot.

The way to the Odinhome was barred. A dozen trolls prowled that way and jumped every man that came near. A meat grinder it was. They could die there fighting beside their fellows, but they'd never get through.

By the Vanyar's luck, a clear enough path to the citadel remained open. So that's where they went.

A bunch of soldiers rushed through the citadel doors ahead of Malcolm. Even more behind. A full squadron held the doors. Several trolls had been cut down around the entryway; several men too.

The entry hall was packed with soldiers. Wide eyed but angry. A lot of them young, inexperienced. Not any older than Malcolm. For some, this was their first fight. None of them had fought trolls before.

Men pulled the great doors closed. A few soldiers dived through at the last moment. The guardsmen held the doors ajar for as long as they could. Not two seconds after they pulled them closed, the first troll slammed into it. The officers, what few there were, shouted to barricade the doors. They put the great crossbar in place, and tied the iron pull rings together with heavy chains. Then Malcolm saw that someone had installed anchors for more crossbars, every foot or so, from the very bottom of the doors, to their tops.

Men heaved great timbers into place. Others rolled heavy barrels filled with rocks up against the doors.

Malcolm didn't know what to do.
He wasn't supposed to be there.
None of them were.

20
HOUSE ALDER LOMION CITY

YEAR 1267, 4TH AGE
LAST YEAR OF KING TENZIVEL'S RULE

THE GRANDMISTRESS

When you command the most feared assassin's guild in the known world, every once in a while you need to do something unexpected. Something odd. To keep them guessing. The moment you become too predictable, someone hangs a target on your back, and people line up to start taking shots.

Weater pleaded with her not to go to House Alder herself, little less alone.

"*The most conniving family in all Lomion City will know your face and be able to take your measure*," he said. "*That will weaken your position. Make you more vulnerable.*"

He was right, of course, but he didn't have all the information needed to realize that the upside outweighed the downside. Still, maybe the little worm did care for her — beyond the effects of the perfume. It was hard to tell with that one. Well, with anyone. She only saw people through the veil of the perfume. What they were otherwise like was always a bit of a mystery. Every magic had its downsides, its costs. That was one of the perfume's.

The Grandmistress figured that her best chance to get the Malvegil contract paid was to visit Mother Alder herself. If she sent her flunkies or leg breakers like Weater, Coburn, or The Rat, Mother Alder might get insulted and refuse to pay. That might start a war, because if they refused to pay, she'd be obliged to hurt them — or else look weak. She didn't want it to come to that. No profit in it.

Besides, the Alders were powerful and dangerous folk. Not that she couldn't deal with the whole clan if she had to, for she could, but it was best for any number of reasons to keep the peace. If there was any killing to be done, she wanted to do it for coin, not for a feud.

Getting paid on that contract was only one of the reasons she wanted to visit House Alder herself.

She knew that Mother Alder was a true seer. And she needed one of those to operate the Malvegil Stone, as she came to call the seer stone that her brethren seized from the cold dead hands of old Torbin Malvegil. Where he got the thing, and what he was doing carrying it around, remained a mystery. But one that she eventually wanted to solve. She'd forge a deal with Mother Alder. Shared use of the Stone — as a thank you for prompt payment on the contract. What seer would pass up a chance to use a real seer stone? To have regular access to it? Not a one.

The other reason was personal. She'd seen the Witch Mother about the town at social gatherings any number of times over the years. She was older than her preference, and surely a lot older than even she looked, but she was stunning nonetheless.

The Grandmistress wanted to sink her teeth into her. With the perfume, success was a given. More than the pure fun of it, she suspected the Witch Mother was a kindred spirit. She hadn't found someone like that in a long time. Maybe a waste of time on that front, but she wouldn't know until she met the woman.

A stormy night it was. That suited the Grandmistress. She liked to cover up in public. Keep her identity, her face, a secret. And of course, not garner unwarranted attention. The heavy, unflattering overcoat and scarf did the trick, the big pointy hat, not so much. She couldn't throw fashion completely aside.

The Rat and a dozen of the brethren lurked about the streets, just in case. She usually didn't travel with more than half that many, but Weater had insisted.

The butler ushered her into the parlor after but a few moments delay, her outer garments left in the anteroom; she wanted to make an entrance. An impression. Heck, she wanted Mother Alder to see the curves. While waiting, she'd dabbed more of the perfume about her neck and wrists. Twice as much as needed. She intended to get everything she came for and was prepared to use all her assets to accomplish that.

"Mother Alder," said the Grandmistress, gifting her with her most sparkling smile as she strolled into the room, the large wicker basket that concealed the Malvegil Stone in hand.

She wore her tightest red dress. The one that was especially low cut. That would get the witch's attention, though she feared she over-painted her face. The perfume wafted around her.

"How is it possible that we haven't met?" she said extending her hand toward Mother Alder. "I've heard so much about you."

"Your reputation precedes you as well," said Mother Alder, her voice confident, her face, devoid of fake smiles. The Grandmistress held her hand hostage twice as long as customary and stood a step closer than most folks would. Mother Alder's eyes dilated right on cue, the perfume wasting no time. She had her!

She looked older up close. And lacked curves. But her face was beautiful and exotic, her skin darker than Lomerians, and flawless. The grandmistress's heart thumped in her chest and she salivated. If they'd been alone, she'd have taken her right then and there. But decorum must be preserved. The pitfalls of polite society. Someday she'd move her operations out to the country and do as she will. Oh, the harem that she'd have.

"My son, Chancellor Barusa," said Mother Alder, her voice weaker than before, her eyes never straying from the Grandmistress.

"Delighted," said the grandmistress with a quick curtsy, though she barely glanced his way. Barusa did not move from his spot by the fireplace, brandy still in hand. Maybe she'd take him too. Now that would be scandalous. "That handsome devil I've seen before." She leaned in closer and dropped her voice. "I attend the odd council meeting every now and then. Incognito, of course. It's important to stay up on current events, don't you think?" Up close, Mother Alder smelled vaguely of mothballs — a sure sign that she was no common seer, but a master. She'd made the right decision coming there, she was certain of it. Mother Alder would never turn down the chance to get her hands on the Malvegil Stone.

"Why are you here?" said Chancellor Barusa.

"Now, now, firstborn," said Mother Alder. "Let's not be hasty with our guest. Pour her a brandy and let's sit. By what name do you go by, my dear?"

"Oh, I have many names. Evil Witch, Bitch Queen, Goddess, Goddess of Beauty, Mother of Assassins, and several more colorful ones less fit for polite company. Personally, I prefer, Grandmistress. At least until we get to know each other a lot better. Which I hope we do. Then you can call me the colorful ones."

Barusa brought over the brandy. He stumbled a half step back after a single whiff of the perfume. Its effects started working on him the moment she entered the room, but up close, he noticed its effects and resisted. Curious. A strong will that one. She was wise to double the dosage.

"I trust this isn't merely a social call," said Mother Alder, "not that I wouldn't welcome it if it were."

"Sad to say that I came on business." She took Mother Alder's hand in hers and stroked it. "But now that we've met, I truly hope we can be fast friends."

"That would be wonderful," said Mother Alder as she squeezed her hand.

Dead gods, she wished Barusa would leave. The old girl was fully in her power now. She could do anything to her, at least in regard to the physical. But that would have to wait.

"There is a small matter of a debt," said the Grandmistress.

21

ISLE OF JUTENHEIM THE INTERIOR

YEAR 1267, 4TH AGE
LAST YEAR OF KING TENZIVEL'S RULE

The Eotrus expedition's climb down the cliffs was less eventful than it could have been. Their local guides, Darmod Rikenguard and his two sons, led them to a spot easier to descend than elsewhere. The Rikenguards had the right gear and were expert is its use. It was the sheer number of men and the amount of supplies that they hauled down that slowed their progress. It took the entire day to get the whole of the expedition down to the valley floor. Thanks to the Rikenguards, they all made it down unscathed. The guides passed out odd-shaped nuts to the men and instructed them to eat them as protection against the fever. Then they gave them each a leaf to fold over and hold under their tongues as they marched, a sip of water to soften them. Protection against some other fever born of the bog.

Close to the cliffs, the land was dry. In some spots rocky, grassy sloped in others. As one moved farther from the stone cliffs, the land grew softer and muddy. Then began the swamp. The Rikenguard's plan was to skirt the edge of the swamp by steering far to the east. That track would bring them out at the front edge of the swamp in half the time it would take to traverse the direct route — and that was assuming that they had a canoe to cross the water. Rikenguard had brought down two, just in case, though they had no use for them. They'd have needed near a hundred canoes to ferry all the men and supplies they carried. There weren't that many in all of Jutenhiem. They'd have had to drop men off and circle back over and over to make do with fewer boats. They didn't have time for that. And Theta didn't want to split his force, with a handful of men going on ahead, unless he had to.

So around the swamp they went. *It was the smart path*, said Rikenguard. *Not only the quicker, but far fewer dangers.*

"But is it faster than the underground route?" said Ob. "Them Svarts may have chewed a tunnel straight and true under the swamp. If that's the case, we'll lose another day on them, maybe two, going the way we're going."

"There's no choice," said Theta. "The underground road is blocked. Rikenguard's path is the quickest open to us."

"Which way does your ankh thingy tell us to go?" said Ob.

"Hard to say," said Theta as he held the artifact in his hand. "Generally southeast, but the distance still seems far."

"Well, Rikenguard's track takes us southeast eventually. That sounds about where we want to go. So let's have at it."

***

Most of the first day held few hardships save for hiking the uneven rocky ground along the base of the cliffs. Ever-present were the sounds of the swamp. The Lomerians had experience in the swamps of their homeland, but even at its outskirts, the Jutenheim bog was different. The sounds of insect and bird were routinely eclipsed by the roar and howl of who-knows-what. Rikenguard called them swamp creatures. Deadly. To be avoided. But he offered no more.

The air was heavy, stagnant. It reeked of decay. The mosquitoes were thick and hungry. The men all wore their gloves, and tied cloths over their faces for protection. Still, they felt crawled upon. Every man amongst them dreaded the thought of spending the night in that place, for they all knew that night was when a swamp truly came alive.

The men took comfort that they walked on mostly dry ground and out of the tall grass. They'd not accidentally stumble upon some creature unnoticed. More so, they took comfort in their numbers. No swamp creature, whatever its attributes, save perhaps the smallest of insects, could survive a battle with more than two hundred Lomerian soldiers. Even so, not one man amongst them wanted to be the first one who some creature took a bite out of.

The men's moods grew grim when they came upon the lake. Its waters reached the cliff face and stretched east for a mile and south for many miles. Small islands dotted its expanse here and there.

Rikenguard stood silently at the water's edge. He shook his head. Theta stepped up beside him.

Claradon and Ob followed.

"Did this gigantic lake slip your mind, Mister I-Know-Every-Blade-of-Grass Over-the-Rock?" said Ob.

"Didn't expect this," said Rikenguard. "A rainy year. More in the mountains it seems. Times past, there's always been a wide track between the lake and the rocks. I leave a canoe here, just in case," he said as he looked around. "The waters took it, it seems."

"It can't be very deep," said Claradon.

"One foot is deep for some of us, Mister Long Shanks," said Ob.

"Deep is not the problem," said Rikenguard. "Water serpents. Large. Dangerous. And gators — big jaws, big teeth. Biting fish, small but deadly in numbers."

"What are our options?" said Theta.

"Wade the lake edge," said Rikenguard, "or backtrack and use the canoes. Else, give up and head home."

"What's your advice?" said Claradon.

"At this point, I'd use the canoes," said Rikenguard, "instead to walk that water. Canoes would be safer."

"But a lot slower," said Theta. "We can't afford the time to go back. We wade the lake's edge. It's the only viable option. Let's move."

Rikenguard and his sons, Theta, Ob, Claradon, and their officers were near the front of the line. The Alders and Kalathans made up the middle, and Seran Harringgold and his soldiers were the troop's rear guard.

The expedition had walked the water's edge for a hundred yards when they saw the snake. Or they assumed it was a snake. A disturbance in the water caught the men's attention. A snakelike hump or coil rose up out of the water, perhaps fifty feet from the lead men. It formed an arch that spanned a couple of feet above the water as the thing slithered through the lake. No head was visible. But the trunk of that serpent must have been five feet around. Its tail end showed itself for a moment before it disappeared beneath the murky surface.

"How long is that thing?" said Ob.

"Fifty feet at least," said Rikenguard.

"Nearer eighty, I'd mark it," said Theta.

"What do we do if it comes at us?" said one soldier. Others echoed him.

"We kill the bugger," shouted Ob. "And we'll have fresh meat for dinner, and for the morrow. So stop your bellyaching or I'll feed your sorry hides to it." That stopped the grumbling. But it didn't stop anyone from worrying. The water was about two feet deep most of the way along the lake's edge. It never grew deeper than three feet — though that was deep enough that Artol had to carry Ob. The gnome had no like of that.

Rikenguard spotted gators several times along the way. Most of the time, only their eyes were visible above the water's surface as the creatures floated silently and motionless. By the size and spacing of their eyes, Rikenguard said that their size varied. Most were smaller than a man. Some larger. Some few were giants. Some of the gators were oblivious of the men's presence. Others watched them intently. But not a one dared to molest them. The benefit of traveling in large numbers.

The attack came when the expedition's lead men were two-thirds of the way across the lake.

Shouts rang out a third of the way back down the line. Men kicked at the water. Weapons were out. Cursing. Shouting. Some men sprinted through the water to get clear, but were slowed by the water's depth and the muddy and rocky bottom. To get by their fellows they had to step into still deeper water that further slowed them. Some men tripped or slipped and fell, fouling those behind them. Others scrambled up onto the rocky face of the cliff, dangling from puny toe and finger holds.

"What in Helheim?" said Ob. "I can't see what's happening. What are they fighting?"

"A gator or serpent if we're lucky," said Rikenguard.

"Why lucky?" said Ob.

"They act alone," said Rikenguard. "And the commotion will scare off others of their kind. But if it's the biters — the biting fish — the commotion will attract more. They move in schools of dozens or hundreds. I've seen them take down a horse. Chew it to the bone in minutes."

"Find out which it is," said Theta. "Let's keep the men moving, double-time." Theta stood his ground. Let the others pass. Claradon paused beside him.

"Gnome, get Claradon to the far shore."

"I need no babysitter," said Claradon.

"Pick him up and carry him," said Theta as he moved down the line. He tapped Glimador on the arm to follow him. "You too wizard," he said to Tanch as he passed.

Ob looked Claradon up and down. Claradon

was fully twice his height and more than three times his weight. "Kelbor, Paldor, Trelman, get your liege to dry land," said Ob. "Kayla, you too. Double-time it."

22

ANGLOTOR
THE OLDEN DOME
JUTENHEIM

YEAR 1267, 4TH AGE
LAST YEAR OF KING TENZIVEL'S RULE

URIEL THE BOLD

Mysinious groaned. She tried to grab the long blade that stuck through her belly. Her face turned toward Uriel.

Her attacker pulled its blade clear. Mysinious staggered two steps backward, then dropped.

Kapte was screaming. Backing up. Hands to her face. Screaming.

Uriel's sword was out. A blade of medium length, wider and thicker than common make. Engraved of stylish symbols of archaic style. A hand axe of similar style in his right hand. Even in his own redoubt, Uriel was ever armed, though the only armor he wore was his light steel breastplate, more style than substance.

The figure advanced. Out in the hallway, beyond the domed room's door, the stone flooring was melted and depressed from the attacker's passage. As if its very feet burned through the stone. Warped it. Whether that was from unimaginable heat, or great weight, or some other strange phenomenon, Uriel could not immediately say.

Uriel blocked its way. *Who was the figure? Why was he there?* A million questions sprang to mind. And anger welled over its attack on Mysinious. As Uriel's mouth opened to speak, he spied another figure behind the first. It was no lone assassin or spy. His fortress, his home, was under attack. Infiltrated silently. Without warning. How?

"Your time has come, traitor named Uriel," said the indistinct figure; its voice, deep and gravelly; its accent, odd. "A reckoning long past due. We have prepared for years beyond count. You cannot withstand us."

Uriel did not respond. He clamped his jaw shut and went to war.

Kapte backed up. Kept backing up until her backside hit the chamber's wall. She couldn't believe what she'd just witnessed. It couldn't be happening. Couldn't be real. Mysinious stabbed. Blood gushing everywhere. She wanted to rush to her side. Staunch the bleeding. Help her. Comfort her. Profess her love, despite all their sparring. But she couldn't get to her. The thing was in the room. More than one. Uriel launched himself at them.

Kapte expected her master's first strike to kill or incapacitate the assassin. The second blow would take off its head. He'd do the same to the next one, and the next after that if there were more. And then it would be over. They'd help Mysinious and everything would be alright. Uriel's strikes were too fast, too powerful for anyone to block, anyone to survive. He could kill as fast as he could swing his weapons, and that was almost faster than the eye could follow.

But that didn't happen.

The assassin parried Uriel's sword strike. A great clanking of metal rang out when it did so.

Uriel blocked its counterattack with his axe.

Then began a duel of sword masters beyond the modern ken. A dance of death the likes of which Kapte had never before seen and only heard of in Uriel's tales of ancient days.

Kapte didn't know what to do. She had her magics. But what to throw? She couldn't chance hurting Uriel. He might be angry if she interfered. He never needed help from anyone. Why would he now?

Kapte had no healing magic. She couldn't even escape the room. A second sinister figure blocked the door — cloaked in smoke and shadow, same as the first. She couldn't even tell if they were men or creatures — demons called up from the Nether Realms. The clash of steel was so loud in the domed chamber that it pained her ears. *Clang*, *clang*, *bang*, *bash*, over and again. A blur of movement were the combatants.

Malth'Urn dropped down from her perch and landed catlike, ready to bound this way or that. She clutched the seer stone to her breast. She must have felt vulnerable atop her stool. Surely, she knew that Uriel would protect her. She was as beloved of Uriel as was Mysinious, Kapte, and the other consorts. Did Malth'Urn think that Uriel might lose this battle? Is that why she slid down from her seat, and removed the stone from the spot it had sat for untold ages, studied by seer after seer before her, back into olden times? There was nowhere for Malth'Urn to flee. Nowhere to hide. The chamber, bare save for the stone's tall table and her stool. Nowhere to safeguard the stone. So she kept it close. And then Kapte realized her mind. If all was lost, Malth'Urn would smash the stone asunder. Shatter it against the cold stone of the chamber's floor. No doubt the vast release of mystical energy would kill anyone inside the chamber. It may well vaporize them to little more than dust and ash. Dead gods, could that happen? Could Uriel be defeated? Was it that desperate? Were they all about to die?

Kapte was paralyzed with fear. Sorcery swirled about her thoughts. But she couldn't focus those thoughts. She couldn't force order out of that chaos and select the appropriate spell to support her master or safeguard herself, the stone, Malth'Urn, or anything. She was useless. She could barely breathe. The metal banged and banged. How could that be? How could anyone stand against Uriel? Why hadn't he killed them already? What was wrong with him? It didn't make any sense.

Then Uriel's sword slowed as it sank deep across the creature's chest. Sliced its right shoulder. The cut went diagonally down across its torso.

Uriel's axe slammed into the assassin's forehead. The creature dropped.

Its twin came on.

Kapte's breath steamed before her. Much more so than was normal for the domed chamber. She realized that the temperature in the room had plunged after the creatures entered. Twenty degrees at least. Her bare skin was going numb. Creatures of the Nether Realms they had to be. Icy terrors out of frozen Nifleheim. Or dread Helheim. Dead gods, had the portal already been opened? Had the Azathothians infiltrated the fortress unseen and unknown to all? Did they already perform their vile rituals and succeed it tearing open a gateway to the beyond? How could that have happened unbeknownst to them all? Without Malth'Urn sensing it? Without Uriel knowing it? With no alarm raised? She couldn't catch her breath. The air was so thin. Uriel's sword clanged against the creature's. *Bang. Bang. Clang. Crash. Clang.*

And then the creature's head flew from its body; Uriel's sword had sliced through its neck.

And then Kapte's limbs functioned again. She could move. She made to rush forward. To throw herself into Uriel's arms. But his hand flashed out toward her.

"No!" he commanded in a voice as harsh as she had ever heard from him. It stopped her in her tracks.

Then she witnessed another impossible wonder, terrible to behold. The creatures' bodies dissolved; collapsed into a thick goo where they lay.

"Touch not their remains to your peril," said Uriel as he pulled Mysinious away from the corpses. "A single touch of their ichor will be your death. Heed me well."

Kapte moved to Mysinious's side, keeping clear of the ichor. She pulled off her shirt and applied pressure to the wound. The shirt turned red. Blood pooled about the cold stones.

Even as he held the wounded girl, Uriel's eyes returned time and again to the open door. There was no more fog there. No more blackness. Were they gone? Were there only two?

"Master, forgive me," said Mysinious, her voice weak.

"Forgive what?" said Uriel as he held her gently.

"I failed you," said Mysinious. "My beloved Master. I failed you. All my training and I could not defend myself. I am useless."

"The fiends surprised us all," said Uriel.

"One artery at least is severed," whispered Malth'Urn.

"Stay with us," said Kapte as she squeezed the other girl's hand.

"Kapte, get the Leren," said Uriel. Even as he said that, Mysinious's eyes fluttered, then closed, and did not open again. She was gone.

"I must get to the temple," said Uriel, "before all Midgaard is lost."

23

DOR EOTRUS
THE CENTRAL TOWER

*YEAR 1267, 4TH AGE
LAST YEAR OF KING TENZIVEL'S RULE*

MALCOLM EOTRUS

There were no windows on the first floor of the citadel. Only stout oaken doors, front and back. If they held, the only fighting to be done would be launching arrows from the upper windows. Before his injury, Malcolm had been a crack shot. He'd have done the troll damage from a window perch. But now, he couldn't draw a bow. All he could do was bumble about with a short sword in his off hand.

He hated having to give up using a long sword. That's the weapon his training had focused on; what he'd always felt most comfortable with. But he couldn't wield one anymore. His off hand didn't have the proper coordination. Or even the strength. But the shorter blade, he could manage. He could chop with it quite well. Thrust too. Slicing, slashing was tougher. He didn't have the coordination. The finesse. Parrying anything was next to impossible. Without those skills, how could he survive in real battle?

He couldn't. He knew that.

He didn't belong on the battlefield. Not any

longer. Ector and Sarbek were right. He should have stayed with them at the command post.

It looked like Lieutenant Krander was in charge of the citadel's defense. Problem was, he was a kid. The same age as Malcolm. His father was an Eotrus bannerman. His pedigree got him his position, not his skills.

There were at least a hundred men in the entry hall, and probably several times that many on the upper levels. Krander had no business leading such a troop. He wasn't ready. He didn't have the respect of the men. Hadn't earned it yet. Yet there he was, barking orders best he could. And so far at least, the men were following him. Good for him.

A group of soldiers rushed down the stairs, past Malcolm. Captain Haden amongst them.

That was a relief.

Of all the men in the archer corps, Haden was the officer most respected. A tough man, but well liked. He knew the ways of war. He stood with Malcolm's father at Karthune Gorge. And he came back alive. Little more need be said about his skills.

Malcolm didn't expect to see Haden there. Two-thirds of the archers were supposed to go to the Underhalls. Malcolm figured Haden would be there, with the majority of his men, protecting the noncombatants. Maybe he got trapped in the citadel too. Or else maybe, he figured, he could do more good from there. Either way, the men stuck in the citadel were far the better off for his presence.

The trolls pounded on the citadel doors; they rumbled and shuddered with each furious impact.

Malcolm stood there not knowing what to do. *What could he do?* What could any man do against those things? Baret was shouting, shouting something. Shouting in his ear. Baret grabbed him by the arm. But Malcolm didn't absorb his words. He couldn't take his eyes off the doors. The oak was splintering. The metal bands were bending, screaming. The men pushed heavy loads against those doors to brace them. They leaned timbers against them; shored them up with whatever they had on hand. Spears filled the room, leveled and ready; the men rock solid. Their courage would hold.

But Malcolm couldn't move.

He couldn't move his feet. He didn't know what to do. And then Graham was in front of him. The corporal grabbed his face.

"We've got to move, your lordship," said Graham. "We've got to head upstairs. Them things will be in here in a moment. We've got to get you clear. Let's go."

And then Malcolm was moving up the stairs. Graham was in front; Baret was behind, a hand on his back. They were running now. Running up the steps. The men made way for him, for them. They knew who he was. He felt ashamed that he ran while they stood firm. He didn't want to run. He wanted to stand with them. He would've. But the others pulled him along, up to the second level. There must've been two hundred, maybe three hundred men between them and the citadel doors on the first floor. And then Graham stopped. Turned around.

"Where do we go, Sarge?" said Graham.

"Up higher," said Baret. "All the way up."

"I want to fight," said Malcolm. "I've been fighting all morning.

"No one's questioning your skills or your courage, young master," said Baret. "But I've orders to keep you alive, and I aim to fulfill them."

"We had orders to bring him to the Underhalls," said Graham. "Sarbek didn't say anything about keeping him alive, not strictly."

"It was implied," said Baret. "Besides, what would you have me do, let the boy die?"

"Never," said Graham as he turned toward Malcolm. "We'll keep you safe, lad. Old Baret's the best, and I'm a close second. We'll get through this fight, you'll see."

24

HOUSE ALDER LOMION CITY

YEAR 1267, 4TH AGE
LAST YEAR OF KING TENZIVEL'S RULE

THE GRANDMISTRESS

"**W**hose debt?" said Barusa.

"Yours," said the Grandmistress. "Or rather, House Alder's. As you know, some time ago, Rom Alder placed a contract on the life of Torbin Malvegil. That contract has been fulfilled. I'm here to collect what's owed."

She looked back and forth between Barusa and his mother. "Oh my, have I spoken out of turn? I see that you didn't know about this matter," she said to Barusa. "But did you?" she said to Mother Alder.

"Very little that concerns House Alder escapes my notice," said Mother Alder. Then she stood and stepped away.

The old girl's head was not fully muddled. She moved away to buy time to think. Strong willed that family.

"You have the proper paperwork, of course," said Mother Alder.

She handed Mother Alder a folded parchment that she plucked from her basket.

Mother Alder opened it. Read it quickly. "Fifty

thousand silver stars is a weighty sum."

"It was a weighty deed."

"Why come to me with this?" said Mother Alder. "Your agreement is with Rom."

They didn't know. About the trolls. About the Alder brigade. Surprising. She'd heard the Alders network of spies and messengers was the best amongst the noble Houses. And being that she was a seer. . .

"You haven't heard?"

"Heard what?" said Barusa. He sounded agitated.

"It may be nothing, of course," said the Grandmistress, "but there have been reports of trouble in the northlands. Seems that a pack of trolls has gone on a rampage up in Eotrus lands. Your dear brother may be delayed in his return."

"Trolls you say?" said Barusa. "Is that a jest? Are you referring to the Eotrus?"

"No, Lord Chancellor. Actual trolls. Ugly, wild things, with claws and such."

"Rom has an entire brigade with him," said Mother Alder.

"And that's sure to be enough to safeguard him," said the grandmistress. "But the reports imply that there are a great many trolls. No doubt, your brother will return in good time. But as you can imagine, with a debt as weighty as this, The Hand requires prompt payment. I'm certain that we can work out something that's mutually agreeable."

"Rom will pay his own debts upon his return," said Barusa. "His debts are not ours."

"And if he doesn't return, then what?" said the Grandmistress. "His debt passes to his heirs. Is that someone other than his House?"

"I would know if my brother is dead," said Mother Alder. "He is not."

"So the debt remains with him," said the Grandmistress. "I'm relieved to hear that, but the debt will not wait. Though I do have something to offer that may make the payment more palatable."

"What's that, my dear?" said Mother Alder as she squeezed the Grandmistress's hand again and leaned closer to her.

Rom's brow furrowed. He didn't like seeing Mother Alder getting all cozy with the Queen of Assassins. A strong will.

"I have a curious artifact that you might find interesting," said the Grandmistress. She extracted the Malvegil Stone's box from the wicker basket and placed it on Mother Alder's lap. "Open it," she said, though she stood up and readied herself to step back.

"What's in that?" said Barusa.

"A relic, rare and powerful. Open it. Do not fear, it will do you no harm."

Mother Alder ran her hand over the box. Could she tell what it was? Even through the box? Lead lining be damned?

She opened it and her eyes went wide. "A seer stone."

The Grandmistress stepped back and back again. Barusa moved closer to take a look. A few seconds passed and he backed away, gagging.

"I hoped that you would know what it is. Have you ever seen one before? A real one?"

"Never," said Mother Alder. "As far as I know, there hasn't been one in Lomion City in hundreds of years. How in the world did you come by it?"

"In my profession, I come by all sorts of things."

"And what did you have in mind?" said Mother Alder.

"Straight to the point. I like that. You pay your brother's debt and I will give you access to the stone. Imagine that, Mother Alder. Your seer powers will be tenfold more powerful than ever before."

"Are you offering to sell it to us?" said Barusa.

"Access only," said the Grandmistress. "When Mother Alder wishes to use it, she'll visit me at Black Hall, at a mutually convenient time, and she can spy away. In return, from time to time, I'll ask her to use the stone on my behalf. A mutually beneficial arrangement, don't you think?"

"Using such a thing is not easy," said Mother Alder. "A seer pays a price every time she uses such a tool."

"Such is the burden of magic," said the Grandmistress.

Mother Alder tentatively ran her hand over the stone. As she did, eruptions of light shone from within. The thing came to life with her touch.

"Do we have a deal?" said the Grandmistress.

"We do," said Mother Alder.

"Excellent," said the Grandmistress gifting her with another sparkling smile. She leaned in, closed the lid on the seer stone's box, and snatched it from Mother Alder's lap. "I promise that I'll be most generous with providing you access to the stone. In fact, I have a feeling we'll be spending a great deal of time together."

"I think so too," said Mother Alder. "Perhaps

we can spend a bit of time together now."

"I would like nothing more," said the Grandmistress. She turned to Barusa. "It was a pleasure meeting you, Chancellor," she said.

"Yes, do run along, Barusa," said Mother Alder.

Barusa hesitated.

"Get out," said Mother Alder sharply.

He left the room and closed the doors behind him, his expression grim and disapproving.

"So jealous he is," said the Grandmistress as she placed the seer stone's box back into her basket.

"Let's not let that silly boy spoil our getting properly acquainted," said Mother Alder as she moved up behind the Grandmistress and gently placed her hand on her shoulder. Then she put her arms around the Grandmistress's waist, cupped her breasts, her hands barely covering a fraction of them, and nuzzled her neck, her face right where the perfume was strongest. She lingered there, fully under its spell.

"We should go up to my chambers at once," said Mother Alder panting. "More private and comfortable."

"Yes, we must," said the Grandmistress.

Mother Alder kissed her neck, then reached down with a hand to pull up her dress. They weren't going anywhere except maybe the couch. And they both knew it. Then Mother Alder reached around to turn the Grandmistress's head for a kiss on the lips — but instead, sliced her throat ear to ear with a short blade.

25

ISLE OF JUTENHEIM THE INTERIOR

*YEAR 1267, 4TH AGE
LAST YEAR OF KING TENZIVEL'S RULE*

EOTRUS EXPEDITION

As Theta moved toward the conflict at the lake's edge, the other soldiers fled it. "Man-eating fish," or the equivalent, warned several men.

A number of men limped along, obviously in pain, helped by others. The Eotrus men and the Kalathens fared well due to their heavy armor, but the Alders' lighter gear made them vulnerable.

"Can you send a bolt of electricity through the water? Either of you?" said Theta to Glimador and Tanch.

"I can," said Glimador, but I have to get closer.

"Let's not fry our men," said Theta.

There was no battle per se, just a bunch of soldiers trying to get away and trying to help their fellows. The water ran red with blood. Several Alder marines were down on their knees or their rumps kicking and slapping at the water, screaming as the fish went at them. One man was face down, floating, some feet from the others. His body bobbed and rocked as the fish struck it over and over, the water roiling all about him. Other men dragged their injured fellows to safety and were themselves beset.

A fish slammed hard into Theta's leg. He felt and heard its teeth scrape against his greaves. He reached down with speed and dexterity that few men could match and plucked the fish from the water. He lifted it up before his face, his mighty grip holding it firm. Not more than a foot long was it. A tiny thing. But a dozen teeth longer than a man's it had, each tapered to a razor's point. The thing wriggled in his hand, trying to get free, its jaws opened and closed frantically, teeth clicking together in manic fashion. Theta closed his fist and the fish burst to pieces. "Fry them," said Theta.

Glimador spoke his words. Tanch spoke some too. The injured men rose up out of the water, courtesy of Tanch's sorcery. Some dozen men hung suspended in the air. Several fish clung to the men; their jaws unwilling to slacken. One man's guts hung out from his belly. He was still alive. Tried to hold his intestines in as he cried out in agony. Another man's foot was gone. Others, bitten to the bone all about their legs. Some few on their arms or torsos. A scene of carnage, pain, horror.

Glimador completed his spell. Shouted elvish words from bygone times. A beam of white numinous energy erupted from his hands, shot into the water, branched out in tendrils. Struck one fish, then another. Each glowed brightly as the magic assailed them. More tendrils split off. Sought out the fish wherever they were. The water roiled and steamed, though the energy did not afflict Theta or Glimador or those few men that stood with them. It killed in an instant every biting fish that it touched. They rose to the surface. Lifeless. The water bubbled about them. The scent of cooked fish filled the air.

Glimador's magic killed every biter within a dozen yards in all directions. Even a couple of onlooking gators were caught by the magic and sizzled as their lifeless heads bobbed the surface. But they didn't get all the biters. More fish slammed into Theta's armor. Glimador's too. Testing. Probing. Searching for any flesh their teeth could reach.

"Can you hold them up?" said Theta to Tanch. "No," he said even as the men dropped back into the water.

"Pull them clear," shouted Theta.

And they did.

When they reached dry land, ten minutes later, the man whose foot had been taken was dead. Blood loss. The eviscerated man still lived. Still breathed. A length of intestine trailed behind him. Theta had pulled him along.

"What do they call you?" said Theta to the man. A youngster. Not more than twenty.

"Finnias of Alder," said the man through clenched teeth, biting back the pain. "Am I dying?"

"Yes," said Theta. "But you showed bravery and strength. You'll feast in Odin's hall tonight. You've earned your place."

Finnias attempted a smile, but a groan passed his lips. "Odin's hall," he said.

"No man can save you," said Theta, "but I can speed your journey. End your suffering now."

"No," said Finnias, barely able to get his words out. "That's the coward's way out. Not for me. Not for me. I will sit here until the Valkyries come for me. I will sit here."

"There is nothing to be gained from that, lad," said Theta. "You've proved your quality. Your suffering need not continue."

"I will die as the gods decree," said Finnias. "Leave me be."

And Theta did.

"A brave lad," said Ob.

"He will be a long time dying," said Theta. "Where are the Alders?"

"Seems their whelp got a boo-boo and they ran for it," said Ob. "Left their men to fend for themselves."

Two men were dead. Finnias dying. Another man about to join him. Three others were badly bitten, unable to walk. Another fifteen were injured but mobile.

In the end, they decided to leave Finnias and the three that were badly wounded. Six of the most injured walking wounded would stay with them to guard them.

The expedition set out to the south, skirting the eastern edge of the lake, though they kept at a respectable distance from the water for Rikenguard warned of gators that lurked and hunted the water's edge.

"What lies beyond these waters?" said Ob to Rikenguard as they and the expedition's senior men sat about one of two dozen campfires that dotted the low hill some two hundred yards from the lake.

"More bog," said Rikenguard. "As thick and deadly as that which we skirted. To avoid it, we'll have to turn east again until we pass its edge.

Two days it'll take to sidestep it. Assuming no holdups."

"And if we plow straight through to the south?" said Theta. "The bog be damned."

"Shorter distance but slower going," said Rikenguard. "Four or five days at least. But given the high water in the lake, we'll see the same in the bog. We won't be able to wade it. Have to swim. Snakes, gators, biters, and such. Some worse things back there in the deeps. We go that way without boats, we're dead."

"What's your thingy say?" said Ob to Theta.

Theta grasped his ankh in his left hand and held it up. He closed his eyes for a few moments. Held his breath. "South, south-east."

"So we're headed the right way, still?" said Ob.

"So it seems," said Theta.

"Some kind of charm?" said Rikenguard to Ob after Theta went off to check on the camp guards.

"It's just a lump of petrified wood," said Ob. "Helps him to get his way to pretend it's some mystical artifact from olden times. We indulge him."

"We've anything to worry about tonight?" said Claradon.

"The fever is our worst enemy out here," said Rikenguard. "With the nuts and herbs we took we should be safe enough, so long as we don't drink the lake water. I'll pass around another dose of herbs in the morning. Should keep us clean."

"I meant the gators or whatever else is in that water," said Claradon.

"Only things what come out of there in numbers is hippos," said Rikenguard. "A pack of them would be hell to deal with in the dark. But they wouldn't come at us on purpose; only if they stumbled upon us. Lions are different. I've seen them in the grasslands east of here. They're not afraid of men. Travel in packs. Always hungry. They'd do us some damage if they had a mind to.

"You mentioned Lugron," said Ob.

"Not here," said Rikenguard. "They roam the hills south of the swamp."

26

ANGLOTOR URIEL'S CHAMBERS JUTENHEIM

YEAR 1267, 4TH AGE
LAST YEAR OF KING TENZIVEL'S RULE

URIEL THE BOLD

Uriel leaned back on a couch in his chambers wearing only his silken shorts, all his armor and weapons stowed away in their proper places. The consorts, Malth'Urn included, lounged beside him, on the floor before him, and in the wading pool that dominated the center of the large room. His favorites, including Kapte, were closest to him. No one sat in Mysinious's usual spot.

The place was silent. And that felt strange, for the consorts were never quiet, not even during the most intimate times.

All eyes were on Uriel. Concern on some faces. Fear on others. One or two of Mysinious's rivals may even have been happy. Uriel tried not to think about that, for it made him angry. He had no time for distractions like that.

The consorts all waited for Uriel to disclose what happened. Tell them what they needed to know. Reassure and comfort them. He needed to protect them. Safeguard them from what was coming. For in his own way, he loved them all.

"The things that murdered Mys were Einheriar," said Uriel. "Warriors out of Nifleheim. The knights of the Nether Realms. Rare it is that such beings walk Midgaard. Rarer still for there to be more than one. They can be conjured up by certain wizards of great power using ancient, blasphemous rituals that include blood sacrifices. The Nifleheimer that recently landed in Jutenheim Town has done this thing. He or one of his minions."

"Did the Einheriar come through the temple?" said one girl that lay in the pool, older than most, but still beautiful.

"The conjuring would not require that," said Uriel. "They could have manifested anywhere. Probably they were set to appear right next to me. To grab me before I knew what was happening. The ancient magics of the Olden Dome stopped that. They could not manifest within, so instead they appeared outside the door."

"Surely, you would have overcome them anyway, Master," said Brithlinda, a buxom girl of flaxen hair and great height.

"Their merest touch is death," said Uriel. "Perhaps even for me."

Gasps all around. *No, no, it cannot be,* spoke the women.

"They are immune to most weapons," said Uriel. "Though some ensorcelled weapons will affect them, as will weapons made of ranal. We will open the armory, and distribute the ranal weapons to all of you. Even the ones that hang in my collection. I want you as protected as possible."

"You cannot protect us from what comes, Master," said Malth'Urn.

The girls turned fearfully toward the seer, confusion and trepidation on their faces.

"Enough of such talk," said Uriel.

"They need to know the truth," said Malth'Urn.

"What truth?" said Uriel. "They already know it. Azothothians come to open a portal. To bring forth the old god and his hosts. I will stop them."

"Tell them of the Nifleheimer," said Malth'Urn. "They don't know what he is. What a threat he poses."

Uriel's jaw clenched. His face darkened. He had not planned to go into such things.

"A lord of Nifleheim leads them," said Uriel to fearful gasps.

"A lord?" said Kapte. "Is there more than one?"

"There are many. Which one comes, I know not."

"Such things are as gods in the old stories," said Brithlinda.

"As is the Master," said Trilda, a dark-haired beauty.

"I am not a god," said Uriel. "I am a man."

"The greatest man," said Trilda.

"Aye," said the other consorts.

"Where did the Nifleheim Lord come from?" said Brithlinda. "There are no such beings on Midgaard, are there?"

"I don't know how he got here," said Uriel. "But he is here. And we must put him down."

"There are archwizards with the Nifleheimer," said Malth'Urn. "Four or five of them at the least."

More gasps and fearful looks all around.

"How can we overcome so many?" said Kapte.

"I have a plan," said Uriel. "I've had a long time to plan."

"Are they still in Jutenheim Town?" said Brithlinda.

"We've lost contact with the Ivaldis," said Uriel. "More than likely, they are all dead. So too have we lost contact with Starkbarrow. They were under attack. Before we got the details, they went silent."

"Perhaps the Svart have gone into hiding," said Kapte. "Abandoned the city to take refuge in the deep caverns."

"They are dead," said Uriel. "Starkbarrow is finished."

"How can you know that, Master?" said Kapte.

Uriel did not respond, he merely fingered the ankh that hung from a golden chain about his neck.

"It was the Svarts' purpose to stop any assault across the island," said Brithlinda. "They have thousands of warriors. Surely they could not have been defeated so easily."

"Yet defeated they were," said Uriel.

"Our other allies will help us, of course?" said Trilda.

"I have called for them all," said Uriel.

"Tell them of the primitives," said Malth'Urn.

Uriel's brow furrowed again and his eyes bore into the Svart seer. The women closest to Uriel inched away.

"Sometimes, in desperate times," said Uriel, his voice calm, "one must do questionable deeds for the greater good. Such is not my nature. But this is a desperate time."

"What have you done, Master?" said Brithlinda, dread in her voice.

"Agents of mine have taken the wife of the Ettin king. They bring her here even now as hostage. If the Ettin aid us as I've ordered, they will win her safe return."

Disbelief filled the faces of many of the girls. Shock. Sadness.

"And if they do not aid us?" said Kapte.

"I will worry about that only if it happens," said Uriel. "There is more. My minions have taken the firstborn children of each of the high chiefs of the Juten Lugron tribes. They too are being brought here as hostages."

The women looked shocked. Some downcast their eyes.

"Children?" said Brithlinda. "We abduct children? That is not right."

"They're just primitives," said Trilda. "They breed like rabbits. What does it matter?"

A look of horror filled Brithlinda's face. "What does it matter, you say? What a shallow, stupid little thing you are."

"But for the luck of birth, go you there, Trilda," said Malth'Urn.

Trilda turned up her nose to them and looked away.

"Did you ask the Ettin or the Lugron to cooperate before you took these steps?" said Brithlinda.

Girthmagen, the oldest of the women, gray haired but stately, broke her silence. "Uriel does only what he must do to protect all Midgaard. It is not for us to question him. But rather, to support him. I expect you all to do no less."

"Have the primitives agreed to cooperate?" said Brithlinda.

"They say they do," said Uriel. "The Ettin trust that I will not harm their queen. One or two of the Lugron swear they'll kill me no matter how this plays out. But neretheless, even now, they march toward the Plain of Engelroth to meet the Azatothians."

"I did not do these deeds lightly," said Uriel. "As Girthmagen said, all of Midgaard is imperiled by the Nifleheimer's plans. That portal must remain closed, now and forever."

27

DOR EOTRUS THE CENTRAL TOWER

YEAR 1267, 4TH AGE
LAST YEAR OF KING TENZIVEL'S RULE

MALCOLM EOTRUS

Malcolm thought that he heard the citadel doors burst inward. It was impossible, of course, up ten levels as they were, and all the shouting and screaming from without and within. Heard it or not, he knew the precise moment that the trolls sundered the doors. So did Baret and Graham. What sense told them so — sound or something else — some sixth sense, Malcolm didn't know. But they all stopped running at the same moment and turned about. A moment later, they heard the roars of the trolls as they flooded into the entry hall. They heard the twang of scores of arrows and bolts being fired.

The howls of wounded trolls.

The screams of dying men.

And then they were running again. Up and up the stair. Fast as they could manage. Malcolm had raced up those stairs a thousand times, nipping at his brothers' heels. The citadel was their home. The heart of the Dor. He knew its every hallway and room, every crack, divot, and spall. Every hidey hole was an old friend forged over long years of hide-and-seek with Ector, Jude, Claradon, and the servants' children.

Malcolm could run to the top of that stair, take a few breaths and sprint right back down again, barely a drop of sweat from his brow. But that day, when the trolls came, was different. Malcolm struggled with every step, his legs stiff and burning with pain. It wasn't just the fatigue from standing the wall all morning. The fear, the tension of the battle had seized up his leg muscles. They felt so stiff that he barely made half his normal speed and yet that took twice the effort. Baret was winded, huffing badly by the eighth level, and in trouble by the twelfth. But he kept going. So did Graham, despite the extra weight he carried on his frame. Graham's face flushed beet red, but he kept running. If those two could keep going, then so could Malcolm.

As they passed the twelfth floor, glass broke and shards flew all around them. Something grabbed Malcolm's shoulder and stopped him in midstride. A grip of iron lifted him into the air, legs dangling.

A troll!

The beast was at the stairwell window. Its arm stretched through the broken glass. Its body held back by bars that criss-crossed the opening.

Graham crashed into Malcolm. Pulled him down; broke the troll's grip.

Malcolm rolled over, pulled out his dagger. Baret had his sword raised high, the troll's arm still straining toward Malcolm, though now hopelessly out of reach. Baret's sword came down and sliced the troll's arm in two, up high, past the elbow. For a moment, the troll tried to hold on to the bars as blood spurted from its wound. But it lost its grip. Fell away from sight.

"Dead gods, that was close," said Baret.

"How in Odin's name did it scale the bloody tower?" said Graham.

Baret shook his head. "Nearly two hundred feet up smooth stone and faster than we could run it. What are these things?"

Only the bars kept that troll out. Bars newly installed on Sarbek's orders. He'd had them put in after another creature, a reskalan out of Nifleheim, had scaled the Dor's walls and attacked Claradon in his chambers months before. The men had thought Sarbek crazy for ordering such a thing. Ector went along with it. Malcolm wouldn't have. But the bars had saved them. Sarbek had been right.

"Where do we go?" said Graham. "Up farther or no?"

"I thought the roof," said Baret, "but if they can climb this high, then mayhap they can make the roof too."

"Then where?" said Graham. "We've got to get off this stair."

"My father's chambers," said Malcolm. "He has a safe room."

Up they went. Before they'd reached the thirteenth floor, they heard more glass break, both above and below them. Men yelled up on the higher floors. Archers were up there. Moments later, a soldier's body fell down the center of the stairwell past them. The trolls were in the tower. Above them!

Men ran down the steps toward them. Four archers, bows in hand. One was a sergeant.

"They're on the roof and coming in the windows," said the man, breathless. "They're ripping out the bars. And they don't die. Shoot them. Stab them. They don't die."

"We'll not make the sixteenth," said Baret as he looked to Malcolm. "Is there another place?" The sounds of battle filled the stair, mostly from below, but now also from above.

Malcolm's mind was muddled. He couldn't think. Brother Donnelin had reinforced his father's safe room. The secret room had always been there, but Donnelin lined it with steel plate and replaced the door. He'd outfitted it with all sorts of contraptions. And then it hit Malcolm — Donnelin had his own safe room. Malcolm had never been in it, but he saw Donnelin step out of it once when he'd scurried into the priest's chambers to hide from his brothers.

"This way," said Malcolm as he pushed past the archers. "We're going to fourteen. Donnelin's chambers."

They made it to that floor unmolested, though the fighting drew closer above and perhaps below. Baret grabbed Malcolm's arm and pushed him aside as he sought to open the door to the fourteenth floor. Baret thrust the door open, poised to strike. The hall was clear.

They ran past Ob's chambers, and then reached Donnelin's door. Locked as always. Malcolm didn't carry a master key but he didn't need it. He could pick it. The Eotrus boys had found their way into every room in the Citadel, one way or another. He went to one knee to get at the lock.

"Troll!" shouted someone.

Then came the twang of a bowstring.

A heartbeat later came another.

Malcolm felt a rush of air, then a troll blasted into him. A grazing blow, but it knocked him to his rump. The other men were bowled over, one and all. The troll hit them at a flat-out charge.

Malcolm bounced up to his knees before the door. The troll and the soldiers were fighting. A desperate tangle of limbs and weapons. Malcolm figured that Baret, Graham, and four archers could take one troll, so he gave the lock his attention. If they couldn't take it, he supposed his help wouldn't make the difference anyway. But getting them in Donnelin's room before any more trolls showed up would save them all.

Ten seconds and he was in.

Two archers were down, including the sergeant. Both dead. The others were at the thing, sword and dagger. The battle, desperate and close. Malcolm hadn't seen Baret fight before that day. Not for real, in a full on melee. The man moved like Gabriel or Sarbek. An expert. Gray haired or no, his sword was swift, far swifter than Malcolm could manage, even before he lost his arm. Baret slashed the troll across the chest. Once and then again. The thing already bled from a dozen wounds. Graham's sword came down hard on the back of its shoulder. That strike nearly severed its arm; only a string of ruined flesh held it on.

The troll had had enough. It tried to run. Baret tripped it. It went down face first. Baret leaped upon its back and put a dagger through the base of its skull. That ended it.

"Inside," shouted Malcolm. The five of them

scurried in.

"More coming," said Graham, the last through the door. "And that one we fought is getting up," he said as he grabbed the crossbar and set it in place.

"I took it through the brain," said Baret, his eyes wide.

"Maybe it keeps its brain somewhere else," said Graham. "Its feet, maybe? Or its ass?"

A moment later, a troll crashed into the door. The impact made a loud thump and the frame rattled, but it held. Thick oak, banded and framed in iron; it wouldn't give up quick.

The men backed away, weapons ready, as the troll crashed into the door over and over.

"It can't be the same one," said Baret.

"I saw two more coming down the hall," said Graham. "One was a lot bigger. It had a big club."

The door frame groaned. It started to bend.

"It's not going to hold," said Graham.

"There's a safe room," said Malcolm, barely able to get the words out. His feet felt rooted to the floor. "This way," he said. He turned and forced himself toward Donnelin's bedchamber.

As he entered, a troll, stepped through a broken window across the room. It had pulled out one of the window bars. Bent the other aside just enough for it to squeeze through.

"Shit!" said Malcolm.

28

HOUSE ALDER LOMION CITY

YEAR 1267, 4TH AGE
LAST YEAR OF KING TENZIVEL'S RULE

BARUSA ALDER

Barusa wrapped a wet cloth around his face as he walked down the grand stair in Alder Manor, Sirnick Butler a few steps ahead of him. He didn't know if the cloth would block the effects of that witch's magic, but he had to give it a try. Whatever sorcery her perfume contained sought to sap his will every moment he was in her presence. It influenced him to bend to her every whim and to physically desire her above all others. Even now she was doing who knows what with Mother Alder — his mother! The thought of that twisted knots in his stomach. Now Mother Alder had called him back. Insisted on it. Dead gods, what sordid plans did they have? He'd not get involved in anything inappropriate. Certainly not anything obscene. Even if it were only with the Grandmistress, he could never. He was a married man. He'd not dishonor himself, his wife, or his House. But at the same time, he could not ignore Mother Alder's summons. If they had dark purposes for it, he'd flee, her wrath be damned.

Sirnick paused as they approached the door

to the grand parlor.

The butler had an odd expression on his face. Amusement? Disgust? Some combination of both? "Mother Alder requested that you return alone," he said, explaining why he'd not be opening the door for Barusa. He retreated back to the foyer.

Barusa watched him go. If he dared to turn about with the slightest glimmer of a snicker on his face, Barusa would give him what for. Wisely, Sirnick didn't.

The parlor's door was locked.

Mother Alder responded to his knock and opened the door a crack. She confirmed that he was alone before she opened the door wider and pulled him in.

"Mother, I will not get involved in any . . ."

The grandmistress lay face down in a pool of blood in the middle of the parlor floor.

"Dead gods!" said Barusa. "What happened?"

"That should be obvious even to a dullard like you, firstborn."

"You killed her?"

"Yes, I killed her, you moron. I need you to fetch a mop and a bucket of water here at once. We need to clean this mess up. You must tell no one, including Sirnick. Including everyone. You must act natural, normal, to any and all you see. Smile. No don't smile. If you do, everyone will know that something is up. Just act yourself and get that cleaning stuff now. No servants. We'll clean it up ourselves. Are you listening?"

Barusa couldn't take his eyes off the Grandmistress's body. He shook his head, not understanding how it came to that.

"Did she try to harm you?"

"No."

"Then why? We could have just paid Uncle Rom's debt. It's a trifling to us. Now we'll have The Black Hand out to kill us. All of us. This will destroy our House."

"Not if you keep your head and do precisely as I say. If you don't, it will be your stupidity that destroys us."

"But why do this?"

Mother Alder pointed to the wicker basket.

"For the stone?"

"Of course, for the stone, you idiot."

"But we already have two seer stones, for Odin's sake."

"Now we have three."

"This is madness."

"Do you know what I can do with three seer stones? Do you have any idea of what power that represents?"

Barusa shook his head.

"Well I do. This changes everything for our House.

"How did you escape her spell? How could you even think of harming her?"

"She held no power over me. Not for a moment. To me, her magic is petty and juvenile. I played along to get her to reveal whatever I could. Once she showed me the stone, she had signed her own death warrant."

Barusa shook his head.

"That's right, firstborn. She wasn't the Bitch Queen. I am. Be happy you're on my team."

"What of the Hand?"

"Once we get this cleaned up and the body

disposed of, you'll fetch Zilda here."

"She's leaving for Dyvers in the morning. Her studies."

"Precisely. And she'll leave on schedule, just as planned. But tonight, she will impersonate the Grandbitch for us, though she won't know it. Just do exactly as I say and we'll get through this."

29

ISLE OF JUTENHEIM THE INTERIOR

YEAR 1267, 4TH AGE
LAST YEAR OF KING TENZIVEL'S RULE

THETA

Theta's eyes burst open. A distant pinging woke him. Pebbles thrown against metal. Not loud, but incongruous in the night, otherwise silent save for bug and frog. Theta scrambled to one knee. The campfire to see by. Dolan, already up, weapons to hand. He heard it too.

More pinging; from this way and that. Metal was being hit for certain. What was going on?

A camp guard shouted the alarm from the south side of camp.

A moment later, an alarm from the north.

Now strange sounds broke out from all around.

A hoarse hissing from many throats out in the darkness.

A thumping of many feet.

A charge!

The camp was being charged.

"Up," shouted Theta. "We're attacked. Up! Up!" Many of the men were woken by the noise and the alarm but few were quick to their feet — it was two hours past midnight and the men were finally deep in their slumbers. "Get up, they're on us!" Theta donned his helmet; hefted his shield; drew his falchion, all in a flash, though not too soon. "Get up."

Even as the others reached for their weapons, sleep in their eyes, the wild roared into camp. They were everywhere. From all sides.

They were not animals.

Not men.

Nor any cousin of man.

Bipedal lizards they were. Gatormen, they came to be called. Thinner framed than a Volsung. Longer limbed. Spiked tails. Claws. Teeth like daggers; lots of them. Forked tongues lagging. Wide jawed like snakes. A reptile smell about them.

The gatormen raced through the camp. Shadows in the dark. Pounced. Stabbed. Killed.

Motion everywhere.

How many were there?

Hundreds?

Thousands?

Too dark. Theta couldn't tell.

Dolan's arrows flew. Two shots to the chest didn't stop the nearest gatorman. It charged up the hummock upon which most of the expedition's core group had been sleeping. An arrow through the eye finished it.

The next gatorman, but a few strides behind the first, weathered two arrows to the upper chest and came on toward Theta, oblivious of his wounds. Theta sidestepped. Thrust aside the spear's head with this shield. Slashed the creature's side with his falchion.

That blow should have ended it.

But it didn't.

The thing's scabrous hide was thick, tough, stoney. More armor than skin.

Its forked tongue flicked out. Shockingly long was it. Two feet or more. Aimed for Theta's eyes, but the knight dodged clear. Theta's next blow caught the lizard's neck. Its head should have gone tumbling away from its body. But it didn't. The heavy stroke took the gatorman from his feet, but failed to cut deep.

Theta stepped in. Shield bashed the gatorman in the face as it tried to rise, once and then again. That sent the lizard tumbling down the hummock.

Theta felt and heard the spear tip slam into his back. The blow pushed him forward and lifted him off his feet for a moment. The power of that strike shocked him. Pound for pound, the gatormen had several times the strength of a Volsung. Theta spun. His shield arced wide. The lizard drew back, avoided the blow. Its speed uncanny.

Men fought all around. The battle desperate, close. They weren't ready. Not for a full-on assault by a large force without warning in the middle of the night. And they were dying for it. Losing. Theta felt the fool to leave him and his open to such a thing. Fifteen guards at the camp's perimeter. Another half dozen scattered throughout the camp. Still they only had a few seconds warning. How had such a large force taken them unawares? It should never have happened.

Theta had no time to pull his hammer out. The creature was at him. Fast and angry. Unrelenting. He had to stay with the falchion, as ineffective as it was.

Ping. Ping. That sound again. Something had struck his armor. Not a spear. Much too weak a blow. His armor held so he ignored it.

Theta blocked the lizard's lightning spear thrusts with falchion and shield. Waited for an opening. But he couldn't afford to wait. His ears told him all he needed. The gatormen attacked them en masse from all sides. There were too many of them. Off-guard, in the dark, his men were at great disadvantage. And were dying for it. He heard the screams. His position, at the very center of the camp was the least affected so far. Only a few lizards had made the hummock. And his men were on them. He had to rally them. Get them into a formation. Use the wizards to best affect. But he couldn't do any of that until he put down the lizard that was at him. The thing had reflexes ten times faster than a man's. It bounced back too quickly every time he sought to bash it with his shield.

And then a big weighted net came down over Theta's head.

In the darkness, he didn't see it until it was on him. With a lightning slash and slice with the falchion, he cut a big hole in it, ducked, and tried to scramble out, but was pulled from his feet. They dragged him down the hummock. He saw nets flying in all directions. Ob was trussed up — two lizards atop him. He saw Claradon on one knee — a great mantle of magical light about him and Kayla, the lizards beating on it with clubs.

In the confines of the net, Theta couldn't bring his sword to bear. Ping. Bang. Ping. More impacts to his armor. Darts? Were they using darts?

The strength they had. He saw two gatormen fly by on his left dragging another netted man down the hummock. He couldn't tell who it was. And two more groups of two gators dragged two other men, flying by on his right. Theta's weight slowed the ones that dragged him by half at least. Still they raced across the ground, battering him.

Theta's anger rose. He let drop the falchion. Grabbed the net and pulled. It didn't yield. He didn't have the leverage. Couldn't get a sound enough grip with one hand. His own shield tied up his other. He thrust both arms forward and pushed the net back. Got his arm clear of his shield, even as his forward slide stopped for some reason. Both hands on the net, he pulled, and tore the thing in half. He came up growling.

DeBoors was there. He smashed one lizard's head with a hammer. Cracked it open. Blood and brain bits flying, even as a second gatorman jumped onto his back. Its jaws clamped down atop his helmet. He grabbed at the thing. Pulled it up and over him. The helmet going with it. Lifted the thing over his head. Brought its back down across his knee. For a split second, the snap of its bone outmatched the roar of battle around them. Theta extricated himself from the remnants of the net. His hammer to hand.

DeBoors grappled with another lizard, his hands to its throat. With a great wrench, he snapped the creature's neck.

Theta caught a spear thrust in his bare hand. Pulled the creature close. Dropped his hammer atop its head, crushing it to pulp. Another creature leaped at him from behind. He spun. Ducked. The creature landed beyond him. He brought his hammer down on the back of its neck. Once. Then again. Bone crunched beneath those blows. And then the lizards were running off. Disappearing into the night. Dragging nets.

"Stop them," shouted Theta. "The nets. Stop them."

Theta charged after the closest net. DeBoors went after another.

The lizards were lightning quick — even burdened with dragging a man in a net. But Theta was the quicker. He leaped over the net, landed on the backs of the two gatormen that dragged it. As they all smashed to the ground, one clamped its jaws on Theta's forearm. Wouldn't let go. Theta couldn't wrench his arm free. He bashed the thing twice to the back of its head and neck. Still it held on. He had the other gatorman pinned, but it squirmed and thrashed. Its spiked tail walloped Theta in the back, over and again, jarring him, threatening to take the wind from his lungs. He put his knee to the clinging gatorman's back and pulled up hard and fast until he heard the sickening snap of its spine. The other lizard was up.

And dragging the net away.

A man trapped inside.

Glimador. Theta recognized the armor. He fought to get free, a dagger sliced ineffectually at the net's fibers. Theta bounded after them. In five strides he caught them. Bashed the gatorman in the shoulder. It dropped the net. Fell. Rolled. Was up running in a flash. Its prey forgotten in its flight. Gatormen raced by on all sides. Dragging more nets. Theta leaped at another. Landed on the net and the man in it. The lizards lost their grip. They bounded off into the night. Theta tripped another group. Scrambled atop one gatorman and twisted his neck around until it snapped.

Theta jumped up. Moved as fast as he could possibly move. Barreled into another net group. Punched one lizard in the face so hard its bones shattered and its skull staved in. The other gatorman dropped the net and ran.

Another gatorman appeared. A huge beast. A foot taller and a hundred pounds heavier than most of its fellows. It opened its jaws wide. Leapt at Theta's face. Theta caught those jaws with the haft of his hammer. Its teeth crunched down on the haft but could not break it. Whatever ancient charms lived within the hammer were beyond damage from mortal strength. Theta grabbed the thing's jaw and pulled, his face snarling now with anger. He ripped those jaws apart. Tore the creature's head in half.

Gatormen raced past him on both sides. He was near the lake now. No lizards with nets were close. At the limits of his vision, he saw them. Gatormen dragged netted men into the water and disappeared into the night. There was nothing he could do. No way to save them.

As quickly as they came, they were gone. The gatormen. Fled back into the swamp and the lake from which they sprang.

Theta turned his gaze back toward camp. He saw a group of men gathered atop the very hummock upon which he'd been sleeping. Another group was atop another small rise. Beyond that, men were scattered all around. Some few bashed and sliced wounded gatormen.

A desperate struggle went on here and there. Theta raced to the nearest. Blain Alder had his hands clamped about a gatorman's neck. A huge creature. Bigger even than the one Theta had just killed. The creature had its hand on Blain's throat too. Theta pulled out his dirk and sank it into the base of the gatorman's neck as he strode by. Blain's face was twisted in pain or anguish.

"They took my boy," said Blain as he looked toward the lake, where no fleeing gatormen remained in sight. "They took Edwin."

Theta helped the men kill a half dozen more gatormen. He took two more as prisoners. He had the men hog-tie and gag them.

Soon the night was silent again. Save for bug and frog. And the wails of wounded and dying men.

30

JUTENHEIM

YEAR 1267, 4TH AGE
LAST YEAR OF KING TENZIVEL'S RULE

JUDE EOTRUS

Before his ordeal began Jude had only half believed that magic was real rather than just sleight of hand and trickery. Now it seemed to be everywhere. Wizards as common as dirt. The stuff of song and story. Sorcery was real. There was no denying it. Not any longer. He'd heard the stories. But it was always kept so secret. Even with Par Talbon and his apprentices living at the Dor; knowing them his whole life. They never did any magic in front of the family. At least not in front of him. They only talked about it in abstract terms. Even then in hushed tones in trusted company. Jude had thought it mostly bunk.

Now he knew better.

Jude looked around at the cordon of steel that surrounded him. The Sithian mercenaries marched along, shoulder to shoulder. More than half of them that were left were knights in brick-red armor. Only one in four or five of the Sithians had been knights at the start of this thing, but most of the regulars, who wore lesser armor, had been killed along the way. The knights were tanks in that battle armor. It wasn't as thick as that worn by the Eotrus, but it was well-sculpted and individually fitted to each man. No small expense had been spent in putting those suits together.

The Sithians had kept up their discipline through terrible trials. As skilled and well-trained as were the knights of Dor Eotrus, the Sithians may well have surpassed them.

At the rear of the troop were what Stowron were left. Maybe two dozen of them all together. What the Stowron were under those cowls they wore, Jude didn't know. Were they even human? Covered up as they were, he never got a clear enough look at them to make a judgment. Where Master Thorn had found them, Jude couldn't imagine. There was no denying that they could hold their own in a fight. Their agility was uncanny. Superior to any race of man that Jude knew. Skilled of blade and staff. Determined. They never gave up. They'd fight to the end.

In the center of the expedition was everybody else: Lord Korrgonn, son of Azathoth or so they claimed; Master Glus Thorn, that pasty-faced ancient wizard that everybody feared; Father Ginalli, the smooth talking lie-master of the band; Par Brackta, the beautiful sorceress; Par Keld who nobody liked; Par Rhund who kept to himself; Stev Keevis, an elven archwizard that seemed less dark than the rest; Mort Zag (aka Big Red), a ten foot tall giant with two horns on his forehead, fangs that protruded from his mouth, and red fur that covered him, head to toe. What he was, Jude could not imagine. When Jude looked into the eyes of that creature, he saw evil. Cold, dark evil. A heartless, soulless thing. But intelligent. Calculating. Not some mindless minion. Big Red had his own agenda. One that may or may not align with the League's or even with Korrgonn's. Jude wondered if the Leaguers were smart enough to have figured that. Nowhere on Midgaard that Jude had ever heard of could have birthed that fellow. He was the very image of the devils and demons of legend. A beast conjured from the Nether Realms. Or from a nightmare. Seeing him made Jude think that the mad mission that the League was on might actually be possible. That in truth there may be other worlds. That a wizard with the right knowledge and skill might be able to open a passage between Midgaard and somewhere else. And then bring something through. Maybe that is where Azathoth went. Why he disappeared from the world millennia ago. That is, if he were ever real to begin with. Those stories were so old, so ancient — who knows whether they were ever true, or just some fable or allegory. But there Mort Zag stood. Maybe his kind was the last of a strange breed that long ago died out but gave rise to the demonic legends. Mayhap a small tribe of them remain in some remote location that the League happened upon. Maybe there was nothing unnatural about him at all. Who could say? Jude didn't know. But he wanted to. It mattered. If other realms were not real, at least he could rest easy that the League's mission would fail. That there was no Azathoth to conjure up and no place to conjure him from. But the Leaguers believed there was. Believed that Azathoth was real. That Nifleheim was a real place. That Azathoth was there, waiting to be called home if only the conditions were right. And the Leaguers believed that Korrgonn was Azathoth's son.

But was he?

Jude had long ago stopped thinking of Korrgonn as Sir Gabriel Garn. Even though he wore Gabriel's face, his body, even some of his mannerisms. He wasn't Gabriel. A different person entirely. Jude had no doubt of that. None at all.

But did that mean that he was some divine or demonic creature from another world?

That was a stretch.

A big one.

But that's what the Leaguers believed.

In part, because that's what Korrgonn told them. Jude could see Ginalli being fooled. Shrewd as that character was, tell him what he wanted to hear, and he might well be duped. Glus Thorn was another matter. That fellow was a fountain of knowledge and wisdom. A man to be respected. And feared. Whether you liked him or not. Jude couldn't imagine the likes of him being duped by some charlatan. Yet Thorn believed Korrgonn was the real deal. And that opening a gateway to the realm of Nifleheim was possible. That bringing Azathoth back over to Midgaard was possible. And that it was something that should be done. That must be done. Or so Thorn claimed.

Jude didn't know what the truth was. He was captive in a den of professional liars. Of villains. Though they thought themselves heroes. Heroes of their faith. True believers. They thought that their cause was righteous. That they were the good guys. They knew that their methods were harsh at times, but they justified them. The ends justifying the means. An olden philosophy. Jude's father named it the refuge of those sorry souls with no moral center.

The Leaguers would never accept that. They truly thought that all those who opposed them were bad. Evil. Especially the so-called Harbinger of Doom.

All that swirled about Jude's head. He wrestled with it daily. Tried to sort reality from fiction. Tried to puzzle out the truth. But none of it mattered if he ended up dead somewhere in Jutenheim where his body would never even be found by civilized men.

Also with the expedition was Mason, a man made of solid stone, a creature brought to life by sorcery — of that, there was no denying. Lord Ezerhauten was there too, the commander of the Sithian Mercenary Company that the League had hired as their muscle. In addition to them, a squad of assorted Lugron mercenaries served as bodyguards to the wizards. There had been scores of those Lugron mercs at the mission's start, less than a dozen left. With them, Jude had little interaction, save for the one called Teek. He watched and guarded Jude day and night. Not a bad sort was Teek, considering.

The aforementioned group were all that was left of the League's grand expedition. The tunnels of Svartleheim, not to mention all the trials they'd weathered getting there, had done their damage. Thorn and Ginalli had lost most of their wizards. Ezerhauten had lost at least two-thirds of his company, including his famed Pointmen squadrons. The Black Elves had bled the expedition dry, harrying them all through the cavern system. After the League had defeated the initial assault by the elves, the little buggers didn't give up, they just changed their tactics. They avoided direct massed combat, and instead popped out from ambush, sniped or cut at the Leaguers, and then disappeared back into the dark. Many a man had taken an arrow from their bows. The Stowron had it the worst, for they wore no heavy armor that could deflect missiles. They'd lost men for every hundred yards they traversed in the tunnels of Svartleheim.

Once they finally got out, they all breathed a great sigh of relief. To see the sun again. To feel it on their faces. A wonderful thing. Even better, that the Black Elves didn't follow them out into the wide world. The Leaguers figured that the Elfs avoided the daylight. That mayhap it even did them harm. But they had no illusions that the Elfs wouldn't come out of their caverns once the sun went down. They had to get far enough away by then. And hope that the Elfs had no other exits farther south that would allow them to come up in front of the expedition. Nothing to do about that. Save to move with all possible speed.

31

DOR EOTRUS THE CENTRAL TOWER BROTHER DONNELIN'S CHAMBERS

YEAR 1267, 4TH AGE
LAST YEAR OF KING TENZIVEL'S RULE

MALCOLM EOTRUS

Graham shoved Malcolm out of the way and went at the troll that came through Donnelin's window, sword swinging. No hesitation.

The troll ducked Graham's powerful slash.

Its claws raked Graham's chest.

Graham spun around and whipped his sword in a tight arc.

Somehow, the troll dodged it. Then raked its claws across Graham's torso again. His chainmail shrieked. Squadrons of metal links flew across the room. Graham started to step back. He brought up his sword for another swing, but was too slow.

The troll's third slash ripped Graham open, belly to chest.

He staggered back, fell to his rump. His mouth open in disbelief.

An archer put a shaft through the troll's neck.

Baret and another soldier retreated into the

bedchamber. Slammed and bared the door behind them.

The troll leapt through the air. To Malcolm, it looked like the thing flew. Its claws held out before i. They caught the archer in the throat. Blood spurted everywhere and the man crumpled.

Malcolm swung his sword. He was so close that he couldn't help but hit the beast. But there was no power behind the strike. The blade merely bounced off the thing's scabrous hide. The stench that came off it was terrible. A foul fume that could make a man puke. The teeth it had! Incisors bigger than a winter wolf's.

Baret's sword worked up and down. The creature's attention on him. It matched him shot for shot. The beast's hide so thick, so tough, that its arms could parry a sword blow.

As Malcolm readied himself to take another swing, suddenly, the troll turned. Lunged. Its kick slammed into Malcolm's breastplate. He barely saw it coming. Had no time to react, to dodge, or block. It happened so fast, yet strangely, as the blow came in, it was as if it were in slow motion. Malcolm flew through the air. Crashed into the wall. His steel breastplate gifted with a huge dent at its center, as if Artol had taken his hammer to it.

Malcolm couldn't breathe. His back was against the wall, his legs out in front of him. He felt as if he were floating. His vision dimmed. Narrowed. Blackness crept in from the edges.

Malcolm regained his senses as someone dragged him backward; gripped under his arms. The fight was still on. The troll had just ripped the throat out of the last archer. Blood and flesh dangled from the creature's maw. Baret had lost his sword and his helmet, but held a dagger in each hand. His forehead ran red with blood.

A huge impact struck the bedchamber's door. The frame creaked, cracked, and bent. The door bulged and buckled. Only the reinforcements that Donnelin had installed kept it together. A few more impacts and it would collapse, just as the outer door to the apartment must have.

Baret's breastplate was gouged and dented. He was hurt. Wounded in more than one spot, but Malcolm couldn't tell how badly. Baret and the troll went at each other like madmen. Baret's daggers slashed back and forth, this way and that, using all the maneuvers that Eotrus men mastered. Except that Baret did them faster than almost anyone. The troll matched him, nearly. The thing bled from a dozen wounds. Every second or third dagger slash drew more of its blood. But the thing didn't slow. It didn't die.

It was Claradon's manservant Humphrey that was behind Malcolm. Good old Humph. He pulled Malcolm into the safe room. Humph had been hiding there.

"We've got to help him," said Malcolm.

Humph thrust the safe room door open, and simultaneously shouted a battle cry and slammed a war hammer into a shield that he held.

The troll's head snapped in Humph's direction.

Baret's dagger slammed into the troll's eye. His second blade sank into its neck. The troll spun around, howling. Somehow, Baret found a sword. Swung it.

The troll's head tipped off its neck. Its body

crumbled.

Baret glanced over at Graham who was still on his knees. Alive. Bleeding. In terrible pain. His guts hanging out. There was no time to do anything to help him. No way to save him. Baret dived for the safe room door. Humph and Malcolm slammed it behind him. Graham's eyes met theirs as the door closed. Two seconds later, they heard the bedchamber's door break. The trolls were in.

And then Graham screamed.

32

HOUSE ALDER LOMION CITY

***YEAR 1267, 4TH AGE
LAST YEAR OF KING TENZIVEL'S RULE***

MOTHER ALDER

Mother Alder and Zilda Alder, dressed as the Grandmistress: overcoat, pointy hat, shoes, leggings, scarf, and veil, stepped out onto House Alder's porch. Zilda was a match to the Grandmistress in height and general form, though she lacked her upper curves, which Mother Alder fixed with padding. She told Zilda that it would make the coat fit her better. Zilda, Bartol's first daughter, and thus Mother Alder's granddaughter, was sworn to secrecy over the whole event. And told she wouldn't be asking any questions. All she knew was that she was required to put on some odd clothes and accompany Mother Alder in their carriage for a ride. An odd thing to be certain. But when you're an Alder, you come to expect odd happenings from time to time. And if Mother Alder is involved, you learn fast not to ask many questions. She'll tell you whatever she thinks that you need to know. Best to consider that enough.

They paused on the porch long enough to make certain that the Grandmistress's people saw them together, and saw that their mistress was in no distress. Mother Alder was careful to stand closest to the light, keeping the fake Grandmistress more to the shadows. After a few moments, the carriage pulled up. Grontor the Bonebreaker, a Lugron mercenary captain in House Alder's guard, and a few of his men would follow behind on horses — an appropriate escort for two prominent ladies heading out into town. Mother Alder didn't see any of the brethren skulking about, but she was certain that they were there. In fact, she prayed that they were. Her whole plan depended on it.

"You haven't asked where we're going," said Mother Alder to Zilda when the coach started moving, just the two of them in the back, hidden from view and from the elements in the richly appointed coach.

"I trust you to tell me whatever I need to know," said Zilda.

Mother Alder laughed. "Shrewdly worded. That's why you've always been one of my favorites, my dear. We're going to the bazaar, or rather, you are. When we arrive, we'll both step out of the coach, exchange a few pleasantries, including a long hug and kiss on the cheek. I'll get back into the coach while we're still talking about what a lovely visit we had. The very moment the coach starts to pull away, you'll head into the bazaar through the revolving door. You'll keep going straight around, and immediately exit through the same doors. You'll walk up the street to Smidgewick Tavern, walk through to the back, out the back door, and into one of our coaches that will be waiting for you. Then off home you'll go, to bed, and up tomorrow as planned for your trip."

"And you're not going to tell me why we're doing this?" said Zilda.

"No, and you'll never mention it to anyone, including me, that it ever happened. Not one bit of it. Ever. Do you understand?"

"Yes, Mother Alder."

"When you step out of that revolving door, back onto the street, your clothes will look different. Pay that no heed. No heed at all. Not even a glance down to your coat or shoes. Do you understand that?"

"Not even a glance."

33

ISLE OF JUTENHEIM THE INTERIOR

***YEAR 1267, 4TH AGE
LAST YEAR OF KING TENZIVEL'S RULE***

CLARADON EOTRUS

Claradon stood atop the hummock, Kayla at his side. "To me," he called out in loud voice. "Rally here. Here," he shouted. From all sides of the camp men appeared from the darkness. Alder marines. Malvegils. Harringgolds. Kalathan knights. And Eotrus men. But not many. Not so many as there should have been.

Claradon's knights and comrades stood close about him. Sir Kelbor at his right hand. Kayla at his left. The Bull was there. Sergeants Lant and Vid. Artol.

"What in Helheim were those things?" said Kelbor.

"Where is Ob?" said Claradon. No one answered for a moment. No one wanted to say it. To make it real.

"They took him," said Artol. "I saw it. Dragged him away. Glimador too."

"What?" said Claradon, his face in a panic. "You saw it? Are you certain?"

"I saw it," said Artol.

"I saw it too," said Kelbor. "They took Trelman

too. I couldn't get to any of them."

"Dammit!" shouted Claradon as he slammed his foot to the ground.

"They dragged a lot of men away," said Kayla.

"They took Theta too," said Artol.

Every eye turned to Artol. Disbelief on their faces.

"He was just to my right," said Artol, "fighting a couple of them. They dropped a net over him and knocked him from his feet. Same as Ob and Glimador."

"They'd never hold him," said Ganton the Bull. "Not him."

Then came a grunting. Little Tug came into view as he trudged up the hummock, his great hammer, Old Fogey, to hand, though its bloody head dragged along the ground as he walked. The man looked battered. Out on his feet. "They took my captain," he said. "They took Slaayde." Tug collapsed face first to the ground and lay unmoving.

Kayla and Artol checked him.

"Still breathing," said Artol as he looked the giant over.

"I don't see any serious wounds," said Kayla, "but look here — a dart in his shoulder."

"Two more in his back," said Artol. He carefully plucked them out and examined them. "Poison. That's how they took our men. Some kind of poison. It knocked them out."

"Mayhap we can counter its effects," said Claradon as he turned and looked around for the wizard. "Tanch? Where is Tanch?"

They looked around. He was nowhere to be found.

"And Dolan?" said Claradon. "Has anyone seen Dolan?"

"Without Theta and the wizard, we're finished," said Artol. "We'll not survive this place, little less accomplish our mission."

Claradon frowned at the big warrior, and his voice went stern. "As Ob would say, stow that stinking talk, Mister Too Tall, or I'll knock you on your butt."

"My lord," said the Bull as he gestured toward Sir Paldor who lay on his back not far away. A spear was broken off in the young knight's side. Somehow it had found the seam between steel plates and penetrated the chainmail below. Paldor's face was ghostly pale. Efforts to staunch his bleeding were ineffective.

Claradon went to his side. Took his hand in his. The Eotrus soldiers gathered close around. These men, they were like brothers before the expedition. Living, working, training together for years. For some, for all their lives. All the closer now after what they'd been through.

"You took that spear to save me," said Claradon. "I saw it. You're a hero. I can see the look on Sire Brondel's face when you tell him this tale."

"I'm no hero," said Paldor. "I thought my armor would hold. It should have. And you'll have to tell the tale for me. I'm done for."

"We'll get the spear tip out," said Claradon. "Then we can stop this bleeding and sew you up right and proper. Once we do that, you'll be fine. Out of action for a while, mayhap, but fine."

"You'll have a nice scar to go with your stories about this trip," said Kayla. "The girls back home will like that."

"That spear is not coming out," said Paldor. "Not without tearing me apart."

"We have to try," said Claradon.

"No," said Paldor, his voice growing weaker. "Valhalla beckons. I can feel its pull. We can't fight fate, my lord. Anything else. But not fate. The Norns have decreed it. Tell my mother and my sisters that I love them and that I didn't suffer. Promise me that."

"I will," said Claradon, though the words barely escaped his lips, his throat constricting, his mouth going dry. He'd known Paldor since he was a small child.

"And tell my father, I died a warrior's death, doing my duty and such."

"I will," said Claradon, his voice a crackling whisper, his eyes wet. Claradon and the Eotrus soldiers remained with Paldor for some minutes until his grip went slack and he breathed no more.

34

PLAIN OF ENGELROTH JUTENHEIM

YEAR 1267, 4TH AGE
LAST YEAR OF KING TENZIVEL'S RULE

JUDE EOTRUS

Father Ginalli, foolish as he was, acted as if they were home free once they escaped from Svartleheim. Once they were in the open air and the light of day again. Ordered a double-time march to stay clear of the Black Elves, but that was it. He didn't even want Ezerhauten to send out scouts or flankers. *Keep everyone together and keep moving* were his orders. *We're close now*, he said. Well that wonderful strategy landed them in their current predicament. Trapped in the center of a valley, with two enemy armies surrounding them. Wild Juten Lugron on three sides. Giants on the other.

Giants, for Odin's sake!

Many of them as tall as Mort Zag. Many, a lot taller. Hairy creatures, though not shaggy like Big Red. These giants were men of a sort. Ape-like in their features and movements. But some primitive race of men nonetheless. The legends of the giants of Jutenheim were true.

For all appearances, it seemed that the giants and the local Lugron tribesmen had decided to wipe each other out. And they just happened to pick the day that the League was ambling by to do it. And by all rotten luck, the expedition ended up right between the opposing forces. What were the odds of that? Pretty low, Jude figured. But a lot of unlikely things had befallen them since they left Lomion. As if someone or something of great power were acting against them. Manipulating things to hinder them. Some wizard? Some traitor in the League's midst? The Norns? Or the gods themselves? Jude couldn't guess. He just wanted to survive the day.

And that was looking unlikely.

When they were a third of the way across the valley, a horde of Lugron appeared on the eastern hills. They streamed toward the expedition, hooting and howling. Hundreds of them.

Ezerhauten urged that they turn around and flee the valley at top speed. They'd go around. He feared a trap.

Ginalli would hear none of it. Demanded that they move forward at their best speed. Thorn went along. Korrgonn kept his thoughts to himself and stared off into the distance as he often did, as if he weren't with them at all — or perhaps, as if he were somewhere else at the same time, and that other place currently held his attention.

So they plowed forward, Ezerhauten cursing under his breath. Then the Lugron appeared in front of them. A smaller force but backed by siege engines. Ballistae of various sizes. Catapults, small and large. Of primitive design, but presumably in working order. In the back, even a few trebuchet. Ezerhauten had no interest in charging any further on open ground into that. He ordered the troop to turn around, Ginalli be damned.

Before the priest had a chance to protest, they saw the Lugron coming up from behind them, from the north. Cavalry. Though it was cavalry the like of which Jude had never before seen. The Lugron rode lizards. Lizards as wide and stout as horses, though of much shorter legs, so that they were low to the ground. There were a couple of hundred of them. Well equipped with spears, bows, and clubs. All their gear was of primitive design. Wood mostly. Leather of some type. Not much metal to be found and what little there was, was unskillfully crafted. Even the Lugron themselves were different from those the Lomerians knew from the north. Different from those few left amongst the expedition. The Juten Lugron were shorter and thicker of limb in the main. Though some few were as tall as Volsungs. Aberrations, mayhap, or else of a different breed. They had a wildness to them. A primitive fierceness few of the Lomion Lugron retained.

But one direction remained open to the expedition. West. Up the far western slopes, over and out of the valley. The way was rocky and steep in places, but definitely passable. The only question was, how to stay ahead of the Lugron? The lizards plodded along a good deal slower than horses, or at least, so it seemed, but they were still likely too fast for the men to outrun on foot. At least for long.

They had to chance it. There was no choice, save for open battle against hopeless odds. They shifted west and made their best speed. They'd gone but a hundred yards — they hadn't even hit the slope yet, still on flat ground, when they saw the first giant standing atop a rocky promontory most of the way up the hill.

Big Red spotted it first. Raised the alarm. He wasn't even near the front line. Maybe he smelled the thing. Or maybe his eyesight was a lot better than anyone else's. The thing had fur like a bear. In fact, that's what it looked like at first from the distance. A big brown bear.

That wasn't going to stop the Sithians.

They saw it, paused, then started right up again. They'd run by it or over it, but they were going to get up that damned hill.

Then another giant appeared. And another. Then a whole horde of them. They weren't bears. That became clear quickly. The smallest of them had to be seven feet tall and three hundred fifty pounds. Most were about nine or ten feet tall. Some more than that. Twelve feet perhaps. Maybe a thousand pounds. As large or larger than the largest brown bear. The sight of that group stopped the company in its tracks.

Ezer's men weren't interested in wading into that.

Then appeared the giant's chieftain.

Oh boy!

Maybe fifteen feet tall. Maybe even more. And twice as broad as most of the others. A shaggy gray beard dangled from his chin.

"What do we do?" shouted Ginalli. "Which way can we go? We've got to get Lord Korrgonn clear of here."

He was looking to Ezerhauten, whose eyes scanned all around, though Ezer failed to reply.

"How do we get clear?" shouted Ginalli again.

"We don't," said Ezer. "We're surrounded. We're outnumbered. We're in the deep shit now."

"You should have never led us into this valley," said Ginalli.

"Me?" said Ezerhauten. "You're blaming me, you sniveling shit? Get your spells ready and keep your mouth shut. We have to wipe out whatever force they send at us, and quickly. Maybe that will give them pause. Maybe they'll back off or give up altogether. Figure that we're more trouble than we're worth."

"Don't dare to give me orders, mercenary," said Ginalli. "Or to insult me again. You work for me. Don't forget that."

Ezerhauten's jaw clenched. Jude figured he must have bitten through his tongue the way his face looked pained and red.

"How did they know we were coming?" said Par Keld. "Who betrayed us? Someone must have. Who was it?"

"No one betrayed us, you fool," said Master Thorn. "They gathered to battle each other. We're just in the way."

"So let's get out of the way," said Ginalli.

"Maybe they'll let us go," said Keld. "Maybe we can buy our way out?"

"Each side probably thinks we work for the other," said Ezerhauten.

"Then we should attack one side," said Ginalli. "Then pull back. The other side will think we're on their side and leave us be. We'll be able to flee."

"If we attack one side," said Ezerhauten, "that side will throw their full force at us, not knowing of what we're capable. The other side will sit back and watch us get slaughtered. Every one of their enemies that we bring down will be one less for them to deal with. When we're out of action, they'll continue their little war."

"Then what are we supposed to do?" said Keld.

"Let them come to us," said Ezerhauten. "Then kill them quickly and without mercy. Give the others pause, just as I said. It's all we can do. Other than to try to run. If we do, one side or both will run us down."

35

DOR EOTRUS THE UNDERHALLS

***YEAR 1267, 4TH AGE
LAST YEAR OF KING TENZIVEL'S RULE***

SARBEK DU MARTEGRAN

Sir Sarbek du Martegran, acting castellan of Dor Eotrus, and knight commander of the Odion Knights, stood in the First Underhall beneath Dor Eotrus's Odinhome. Hundreds of soldiers flooded through the great steel doors and parted around Sarbek and the clutch of knights aligned behind him. Sarbek wore his Odion battle armor that day: a full suit of plate forged by the master metalsmithes of the Odion Chapterhouse in Lomion City. Of an exotic alloy it was made, heat treated and quenched, one-third lighter than common steel but just as strong, the plates half again thicker than that worn by other Lomerian knights. That plate was supplemented by the stoutest Dyvers chainmail at every joint and juncture. Well over a hundred pounds of steel all told. No other militant order wore anything like it.

Sarbek's face was hard. Angry. In his right hand he gripped a long sword of wide blade, heaviest at its end — the signature weapon of the Odions. A sword that had served him well for forty years. A steel battle shield in his left hand, tall and rectangular, polished to a shine, the Martegran sigil embossed in bright hues at its center, the Eotrus colors adorned the ribbons at its edges.

Six soldiers stood behind each side of the double doors, awaiting Sarbek's command to close and bar the way.

Ector Eotrus was there, clad in the stout plate armor of the Tyrians, his knightly order. Captain Pellan, the beardless dwarf, stood beside Sarbek. Her armor wasn't nearly as heavy, and didn't fit nearly as well (as it wasn't made for a dwarf, but rather, a short Volsung), but was stout and sturdy all the same.

"What the heck happened?" said Pellan. "Could they have breached the gates so quickly?"

Sarbek made no answer. He stood there, jaw clenched.

Over the din of the men, now came the roaring of trolls. By the sound of it, some few at least were inside the Odinhome. Sarbek stood a fighting stance; Pellan did the same.

Sarbek heard the clash of weapons. The twang of bows.

He looked over his shoulder. Ready to support him, along both walls of the corridor stood archers, one behind the other. Two hundred strong. They waited for the flood of soldiers to pass. Then they'd array themselves behind Sarbek — kneelers in the front row, standing in the second, atop benches in the third, ready to fire either en masse or in three alternating waves to provide continuous attacks.

The last men through the doors was a battered and bloody squad led by Sir Indigo. They ran in, weapons dripping of gore, and dodged to the side, leaving wide open the center. Four trolls came through the doors on their heels. Sarbek didn't need to give the order. He merely dropped low, as did the soldiers behind him. The men knew what to do. All three rows of archers opened up. A blistering torrent of arrows pincushioned the trolls. No less than a dozen shafts struck each. All but one troll went down, though not one of them was dead.

"Bar the doors," shouted Sarbek as Indigo and his men pounced on the wounded trolls. The knights with Sarbek joined them.

A single slash of Indigo's sword took the head from the one troll that still stood. He ignored the rest, trusting to the others to finish them off and strode up to Sarbek and Pellan.

"What happened?" said Sarbek.

"They scaled the walls, like squirrels up trees," said Indigo. "Within ten seconds of their charge, some were up and over. Only the oil and pitch stopped them, but they went around. Found whatever openings there were. Got enough of them on the battlements to disrupt us within a minute or two. Whoever stood and fought them, got dead. They could have come over hours ago if they had wanted. They could have come over at any time."

"Then why wait?" said Ector.

"They wanted to come all at once," said Sarbek. "Overwhelm our defenses, minimize their losses. Seems it worked. Stinking buggers."

"They wanted to put the fear in us," said Pellan. "They wanted us to see what they did to the Outer Dor and the sorry fools that wouldn't leave her. They wanted us to fear them."

"Was that all what got in?" said Sarbek pointing to what was left of the trolls on the corridor floor. Some few men were still hacking them to pieces. There was a lot of anger to loose.

"All that we didn't kill in the sanctuary," said Indigo, "or on the way down. I lost a lot of good men up there. We got the sanctuary doors closed and barred, but six or eight of them got through. We also managed to bar the Underhall door. Locked it up tight."

"They'll be in the sanctuary by now," said Sarbek. "Those doors were not meant to hold back such as them."

"But the first underdoor is," said Pellan.

"It may hold for a while," said Sarbek, "but they'll be through it soon enough. The real question is whether they can get through *this* door," he said as he pointed to the door they just closed. The men were still setting the crossbars, one every two feet, floor to ceiling. Each one was solid steel and weighed many hundreds of pounds, four or more men to each side to lift them into place.

"Malcolm is still out there," said Ector.

"I know," said Sarbek. "Baret should've brought him back the first time."

"There's nothing we can do to find him, to help him, is there?" said Ector.

"Nothing," said Sarbek.

"How do we win this?" said Ector.

Sarbek's voice dropped to a whisper so that only Ector, Pellan, and Indigo could hear him. "We've already lost," he said.

36

LOMION CITY

YEAR 1267, 4TH AGE
LAST YEAR OF KING TENZIVEL'S RULE

THE RAT

"How long do you think she'll be in there?" said Rifkin as he lurked in the shadows across the lane from Alder Manor.

"You've asked that ten times already," said the Rat. "She'll be out when she's through having her fun with the old lady."

"That Mother Alder is a grandmother," said Rifkin, "but not very old. Forty-five at most, I'd mark her, but probably only forty."

"I've been in this business for thirty years, sonny boy," said the Rat. "And thirty years ago, she looked the same as she does now — a pretty faced woman past forty."

"So you're telling me she's a wizard?" said Rifkin.

"Must be, but what do I know?"

"Here she comes," said Rifkin as Mother Alder and the Grandmistress (carrying her basket) stepped out onto the porch, all smiles and best friends. A coach pulled up and they both got in it, headed downtown. Four Lugron on horses followed — all wearing Alder livery. But the Rat knew them to be mercenaries. Grontor's Bonebreakers. A tough bunch of killers — long employed by the Alders. Grontor himself was amongst them. Mother Alder wasn't taking any chances on security.

"Where in Helheim are they going?" said Rifkin. "This isn't part of the plan."

"The Mistress is improvising. Let's go. Hopefully the coach takes it slow or this will be a painful run."

The Rat and Rifkin managed to keep up. Luckily the coach stopped after only about a mile. At the bazaar.

In the evening, most of the bazaar's stalls were shut down, but a few, food stands mostly, stayed open late into the night. Inside, however, was where the action was. A series of revolving doors led inside to a maze of shops, eateries, and entertainment venues. Most appealed to common folk, some to those of esoteric tastes, others to the refined noblefolk, and some few to the fringe. It was said that if you couldn't find it in Lomion City's bazaar, then it didn't exist. The place was crowded as always. People going in every direction. A good place to people watch. An even better place to get lost in a crowd.

Rifkin and the Rat watched the Grandmistress and Mother Alder exit the coach.

"Dinner, you think?" said Rifkin.

"Doubtful," said the Rat. "They're probably headed down Red Alley, if I know the Mistress. Wait, Mother Alder is getting back into the coach."

"A hug and kiss and off she goes," said Rifkin. "Do we follow the coach?"

"You do," said the Rat. "Just in case something is fishy. I'm going to catch up to the Grandmistress and see what she's up to."

37

ISLE OF JUTENHEIM THE INTERIOR

YEAR 1267, 4TH AGE
LAST YEAR OF KING TENZIVEL'S RULE

EOTRUS EXPEDITION

The survivors of the Eotrus expedition gathered atop the hummock where the center of their camp had been. The Eotrus men were relieved to see that Theta and Glimador had escaped the gatormen's clutches, though Glimador was unconscious. Try as they might, they couldn't rouse him.

The men ringed the little hill with fire to keep the gatormen and whatever else at bay.

The expedition's losses were staggering. Two out of every three men, dead or taken.

Of those who remained, nearly twenty were unconscious, laid out in rows, incapacitated by the gatormen's poison. The rest sat in a circle, facing each other.

"I found Bartol by the lake," said Blain Alder, a hard edge to his voice, his jaw clenched. "Four of those lizards dead about him. He tried to free Edwin. He failed."

"We all failed," said Claradon.

"They wiped the floor with us," said Artol. "Made us look like amateurs. A hard lesson. A costly lesson. Next time will be different."

"Will it?" said Kelbor. "My sword couldn't cut them. My dagger couldn't stab them. Their hide is harder than armor. How are we supposed to fight things like that?"

"Use a hammer," said Little Tug, his voice slurred and groggy. He was the only man hit by the gatormen's darts that was awake, though barely. "Mine stopped them good and proper. Or else, just hit them harder, little man."

"We have to adapt our tactics," said Claradon. "Use what we learned about them to our advantage."

"You're crazy if you want to tangle with those lizards again," said N'Paag, *The Black Falcon's* first mate. "It's suicide. We need to get out of this valley and back to Jutenheim Town before we're all dead. How many men did we lose? Two-thirds of us? More? And this is just our first day here."

"I walked the camp," said DeBoors. "Checked the bodies. We lost forty-one men here. Most to their spears. All the rest were taken. Look around. Most of us that are left wear plate armor or finely woven chain — heavier stuff than most of those taken. That's what saved us from their darts. They couldn't penetrate our armor and so their poison couldn't get to us. Not easily, anyway. Whatever they use causes immediate weakness, and soon, unconsciousness."

"Are they going to wake up?" said Kelbor.

"I'm no Leren," said DeBoors with a shrug.

"How many of them did we kill?" said Artol.

"They left twenty-odd bodies behind," said DeBoors. "But I suspect we killed no less than twice that many, and they dragged the rest away."

"They whipped us, and good," said Artol as he shook his head. "Caught us with our pants down."

"Their darts took out our sentries," said Theta. "That's what did it. Why we had so little warning."

"Why take our people?" said Claradon. "To what end?"

"If men had attacked us," said Artol, "I'd mark them as slavers. Possibly they'd demand ransom, though you wouldn't need so many hostages for that."

"Large animals take men for food," said DeBoors.

"Which is it here?" said Claradon.

"Mayhap both," said Artol. "Or neither. Who can know the mind of a walking alligator."

"Gatormen," said Kayla. "That's what they were."

"Gatormen?" said Artol. "You make that up or have you heard it before?"

Kayla shrugged. "As good a name as any."

"They had warm blood," said DeBoors. "The look of lizards, but warm blood. I've not seen their like."

"I've never even heard of such creatures," said Claradon. "Could the League have opened a gateway already? Could these things have been the first wave through the portal?"

"The dark corners of the world harbor creatures not known to the modern world," said Theta. "I think these gatormen are swamp creatures. Nothing more. But we'll find out for certain when we find them."

"That's crazy talk," said N'Paag.

Artol put his hand on N'Paag's shoulder and

squeezed until the man doubled over in pain.

"You're advising we go after them?" said DeBoors. "Track the gatormen? What of your mission?"

"They fled to the south," said Theta. "We are headed south anyway."

"What if the League gets that portal open while we're delayed chasing them?" said DeBoors.

"Then we'll deal with that," said Theta. "I'll not abandon our men. Not so long as there's a chance they're alive."

"Nor will I," said Claradon.

"So what do you propose?" said DeBoors.

"We track the gatormen to their lair," said Theta. "And rescue any of our people still alive."

"And what of the gatormen?" said Artol.

"I'm going to kill them all," said Theta.

38

ANGLOTOR
THE OLDEN DOME
JUTENHEIM

YEAR 1267, 4TH AGE
LAST YEAR OF KING TENZIVEL'S RULE

URIEL THE BOLD

Atop her perch in the Olden Dome, Malth'Urn's long spindly fingers caressed the seer stone. It hummed to her touch. Small streaks of lightning — white, blue, and gold erupted from within the stone's depths and leaped to her fingertips. She leaned in close and gazed deeply into the swirling mists that filled the stone.

"Seeing the Azathothians proves difficult, my master," said Malth'Urn. "Sorcery swirls about them. Cloaks them. I can feel the power of the wizards, their connection to the grand weave. The Nifleheimer is with them. Layers of magic cloak them, obscuring all detail."

"Is the outre' creature still with them?" said Uriel.

"I sense it no longer," said Malth'Urn. "And have not since they left Jutenheim Town. If on Jutenheim it be, cloaked it is beyond my sight."

"Where are the Azathothians now?" said Uriel.

"They approach the Plain of Engelroth," said

Malth'Urn.

"Just as you predicted, Master," said Kapte.

"Are the Lugron in position?" said Uriel.

"Four thousand strong," said Malth'Urn.

"And the Ettins?" said Uriel.

"This time, late they are not," said Malth'Urn. "All the tribes have gathered."

"And Koobtak?"

"He leads them," said Malth'Urn. "Deceived you, he has not."

"Your plan is working perfectly, Master," said Kapte. "The primitives will stop them and we will be safe. The temple will remain sacrosanct."

"The primitives will not be enough," said Malth'Urn. "The brutes cannot stop the Nifleheimer or his wizards. Together, their power is too great. Though great damage they may do."

"Time will tell," said Uriel. "Once battle begins, nothing is certain but uncertainty."

"What is this?" said Malth'Urn, surprise in her voice.

"Don't tell me that Koobtak is turning back," said Uriel.

"No, master," said Malth'Urn. "Other powers have entered Jutenheim. They skirt the northern swamps. A large group of men."

"Who?" said Uriel.

"There is a veil of shadow over them. More sorcery. I cannot judge its nature. They have a wizard of power."

"More Azathothians?" said Kapte.

"I cannot tell," said Malth'Urn.

"Can you tell if they are friends or foes to us?" said Kapte. "Are they good or evil?"

"I cannot tell," said Malth'Urn.

"Any that march toward us in force are foes," said Uriel. "All my friends that endure are here, in Anglotor and its surrounds. So now we must prepare for not one attack, but two."

"Can we win this, Master?" said Kapte.

"If the primitives weaken them enough, there is a chance," said Uriel.

"Why not destroy the temple?" said Kapte. "Throw down its walls before the Azathothians get here."

"I would have done that at the first if it would work," said Uriel. "The power is in the location, not the walls. The fabric between the worlds is weakest there. It lies at the intersection of lay lines of power. One of several about Midgaard. The temple merely marks the location. Collapse the walls and the weak spot between the worlds remains."

"Then let's throw down the castle atop it," said Kapte. "Bury the spot beneath tons of stone so that they can't reach it."

"That will not stop them," said Uriel. "It will only delay things. They will dig to the spot or magic the stones aside. Buying that time achieves us nothing. There is no help that is coming. We are on our own in this. If we fail to stop them head on. If we fail to kill the Nifleheimer and every wizard of power with him, they will wrench that portal open eventually. There is no one to stop them here save us and our allies."

"And if we drive them away?" said Malth'Urn.

"Then they venture to one of the other temples of power about the world," said Uriel. "For all I know, this one may well be the only one still guarded. There may be nothing to stop them at the other locations. For long years my hope has been that the other temples remain hidden, forgotten by the world. But that is a vain hope. For their kind, adventurers, cultists, or crazies, find us here time and again. There is always someone who remembers. Someone who seeks this place out. Mayhap it's the same at the other temples. Perhaps their guardians remain, diligent and enduring as I. I do not know. I suppose, I will never know."

39

TROLLHEIM

YEAR 1267, 4TH AGE
LAST YEAR OF KING TENZIVEL'S RULE

GOTRAK OF GOTHMAGORN

In the heart of Mount Troglestyre, tallest peak of the Kronar Range, and far north of any lands frequented by Volsung, Lugron, or Gnome, was the troll kingdom of Gothmagorn. Gotrak, son of Tirg the Bold, was their high chieftain.

Gotrak stood in the grand lair's nursery, his eyes downcast, his shoulders slumped. He'd stood there a long time.

Hours.

Naked, save for his loincloth.

Called from his nest when the black deed was discovered. He only took time to pick up his bone club. No trappings of his office did he take. Not even his bracelets or bracers.

All the nursery's nests were empty. All save one. The menials had carried away the littlelin's bodies to prepare them for proper burial in accord with olden custom.

No one had told them to take the bedding.

Someone should have; they were soaked of blood, as was the floor beneath each tiny nest. Gotrak knew the menials could remove the bloodstains from the nests, from the floor, but only death could wipe them from his mind's eye.

Gotrak couldn't bear to look at those nests, those stains, but he couldn't look away.

For the first time in hours, the nursery was silent, save for Terna's quiet sobbing. The wailing of the other mothers retreated with them to their dens. One by one, they'd shuffled away to grieve by themselves or with their mates and other littles.

Terna wouldn't leave. Gotrak stood behind her. He didn't know how to comfort her. What to say. So he just stood there. Simmering. Grieving. His heart torn to shreds. Never one for emotion, still his eyes were wet. Wet like they'd been on only two other days in his life. The day his Mommap died. And the day the fever took their first littlelin.

Terna wouldn't leave the littlelin's side. She knelt before the nest, her hand on his tiny chest, willing him back to life.

Finally, Terna turned her head toward Gotrak. "He didn't make his naming day," she said. "He's gone to the afterlife with no name. How will the gods know him? How will he know himself? Where he came from? Who we are?"

"Choose him a name," said Gotrak. "With Karmagarg's blessing, he'll carry it with him to the spirit realm."

"Gotrak," said Terna, "is the name I planned for him. After you."

Gotrak made no response, but his jaw stiffened.

Terna gently lifted little Gotrak from his nest and clutched him tightly to her chest. After a time, she turned and began to shuffle toward the exit, the littlelin still in her arms.

"Terna, you—"

"Don't say it," she shouted. "Don't say it. I will take him to our den. I will show him the room that was to be his. I will show him his nest, his things, the toys that Shevtak made for him. I know what needs to be done." She turned toward Gotrak and her eyes bore into his. "As I know that you do. Do what must be done, Chieftain."

As she walked out, another troll entered the chamber. That one was wizened and stooped and wore a long brown robe that reached to the floor. In his hand, a long staff carved with a bear's head. He was Tarmain, the High Magus of all Trollheim. Gotrak was lost in his thoughts.

"Three saw he who did this evil deed," said Tarmain.

"Who was it?" said Gotrak.

"Not who, my chief," said Tarmain. "But what."

Gotrak locked his gaze on the Magus, his eyes demanding more.

"A manling from the southern lands," he said.

"What?" said Gotrak. "Impossible. No manlings have ventured within a hundred leagues of here for three hundred years."

"This one did."

"And no one stopped him?"

"Several tried, but he moved like the wind. They didn't know what he'd done. Thought him a wanderer or hunter, so no one tried overhard to capture him."

"Send a troop of hunters on his trail," said Gotrak. "Bring him to heel. Then bring him back to me. Alive."

"They've already left. We found this as we searched the city," said Tarmain as he held out a dagger crusted with blood. "See the inscription?"

Gotrak wouldn't touch the dagger, but he looked at it closely as Tarmain held it. "The sigil of the big Volsung city far to the south. What do they call it?"

"Lomion City," said Tarmain.

"Why would they do this?" said Gotrak. "This was no random act. It was carefully planned. They must have been spying on us, maybe even infiltrated the warrens before today. Why do this?"

"They're evil, my chieftain," said Tarmain. "Every time we encounter the soft people of the south, they try to kill us on sight. They fear us. They fear our strength. Our power. Our riches. Our knowledge. They hate us for it."

Tarmain paused for some moments before he continued. "They know that we must respond to this. That we won't let this stand. That's what they want."

"War?" said Gotrak.

"War, my chieftain."

"They are many more than us," said Gotrak. "Their lands, far away. I would go to the ends of Midgaard to find this killer, but to war? It could be the end of us."

"They are weak, my chieftain."

"Yet they provoke us so," said Gotrak.

Several trolls wearing ornate metal armor loped into the chamber, distressed looks on their faces.

"Speak," said Gotrak.

"The winter stores, Chieftain," said the soldier, his voice crackling with nerves. "All tainted with poison. Every barrel. Every box. Nothing is safe."

"All of Gothmagorn has only what lies in their pantries," said Gotrak. "A few days of food. A week at best."

"We can forage," said Tarmain. "We can hunt."

"Hundreds will starve over the winter, no matter what we do," said Gotrak. "Maybe thousands."

"The fiend did his work well," said Tarmain. "They've left us no choice."

"I smell a trap or ruse in this," said Gotrak. "We are being manipulated. Used. For some dark purpose."

"Mayhap, my chieftain," said Tarmain, "or mayhap, they simply want to provoke war, for their own glory or to collect some treasure that they imagine we possess. Yet, it remains, we must act."

"Helheim will drown in Volsung blood before this crime is paid back in full," said Gotrak.

"One out of every five hunters will remain at Gothmagorn to guard the lairs, the females, and the littles," said Gotrak. "Gather all the rest, girded for long travel and for war. We'll take no more than a single day's rations. We'll hunt on the way."

"What revenge do you plan, my chieftain?"

"They killed our littlelins and tried to murder us all," said Gotrak. "Now we will return the favor. We range to the southlands. And there we will remain until we kill every last Volsung in Lomion, or until they kill us. They started this madness. I will end it. I will make them pay."

40

BLACK HALL LOMION CITY

YEAR 1267, 4TH AGE
LAST YEAR OF KING TENZIVEL'S RULE

WEATER THE MOUSE

"Tell me what happened after Mother Alder got back into the coach," said Weater the Mouse.

"I followed the Grandmistress into the bazaar," said the Rat. "Rifkin followed the Alder coach.

"Where did the coach go?" said Weater.

"Blackron's Tavern," said Rifkin. "Just as I told you before."

"And you'll tell me again, if I tell you to," said Weater. "Keep going."

"She met some noblewomen for dinner. I think one was Lady Marbon, the mother, not the daughter. Not sure about the other woman, but she was blonde, wrinkly, and rich. They stayed about an hour. The coach waited outside for her."

"What of the Lugron?" said Weater.

"All four of them hung about the coach."

"The whole time?"

"Every minute. When she came out, they drove her home."

"You followed the whole way?"

"Every step. I saw Mother Alder get out and

go inside. She was alone."

"And you?" said Weater, speaking to the Rat.

"The Grandmistress went inside the bazaar. I was about a minute behind her. I figured she'd be waiting for me inside, to check in, if nothing more. But there was no sign of her. I looked everywhere about the halls and alleys. Nothing. So I went to each of her haunts in turn. Even the sketchy ones. Nothing."

"There's a million places in there that she could have gone that you'd have missed her," said Weater.

"What do you think happened?" said the Rat.

"I think somebody snatched her," said Weater.

"She'd make short work of anybody what tried," said Rifkin.

"Anybody can get knocked silly or taken by numbers," said Weater. "Even her. I'm going to send a clutch of the brethren round to the bazaar to see what we can find out. Somebody had to see her go in, and which alley she went down."

"What do we do if she got snatched?" said Riftin.

"We get her back, one way or the other," said Weater.

"And what if she's dead?" said the Rat.

"We make somebody pay dearly in blood. We make an example of them. Wipe out whatever they represent: a noble House, a guild, a mercenary company, a family, whatever. Then we elect a new Grandmaster or Grandmistress."

A loud crash sounded somewhere in the distance, inside Black House.

Then shouts.

"What in Helheim?" said Weater.

The three raced into the hallway outside the room, checking their weapons as they went.

The shouting came from the floor below — the barracks. At first it seemed to be coming from the south side of the building. As they made their way down the hall, shouting and what may have been a clash of arms sounded from the north side too.

When they neared the stairwell, Coburn and two brethren raced toward them, having dashed up from the second floor.

"We're getting hit," shouted Coburn. "A crossbow bolt was stuck in his shoulder."

"Shit," said Weater. "Who is it?"

"Duck!" shouted the Rat as crossbows twanged from within the stairwell. Both brethren with Coburn went down.

Men clad in black charged into the hall, swords drawn.

Coburn turned and raised his sword as a big man came toward him. The man's swing went under Coburn's blade, and ripped open his abdomen. Fast as lightning, he kicked Coburn in the groin so hard that he left the floor and crashed into the wall. A dozen men at least were behind the big man.

Weater and the others turned and ran for it. As they neared Weater's den, more attackers burst from the north stairwell.

Weater ducked into his office, the others on his heels as crossbow bolts flew like buzzing bees.

Rifkin took one in the gut and stopped running.

The Rat slammed Weater's door closed even as a battle axe cut Rifkin's head in two, just above the nose.

The Rat bolted the door. Weater went straight for the window. He flung it open and a crossbow bolt flew in, but missed him. Another bolt went high and shattered the glass.

The door burst open from a single kick. The big swordsman was there, his fellows behind. They didn't look like they were taking prisoners.

The Rat went straight at the swordsman. Their blades danced. If the swordsman was a skilled soldier, he should've dropped within the first two strikes. If he were a swordmaster, he should've been dead within five flicks of the Rat's sword. Problem was, he was better than that, twice the size of the Rat, and just as fast. It might not end well. A dozen men flooded the room. There was nowhere to go.

Weater waded into the others. The Rat would have to deal with the big man.

Many of the brethren were subtle killers. Poison. Arranged "accidents". Traps. A well-placed dagger to the back. A garrote. Weater was a swordsman. A straight-up fighter. Lithe, fast, deadly. Same as the Rat. He went to work, doing what he did best.

The problem was, the attackers were no ordinary freeswords or mercs. They were skilled. Professionals. And there were a lot of them.

Weater sized them up. Parley was no good — they were in a killing mode. Giving up would most likely get him cut down. Weater figured he'd go down fighting, or maybe he and the Rat would kill them all. Too early to tell. Too bad Coburn had bitten it. The three of them together would have cleared the room.

41

THE BLACK FALCON

CAPTAIN DYLAN SLAAYDE

Slaayde awoke with a start. A sound echoed in his head. A scream? His own? Groggy from sleep, he didn't know. The place was pitch black; Slaayde couldn't see a thing. He felt the sway of the ship. The softness of a mattress. The smell of the sheets. Bertha's perfume still on them. He was in their cabin aboard *The Black Falcon*. For a moment, that didn't seem right. As if he shouldn't be there. He should be somewhere else. But that made no sense. Where else would he be?

No light filtered in through the shuttered portholes. Nighttime outside. The cabin was silent and still. Yet he sensed something lurking in the dark.

He didn't see it of course. Nor did he hear or smell it, but he knew that it was there by some warrior's sense born of long years of battle and strife.

He reached out his hand to Bertha's side of the bed. Had to wake her. To warn her. Protect her.

Empty.

That's when his heart began thumping in his chest and his stomach churned. Where could she be? Was she in danger? He wanted to call out to her. Maybe she had gotten up, unable to sleep, and was sitting in the armchair. But he quickly decided that wasn't the case.

What lurked somewhere in the dark recesses of the captain's cabin was not Bertha or any other member of *The Falcon's* crew. It was something malevolent. Something evil.

Slaayde was not surprised when he heard a slight intake of breath. A raspy sound from somewhere across the room. His imagination? Some normal ship sound? Or something more?

It was more. He knew it as surely as he knew anything. In his bones he felt it. Something depraved. Something that meant him harm. Could it see him? Did it know that he was awake? Had he called out as he jerked awake, and given himself away? Was the thing creeping up on him, readying to strike?

And how did it get in?

Was it sneak thief or assassin?

Slaayde kept the cabin locked tight whether he or Bertha were inside or not. Only Bertha and he had keys. No one could have broken through the door without waking him; he was far too light a sleeper for that.

Could someone have picked the lock? He doubted it; not without him hearing. He had that lock installed special. Made by a dwarven tinker; cost him sixty silver stars. Then how? Was it all his imagination?

And then a more disturbing thought sprang to mind. Could they have wrested the key from Bertha when she left the cabin? Did they hold her prisoner even now? Had they harmed her? Dead gods, he had to know.

Slaayde moved his hand to the edge of the

bed and attempted to gauge his exact location. He kept his sabre at the bedside. He knew exactly how far he had to reach to grab it.

But what good would that do without light?

He moved his hand ever so slowly toward the nightstand. His fingers fell lightly upon his logbook, which rested in its usual place. He prayed that whatever horror lurked within his abode had no power to see in the dark. He had to be fast.

He grabbed up the logbook. Flung it hard across the room, toward the room's opposite corner.

As the book fluttered through the air, he heard something start. When the book hit the ground, the thing moved. Leaped toward the book. He heard it! There was no longer any doubt.

Slaayde leaped from the bed in a single motion, his agility surprising for a man of his bulk. Grabbed for his sabre with one hand; the lantern with the other. His left hand snatched up the lantern, but his right fell upon empty air. The sabre wasn't in its proper place or else he'd misjudged the distance.

The thing moved toward him. He heard the creaking of the floorboards.

He thrust the lantern out before him at arm's length. Turned up the knob and flipped open the shutter. A beam of light shot across the room; everything before him bathed in its soft glow.

When he saw it, Slaayde startled back in shock. Slammed into the nightstand. Somehow his feet came out from under him. He crashed hard on his rump.

Lantern still in hand. He could see. But he

wished he couldn't. The image of the thing burned into his mind's eye forevermore.

It hovered over him.

A creature.

An abomination.

Too terrible to contemplate. Too painful to bear.

An evil shadow of the woman that he had once loved.

Bertha.

But not Bertha. It had her form. Her face. But its eyes were black as tar, no whites to them at all. Long canine teeth protruded from her mouth. A mouth that dripped of blood and gore. It ran down her shirt and pants. Puddled at her feet. So much blood. Where did it come from?

And then Slaayde saw. Beyond her, bodies sprawled on the cabin's floor. Guj was there. Neck torn open. Spouting blood. Lifeless eyes stared into nothingness. Slaayde's old friend Alpan Ravel, ship's trader, was there beside Guj. His face and chest slashed. Just as dead. Seaman Gurt lay twisted in the corner. Bloodied. Broken.

She — no, it — for it was not Bertha. It was no living woman. Rather, a thing. A beast of the pit. A creature of the Nether Realms. It growled and shifted from side to side, breathing heavily as it leered at Slaayde.

Why it didn't pounce, at first Slaayde didn't understand. He was unarmed. Vulnerable. In naught but his nightclothes. He could call out, but no one could possibly come in time. He'd end up just like the others. Dead. Bloody. His time had come.

What had done this to Bertha? And then he

remembered the red woman. The Duchess Morgovia of Evermere. And the creatures that she commanded.

Bertha was one of them now. One of them! A creature of the night. A bloodthirsty fiend. Dead gods. How he failed. Failed to protect her. His most important job.

It wanted him to see. To take in that scene of horror. To suffer it. For the fear to build to bursting within him. That's why it waited and watched. It enjoyed his suffering.

And then Ravel stirred. Gurt opened his eyes. Guj sat straight up. As one, they turned toward him. Eyes black as Bertha's. Fangs grew before his eyes. Those broken corpses pulled themselves to their feet. Moved stiffly at first, then more fluidly. They came toward him.

The thing that was Bertha smiled at their approach. She had bitten them. Turned them into her kind. Into monsters. And now she was gifting Slaayde to them. To sate their bloodlust. They'd tear him to pieces. Drink dry his blood. Dead gods. Slaayde tried to bound to his feet. To run. To fight. But his limbs wouldn't respond. He couldn't move. Frozen. Not with fear, but something paralyzed him. Held him still.

The creatures closed in.

Slaayde fought to break free of whatever curse held him. Strained as hard as he could, but could not lift a finger. He couldn't even scream.

Then his eyes burst open and that scream finally escaped his lips. Still the place was black. But now, Slaayde hung suspended in a net.

42

JUTENHEIM

YEAR 1267, 4TH AGE
LAST YEAR OF KING TENZIVEL'S RULE

FREM SORLONS

Seventeen men. That's all Captain Frem Sorlons had left. All that remained of his Pointmen, plus a few men from second and fourth squadrons, and Ma-Grak Stowron, the last of his company. All of them exhausted. Bruised. Battered. A few wounded but good. Luckily, all of them were mobile. All could fight. They were some of the toughest men of the Sithian Mercenary Company. A troop where even the weakest was more than a match for most soldiers considered "elite". That's why they'd survived that long.

Frem always knew that it would end up like this. Heavy losses.

Maybe even the whole company.

But he figured most of those losses would happen when they got where they were going — that temple of power. He never dreamed it would be so difficult and dangerous just traveling there.

Frem stood atop a ledge high on the wall within the hidden cave at Svartleheim's exit. As he peered out the spy hole in the cave's wall, he figured that if he had about five hundred more men just like those with him, his chances of surviving the day might run as high as fifty-fifty.

Even that was probably optimistic.

Outside the cave in which they hid, a great battle was beginning. A horde of Lugron: footmen, lizard-mounted cavalry, and siege engines were assembling on the western side of the valley that the cave overlooked. More Lugron stormed into the valley from the north and from the south. How many of them there were in total was hard to say, except that their numbers certainly reached into the thousands.

Assembled on Frem's side of the valley was an army of giants, shaggy and primitive in their look. In general form, they were much like men, but they stood no less than eight feet tall, and some topped twelve feet. Frem had never encountered their kind before, but he knew what they were. Ettins. Olden giants from days long past, now remembered only in song and story, phrase and fable. Isolated there, deep within the unexplored interior of Jutenheim, they survived long past their time.

Trapped in the middle of the valley, between those two forces, Lugron and Ettin, was all that was left of the Shadow League's main expedition, save for Frem's small force.

Frem and his men were trapped too. They were in a hidden cave — a passage from the outside world into Svartleheim, the forbidden domain of the Black Elves. Outside the cave, the Lugron and the Ettin. Coming up the long subterranean stair behind them, the surviving remnants of the Svart army. Frem couldn't sally forth to aid Ezerhauten without engaging the Ettin. He couldn't go back into Svartleheim, for the Elfs commanded the stair, and he couldn't remain hidden where he was, for the Elfs were approaching. What was he supposed to do?

"They be coming," said Moag Lugron, Frem's lead scout. "Another ten minutes if we're lucky, five if we're not, and they'll be knocking at the door."

"How many?" said Frem.

"All of them," said Moag.

"How many?" said Frem.

"Hundreds, Captain," said Moag. "Too many."

"We're in the deep stuff this time," said Sergeant Putnam, Frem's second-in-command.

"I'd rather fight more Elfs than giants," said Sir Carroll.

"I'd rather die with the sun on my face than in these damn caverns," said Sir Royce.

"I'd rather not die at all," said Putnam. "Holding the stair is our best bet, Captain."

"The giants will hear the battle," said Royce.

"If they do, they won't be able to get in," said Putnam. "They're too big to squeeze their hairy butts in here. If we're lucky, they won't be able to figure where the sounds are coming from. But I doubt they'll hear it. All hell's about to break loose out there. Once it does, nobody will pay any attention to us."

"They can block up the exit," said Royce. "Or lie in wait for us to come out. Then even if we defeat the elves, we'll still be trapped in here. I'm not heading through those tunnels again. No way, no how."

"None of us want that," said Frem. "But Putnam's right, our best chance is to hold the stair. We'll close the door behind us. Maybe that'll mute the noise enough and the giants won't hear."

"What of Ezer?" said Par Sevare. "Are you saying we're abandoning him?"

"I'm saying that right now, we can't help him," said Frem. "Besides, he's got a lot more firepower with him than we have with us. No offense, Sevare."

"None taken," said the wizard.

"Wikkle," said Frem, "you keep watch on the battle outside. The rest of us will hold the top portion of the stair. We'll fight by twos and switch men out every minute or so, or whenever anyone takes a hit."

Moag opened wider the secret door to Svartleheim. The howls of the Elfs roared through. The pounding of hundreds of feet racing up the great stair. "They're moving fast," said Moag. "We best get in position right quick."

"Everybody in," said Frem.

Moag propped the door open a fraction of an inch, just wide enough to keep the mechanism from locking. The men filled the top of the great spiral stair down to the first landing.

"Keep going down," said Frem. "We need to get down to a lower landing, so that we can give ground as needed."

"And we need to keep the sounds of battle as far from that door as possible," said Putnam.

Sir Lex found himself at the head of the line. Trooper Drift beside him. Lex looked back at his fellows.

"Anyone want the point?" he said. "Step right up. Anybody?"

Torak Lugron, just behind him, stared at him, an amused look on his face.

Brave, battle-hardened men every one, but not one of the Sithians wanted to be the lead man to engage the Black Elves.

Ma-Grak Stowron stepped up. Passed through the ranks of the others until he stood at the van of the small troop. Lex looked visibly relieved when Ma-Grak stepped in front of him.

"Thanks," he said.

"You'll have your turn, I expect," said Ma-Grak in an oddly clicky but deep voice, heavily accented. Maybe Ma-Grak was fearless. Or maybe he had nothing more to live for — since all his men were dead. Frem figured the fellow had the bloodlust. He wanted to kill more Elfs — all the Elfs — for the slaughter they'd inflicted on his people. So be it. He'd get his chance. Trooper Drift took up position next to him. The youngest of Frem's band, Drift was still out to prove himself. To show his quality. Earn the respect of the squadron's veterans. Frem had noted he'd done his share so far and then some. If the boy survived this campaign (assuming any of them did), Frem might stick a corporal's stripe on his arm. He was that good.

Frem moved close to Sevare. "You got anything left?"

"I can throw a few," said Sevare through gritted teeth. The man was still in pain. Mayhap a lot of pain. He smelled like meat burnt crispy.

"Anything big?" said Frem. "Something that could knock the lot of them off the stair? Or better yet, knock down the stair itself?"

"Fresh and at my best, I might be able to collapse the stair. Not with one spell mind you, but a bunch. Right now, there's no chance of it.

None at all. I can take more than a few Elfs down, though."

"Do you need to be at the van?" said Frem, his voice rising as the Elfs came closer, now but two switchbacks away from the lead men. Frem and Sevare stood one full landing up from the front line. Most of the squadron in front of them.

"I can toss it from here" said Sevare. "Now leave me be so that I can ready it."

"Steady boys," said Putnam. "Sit tight and wait for them. They'll be nice and tired by the time they reach us. So let them come."

43

THE REGENT'S EXPEDITIONARY FORCE (THE ALDER BRIGADE)

YEAR 1267, 4TH AGE
LAST YEAR OF KING TENZIVEL'S RULE

DIRK ALDER

Sir Dirk Alder had never run so far in field armor in his life. Staying ahead of the trolls that hunted him and his fellows was a powerful incentive to keep moving, for he knew if he stopped for a rest, even for but a minute, the trolls would be on him, and he'd be dead.

Heavy as his armor was, he thanked the gods that he'd adopted his Uncle Rom's practice of wearing it to sleep when in the field. If he hadn't, he'd have died during the troll attack on the Alder encampment outside Dor Eotrus, for at least two or three blows that the stout steel of his breastplate had absorbed would have been the death of him.

Bad as it was running from the trolls, it could have been worse. At least there was enough moonlight that night to see by. If not, he and his men would have blundered around blindly after the last of their torches went out. At least with the moonlight they could keep moving, though it limited them to the road; the woods were too dark. That meant they had no chance to lose the trolls. Their only hope was to outpace them. So far, that wasn't going very well.

There were about ten men ahead of Dirk, and from the sounds of it, he figured an equal number were still alive behind him. Could have been more. Could have been less. He dared not slow or turn to take a count of who and how many still hung on. The trolls had been picking them off all too regularly. There had been some fifty of them that fled the Alder camp together after the trolls overran it. Only those twenty or so remained.

Dirk wanted to be nearer to the vanguard, but he couldn't gain ground on the men in front of him. They were too fast.

Motivated.

And well trained.

Every man in front of him was a mercenary from Bald Boddrick's crew. The Alder men, for all their training, couldn't keep up with the mercenaries. Dirk wondered whether there were any of his fellows left, or had the trolls picked the last of them off?

Boddrick himself ran just behind Dirk. How that fat old man managed to run so fast and so long, Dirk couldn't imagine. Proper motivation probably. Boddrick was an expert at staying alive. And was darned hard to kill — or so claimed his storied reputation. Might have been naught but bunk and bother. Dirk didn't know. But he hoped that the stories about him were true. If they were, maybe with Boddrick's help, he'd survive the night.

Dirk heard a scream from a ways back. Then

came the shouting for help. The trolls had picked off another man, probably a straggler at the very back of the ragtag bunch. Every couple of minutes, the trolls brought down another man from their line. They came out of nowhere, the trolls did. Jumping from the trees, or charging from the brush. They blended into the background so well, you couldn't see them until they were right on top of you. They never killed the men they jumped right away. They always let them call out for help, several times at least. The more the men said, the more they begged and pleaded, the longer the trolls let them live. In the end though, if the trolls got you, you were a dead man. That much was plain enough.

Boddrick tried to pass Dirk again, coming up on his left. Dirk forced himself to run faster.

Dirk wasn't certain of where they were running to. He thought that they were on the main road heading south from Eotrus lands, but he didn't know the ground, and in the dark it was impossible to get his bearings. If he was on the road that he thought, then eventually they'd reach Riker's Crossroads, a trading post and village on the main road between Lomion City and Kern. Riker's wasn't fortified, but some of the buildings had stone walls and stout doors, or so Dirk thought he recalled. He'd only been through there the once. If he and the men could take refuge there, then they had a chance. A chance to hold out until morning.

Maybe the trolls would flee from the light of day and then he could escape back to Lomion City. He thought he remembered something about trolls shunning the sun in the old stories.

The ones Mother Alder told the children on cold nights when they gathered close about the big hearth in Alder Manor. Dirk was certain that there was something in those stories about trolls turning to stone under the cleansing light of the sun. Or mayhap it was men turning to jelly when trolls touched them. He couldn't recall the details.

Then appeared a rider before them. No, several. Came out of the woods.

They shouted and waved the men off the road, directing them onto a narrower path, barely wide enough for a wagon. Dirk wasn't close enough to tell who they were.

Did this mean salvation? Or ambush? Dirk didn't know, but he followed the others as they ran after the riders.

"Who are they?" said Bithel the Piper from somewhere behind Dirk.

"I think it was some of our men," said Sentry of Allendale.

"It doesn't matter," said Bald Boddrick, his words breaking up as he huffed and puffed. "Save your breath and follow them."

A hundred yards down the track they came upon a hunter's cabin, a large one. Multiple torches were ensconced along the porch's rail, the front of the cabin and its front yard brightly lit. The trees were so thick down that lane, they might have run right past the place and not seen the light.

The riders dismounted. Dirk saw the Alder colors. They were his men. They waved them on toward the building. Other men came out through the cabin's front door. A big man filled the doorway, his shoulders as broad as the door,

though not nearly as tall as Boddrick.
   Gar Pullman.
   Now they had a chance.

44

DOR EOTRUS THE UNDERHALLS

***YEAR 1267, 4TH AGE
LAST YEAR OF KING TENZIVEL'S RULE***

ECTOR EOTRUS

Ector's brow furled as he and the key officers gathered in Donnelin's workshop, which was not far from the main entry to the Underhalls. "Sarbek, you said we've already lost," said Ector. "What did you mean? We've got most of our soldiers down here. A defensible position. Plenty of supplies."

"Keep your voice down," said Sarbek. "We left at least a thousand men up there. A thousand of our own. Left to die. And that's not counting the men defending the citadel."

"They'll scale the tower, same as the walls," said Indigo.

"And the window bars won't hold them for long," said Sarbek. "Then the tower will fall. Not as quick as the walls, but it will fall all the same."

"And us?" said Ector.

"Dor Eotrus has fallen," said Sarbek. "Once the trolls clear the tower, we'll be all that's left. And we're trapped underground. We're screwed. Once they pass us, they'll kill the civilians. The women. The old folks. The children. You saw what they did to them folks in the Outer Dor. It'll be just as bad for everyone here."

"But we've got defenses," said Ector. "Traps. And steel doors. Surely, we'll be able to hold out until help arrives."

"Dor Eotrus has fallen," said Sarbek as he shook his head. "And on my watch. On my watch!"

Trooper Gorned stuck his head into the workshop. "Castellan, they're at the door. Pounding it but good."

"Archers and pikemen at the ready, just as we planned," said Sarbek.

"Aye," said Gorned, and he was off.

"They can pound their fists to the bone on that door," said Indigo. "It's not going anywhere."

"They'll find a way in," said Captain Pellan. "They're as smart as any of us. How would you get in?"

"A battering ram is what I'd try," said Indigo. "Or dig through the walls on either side or both."

"The door, walls, and frame are reinforced against that," said Sarbek. "But if they keep at it long enough, they'll breach it. Only a matter of time."

"How would you get in?" said Pellan to Sarbek.

"I'd look for the escape tunnel," said Sarbek. "I'd come in from that way with everything I had. We've got men guarding every passage. That won't keep them out, but it will keep them from catching us unawares. How would you get in?"

"I wouldn't," said Pellan. "I'd find the exits and block them all. Find the air shafts and block them too, but not until I threw whatever fire I could down them. Then I'd let you rot."

"I've got men guarding the shafts," said Sarbek. "They're too small by design for anyone to get through. But the guards have plenty of sand and water buckets. We're ready for whatever they throw at us."

"It won't be enough," said Pellan.

"It's all we can do," said Sarbek. "We can't sally forth, and hope to accomplish anything."

"So what chance do we have?" said Ector.

"If they break through, from one way or another," said Sarbek, "we'll have the chance of a warrior's death and a one way trip to Valhalla. We'll bleed them in here. We'll make them pay in blood for every step they take in these Underhalls. We're prepared for just this sort of siege. Always have been, but much more so in recent years with the improvements that Donnelin made."

"I'm glad that he did, but why did he spend so much time on that?" said Indigo. "It never made any sense to me."

"Twenty something years ago, Donnelin went off with Lord Aradon, Sir Gabriel, Par Talbon and some others," said Sarbek. "They fought something old. Something evil. Down in the Dead Fens. Something so dark they'd never tell the tale. Not even to me. That's how Donnelin lost his arm — fighting whatever that evil was. Donnelin was afraid that they hadn't destroyed it completely. That someday that evil might come looking for the Eotrus. And he was determined to keep it out. That's why he designed so many defenses for the Dor. Made it his life's work."

"Fighting them in these halls will only lead to our deaths," said Pellan. "I want my place in

Valhalla as much as anyone, but I'd prefer to put it off for a few more years. We've got to get our people through the tunnels and out into the forest before the trolls sniff out the exits. At least we'll have a chance out there."

"What chance?" said Ector. "Even with fresh horses, run to their deaths, we couldn't stay ahead of them even on the open road. On foot, we'll be slaughtered straightaway."

"If they're as smart as we fear," said Sarbek, "they'll have the roads blocked. With the way they can move through the trees, we could never outdistance them."

"How many escape tunnels are there?" said Ector.

"Six main tunnels," said Sarbek. "They have branches near their ends, in case of blockages. The closest lets out a mile to the south, not too far from the road."

"Split our force," said Indigo. "Send all the civilians south toward Doriath Forest with half our troops to guard them. Split the rest of our forces into three groups and sally out the exits to the west, north, and east. Then converge on the Dor, attacking from three sides."

"Siege our own fortress?" said Ector.

"They'll not stand the walls," said Indigo. "They'll run out to meet us and we'll have it out with them."

"That's suicide," said Pellan.

"It is," said Indigo, "but it might distract the trolls for long enough for the civilians to get clear. If we get lucky, we'll run into our Bannermen coming in from the field. We might assemble enough men to really do some damage. We'd save our folk and secure our places in Odin's hall."

"It might work," said Sarbek, "except that a troop of trolls went off south chasing the remnant of that Alder brigade. We'd be sending our people right into the middle of that. It would be a slaughter."

"Can we send the people out one of the other exits?" said Ector.

"We could, but unless they turn south, there's nowhere for them to go," said Sarbek. "None of the manors, towers, or villages could accommodate them all. If the trolls followed them, they'd all get slaughtered anyway."

"Where does that leave us?" said Pellan.

"It leaves us staying put," said Sarbek. "And bleeding them but good if they get in. We'll kill a lot of them before they finish us. You mark my words."

"I don't understand why they are doing this," said Ector. "What do they want?"

"They want to kill us," said Pellan.

"But why?" said Ector. "What did we ever do to them?"

"What did we do to the Alders?" said Sarbek. "Nothing, yet they've hated us for years. They came here ready to kill us and to take the Dor. They want what we've got. Jealousy. Envy. As simple as that. All evil flows from it. The trolls want something that we have. And they aim to get it, no matter the cost."

"Our bones," said Ector. "That's what Leren Sverdes said. They eat the marrow."

"Could be," said Pellan. "Or else maybe some hunter way up in the mountains killed one of them. Somebody important. Their chief's grandma? Their queen's sister? Now they're on a blood feud. Out to kill every human on Midgaard."

"We'll never know for certain why they're doing this," said Sarbek, "since we can't speak with them. In the end, it doesn't matter anymore. It's kill or be killed. The old way of the sword."

45

BLACK HALL LOMION CITY

YEAR 1267, 4TH AGE
LAST YEAR OF KING TENZIVEL'S RULE

WEATER THE MOUSE

Weater woke up when someone dropped a bucket of water over his head. He was in a world of pain. His arms. His legs. His torso. His head.

His hands were bound. His legs too. They hefted him to a sitting position. There were about a dozen of them in the room. The bodies of a dozen more lay scattered about, blood everywhere. He had gotten in his licks and then some. Somebody must have bashed him in the head from behind, because he never saw the blow that dropped him. That's how it worked most of the time. Lucky he was to be alive.

The Rat's head sat on the edge of the desk, facing him. Poor bastard. They put it there to intimidate him. They wanted something. He could use that. Maybe there was an angle. Maybe he had a chance to get out of this alive.

"Where's the grandmistress?" said the big swordsman.

"Don't know," said Weater.

The man punched him in the jaw. Not too hard. Just hard enough to let him know that this would go badly if he didn't answer.

"Who are you people?" said Weater.

"Who put out the contract on the King and Torbin Malvegil?"

That was it. They must be Dramadeens. But there were too many of them. Or else Malvegils? But where did they come from? The Malvegils had no forces in Lomion City.

"Who are you people?" said Weater again. He risked another punch. He just had to know.

"I'm Karktan of Malvegil. The Hand killed our lord, now you're paying the price. Tell me who put the contract out on him, and I'll kill you quickly, otherwise, I'm going to start cutting pieces off, starting with your toes."

Weater knew it meant death for a member of the Hand to reveal such information, no matter the duress. The thing was, it was the brethren that would kill you for it, under orders from the leadership. Aside from the Grandmistress, most of the Hand leadership was dead. Most of the brethren too if the Malvegils took the whole building. Who'd make him pay? There was room for a deal there. "I'll tell you everything if you let me live."

Several more men burst into the room, led by a red-bearded dwarf with huge muscles. Weater figured he must be McDuff the Mighty, an old Malvegil loyalist, and a legend in his own right. The Hand finally bit off more than it could chew. Behind the dwarf came a tall woman, a cowl covering her head. Even a heavy cloak and cape could not hide that woman's curves. Curves that put the Grandmistress to shame. Really to shame. And that was saying something. And then

Weater realized who she was. Lady Malvegil herself. A witch by all accounts, but with looks that could melt the stoniest heart. She came for revenge. To see those that killed her husband get what they had coming. There had to be an angle here that he could use. Had to think fast.

"Did you find her?" said McDuff.

"Only her toadies," said Karktan. "Is the building secure?"

"We're still routing them out, the stinking rats," said McDuff. "The place is full of hidey holes and trap doors. Our boys will smoke them out, one and all. Who is this sad sack?"

"Tell him," said Karktan.

"I'm Weater the Mouse. First Brother of the Hand."

"Second-in-command to the Grandbitch herself," said McDuff. "A nice prize. Have you cut off any parts yet?"

"I was just about to start," said Karktan.

McDuff pulled out a very long, wide dagger. "I'll do it. It would be a pleasure."

Lady Malvegil pulled the dagger from the dwarf's hand. "I will do it," she said, her voice icy cold.

She wasn't kidding. "I'll tell you," said Weater, his voice choppy as he tried to remain calm. "I didn't know about the hit until after it happened. I swear it. Nothing to do with me. I always respected the both of them. Spare me, and no torture, and I'll tell you all that I know."

Karktan looked to Lady Malvegil

"If your answers are satisfactory, you can live," said Lady Malvegil.

"And no torture?"

"I need to take a few pieces off," said McDuff. "Let me soften him up a bit. More likely he'll spew true." The dwarf stepped forward, retaking his dagger from the lady. "The Alders," said Weater, talking a bit faster. "It was them what put out the contract years ago. Fifty thousand silver stars."

"Which Alder?" said Karktan.

"Rom," said Weater. "The witch mother's brother."

"Where is the Grandmistress?" said Karktan.

"At the bazaar, last we heard," said Weater.

"When is she due back?" said Karktan.

"She's overdue already," said Weater.

"How many Hands are there?" said Karktan.

"Four hundred in Lomion City, give or take."

"How many in this building tonight?" said Karktan.

"No less than two hundred."

"Where is your roster? Duty schedule?"

"In our heads," said Weater. "Each lieutenant runs his own crew. We're the only ones what know who and where they are."

"How many lieutenants are there and what be their names?" said McDuff.

"Twelve there be. One of them is behind you," he said, referring to the Rat's head atop the deck. "Another is the gray-haired fellow you chopped up good down the hall."

Karktan looked over to one of his men. "Get some paper and a quill. Mister Weater — you're going to tell us every name you know. You're going to describe every one of them down to the birthmarks on their butts. You're going to tell us about every haunt and hidey hole that you people have."

"And you'll let me live?"
"Aye," said Karktan.
"And no torture?" said Weater.
"No torture," said Karktan.
"Then get me an inkwell and let's get started."

46

ISLE OF JUTENHEIM
THE GATORMEN'S LAIR

YEAR 1267, 4TH AGE
LAST YEAR OF KING TENZIVEL'S RULE

OB

Ob felt a kick to his side. Best to ignore it, he figured; try to sleep some more. He hadn't gotten enough rest in ages. Not since the League opened that gateway in the Vermion and practically destroyed the world. The stupid bastards. Not since Aradon, Gabe, Talbon, Stern, and Donnelin died. Nothing was the same since then. Nothing would ever be the same again.

Then came another kick. The bastards. The kicker said something too; sounded like gibberish. Stinking no-good mumblers. Why couldn't they just leave him be. Let him get some shut-eye. Ob grew angry. Probably somebody wanted permission to pee. They couldn't do anything without him. Like a bunch of children. Whelps. Let them deal with it themselves. He wasn't their mother. He had more important things to do.

Then came a third kick. It hurt. Now Ob was pissed. He lashed out with his arm. He'd slug whoever was messing with him. That'd teach them.

But he couldn't slug anyone. His arms caught on something close. A mesh of some kind. Somebody's darned curtain. That's when Ob realized that he hurt from head to toe. Moving made the pain all the worse. His mind was muddled. As if he were drunk. And so tired he couldn't even open his eyes. He thrashed his head from side to side to shake loose the cobwebs. Why didn't they just leave him alone? Couldn't anybody do anything without him?

He opened his eyes and his whole body spasmed as the world came back.

"Oh shit," he spat.

He dangled in a net that hung from the ceiling of a dark cave.

A gatorman net.

Captured. The bastards had captured him. Strung him up.

The stinking lizards.

He could barely see through the net — so tightly woven was its mesh. There were torches in the place, so it wasn't completely dark. Other nets hung all around. Other men were trapped in them, same as him. He smelled smoke. Meat. Cooking.

"Mister Ob," said Dolan from close by on his right side. At first, his voice sounded like a buzzing bee. After a moment, he started hearing straight. "Are you all right?"

"No, I'm not alright, you stinking string bean. I'm trapped in a net like a fish. Hanging in a stinking lizard cave. And they're about to barbecue me. There's nothing alright about that. Nothing."

"Are you wounded?" said Dolan.

"Head to toe. You?"

"I'm okay," said Dolan. "Just foggy. They drugged us. Poisoned darts."

"Explains it," said Ob. "Never would've got the best of us otherwise. How many of us did they nick?"

"A lot," said Dolan. "Slaayde is here. So is Sir Trelman. Captain Graybeard. Mister Rikenguard. And a lot of the Alders."

"How many is a lot?" said Ob.

"Over a hundred, I think," said Dolan.

"That's it then," said Ob. "They whipped us. Claradon? Fancy Pants?"

"No sign."

"What about Artol and Wizard Boy?"

"No sign of them either," said Dolan.

"A lot of the men are still knocked out," said Dolan. "Most of them. So they could be here."

"Always hated darts," said Ob. "And lizards. Weapons?"

"I've got a small folding knife that they missed," said Dolan. "They took everything else."

Ob gripped the net and tried to tear it. No chance of that. The stuff was strong.

"Been trying to cut through it for ten minutes," said Dolan. "Slow going, but I'll get it. A few minutes more. They're coming for us, one by one."

"Oh shit," said Ob. "Torture?"

"Food," said Dolan. "Smell it?"

"Dead gods," said Ob. "They really are eating us?"

"Taken six men since I've been awake," said Dolan. "Killed them for certain. Don't know how many more before that."

Ob realized that he was shivering. His clothes soaked through.

Then Ob heard a voice rise up from across the way.

Par Tanch!

Speaking his crazy wizard words. Shouting them.

Odin knows what those words meant, but they hurt Ob's ears like somebody stuck pins in them. Not because they were too loud, which they weren't, but the very sound of them hurt. The tone of it — the pitch, whatever it's called. That didn't make much sense to Ob, but it was the way it was. So too, twisted his stomach into knots, those weird words did. Stinking magic.

And then the room filled with yellow fire.

It erupted in a great plume. A plume that came from Tanch.

The fire roared. Billowed out in all directions. Expanded across the entirety of the cavern.

There was no escape from it.

Ob closed his eyes. Held his breath. Tucked chin to chest. Covered face with forearms. It was all he could do. If the fire fizzled out quick enough, maybe he'd live through it.

Ob felt the fire encompass him. Heard its roar in his ears.

It was hot.

But it didn't burn.

It didn't hurt, not much, anyways. What weird magic humbug was this? And what use was it?

Then Ob was falling.

The net that held him disappeared. It didn't tear or burn or dislodge from the ceiling. Of a sudden, it just wasn't there anymore.

How far down to the cavern floor? Too dark to tell. No time to adjust position; to brace his fall.

He hit hard.

Ob figured he fell from ten, maybe fifteen feet. He heard crashing all about him. All the men had fallen. All their nets were gone. Groans and curses from all around.

The rush of adrenaline got his head back on straight. The fog of poisoned sleep lifted. He bounced up; surprised everything worked. No broken bones. No torn muscles. Just bruises and scrapes on top of bruises and scrapes. He'd deal with that. Ignore it, and carry on. The warrior's way and all that.

Most of the others had fared as well as Ob. The cavern floor was thick with mud; the landing not so hard as it could have been. And with the nets disappearing, the men fell straight down, instead of tumbling. So no one landed on their heads; so no one died. But some came down wrong on their ankles or knees. The crack of bones took over the cavern for a few seconds. Ob always hated that sound. No matter how many times he heard it, it made him cringe. Most of the men pulled themselves to their feet. Many checked their pockets, belts, and pouches for weapons. Not a full-sized weapon amongst the entire group. A few small dirks and daggers, knives and knuckles, here and there. That was it. That's all the lizards had missed.

Ob crouched, picked up a rock, and slipped on some steel knuckles he had tucked deep in a pocket. "Grab some stones," he said. "Better than nothing."

And then the gatormen rushed in. The ones

close enough to have heard the commotion. Thank Odin, it was only a handful of them. Not the whole army.

The men pounced on them. Anger drove them. These were not men accustomed to being bested; the Alders included. The first three gatormen went down under a pile of men. Their spears did them no good.

Two gatormen turned and ran.

Tanch spoke two words. Words from the *Magus Mysterious*. Haunting, alien sounds. Sounds no man's throat should be able to make. They rang in Ob's head for hours. He couldn't shake them. But even a moment after he'd heard them, he couldn't have told you what those words were. How that could be, he couldn't say. Some other strange byproduct of the magic.

A bolt of blue fire shot from the top of Tanch's fingers. It diverged into two bolts as it flew. Those bolts unerringly struck the backs of the two gatormen that fled. One dropped immediately. A deep hole drilled into the center of his back. Smoking. The second gatorman stumbled two or three steps forward before he too went down. Both of them were dead.

The ones that the men jumped did not go so easily. They grappled and slashed. Bit and tore. Smaller than men were they, but twice as strong. And much quicker. The men pinned them. Arms and legs held down by several men each. Those with daggers or dirks came in. Slit their throats. Stabbed them through eye and ear. In ten seconds it was over. The cavern silent save for the whimpering of broken and wounded men.

"Grab those spears," said Ob as he hurried

over and pushed through the men. Ob picked up the last spear. "Arm yourselves with whatever you find; stones, anything."

Edwin of Alder stepped between Ob and the fallen gatormen. He snatched the spear from Ob's hands.

"You're not in charge here, gnome," said Edwin. "I am. Best you mind that, or I'll hand you over to the lizards."

Edwin lurched forward as a spear's tip ripped through his chest from the back. Blood spurted from his mouth and he sank to his knees. Groaning. Gurgling. The life draining from his face.

The gatormen charged into the cavern en masse. Spears held out before them.

"To the death," shouted Ob as he snatched back the spear from Edwin's dying hands. "Don't let them take you alive."

47

PLAIN OF ENGELROTH JUTENHEIM

YEAR 1267, 4TH AGE
LAST YEAR OF KING TENZIVEL'S RULE

JUDE EOTRUS

Those moments before the battle began lasted forever. The sun beat down on Jude's head. He hadn't had a hat or helmet in ages. It was hot and dry. So different from the Svartish tunnels. There was no cover. None at all. Dirt. Small rocks. A bit a grass and low shrubbery. Nothing that you could hide behind. Nothing that would conceal you. And it stunk. It always stunk around the expedition. No one had had regular baths in a very long time. That was a stink that Jude was used to. That he could deal with. Even the smell of the wild Lugron army was not altogether unfamiliar. An unpleasant stink, but not such that he'd puke. The foul stench that came off those shaggy giants was something altogether different. It burned his nose, that stink did. Made his stomach do flops. Even hundreds of yards away. What would it be like up close and personal? Jude didn't want to know, but figured he'd find out soon enough.

The Lugron came first. About two hundred of them. Ezerhauten stood at the center of the circle commanding the troops. He barked orders and every second Sithian on the opposite side of the circle broke off and moved to the side closest to the Lugron. The men in the second row on that side moved up to fill the gaps. The Stowron and Lomerian Lugron were confused but the Sithians pulled them into position.

"Your wizards ready?" said Ezerhauten.

"Aye," said Ginalli.

"No need," said Glus Thorn. He pushed through the ranks of Sithians, his long black cassock stretching to the ground, covering his shoes, such that he appeared to glide or even float just above the ground rather than walk as any normal man. An illusion, of course. Made him more mysterious. More imposing. Jude figured it was by design. He'd probably had that cassock hemmed a dozen times until its bottom cuff lay at just the right height to achieve that floating effect. His garments were dusty but intact, and no gore or bloodstains covered him. His full head of white hair perfectly in place, as always, despite all their recent trials.

"Master Thorn," said Ezerhauten, "best you step back out of the way. Archers, at the ready," he shouted.

Glus Thorn paid Ezerhauten no heed. He stepped out beyond the Sithian line. "Hold your arrows," he said in a deep voice marred with a slight lisp such that he whistled at the end of every phrase. "Or I'll put you right on the floor."

The archers glanced back toward Ezerhauten, seeking direction.

"Hold arrows until my order," said Ezerhauten.

Thorn stood there stoic and still, his white pallor in stark contrast to the ruddy or tanned complexions of most of his fellows. He waited until the Lugron came within ten yards.

Howling and screaming came the Lugron. Battle cries and curses. The pounding of their feet on the rocky ground made the entire area shake.

Jude saw Ezerhauten fidgeting and pacing. It was all he could do not to order the archers to let fly. They should have launched three or four volleys in the time it took the Lugron to advance. They could have dropped dozens of them. That opportunity, squandered. Jude figured that Ezerhauten had little choice. Thorn was not a man to cross. If you did, you'd end up like old Captain Rascelon, with your head bashed in by magics unseen.

Thorn held his staff in his right hand. A full seven feet long it was. And thick around, so that only a man with big hands could grip it comfortably. He'd dragged that thing all through the tunnels of Svartleheim. Jude had thought it a walking stick. After all, Thorn looked old. Jude couldn't guess his age. Seventy perhaps? Seventy five? Mayhap older. Jude knew it was supposed to be a wizard's staff — a thing of magic, but he still couldn't wrap his mind around such things.

"Violation here," said Thorn as he lifted his arm high. The base of the staff a good foot and half above the rocky ground. "One more false move and I'll put you right on the floor," he said. Then he brought the staff down hard.

A gust of air that came from where Thorn stood sent a ripple through the dust on the ground. The ripple, like the passage of some swift beast sped toward the onrushing Lugron. It was something so slight, an effect so small, even the lead Lugron wouldn't have spotted it.

Until it reached them.

When it did, the heads of the nearest fifty Lugron exploded.

Their corpses crashed to the ground.

Fifty men dead instantly. What killed them, unseen, invisible.

As one, the men of the Lugron horde gasped.

"Dead gods," said Brother Donnelin.

Jude's mouth was open; shock on his face. "How?"

The Lugron charge collapsed. Pieces of skull and brain pelted the Lugron behind those who died. Blood covered them. Many went down. Many more threw themselves to the ground, trying to take cover, to avoid whatever unseen death had come for them.

Fear filled the Lugron faces. Some looked back towards the hill where their army stood and watched. Too far away were they for Jude to see their reactions, though he heard their gasps of surprise and their shouted curses.

Several in the Lugron van rallied their men. Urged them up and to action.

They had guts those Juten Lugron. Or else they were dumb as rocks.

On they came again. One hundred and fifty strong.

"Get back you heathen scum," said Thorn. "Or I'll put you right on the floor."

They'd taken but two strides forward when Thorn swiped his staff from right to left in a swift and powerful stroke.

No Lugron was yet within twenty feet of him,

yet the blow struck.

Eight Lugron — every man in the front rank —-was cut deep across the midsection. Two or three were cut completely in half. They fell as if struck by a great sword.

"Violation here," shouted Thorn. What that exactly meant, Jude wasn't certain. The old fart was crazy, but even more deadly than Jude had thought.

Thorn slashed his staff back from left to right. If he also spat any mystical words, Jude didn't hear them. Another ten Lugron fell dead. Two cut in half.

Jude saw wisps of smoke rising off Thorn's hands and arms. The wizard paid that smoke no heed.

On came the other Lugron. They wouldn't give up. They wouldn't retreat. Why? Jude couldn't say. It made no sense in the face of what was befalling them. Blind courage? Greater fear of their fellows if they fled? Sheer stupidity? Some crazed sense of honor? Whatever reason it was, onward they came.

Thorn spun his staff in the air and slammed its base down to the ground once again, the nearest Lugron now only a dozen feet away.

A hundred men's heads exploded at once. Blood, gore, and brains flew in all directions. Some speckled the Sithians' armor, though it was lost in the grime and gore that had soaked them through those last days.

Gasps went up amongst both the expedition's and the Juten Lugron's ranks. The men of the expedition fidgeted. More than a few took a step or two back from Thorn. Some clearly gave more than a passing thought to running. A man that could do what Thorn did was capable of anything. Smoke billowed from Thorn's arms and cloak. Even from his hair. His body seemed to glow red, a stark change from his customary paleness.

Twenty or thirty Lugron still stood. Some inched backward. Most stood their ground. Tried to get up the courage to charge again.

Thorn held his staff now in both hands, spread a foot apart. He held the staff horizontally, up against his chest. Then he thrust it forward, as if to smash it against a man in front of him. Every Lugron that still stood, was lifted into the air and violently flung backward no less than ten yards. They crashed into the ground as if propelled by a catapult. Bones snapped. Bodies broke.

Three or four Lugron still showed some life. The rest were dead or done. Two began to crawl back toward their fellows on the hill. One somehow made his feet, his leg twisted and broken, bone protruding through the skin. He inched along, fearful looks back over his shoulder at Thorn, blood and tears streaming down his face.

Thorn turned back toward the expedition and the men cheered. "Thorn, Thorn, Thorn," they shouted in unison. He slowly walked back within the expedition's ranks, leaning heavily on his staff and staring down any of the men that dared meet his gaze. "You slackers," he said. "You ought to be selling tulips outside Turnberry's, two for a copper. Headman, bring me some water."

Smoke came off Thorn like a campfire. His face was twisted into a snarl. His skin, wherever visible, red and darkening by the moment. It was the first sign of weakness that Jude had seen him display.

Par Keld rushed up to him, canteen in hand.

"You're not the headman," said Thorn, his tone full of derision.

"Water," said Keld. "I brought you water. You called for it."

"On my head, you slacker," said Thorn as he bent forward so that the much shorter man could reach him.

Keld poured the canteen's contents over Thorn's head. The water sizzled and steamed as it touched the old sorcerer. The smoke decreased. Thorn moved to the very center of the expedition and sat down. Called for more water, which the wizards brought him. They looked at him with awe. Shock. Fear.

"I've never seen the like," said Brother Donnelin. "I don't think even Master Pipkorn could have managed that. That man has power, deep and true. Favored of some god he is."

"Azathoth?" said Jude.

Donnelin shook his head. "I know not. Before all this started, I thought that I understood the world. That I knew how things worked. That only in the darkest, most remote corners did ancient evils lie in wait. Now I know that I knew nothing. That I was a naive fool. Nothing in Midgaard is as it seems."

48

DOR EOTRUS THE UNDERHALLS

***YEAR 1267, 4TH AGE
LAST YEAR OF KING TENZIVEL'S RULE***

ECTOR EOTRUS

The pounding on the Underhall's great doors eventually became powerful and rhythmic as the trolls' fists and kicks gave way to a huge battering ram: a tree trunk they stripped and carried in from the forest. How many trolls hefted it, no Eotrus man could say. But each time that it rammed the steel doors, the boom was heard throughout the Underhalls.

The door's thick steel frame shuddered.

Dust fell from the ceiling.

Cracks formed here and there in the Underhall's structure.

The corridor filled with a dusty haze and stank of a strange chemical odor that stung the nose and tickled the throat — a smell not natural to the place.

"They'll be through soon," said Sarbek. "Three inches of steel and it's still not enough. Bloody trolls. You checked everything?"

"We're ready for them," said Indigo.

"It will work."

"Pull everyone back, behind the line," said

Sarbek. "A full company of archers up front and ready. Make certain that they've got a ton of arrows on hand and people in place to distribute them. The more trolls we stop now, the easier it will be later."

"Consider it done," said Indigo.

"Are all the civilians secure?" said Sarbek.

Indigo started, "We have—"

Without warning, the great steel double doors crashed inward. The repeated impact of the ram must have fractured both the crossbars and the door hinges.

"Run!" shouted Sarbek. He, Ector, and those around them dashed down the corridor, away from the doors.

Away from the trolls.

And on came the wild. There was but a moment's pause between when the doors crashed down and when the trolls thundered through, howling and screeching. The lead trolls wore heavy armor and helmets of steel. They carried great axes, hammers, and pole arms. Their equipment lacked the refinement of Lomerian gear, but it was stout, matching, and custom fitted to each troll. The armored trolls were also of a different breed. They stood taller and straighter than their common brethren, their features more chiseled, their limbs heavier, and far less hairy.

Sarbek and Ector were fifty feet from the entry when the doors came down.

That wasn't far enough, for the trolls were faster than men, despite their heavy gear.

A single squad of Eotrus archers was arrayed just behind "the line," some forty feet farther down the corridor. They made a hole amidst their ranks for the fleeing men to plow through.

"Faster," yelled Sarbek. "Don't stop! Don't look back," though he did. As he neared the line, the lead trolls were within three strides of Sarbek's back.

"Pull it," shouted Sarbek. "Pull it!"

There was a great clanking of metal.

A booming sound.

A whoosh.

Sarbek, last in line, dove forward even as the floor fell out from under him. A trap door that ran for a hundred feet along the length of the corridor opened up; the corridor floor split down the middle. It hinged on either edge.

Sarbek hadn't made it far enough. He dove. Got a hand around Ector's ankle while still in midair. Clamped down. Ector crashed hard to the ground, began sliding backward. Sarbek's legs dangled over the edge, his upper torso on solid surface. Two young soldiers, Artol's oldest sons, dived onto Ector's back to stay his slide. Others leaned over and grabbed Sarbek about the arms and tunic, though their eyes were not fixed on him. The trolls and their terrible fate filled their vision.

The huge trap door opened to a long narrow pit that filled the entirety of the corridor.

Eight feet down was death.

Green, murky liquid was its form.

Called hellfire oil by some, Barden's Bane by most, after the ill-fated alchemist that had invented the stuff.

It filled the pit.

Ten feet deep.

And every drop, the most concentrated and destructive acid known to man.

The Eotrus had pumped it into that pit day and night for the previous two days. Siphoned from sealed stone basins they had long stored it in — ready for just such an occasion.

The trolls fell into it en masse. There was no escape. Nothing to cling to, the walls of the pit, smooth and slick. The acid's calm surface roiled and bubbled when it tasted the troll flesh.

Their howls of agony were deafening but brief.

So tightly packed were the trolls in that corridor, no fewer than two hundred of them must have dropped into the acid. More likely, twice that number. Some scrambled upon the backs of their fellows. They sought to step on their heads or shoulders. To move forward or back. To save themselves. But their legs and feet burned out from under them. Their flesh shriveled and fell off the bone like overcooked meat.

Some few trolls made it several strides forward, but then they went down. A man would have lasted in that stuff but a few seconds, paralyzed from its first touch, but the trolls had a resiliency beyond measure. Some struggled to escape for a full minute even as the acid ate their flesh away.

One troll pulled itself up on the pit walls. Found some handhold that a man could never have managed. It got high enough to grab the top of the trap door's edge. Its legs were gone. All the way to its torso. A foot of blackened bone protruded down; so too, the barest strips of burnt flesh. It clung desperately to the wall. And then, inched back toward the entry. How it hung on, no man could say. The effort so heroic, even the Eotrus quietly cheered it on. Not one man raised a bow to pluck it from its perch. Twenty feet it moved toward safety, until at last its grip failed. Down it fell. A final plunge into the acid, from which it would never emerge.

The trolls crowded the doorway, cursing the Eotrus. The Eotrus answered with arrows, sending them back from the opening.

"You're smoking," shouted Ector to Sarbek as they gaped at the terrible scene before them. Smoke trailed from several spots across Sarbek's back and legs where droplets of acid had splashed him.

"Shit!" went Sarbek.

"Get away from the edge," said Ector.

"Water," shouted several of the archers. But Indigo was already on it. He pushed through the ranks, bucket in hand. Two other men similarly burdened only moments behind him. They showered Sarbek with the water, drenching him, neck to heel. The smoke stopped immediately, the acid sufficiently neutralized.

"By Odin," said Ector. "I've never seen anything like that."

"A little trick Ob picked up out east on one of his adventures," said Sarbek. "Donnelin oversaw the building of the thing, the pumps, pipes, and such."

"They'll not get by that pit easily," said Ector.

"They'll find a way," said Indigo. "Just as we would. We have to be ready."

"We've got more tricks up our sleeves," said Sarbek. "Trouble is, now they'll be wary for them. All the harder the next time to catch them unawares."

49

DORIATH HALL LOMION CITY

YEAR 1267, 4TH AGE
LAST YEAR OF KING TENZIVEL'S RULE

"**W**e caught the Hand with their pants down," said McDuff. "Those bastards are so feared that they figured no one would hit them. They didn't have proper defenses, not against a heavy assault."

"We hit them hard," said Torbin Malvegil from where he lay in his bed. "Two thousand of our best. Nobody could stand up to that. How many of them did we get?"

"One hundred ninety inside Black Hall," said Karktan. "Twenty more when they heard about the trouble and rushed back. Another twenty at nearby hideouts, using the information a prisoner gave us. We've got the men hitting all the known safehouses at once. A hundred men went to each. If we're lucky, by dawn the Black Hand will be no more. Even now, it's broken. Half its strength gone."

50

ISLE OF JUTENHEIM THE GATORMEN'S LAIR

YEAR 1267, 4TH AGE
LAST YEAR OF KING TENZIVEL'S RULE

OB

In the gatormen's lair, battle was joined. Tooth and talon, spear and tail, hand and fist. The ravenous hunger of the beast against the Lomerians' unrelenting will to live. Their will to win.

In moments, it became clear, there were too many gatormen. The Lomerians had no chance of victory. Some forty or fifty lizards rushed into the cavern at once, most well armed.

Others straggled in behind them.

Unarmed, and outmatched in strength, speed, and agility the Lomerians could not win against such numbers. Their only chance was escape. Fight their way to the nearest exit. Then run for it. The men instinctively knew this. Veterans all. No discussion was needed. They charged. Even into the hungry spears of the gatormen.

The Lomerians' best chance was the gatormen's disorganization. They didn't fight as a cohesive unit. Didn't stand in formation. If they'd formed a wall of spears they'd have broken the Lomerians' charge and crushed them.

But they didn't.

The gatormen charged in as individuals. Not a care for their fellows. They didn't have their blowguns. No poison darts flew about the cavern. To the Lomerians' good fortune, the gatormen didn't routinely carry those weapons. Same for their nets. Each gatorman came on either barehanded, with a spear, or a stone dagger. No shields and very little armor to speak of.

Ob rushed forward. One row of men was before him. He was proud and amazed at how the men rushed toward the line of spears. Even as he ran, he didn't know if he could have done it, had he been at the very front. What courage. What heroes. And truth be told, what desperation.

The Alder marines were right there with the rest — the Alders making up the vast majority of their group, perhaps a hundred and fifty strong.

The first line of men crashed into the gatormen's spears, each force converging on the other in the dim torchlight of the cavern. And as he ran, Ob realized he'd forgotten the wounded. He gave no order to help them along. To not leave them behind. How could he not have done that?

He hadn't had time to think. Everything was happening so fast. The chaos of battle. But it didn't matter. The men didn't need him to tell them to help their fellows. They knew to do it. And they would if they could. The trouble is, few would be able to help anyone. It wasn't at all clear that any of them would be able to push through the lizards and escape, little less doing so while dragging a wounded comrade.

Ob dodged through the gatorman line. Ducked between the legs of one. Dodged the spear thrust of another. Heard the crash as the man behind him slammed into a lizard. Other men were on Ob's heels. To the left and to the right. They barreled through. The greater size and weight of the Lomerians served them well. Counterbalanced the gatormen's greater strength.

Ob twisted and turned to slip a lizard's grasp. He caught a glimpse of Dolan behind him, spear to hand. Slaayde was there too — that cold, death stare on his face. A welcome sight, considering.

Where the passage narrowed, a huge gatorman blocked Ob's path. The gnome ducked his spear thrust. Kicked him to the groin. Hard — all his strength behind it.

The blow had no effect. The lizards' anatomy made their privates much less vulnerable.

Ob took a kick to the shoulder. Staggered back. Before he recovered, Dolan rammed his spear's tip through the lizard's neck. Pushed the beast up against the wall. The spear's tip burst through the back of its neck. Buried itself in a fissure in the wall.

And stuck fast.

Dolan wrestled with the spear for but a moment before he abandoned it. Scooped up another that the lizard had dropped.

Slaayde grappled with a gatorman. So did Captain Graybeard. Trelman stuck a spear through the chest of a short, squat gatorman.

The Lomerians' charge stalled.

Ob stuck his leg out, tripped a gatorman. It fell on its back. Captain Graybeard sank a spear into its mouth.

Somehow they broke through the line. They

were running again. Ob had a bunch of men with him. Dolan, Slaayde, and Graybeard for certain. At least a handful more. The sounds of the fighting behind them, loud and terrible. The screams and hisses. Growls and shouts. The terrible music of violent death. Sounds Ob was all too familiar with. Sounds that haunted him even in his sleep.

51

PLAIN OF ENGELROTH JUTENHEIM

YEAR 1267, 4TH AGE
LAST YEAR OF KING TENZIVEL'S RULE

JUDE EOTRUS

The Juten Lugron horde stood stoic on the hill after Glus Thorn had single-handedly wiped out their vanguard. They looked down on the expedition. Fear on most of their faces. Anger on others.

"You think they'll come again?" said Jude.

"Depends on how much they understand magic," said Donnelin. "If they have wizards, they'll know Thorn is spent. That he won't be able to throw much more magic anytime soon. They'll charge us with little fear of him. Of course, they don't know that we've got a bunch more wizards in the group. Though I doubt any of the rest could do a tenth of the damage that Thorn just did."

Jude looked to the other side of the valley. The giants shifted slowly toward them.

"They're going to attack," said Jude.

"A stupid move," said Donnelin. "They should act as if we were on their side. They should be cheering us on. Let us do their fighting for them. But they're too stupid for that. Look at them. They're sending a squadron down at us."

Ezerhauten ordered the troops to reposition. He doubled the men up on the giant's side of the defensive ring.

Then on came the giants. Probably twenty of them. They loped down the western hill toward the expedition.

"Archers," shouted Ezerhauten.

Then came some exchange amongst the wizards. A back and forth that took too long. By the time it was done, the giants had closed half the distance to the group, and Ezer's archers had launched three full volleys of arrows. Many shafts struck the giants, but most bounced off their hides. Some few found purchase, but the giants kept coming.

Stev Keevis, Par Rhund, and Par Keld stepped forward past the archers. Stev Keevis had his hand up close to his chest, fingers wiggling. Keevis's face was stern, his taut features, sharp, pointed, characteristically elven, his skin, a grayish green. Par Rhund's arms waved wildly as he muttered his mystic words, his wild black hair standing straight up as always, his black clothes such a contrast against his fair skin that he looked sickly. Keld was short, balding, and a bit stout. He wore spectacles and spoke with a sleight accent, foreign, eastern of some sort. His movements were tentative as if he were afraid. Who could blame him? His sidelong glances returned time and again to the wizards next to him and back to the expedition behind him. It was as if he thought they were going to attack him. Paranoid bastard. Nerethless, his fingers fidgeted, and he mouthed some words, readying whatever sorcery he commanded.

The giants charged in. Each held a primitive spear of sharpened wood — they didn't even have stone tips. No blades to be found.

Par Rhund's spell went off first. A cone of fire. It launched from his fist. Rocketed at the giants. Expanded as it went. The giants didn't know what to do. And had no time to do it. The flames hit them. Enveloped them. And then fizzled out. A half-dozen piles of ash lay on the ground where giants had been. A half-dozen other giants were on fire. Screaming. All but one on the ground. Rolling. Trying to douse the flames. Flames that had no interest in going out. One giant staggered about. Fully engulfed. Wandered this way and that as he screamed. Until finally he dropped to his knees, then sagged back on his haunches. Burned there like a torch, though he moved and screamed no more.

Stev Keevis's magic went off but two seconds after Rhund's. A dozen bolts of silver plasma sped from his hand. One or two struck each of seven or eight giants. Where it hit them, their fur blackened. They dropped. Five or six died instantly. The rest convulsed on the ground.

Last came Keld's magic. He held it until the others' spells went off. An unseen force lifted the giant closest to him off the ground. Then the next closest. Brought them into the air, turned them over. Then rocketed them down to ground. Headfirst. There was a terrible crunching of bones on impact. Both giants were dead. No sooner had they hit the ground than did Keld scurry back behind the Sithian line looking fearful and guilty.

Not one giant was unscathed. Their charge crushed. Two that had been on fire made their feet. Staggered away, back toward their fellows. A few volleys of arrows brought them both down.

"They've got the power, these Leaguers," said Brother Donnelin. "Archwizards every one."

Nothing happened for quite a while. The Lugron stood on the eastern hill. They didn't move. Just glared down at the expedition.

The giants loped about the western hill. Watching. Grumbling.

But no more of either side came on.

"This is our chance," said Keld. "They're afraid. They're confused. Did you see the ones that I killed? I promise you, one of them was their leader. I took him out. That's why they're hesitating. This may be our only chance to get away – not that anyone will give me any credit – before they regroup and select a new chief."

"We should make a run for it while we can," said Ginalli.

"That would be stupid," said Ezerhauten.

"What now?" said Ginalli.

"Run from a pack of wolves, and what do they do?" said Ezerhauten. "Chase you down and maul you to death. That's what these will do. Our movement will rouse them."

"Then let's walk out," said Brackta. "Slow and steady."

"Worth a try," said Ezerhauten. "But if any man runs, I will shoot him down myself."

They made it about a hundred yards before the Lugron and the giants both advanced on them. They were a mile or more from the end of the valley. The Lugron siege engines still between them and the path to potential escape. The Sithians moved quickly into their circular formation, though this time they made a tighter circle, two Sithians deep. The Stowron and the Lomerian Lugron formed a third row behind them. All the rest, remained in the center, though now they were tightly packed together. The Lugron and the Juten giants closed distance. But this time, they didn't charge. They went with missiles instead. Hundreds of arrows flew at the expedition from the east. Scores of spears flew at them from the west.

"Teek, you stinking bastard," spat Jude, "untie my hands and give me a weapon."

"Can't do that, Judy," said Teek. "You're still a prisoner and me got orders."

"Those Lugron are going to crash through the line and be on us," said Jude. "They won't care who's a prisoner and who isn't. They'll kill me all the same."

"I'll protect you, Judy boy," said Teek. "Just sit tight and keep your teeth together."

More spears came down. One clipped the edge of Teek's boot.

"If I get dead," said Jude, "you'll get blamed for certain. They ordered you to guard us. If I'm dead, you've failed. Thorn will skin you alive."

"Button it, Judy boy. I'm not falling for your bull no more. Sides, the old fart is half dead."

Mort Zag, who somehow overheard the conversation despite the din of the Lugron and giant armies, turned toward Teek. "Cut their bonds. Give them weapons." Then to Jude and Donnelin, "Try to escape, I'll eat one of your legs." Then he passed them two shields. "Try not to get dead yet."

Par Brackta came close to Jude. She was

battered badly. Burned. Bruised. But the fire was still in her eyes. She stood close to him. A mystical shield surrounded her, and she extended it about Jude and Donnelin too.

"We're not going to survive this, are we?" she said. "I can't believe it. All the archwizards we had. All that we still have. I'd have told you we could have conquered the world with all that power. And we've been destroyed bit by bit by things that shouldn't even exist. And now we're about to be killed by Lugron of all things."

"Don't forget the giants," said Jude.

"You have any magic left?" said Donnelin.

"I can throw two or three good spells," said Brackta. "One or two more after that and I'll be done for."

"Lord Korrgonn will fight them," said Mort Zag. "He will lay them low. Suck out their souls and spit them into the void. I will chew on their bones tonight."

"Right then," said Jude shaking his head. Behind the mystical energy shield he was able to stand. The sword they'd given him of Lomerian Lugron make. Not very good. But it had an edge to it. He'd make do. He was thankful for his armor and so too for the shield. He'd go down fighting. A warrior's death it would be. Then he'd join his forefathers in Valhalla.

52

THE REGENT'S EXPEDITIONARY FORCE (THE ALDER BRIGADE)

***YEAR 1267, 4TH AGE
LAST YEAR OF KING TENZIVEL'S RULE***

DIRK ALDER

Strictly speaking, Gar Pullman wasn't part of Boddrick's mercenary company, but rather, an associate. A specialist that the Alders brought in when they expected things to get unusually messy. Seeing him standing on that cabin's porch, urging Dirk and his men forward, was a relief. It gave Dirk hope that he might yet survive the night.

As he ran toward the cabin, Dirk heard another thud and a yell. This time from close behind. He risked a head-turn and saw two trolls drag a man into the woods, the soldier kicking and screaming all the while. So close to salvation was that fellow, but he didn't quite make it. A shame. Dirk didn't see the man's face; didn't know who he was — and truth be told, was glad for it. He didn't know very many of the soldiers in the brigade, but which ones he did know, he liked. Probably, they were all dead now. Dirk tried to push those thoughts from his mind. Keep focused on running. On surviving.

Dodging down the side lane hadn't confused the trolls or thrown them off their trail. They were too close for that. Within twenty yards. Closer than they'd been since they fled the brigade's encampment in the shadow of Dor Eotrus.

Dirk noted that only about five men were behind him. The others, all gone. Fallen far behind, turned off the path to take their chances on their own, or more likely, picked off by the trolls. At the rate the trolls were closing, and he was tiring, he'd not have made another mile. Maybe only half that.

With a last burst of speed, Dirk reached the porch. He wanted to run inside the cabin and hunker down, but that wasn't his place —— not until Pullman turned and went in too. Dirk had to stay in the line of danger for as long as any of the others. It was his duty. He was an Alder. A nobleman. The soldiers, regulars and mercenaries, were all in the employ of his House. And he was the only Alder left on the expedition. His uncle, Brock, was dead — murdered by the Eotrus when he sought to parley with them before the walls of their keep. Dirk had had some doubts about just how bad the Eotrus were before he saw his uncle shot down in cold blood, white flag beside him. No longer.

They were the evil, treacherous bastards that he'd heard tell of a hundred times around Alder Manor. They deserved whatever they got. He hoped the trolls killed them all.

Dirk's uncle Rom was gone too. No doubt killed by the trolls along with the rest of the brigade. Dirk didn't think any man could beat

Rom in battle. But the trolls were not men. It all happened so fast. It didn't seem real.

The Alders hadn't lost a whole brigade since the wars. This would be quite a scandal. One to be long remembered. And not in a good way. He wondered whether he'd get blamed.

By rights, he shouldn't. Uncle Rom was in charge. If someone was to blame, it should be him. Next in line was Uncle Brock. Maybe he'd get blamed too, which didn't matter, since he was dead. Dirk wasn't actually in command of anything, so he shouldn't be held accountable. But he might be. Mother Alder could be fickle. Uncle Barusa could be vindictive. Fairness was not one of his qualities.

The more that Dirk thought about it, the more he figured that he'd get blamed. He'd have to come up with some way to steer clear of too much trouble before they got back home.

When Dirk bounded up the porch steps, he dodged to the side, turned, and pulled his sword. Stood to Pullman's right. Boddrick did the same and stood to Pullman's left. No doubt, the brute was trying to show him up. He wasn't very successful, huffing and puffing as he was. He looked as if he were about to collapse. Dirk tried to hide that he was barely able to stand himself.

"How many do you have?" said Boddrick to Pullman.

"My whole troop and more," he said. "How many on your tail?

"Don't know," said Boddrick.

"Get ready to make a stand," said Pullman. A dozen more men filed out of the cabin and joined them on the porch. They were fresh and fully equipped. Dirk figured they'd give the trolls what for before they breathed their last.

The trolls came on, whopping and hollering. They swung out of the trees. They ran out of the woods. But they pulled up on the approach to the cabin, as if wary. As if they wanted to size the place up before charging in.

"Shouldn't we barricade ourselves in?" said Dirk. "Make our stand inside?"

"Shut up," said Pullman.

"The boy has a point," said Boddrick.

"Just stand ready," said Pullman.

Nearly twenty trolls loped toward them, leering. Even with Pullman's men, the Alders barely had a full squadron. That wasn't nearly enough to stand against a score of trolls. Not nearly. But Pullman had said he had his entire troop with him. Where were they?

Pullman stepped to the front edge of the porch, his sword held point first out before him, his shield at the ready.

The trolls started moving forward.

Pullman let his sword's tip drop.

That's when the arrows came. From both sides of the clearing, a hundred shafts flew through the night. They skewered the trolls. Nearly every one of them hit by at least one arrow, most by a handful or more. One troll went down; an arrow through its eye. One troll bounded toward the porch. Pullman stepped out to meet it. The other trolls turned toward the woods, and as they did, another volley of arrows pincushioned them.

The trolls reeled back. Another one or two went down.

The unwounded troll at the front of the pack bounded toward the cabin's porch. Pullman stood his ground until it came within reach. A powerful overhand slice with his sword opened the troll's torso from collarbone to waist as it came in.

The troll crashed into Pullman's shield. Or rather, the shield crashed into it. That terrific impact stopped the troll in its tracks, and did Pullman no happiness. Pullman stepped forward, down the steps, sword swinging. Each blow struck the troll about the arms or torso. His sword bit deep.

The troll staggered back.

Pullman stepped forward again and cut the beast's head from its shoulders with a single powerful slash.

Then came the sound of horses. From the darkness on both sides of the clearing charged Alder and mercenary cavalry, lances lowered. The trolls were still reeling from the arrow shafts, and had no time to maneuver.

The cavalry charged through the trolls from the right flank, crushing many underfoot, skewering many with their lances. They didn't stop. They rode through even as another cavalry troop charged from the left flank. They barreled in and toppled what trolls were left standing, and rode past. The horsemen leaped from their horses on both sides and dashed back to the thick of the trolls, swords swinging. In less than a minute, it was over. The men hacked the trolls to pieces and set fire to their corpses.

The men on the porch needed only to watch.

"Nicely done," said Boddrick.

"We've taken two other groups so far, each

about half as many as those," said Pullman pointing to the carnage before them. "Rom?"

"We don't know for certain," said Boddrick. "But the whole brigade was slaughtered.

"We need to warn the city," said Dirk.

"Already done," said Pullman. "I sent ravens and riders.

"How many men do you have?" said Dirk.

"My troop — two hundred strong, and about one hundred fifty more from 4th Company that got clear. Plus a full squadron that I sent on to Riker's Crossroads to reinforce the place and evacuate what civilians they can."

"We've enough to do some damage," said Dirk.

"Not enough to keep us alive," said Boddrick. "We don't even know how many trolls are out there."

"Too many," said Pullman. "I'm pulling back to Riker's to regroup and resupply."

"Why not keep going straight on to Lomion City?" said Boddrick. "This expedition is lost."

"Because the Alders paid me to see them through this," said Pullman. "To keep them alive and to take down the Eotrus. I aim to fulfill that contract."

53

DOR EOTRUS
THE CENTRAL TOWER
BROTHER DONNELIN'S CHAMBERS

YEAR 1267, 4TH AGE
LAST YEAR OF KING TENZIVEL'S RULE

MALCOLM EOTRUS

As Malcolm sat in Brother Donnelin's secret room, he couldn't expel from his mind the last look on Sergeant Graham's face before they had to slam closed the safe room's door, leaving him behind. Leaving him to the trolls' mercy.

Graham didn't say anything in those last moments. But that look. His eyes. The way his mouth opened, twisted.

Please.

That's what he was trying to say.

Please.

But was he pleading for help? Begging Malcolm not to leave him? Or asking him to kill him before the trolls got at him? Malcolm didn't know. He would never know. But that image and the terrible sound of Graham's screams haunted him until the end of his days.

The trolls lingered in Brother Donnelin's bedroom. Lingered over their meal. They must have tired of the fighting and decided to hunker down and take a rest, their fellows to continue the fight with the Volsung. That is, assuming that any of the Eotrus still fought on. For all Malcolm knew, his tiny group may well be the last. All his people might now be dead. But he didn't believe that. Sarbek would've gotten the Underhalls locked up tight. The trolls would have no easy time breaking in.

Though the safe room wall was stout and thick, Malcolm heard the unmistakable sounds of the trolls devouring their prey: Graham and the two guardsmen that fell in that room.

It seemed as if the trolls would never leave. Malcolm, Baret, and Humphrey, remained as still and silent as they could. Or else draw the trolls' attention. The creatures didn't know they were hiding in that tiny room — didn't know the room existed. Its door was well hidden by design. And by luck and good timing, the trolls didn't see them flee within. For the time being, their hidey hole remained secret.

A narrow crack in the outer wall allowed some light into the room — the only light. They could barely see anything.

Baret was hurt. A troll's claws had gouged clear through his breastplate. He was bleeding. Not so bad that he'd die of blood loss. But bad enough. The trouble was, they dare not remove the breastplate. There was no way to do that silently. The trolls would hear. Then they'd be at the door. They'd be at the walls. One troll. Two. Three. They probably couldn't get through — not that door. But they'd call their fellows. They'd raise all Helheim. Soon there'd be ten trolls out there. Twenty. Maybe even a hundred. Eventually they'd batter their way in. That would be the end of Malcolm and his friends. The only way to avoid that was to remain silent. Silent and still. To wait the trolls out. Eventually they'd leave. They just had to wait.

Humphrey tried to staunch Baret's bleeding as best he could using a towel from Brother Donnelin's stores. It was a help. Baret gritted his teeth and bore it all. Stoically. Man was a rock.

Baret was the kind of man, the kind of soldier — that Malcolm wanted to be. Skilled, fearless, and tough as nails. He knew he'd never be that man, no matter how hard he tried. A one-armed warrior could never achieve Baret's skill at arms.

A long time later, an hour at least – the trolls finally left Donnelin's chambers. Or it seemed so. For the place went quiet. They sat unmoving for another hour, just to be certain. They heard plenty of sounds from outside, but all were distant. Some fighting still went on. The trolls were rooting men out of hidey holes throughout the tower. And killing them when they found them.

After he deemed it safe to move around, Malcolm found a removable panel on the outer wall that concealed two spy holes cut through the tower's outer wall. One angled steeply upward and ushered in the sunlight. The other angled steeply downward and provided them a look at the courtyard and much of the Dor below. The holes were small and tapered from inside to out. Unless a troll was climbing up the outside wall at just the right spot, they'd never see the opening. Another ingenious design of Brother Donnelin's, no doubt.

The courtyard was filled with trolls. They covered nearly every inch of the place. They were on the lower roofs. Atop the wall — all the battlements. Everywhere. And many of them were feasting. Feasting upon fallen men. On the far side of the courtyard, Malcolm spied the trolls building scaffolding from which they hung, upside down, the bodies of men. Dead men.

"They're storing their food," said Humph after he took a look. "Hanging us up like meat after a hunt. Dead gods, the evil bastards. No compassion. No heart at all. No sense of decency. Where did they come from?"

"Helheim," said Baret. "Straight out of Helheim."

Now that they had some light, they looked around the safe room for whatever else they could make use of. They saw that a heavy black curtain was strung from a line by the safe room door. It was designed to be pulled closed over the inside face of the door, presumably to block any light that might escape from the safe room through some crack or seam and give away its location. The curtain was very thick, actually two heavy pieces of cloth, one behind the other. They may well also serve to dampen any sounds within the safe room. Smart. Even though the trolls appeared to be gone, they closed the curtain just in case.

They found candles and lanterns on a shelf. Lit a lantern, the better to see by. The safe room was some six feet wide by about twenty feet long. And well stocked. Shelves and boxes held jugs of water, food: dried, jarred, bags of nuts. It would sustain them for many days if need be. There was even a privy, tucked away in the corner of the room, attached to the tower's plumbing. The room held an assortment of weapons. Several swords, daggers, staffs, an axe, and a battle hammer. Two crossbows and several bundles of bolts hung high on a wall.

Then Malcolm found a secret room within the safe room. A panel in the wall slid open to reveal a congested closet overflowing with clothes of all sorts: Lugron armor and gear; robes of Thothian monks; armor and dress common to mercenaries and bandits; black clothes like that worn by The Black Hand; tabards and cloaks with the sigils of House Alder, House Tenzivel, and many more, domestic, and of parts foreign. Even a full suit of Myrdonian plate armor. A high shelf held an assortment of wigs, fake beards, hats, and more.

"What is this?" said Humph. "A collection?"

"I don't know," said Malcolm. "Very strange."

"Disguises," said Baret. "The old man was prepared for everything. If anybody ever took over the Dor, he had a costume ready to don so that he could slip through their ranks and escape. Paranoid old nutter, but smart."

"What was he afraid of?" said Malcolm. "No one ever took over the Dor before. Before today."

"Started way back after some mission with your father and Sir Gabriel," said Baret. "The campaign when he lost his hand. Came back a different man. Always looking over his shoulder. That's when he started building all sorts of contraptions, gadgets, traps, and such. That's probably when he built this room."

On the floor of the closet they found more

gear of every type imaginable. And a large trunk. Within that trunk were Donnelin's valuables. Had the priest not been dead, Malcolm would not have gone through that. But Donnelin was long gone, and there was little to do to pass the time in the safe room, other than to worry on their situation, and that did them no good.

Donnelin had accumulated an impressive amount of gold and assorted coins over his long career. Much of it was foreign. Much of it was old. No doubt, these were the spoils of war and the bounty of delving deep into old abandoned places. Gathered over the course of three decades of campaigning with Aradon Eotrus.

A lead box within the trunk harbored the most curious prize. Malcolm opened it to find a note written on a piece of parchment in Donnelin's own hand. It read:

Herein lies the ankh of Azrael the Wise — a being of ancient and mysterious origin. The ankh is a relic of the old world and harbors great mystical power. It was gifted to me for safekeeping, in the year 1242, by Sir Gabriel Garn.

— Brother Donnelin, High Cleric to the Eotrus.

"It looks much the same as the talisman worn by Sir Gabriel," said Humph.

"Aye, it does," said Baret. "Lord Theta carries a similar talisman about his neck. I marked it well. I thought it Sir Gabriel's when I first saw it. Each of them is similar, yet all distinct."

"A holy symbol?" said Humph.

"Take the note at its word," said Baret. "It's a

thing of great mystical power. A wizard's ward or some such."

Malcolm picked it up. Turned it over in his hand. "Cold like ice," he said.

He passed it to Baret. "It doesn't feel cold to me at all. Just a lump of stone." Baret looked closer at it. "Maybe not stone? Petrified wood? I don't know."

"Can I see?" said Humph. Baret passed it to him.

"Cold?" said Malcolm.

"Not at all," said Humph. "Just an odd piece of jewelry if you ask me." He passed it back to Malcolm who winced at its touch.

"It's freezing," said Malcolm. "You don't feel that? Tell me true?"

They said they didn't.

"Mayhap you can sense its spark of magic, where we cannot," said Baret. "I've heard it said that Sir Gabriel could foretell things with his ankh. Used it for wayfinding, and for warning of dangers soon to come. See if it works for you."

"Mayhap it can help get us out of this jam," said Humph.

Malcolm held it tightly in his hand. Closed his eyes. Concentrated. After a few seconds he opened his eyes, stumbled, and nearly fell over. "I can feel them," said Malcolm. "The trolls. I can feel them."

"What can you feel?" said Baret.

"That they're not close," said Malcolm. "I sense frustration in them. Something unfulfilled. They're anxious to get on with something."

"The Underhalls?" said Baret.

"Yes, I think that's it," said Malcolm. "They

can't get into the Underhalls and it's pissing them off."

"That means Sarbek and Ector are holding out down there," said Baret. "That means that a lot of our people are still alive. And that we've still got a chance."

"Or it means that Malcolm's gone nutter just like Donnelin," said Humph.

54

HIGH COUNCIL CHAMBER TAMMANIAN HALL LOMION CITY

YEAR 1267, 4TH AGE
LAST YEAR OF KING TENZIVEL'S RULE

BARUSA ALDER

The High Council met in closed session. That meant the councilors were there along with their personal bodyguards, and no one else.

Chancellor Barusa called the meeting to order. Bishop Tobin was there, far more awake than usual. Also present were Field Marshal Balfor, Guildmaster Slyman, the Vizier, Lord Jhensezil, Lady Aramere of Dyvers, Lady Dahlia of Kern, and Lord Aldros.

"My friends," said Barusa. "As you can imagine, after the brazen murder of our beloved king, Prince Cartegian is naturally indisposed. At last word, Duke Harringgold is recovering in Dor Lomion, though the extent of his injuries remain unclear."

"Our king was ill," said Barusa. "Troubled. For many years. We all know this. But he was our king. Let us remember him for the man that he once was, the king that he once was. And let's mourn him accordingly."

"Do we know yet who committed this black deed?" said Bishop Tobin. "The rumors I've heard are inconsistent and disturbing."

"The Black Hand was involved," said Lord Jhensezil. "But they did not act alone. Mercenaries from the Southron Isles were with them."

"Were any captured?" said Lady Aramere.

They all looked to Marshal Balfor who kept close council with the City Watch.

"None," said Balfor. "The assassins killed nearly every member of the king's party, including Lord Torbin Malvegil who had just arrived in the city for a visit, Captain Korvalan, and almost a score of bodyguards. Only the good Duke escaped with one of his men.

"Rumors swirl about traitors amongst the Dramadeens," said Bishop Tobin. "There is also talk that Baron Morfin orchestrated the whole matter to settle some old grudge."

"Though I regret the need to mention this," said Guildmaster Slyman, "in the interest of a full discussion, I feel I must. Some are saying that it was no accident that the good duke survived that attack. That he was in league with the killers."

"That's preposterous," said Jhensezil.

"The duke and I rarely agree on anything," said Barusa. "You all know that there is little love lost between us, but I cannot imagine Harringgold taking part in such treason."

"Is it treason to kill a madman?" said Jhensezil.

"Of course," Barusa snapped.

"I agree," said Lord Jhensezil. "Though our king was troubled, he was the true and rightful king. We owed him our loyalty."

"Unless his troubles threatened the safety and security of the realm," said Bishop Tobin.

"And what is the test for that?" said Jhensezil.

"A difficult question," said Tobin. "By tradition, if the king acts recklessly or out of unsound mind, the High Council is charged with putting their own preferences and prejudices aside and evaluating the matter apolitically. The test is whether the entirety of the Council, in sound manner, devoid of partisanship, can agree that the king's decision is reckless to the point of being unreasoned. If unanimity exists amongst the Council, the king's orders can be set aside. If a pattern of such behavior exists, then the Council can either depose the king and pass the crown to a rightful and true heir, or if one fitting does not exist or is not of age, the Council can appoint a regent to govern the affairs of the kingdom until a rightful heir becomes available."

"And if none does?" said Lady Aramere. "If there is no heir?"

"Then the bloodline is broken," said Tobin. "A new Royal House must be elected by vote of the High Council and the Council of Lords. This has only rarely happened in our history, but it has happened."

"What to do about these rumors of conspiracies?" said Marshal Balfor.

"Disband the Dramadeens," said the Vizier. "Foreigners. Ruffians. Who knows where their loyalties truly lie. It's long past time that they go. The Myrdonians are the Royal Knights, both in name and function. They can take over all duties performed by the Dramadeens."

"The Dramadeens were appointed by the king," said Jhensezil. "It is only the king that can disband them. This lies beyond the prerogative of this Council."

"I'm not certain that I agree with that," said Barusa.

"What of Baron Morfin?" said Tobin. "How does he fit into this?"

"Some claim to have seen him about the city in the last few days," said Barusa. "His son with him. If that be true, the timing of his return is suspicious."

"Would he not present himself to us, if he had returned?" said Tobin.

"Let's not speak of Morfin as if he was on holiday," said Lady Aramere. "We've all believed him dead these past months. Disappeared one night after one of our Council meetings concluded. I for one thought the Black Hand had done him in, and have long wondered who might have been behind such a contract."

"If he lives," said Barusa, "then obviously that theory has no merit. But of the Black Hand we must speak further. What have you heard?"

The Councilors all gave him their attention, but their looks implied they knew not of what he spoke.

"Balfor," said Barusa, "could you please share with the Council what you told me earlier?"

"Some force has moved against the Hand," said Balfor. "Black Hall burned to the ground last night."

"That was the fire last night?" said Lady Aramere.

Balfor nodded. "Black Hall is no more. There

are many bodies in the rubble. We don't think many, if any, were killed by smoke or flame. There was a battle down there, in Black Row. It seems that the Hand lost."

"So were they a paper tiger after all?" said Jhensezil.

"Hard to say," said Balfor. "But there are reports that a very large force attacked their hall."

"How large?" said Lady Aramere.

"By all accounts, over a thousand men stormed the place," said Balfor.

"A thousand!" said Tobin. "That boggles the mind. How could such a thing go unnoticed? Barely reported? Who were they?"

"What sigil did they carry?" said Jhensezil. "What banners?"

"They displayed none," said Balfor. "And they left no dead behind. We don't know who they were."

"There are few Houses that could field such a force," said Tobin.

"I disagree," said Jhensezil. "There are plenty of groups in the city that could assemble such a strike force. The guard; the watch; the Church Knights; at least one or two of the guilds, probably more, and no fewer than five noble Houses that I can think of."

"Could there be any merit to the rumors about the Dramadeens?" said Lady Aramere.

"Captain Korvalan gave his life protecting the king," said Jhensezil. "Along with those of a dozen of his men."

"Or did he betray the king?" said the Vizier. "And was he killed by loyalists?"

"How can we know?" said Slyman.

"Harringgold can tell us," said Tobin.

"Assuming that he wasn't involved in this plot," said Slyman.

"Let's assume that," said Lady Aramere. "For we've no evidence or motive to assume otherwise."

The doors to the Councilors' mezzanine opened, and there stood Cartegian. Haggard, but not unkempt. His clothes were richer than usual, well fitting and pressed. His hair was combed. His posture, straight and tall.

The councilors were silent as the prince made his way to the king's seat, as was his rightful place.

"Have you all been struck dumb?" said Cartegian, his voice stronger, more lucid than usual.

The councilors offered their greetings and condolences.

"We should speak more of—" said Barusa.

"I have an announcement," said Cartegian in bold voice that grabbed everyone's attention. "As heir to the throne, my coronation must soon be planned. It will be a dual event."

He looked around, gauging their response. "It will also be my wedding."

Slyman snickered. "Probably marrying his cat."

"Perhaps the timing of such a blessed event is not appropriate—" said Tobin.

"It's my decision," said Cartegian.

"And who is to be your queen?" said Barusa.

"Marissa Harriggold," said Cartegian.

"A Harringgold?" said Balfor as he shook his head.

"Does he even know this girl?" said Slyman.

"She has accepted," said Cartegian. "And her father has blessed the union."

"Well there is your motive," said Slyman. "With the king dead, his daughter wedded to the prince, Harringgold rules by proxy. We must send for him. He must stand before this Council and explain himself."

"We will have a regent," said Cartegian.

"Harringgold, of course," said Slyman as he shook his head.

"Barusa," said Cartegian. "Barusa of Alder will be regent until such time as Marissa and I produce an heir that comes of age."

Barusa's eyes were wide with shock. A hush came over the hall.

"You all think that my mind is muddled," said Cartegian. "You are right. I know it. There are times, brief times, such as now, when my thoughts grow clear. And when they do, I feel shame at my behavior and curse myself for whatever affliction makes me behave so. To rule this great kingdom, a clear mind is needed. Someone whose first loyalty is to the realm. Chancellor Barusa has long been my mentor and my voice in this Council. I am the first to admit that I often disagree with his positions. But despite that, I have always respected his council, wisdom, and judgment. I believe he is the right man to be regent, and that a regent must be named. If any of you object, best to keep silent. My mind is made up on this."

"I don't know what to say," said Barusa.

"First time for everything," muttered Tobin.

"Say that you accept," said Cartegian.

Barusa looked around the room at the shocked faces of the councilors. "I accept."

In her private chambers in House Alder, Mother Alder let her hands drop from the Alder Stone as a broad smile came over her face. The image of the council chamber quickly faded from view, the sounds soon followed. She stood up, beaming. "At last, our rightful place is at hand. Now, the Alders will rule."

"Excellent," said Cartegian. "I'm certain that you will get on very well with my other ministers."

"What other ministers?" said Barusa.

"My cat and my troll, of course," said Cartegian, his voice beginning to slur. "Cat will be in charge of all milk deliveries and rodent hunts. Troll will be my weapons master. He is a surly sort, but tough as they come. You've no issue with those appointments, do you, my good regent?"

"It will be as you wish, my prince," said Barusa.

"Good. How soon can we get on with the coronation, taking into account that the wedding will be at the same time? I'm thinking, next Thursday would work. I have my haircut and shave scheduled for the day before, so I'll be at my best."

Bishop Tobin cleared his throat to get the room's attention. "Your majesty, if I may, a few days is not normally considered enough time to plan an event of such import, or such magnitude."

"Then let's reduce the magnitude," said Cartegian. "I need no grand ceremony with kings and princes and queens from across Midgaard in attendance. Wait, send them invitations, but send them late, that way they can't attend but will be obligated to send presents. I do enjoy a good present."

"It must be no less than a month," said Bishop Tobin. "The planning takes time. The preparation. Not to mention decorum. One can't hardly schedule a wedding within days of the groom's father's funeral."

"You can if the groom is a prince and orders it," said Cartegian.

"Why the rush?" said Slyman.

"My future father-in-law, the old dukey-duke, says there must be no funny business between me and Marissa until after we're married, all official, before the gods and such. I've no interest in waiting a day more than I have to. So the wedding will be next week. I need you all to help make that happen."

55

ISLE OF JUTENHEIM THE GATORMEN'S LAIR

***YEAR 1267, 4TH AGE
LAST YEAR OF KING TENZIVEL'S RULE***

OB

A gatorman's spear thrust caught Ob in his right side. He never saw it coming. The stone spear, for all its sharpness, couldn't pass good Lomerian steel: his armor held. But the power of that blow tossed Ob up against the wall. Knocked the wind from him. This time, Rikenguard was there. He put a spear through Ob's attacker. Pinned *him* to the wall. Another gatorman's spear thrust caught Rikenguard in the leg. Still another, in the shoulder. Juten chainmail, not as stout as Lomerian steel, the spear tips sank deep. The Juten turned. Pounded his fist atop the closest gatorman's head. Ob saw it as if in slow motion. The gatorman's head compressed and exploded as the bones burst under the power of that blow. A gatorman's spear snapped against Rikenguard's armor. The guide grabbed that gatorman by the throat. Lifted him high.

Dolan grabbed Ob's shoulder, pulled him up.
"We've got to move," Trelman shouted.
"Can you run?" said Dolan.
Ob didn't say anything. Started moving.

Running. Dolan and Trelman beside him. Slaayde was still with them, bloodied and cursing. So were other men. A bunch.

Gatormen rushed at them. Hissing. Howling. Charged them from side passages, this way and that. The Lomerians barreled forward through the main tunnel, twice as wide as the others. But ran they in the right direction? The passage gently sloped upward, steeper in spots. That seemed right. Downhill as you go in, up as you leave. It seemed right. But they didn't know. Not for certain.

They'd run a long way. Or so it seemed. In the thick of battle. The darkness. The adrenaline. The pain. The chaos. Who could tell? Ob couldn't. If all that time they went the wrong way, deeper into the lizards' den, then they were done for. They'd never fight their way out. And with time to prepare, the gatormen would grab their nets and their poison darts and the Lomerians would drop just as easily as they had back in their camp in the swamp.

Were they even still in the swamp? Or beyond? How long had they been unconscious? An hour or two? Longer? What if the gatormen had given them more sleeping poison? They could've been out for days. Not knowing, scared the piss out of Ob.

But not as much as did the onrushing gatormen.

Ob heard drums. A deep bass sound. He realized that he'd heard them for a goodly while. Coming from more than one direction. The gatormen's call to arms. Their alarm. The whole place was being roused. Odin knows how many of the things were in that cavern system. Certainly several times the Lomerians' number at the very least.

Then Ob felt the cool air of the night on this face, in his nose. Thank the gods. An exit was near.

A contingent of gatormen awaited them up ahead. Their door guards. Their normal numbers bolstered no doubt because of their recent raid on the Lomerians, just in case. A dozen lizards were there. And these were equipped for war. They were armor of a primitive type. Crude metal and stone plates tied about their body with cordage. Helmets of tortoise shell. Longer, thicker spears than most. These lizards were taller and thicker than most of their fellows. And packed close together. There would be no shoving past them. This was going to be a fight.

The Lomerians crashed into the lizards. Graybeard and two Alder marines were at the van. The old sea captain fought like a madman with uncanny skill that belied his age. Ob understood at once how that man had survived the Evermerians. Tough as nails was he.

Slaayde was there. Hacked and slashed with a stone dagger that he'd picked up.

Dolan too, spear to hand. The boy was protecting Ob. Staying close at his side. So was Trelman — that man was a juggernaut. But Ob needed no protection. Small in stature, no doubt, but tough as granite, hard as steel, and skilled as an Odion champion was he. But heck, he appreciated the help. In battle, you needed every edge that you could get to stay alive. To make it home in one piece. And there were no guarantees of anything once blood was drawn.

A gatorman lunged at Ob. Missed with his spear — a downward strike. The spear's tip broke off when it slammed into the tunnel floor. While the creature was still bent over, Ob stepped in and gouged its eye with his fingers. In the moment of distraction, Ob dodged by it.

Another gatorman came at Ob, but an Eotrus trooper intercepted him.

Only one more gatorman stood between Ob and the outside.

At the entrance to the cavern stood a giant of its kind. Six and half feet tall — well more than twice Ob's height. More than three times his weight. The beast lunged with the spear. A quick stroke. But the old gnome was the quicker. He dodged. Sidestepped. Spun. Dodged again. Lightning thrust came after lightning thrust. Ob was on his own now. All his fellows, fully engaged with other gatormen. A desperate battle for life. For freedom.

The gatorman was smart. Experienced. A master of the spear. After a half dozen failed attempts to skewer Ob, he anticipated the gnome's movement.

Crash.

Loud was the sound of the gatorman's spear tip when it broke upon Ob's breastplate. Thank the gods that they hadn't stripped him of it when he was captured. Still the blow did some damage. Ob flew backward from the strike. He crashed into someone fighting behind him. Bounced off. Fell to the ground on his rump. The gatorman didn't miss a beat. He lunged in. Struck with the butt of the spear, aimed at Ob's face.

How he conjured the energy to spring out of the way, Ob never knew, but he managed it. Another gatorman tripped over Ob and went sprawling. Ob scrambled out of the way. The big gatorman was still there. Still determined to kill him. He came in again. Swung the spear like a club. Ob dodged. Stepped closer. Punched the gatorman in the knee with all his might. Somehow, the blow overbalanced the lizard. He fell over. Ob pounced on him. Almost a comical sight it was, the little old gnome attacking the huge gatorman. Ob went at him like a madman. Pummeled him about the face. Brass knuckles crashed against the gatorman's jaw, cheeks, nose, and eyes. Over and over. Left and right; right and left. The gatorman's eyes rolled back in his head. Out of the fight. Maybe dead. Ob sprang up.

Ob saw Dolan stab a gatorman in the eye with a spear thrust. A moment later, Dolan swept another gatorman from his feet with the edge of the spear. Together, Dolan and Ob backed toward the entrance.

"Let's go, boys," shouted Ob. "Run for it."

Ob saw three gatormen rip the innards from old Captain Graybeard. Three or four gatormen lay dead or dying about him.

Slaayde extracted himself from the melee. So did Trelman, Trooper Dross, and a Kalathan Knight. The rest of the men were cut off. The entry guards had been reinforced by many more of their kind as the Lomerians fought them.

"Too many," said Dross, one arm hanging limp at his side, blood all over him.

"We've got to move," said Slaayde. "There's

nothing more we can do."

"Which way?" said Ob as he looked around. The night was black. They were on grass, wet, squishy. In or near the bog.

Gatormen crept out of the cave entrance toward them. Taking their time. Waiting for more of their fellows to join them.

"That way," said Ob, pointing directly away from the cave mouth. "Run."

And they did. As fast as their legs could carry them through the high grass. No doubt there were trails through it that would've been quicker, but visibility was too low, and they had no time to search. They only had time to run. A dozen gatormen were after them.

Outnumbered two to one, out in the black, they didn't stand a chance. But they had no choice.

Run.

Run for their lives.

"Stay together," shouted Ob as they ran.

They'd barely covered a hundred yards when they spotted movement ahead of them. Figures out in the darkness.

"Shit," said Ob. "More of them."

They turned to their right, but after fifty feet they hit the water. A wide stretch of it. They'd have to swim.

"That's death," said Dolan. "We can't outswim them." He turned around and waded back to the edge of the water. "I'll make my stand here," he said.

"I've run too long already," said Slaayde. "I'll stand with you."

"And I," said Dross. "I can't swim with this

arm."

Trelman stared at Ob, waiting for orders. Good man, that fellow.

Ob didn't know what to do. If he stayed, he was dead. They all were. If he swam out into that swamp and they followed him, he was just as dead, and wouldn't even be able to defend himself. If they didn't spot him, maybe he'd get away. But he'd have to brave alligators, hippos, snakes, and the darned biting fish all on his lonesome, all in the black of night, and with no idea of which way he was going. Crazy.

But it was a chance. However slim. It was a chance to live.

He couldn't do it.

He couldn't leave Dolan.

Slaayde he could ditch, the bastard. But Trelman? Dolan? Men he respected. Faced death with a dozen times. Men that looked up to him. Could he run away and leave them behind to fight in his place?

Honor was important.

It wasn't everything. But it was important.

Loyalty.

Pride.

Dignity.

After all they'd been through, he wasn't going to leave Dolan behind. Not even for a chance to live.

And that was that.

He pushed his way past the others. Put himself out front. "Come on, you bastards," he bellowed.

56

PLAIN OF ENGELROTH JUTENHEIM

YEAR 1267, 4TH AGE
LAST YEAR OF KING TENZIVEL'S RULE

JUDE EOTRUS

"**W**here is Par Oris?" said Par Keld to Brackta. "When we need him, he isn't here."

Brackta looked confused. "He's on the ship. Don't you remember? He's wounded."

"I'm here, but he is not," said Keld. "Why do I have to do all this fighting when he's back there, lounging on the ship eating coconuts and marzipan, drinking wine? But I'm here. Is it my job to save everyone again? Why should I do that? I don't get any credit. No one cares what I do. Do you think Ginalli cares? Or Thorn? Or Korrgonn? He doesn't even look at me. They don't appreciate me. I'm an archwizard, you know. It doesn't matter that the tower doesn't acknowledge that. I've taken the tests. They robbed me. I studied. Practiced. I've been a wizard for nearly thirty years, not even counting my apprenticeship. They disrespected me. They always have. I've changed. It was never me anyway. They've always been out to get me. You think they're better than me? No. They're not. None of you are." Then he scurried off to the other side of the circle.

"An annoying little man," said Brackta.

It was then that the giants and the Lugron charged. Maybe they were angry for their losses at the hands of the League wizards. Maybe they were stupid. Maybe they just wanted blood. Who knows. But they charged.

All of them. Wizards and magic be damned.

They came down the hills, their pounding feet like thunder. Jude felt the vibration beneath his feet.

The natives decided that they wanted the expedition dead and nothing was going to stand in their way.

The expedition's bowmen let fly as many arrows as they could, but what was the use? Might as well throw a towel into the sea to dry it up.

"My turn," said Brackta as she bounced up from Jude's side and rushed toward the edge of the circle.

Jude looked around. This time Ginalli, Weldin, and Brackta stepped out past the front line.

Ginalli faced the giants. Weldin and Brackta faced the Lugron.

Black spheres shot one after another from Ginalli's hands. It happened so fast, Jude didn't see how he'd conjured them up, not that it mattered. The black spheres grew in an instant to the size of a man's head and arced high into the air, much like an arrow launched long distance, and came down amidst the onrushing giants. Those spheres were not just balls of energy pulled down through the ether. They were solid. They had mass, momentum. When they struck a giant or hit the ground, they exploded. A sharp crack rang out each time accompanied by a great whoosh of air. Shrapnel tore into the giants. Ripped through their bodies. Sheared off limbs; blasted some of the giants into pieces. No fewer than two or three giants went down for each sphere that exploded.

And Ginalli had managed at least two dozen spheres.

Brackta waved her arms. Spat short sharp words in wizard speech. A great streak of white and blue liquid gushed from her right hand. Gallons of it. It fanned out as it went. Grew larger and larger. Hundreds of gallons. Thousands. It spouted from her hand at incredible velocity. How she wasn't thrown back by it, Jude couldn't comprehend. The moment the liquid hit the ground, it solidified into a sheet of smooth blue ice that grew larger and larger at an incredible rate. Fifty yards wide, twenty deep, three or four inches thick was it.

Brackta dropped it in front of the onrushing Lugron horde. So close to them did she place it, they had no opportunity to stop or turn aside. They blundered onto the ice at a full charge. And promptly lost their footing. Staggered. Slipped. Fell sprawling. The rest of the massed troops behind them crashed into them or fell atop them. Their charge collapsed.

Par Weldin held his hands up close to his chest. His chin down, eyes closed. He murmured words in his deep voice as his fingers twitched and moved about in strange patterns, tracing out bizarre shapes in the air. Things with angles that made no sense. Dimensions that defined explanation. Strangely, those shapes lingered in the air, hanging there as if he'd traced them in thick mud. To look at those patterns too closely was to invite madness.

And then, out of nowhere came a high-pitched reverberation and appeared a black rectangle that hung in the air at the near edge of the ice field. That rectangle expanded in but a moment to several feet in height and width. It seemed two-dimensional, no thickness to it at all. Black as darkest night it was.

A summoning was Weldin's spell, for from out of that blackness, leaped a snarling saber cat. The largest of its kind that Jude had ever seen. Ten or twelve feet long it was, five feet tall at the shoulder, two protruding teeth as long as short swords. It must have weighed over a thousand pounds. Weldon's summoning somehow located the beast he desired and transported it there to do his bidding. Jude had never seen such a thing before, but he'd heard stories of conjurers that could call up beasts from far away to serve their purposes. How Weldon did that made no sense to Jude. But he saw it with his own eyes. Weldin brought that cat there, of that, Jude had no doubt. Unless of course, it was all an illusion, a clever trickery that confounded the eye and fooled the judgment. Mayhap the cat wasn't real at all. A mere will-o'-the-wisp conjured up to frighten the natives.

Seeing such magic made Jude question reality. How could such a thing be possible? Mayhap it wasn't. Maybe, this was all some terrible dream, some fevered nightmare. Mayhap he was in his own bed back in Dor Eotrus, sick with the fever, and all that he endured these last months had gone on only in his mind. When the Leaguers ambushed him on the road to Riker's Crossroads months before, and he fell from his horse, perhaps he never got up. Perhaps he still lay unconscious from his wounds. And everything that he'd subsequently experienced was but a dream. Mayhap in reality only hours had passed, or even only minutes, since that fall, and not the long months that it seemed. Perhaps that's the way Jude wanted it to be.

But was that scenario any less likely, any less believable, than saber cats appearing out of the air? Than giants being real? Sea beasts? Magic itself?

Jude's head was spinning. He felt dizzy. Bit down on his tongue. Pounded his fist to his thigh. That slight bit of pain grounded him to the present. He didn't know what was real anymore. But he decided that it didn't matter. Real or not, he had to act as if all he saw was real. Or else he'd have no chance to survive. Or would he?

Weldon's saber cat stalked along the very edge of the ice field, snarling at the Lugron that struggled to cross the ice.

Then the great cat's twin leaped from the mystical black rectangle that still hung in the air. And then another did the same. And another. And another. Nine in all before Weldin's magic was spent. Real or not, nine of them would certainly be a lot more effective than one. Even so, they could never stand for long against so many Lugron. A moment after the last cat leaped from its rim, the black rectangle shrank, and, with a pop, disappeared from existence. The saber cats remained. All their attention focused on the approaching Lugron. Any Lugron that managed their way across that ice field had nine sets of hungry jaws waiting for him.

57

DOR EOTRUS THE UNDERHALLS

***YEAR 1267, 4TH AGE
LAST YEAR OF KING TENZIVEL'S RULE***

ECTOR EOTRUS

The trolls dumped wooden doors and tree trunks into the acid pit that filled the long corridor at the Underhall's entrance, to try to float the pit or bridge it, but the wood charred and fell apart almost as fast as flesh. Then they dumped in stones. Not gravel or small stones. Big, angular rocks. Ones that weighed a hundred pounds or more. Some, a few times that size. A bucket brigade of rocks it was. Every few seconds, another stone when in.

The Eotrus sniped at the trolls, but they stayed well hidden behind a wall of shields. Only the odd shaft or two found purchase, and even they did no good. The trolls were nearly immune to arrows. When hit, they'd howl, then pull the shaft out, and go right about their business.

"Throw enough rocks in there, and they'll bridge it eventually," said Sarbek. "They're smart. Smart as people, I figure."

"It will take a long time to fill that pit," said Ector, "even at the pace they're moving."

"I'd be looking for a back door," said Sarbek

nodding. "Indigo, you go double-check everything. And when you're done, check again. We've got to be certain that they can't bum rush us from behind."

The hours ticked by. The acid level in the pit slowly rose as the trolls piled in the rocks. Eventually, the stone pile rose out of the pit, such that the trolls could safely step upon it. And they did, and tossed more stones farther out, filling up the next section.

"Two days," said Ector. "At the pace they're going, if they keep it up without stop. In two days, they'll have filled the pit enough to walk across to our side."

"It'll be quicker than that," said Indigo. "Once they're within twenty feet of us, they'll bridge the gap with tree trunks, starting with that ram of theirs, and be on us. I give us about thirty-five hours. Still plenty of time to make a run for it out the tunnels."

"We've been through that," said Sarbek. "We're safer in here for the time being."

"Not once they pass the pit," said Ector.

"You just wait and see, boy," said Sarbek.

The trolls were even quicker than Indigo feared. They put more of their fellows on the job and dumped multiple rocks at once. In about twenty hours, they could walk over seventy-five feet of the pit. Another twenty feet or so remained. The Eotrus lined up two rows of pikemen hidden behind a low barricade. They were there to repel any jumpers. Behind them were multiple rows of archers.

The trolls crowded the tunnel. More even than had fallen into the pit. Two rows of stout wooden shields at their van, pincushioned with Eotrus shafts. Behind them were two hundred of their soldiers, all armored. No doubt, an elite troop. Maybe their best. Their leader wore a great crest atop his helmet — a snake intertwined with a lizard. The center of the corridor was not so densely packed as the rest. That was just as the Eotrus suspected.

Under cover of their shields, the Eotrus rolled their ballistae up behind their barricades.

A great roar went up amongst the trolls. Then came the pounding of many feet. They ran their ram or bridge or whatever they'd put together to span those last twenty feet through the outer rooms toward the acid corridor.

At Sarbek's signal, Indigo pulled a steel lever that was embedded in the wall around the corner, out of the line of sight of the acid corridor. There was a great clanking. Then a huge block of granite, five feet thick, fell from the corridor's ceiling. It came down right at the ruined doorway at the acid corridor's entrance and crushed two trolls to pulp beneath it. The huge slab blocked all passage into or out of the corridor, and trapped two hundred trolls within. The Eotrus dropped their barricades and opened fire with their bank of ballistae.

In confusion and shock, the trolls didn't know what hit them. The great bolts blasted through the trolls' shield wall. Several trolls were skewered and sent flying through the air, such was the force of the Eotrus war engines. With the shield wall decimated, the Eotrus archers opened fire. The trolls could not advance, for twenty feet of acid lay between them and the Eotrus. They could not withdraw, for the granite slab blocked their way. They were trapped. Fish in a barrel.

Over the next ten minutes, the Eotrus fired thousands of shafts. Resilient or not, the trolls fell. The ballistae assured that there was no refuge and no escape for a single troll, as those terrible bolts blasted through armor as easily as flesh. Tough as they were, within fifteen minutes, nearly every troll in the corridor was dead. Only a few quivered here and there, but they were out of action. As fate would have it, the troll leader was the last to fall. When he did, a great cheer went up amongst the Eotrus ranks.

Two hundred more trolls down and dead without a single Eotrus casualty.

"The tide turns," said Indigo.

"I told you'd we'd make them bleed for every foot they took. Look at that," shouted Sarbek, pointing at the battlefield. "They're not invincible. They can be beat. They can die, same as anyone. And we can kill them. We can win this, men. We can win this."

The men cheered and shouted.

58

PIPKORN'S RETREAT SOUTHEAST WARD LOMION CITY

YEAR 1267, 4TH AGE
LAST YEAR OF KING TENZIVEL'S RULE

DUKE HARRINGGOLD

"Duke Harringgold is on the stoop," announced the aged retainer.

Grandmaster Pipkorn lounged in a plush leather chair, deep in thought.

"I thought this location was secret? Have we been advertising my address in the gazette?"

"I cannot say, Master," said the retainer.

"Send him in," said Pipkorn.

Harringgold's step was a bit slower than usual. His face was pale and drawn. One arm and shoulder were bandaged and in a sling.

"You look like dung," said Pipkorn. "But I'm happy to see you survived it."

"Barely," said Harringgold.

"Barely happy am I, or did you barely survive it?" said Pipkorn.

"There are things of which we must speak," said Harringgold.

"I hope you didn't venture into Southeast alone," said Pipkorn.

"My men are outside."

"Do you want to talk about the assassinations first, or about Marissa marrying Cartegian, or about Cartegian naming Barusa as regent?"

Harringgold's eyebrows lifted and scrunched his forehead. "It seems I've made the trip to this hellhole for nothing. How do you always know everything so fast? Wait," he said holding up his hand. "I know, it's because you're a wizard."

"Were they after Tenzivel or Malvegil?" said Pipkorn.

"They killed our whole party with equal enthusiasm, so who can say," said Harringgold. "The ones that you captured — Black Hand or no?"

"They bore the tokens, and the tattoos," said Pipkorn.

"I trust that you got them to speak?" said Harringgold. "To reveal who held the contract on the king?"

"They were low-level men, the ones we caught," said Pipkorn. "They would not have known who held the contract."

"What do they know?" said Harringgold.

"They kept poison in small capsules held in their mouths," said Pipkorn. "They chose to die rather than be interrogated."

"You got nothing?" said Harringgold, obviously surprised.

"Nothing."

"Unfortunate."

"The Hand got their comeuppance anyway," said Pipkorn. "Black Hall burned last night."

Harringgold's face betrayed that he had not heard that news.

"Whatever brethren were about, got dead. At least most of them."

"Someone set fire to it and ran?" said Harringgold.

"Someone sacked the place with untold hundreds of fighters, and when they were done, they burned the place to the ground."

Harringgold looked shocked.

"The Malvegils," said Pipkorn. "It had to be."

"A darned bold maneuver," said Harringgold. "Malvegil's lieutenants are loyal men. What of the Grandmistress?"

"Her fate is unknown as yet," said Pipkorn. "She may well have burned with her cabal or she may be out there still, trying to reconstitute her guild."

"I've a feeling that the Malvegils will not rest until she's dead," said Harringgold.

"The battle at Black Hall was well contained," said Pipkorn. "We can't have civil war on the streets, which is exactly what we will have if the Malvegils stay in the city and try to track down the Hand survivors. Their victory was one of surprise more than anything else. The Hand knows the city a thousandfold better than the Malvegils. And now they're ready for them. They'll pick the Malvegils off a few at a time. It'll be a bloodbath. You must talk to them. Urge them to head home. It they flee the city quietly and in small groups, it may be that Malvegil involvement will never become known. Linger and lurk about for a few more days and the Hand will notice them. They'll snatch one of their men off the streets, and ply him until he talks and then they'll know. The Hand will put their own contract out on

House Malvegil. They'll not rest until every member of the family is dead and Dor Malvegil lies in ruins. We must prevent that possibility from happening."

"I'll speak to them, if I can find them," said Harringgold.

"Cartegian's naming of Barusa as regent was a stroke of genius, don't you think?" said Pipkorn.

"Agreed," said Harringgold. "It keeps Barusa from acting against Cartegian, and it counters any plans that Barusa had to blame me for the assassinations. The downside, of course, being that Barusa is now regent."

"A small enough problem given that Cartegian is with us," said Pipkorn. "Barusa will think that he's in control, and he will be, for the small things, but Cartegian can still block him. Ingenious. That single maneuver gives the realm its best chance to whether this storm intact."

"What a sad place we've reached," said Harringgold. "That the thought of Barusa rising to regent gives us comfort."

"Sad indeed," said Pipkorn.

"What hear you of Claradon Eotrus and his quest?" said Harringgold.

"He and his are in Jutenheim, still on the trail of the League. We shall have to wait and see how that drama plays out. The Eotrus are equally troubled at home. And I'm not just referencing the regent that Barusa sent to Dor Eotrus to assume power. A cloak of darkness lies over the northlands. But through it I sense an ancient evil. Something held over from olden days."

"What now?" said Harringgold.

"I cannot yet name it," said Pipkorn. "But soon

I will. Even now my agents grow near."

59

ISLE OF JUTENHEIM THE GATORMEN'S LAIR

YEAR 1267, 4TH AGE
LAST YEAR OF KING TENZIVEL'S RULE

OB

As Ob stood cursing at the gatormen, the group that pursued them from the cave mouth abruptly changed course and charged the figures coming in from the swamp.

"Well, what do you know?" mumbled Ob as the other figures drew close enough that the moonlight revealed them.

"It's Theta," shouted Slaayde. "That no-good bastard. It's our men."

Ob and his squad surged forward. They were exhausted and had had their fill of fighting, but they had to see what went on.

Theta was out in front of what remained of their expedition. No doubt, the gatormen hadn't realized just how many men they were charging. The lizards didn't stand a chance. Artol was at Theta's side. So was DeBoors. And Claradon. Little Tug. Blain Alder. The Kalathan Knights. And the rest. They crashed into the gatormen, hammers and axes. Crunch. Bang. Crash. Ten seconds into it, sixteen gatormen were down and dead. Theta, DeBoors, Artol, and Little Tug killed two or three each. Those four alone could have killed the whole pack and barely broken a sweat.

Blain Alder hurried over to Ob and company as they rejoined the others. "Edwin, my boy?"

No one responded immediately.

"He's gone, lad," said Ob. "He went down fighting them, as best he could." Ob figured, why tell the father that his son was rotten to the end, and got dead, stabbed in the back. Give him a memory he could be proud of. Ob didn't owe Blain Alder a thing. Well, maybe a butt-kicking, but telling him that — it was the decent thing to do. So that's what Ob did.

Blain closed his eyes and let out an anguished roar.

The sounds of fighting from the cavern drifted over to them. The battle still raged, though it was less than it was.

Theta looked them over as they began their march toward the gatormen's caverns. It was clear enough that he was checking who was still standing.

"Where's the wizard?" said Theta. "Where's Tanch?"

"We got separated," said Ob. "But he's somewhere in the caves, if he's still alive. There're too many of them in there. Even for the whole lot of us. If they get their blowguns out, it'll be just like before. I don't like leaving men behind, but we engage them again, and we're probably all dead."

Theta stopped and turned toward the men. "I'm going in there to put these things down. Come with me or not, as you will. But if you do, get some torches lit. There's no more need for stealth."

With that, he turned and marched toward the cavern at a brisk pace. Every man in the troop followed. Someone handed Dolan his bow. Ob his axe. They passed good Lomerian weapons to each man in Ob's squad. Tug had even salvaged Slaayde's saber.

By the time they neared the cave entrance, the fighting there was over. The Lomerians had lost.

It was inevitable. They had no weapons save for what they took from the gatormen that they fought. Stone spears and daggers were less effective at cutting through the gatormen's hides then was Lomerian steel.

Some twenty gatormen haunted the cavern entrance. They stood there, shoulder to shoulder awaiting the approaching Lomerians. They had enough sense or discipline to not charge out like a rabble. They called back to their fellows and their ranks thickened by the moment. Thirty, forty, fifty strong. Ten paces from them, Ob heard sounds of battle again, from deep within the caverns.

"Some of our boys are still at it," said Ob.

"We fight our way to them," said Theta. "Slow and deliberate. We kill every lizard we find. Don't let a single one get behind us."

Then came the roar of an explosion from deep within the cave.

"Get down," said Theta even as he dived to the ground.

A billowing blast of yellow and orange fire roared up the tunnel behind the gatormen. Some had time to turn and see it coming. But not a one had the chance to move out of the way. The blast crashed into them and roared out into the night. The flames came within ten feet of Theta, at the van of the Eotrus group. The heat was terrible. Ob held his breath to keep the superheated air from his lungs. Even so, he felt as if he might burst into flame.

In a few seconds it was over. Every gatorman at the entry was down. And dead. They were charred, blackened, head to toe. Smoking ruins. Some flames still licked their corpses.

After some moments, the heat died down enough that they could enter the caverns. And they did. Theta at the van. Scores of corpses littered the entry tunnel. All burned beyond recognition. They were barely able to tell Lomerian corpse from gatorman, and sometimes, not even that.

"The wizard, you figure?" said Ob.

"Had to be," said Theta. "Keep your shields up. Beware their darts. And watch out for nets."

They walked and walked down that main passage. Nothing but charred, smoking death. The side tunnels were the same. Everything burned. Ash. It was hard to breathe. The air was thin. But there was surprisingly little smoke.

Deep within the place, very near the cavern within which Ob and company had been hung from the ceiling, they came upon Tanch. He sat with his back up against a wall. Eyes closed. The flesh of his arms, blackened and smoking. No remnants of the bandages he wore over his arms remained. Two Eotrus troopers lay beside him; several Alder marines nearby. Each of those corpses was untouched by the fire, but everything else in the large room was ash. Ash that crushed under the Lomerians' feet as they entered. And when they did, Tanch's eyes opened, his body shuddered, and he looked poised to leap to his feet, his arms moving as if to throw some sorcery.

"It's us, Magic Boy," shouted Ob. "Stand down."

A semblance of a smile crossed Tanch's face, his eyes closed, and he slumped down into a troubled sleep.

"It was him, just as we thought," said Ob to Theta. "Magic Boy blasted them lizards all to Helheim. Dead gods. He killed them all."

Claradon and Dolan hurried to Tanch's side.

"He's still breathing," said Claradon. "But hot as an oven. Could cook an egg on him."

Nothing moved within that cavern save for the Eotrus party. Tanch's magic left nothing but death in its wake.

"By Odin," said Ob. "This rivals what he did at Evermere. Where does he get the power?"

"From within," said Theta. "But at a costly price."

"Too bad he couldn't toss that spell at the beginning of the fight," said Ob.

"He waited until the last men with him went down," said Theta. "He couldn't control the magic. Have it affect only the gatormen. It burned everyone and everything within its range."

"Let's get out of here while we can," said Ob.

The men picked up Tanch, carrying him carefully, gently. Theta started down an opening to a long passage that led deeper in the cavern system.

"You coming or not?" said Ob.

"There's more of them down there," said Theta.

Ob looked down the passage. There'd been a door there, blocking off that way. Nothing left of it but ash. The passage itself was scorched of floor, walls, and ceiling, but only for a dozen feet down. Two gatormen lay dead there. Badly burned. But not blasted to ash like the others. "Best we cut our losses," said Ob. "Could be a lot of them left hold up down there. They might be regrouping even now to come at us. We should get clear while we can."

"And if we do," said Theta, "they'll ambush the next group of people that enters the valley. These gatormen are what kills off everyone that ventures across Jutenheim. Rikenguard just got lucky to not run into them before."

"His luck ran out this time," said Ob. "So what are you going to do?"

"I'm going to kill them all," said Theta.

60

PLAIN OF ENGELROTH JUTENHEIM

YEAR 1267, 4TH AGE
LAST YEAR OF KING TENZIVEL'S RULE

JUDE EOTRUS

Mort Zag grabbed Jude by the collar and pulled him toward Korrgonn, who stood at the very center of the expedition. At over two hundred and fifty pounds, Jude wasn't accustomed to anyone dragging him anywhere. Mort Zag did it effortlessly. There wasn't much point in trying to resist, so Jude didn't. Better to save his strength for when he really needed it. Donnelin stayed close by Jude's side; Teek Lugron a step behind him.

Mason strode over to Korrgonn carrying the trunk that held the Orb of Wisdom.

Glus Thorn sat on the ground next to Korrgonn. Smoke rose from the old wizard. From his arms, his collar, his chest. Jude smelled the burnt flesh. Dust covered the wizard's cassock, though against all reason it had remained spotless all through Svartleheim. For the first time, that man seemed human to Jude, though no less frightening. Thorn could be hurt. He felt pain. He was vulnerable. If he was vulnerable, then surely all the Leaguers were. Mayhap even

Korrgonn.

"Move the Eotrus close," said Thorn. "I would make the shield no larger than it need be."

Mort Zag shoved Jude, and pushed him down, depositing him next to Thorn.

Thorn put his hand on Jude's shoulder. His touch was gentle, almost comforting. "Do not think to interrupt my casting, Mister Eotrus, and dare not make any false moves. If you do, I'll put you right on the floor."

Jude nodded, wide-eyed.

"Place the holy vessel at Lord Korrgonn's feet," said Thorn to Mason, "then step back quickly. Mort Zag, you step back too."

Mort Zag did, and shoved Donnelin back as well.

Thorn spoke his spell. The words were unknown to Jude, unintelligible, but for some reason they made his ears tingle and itch, and his nose and throat felt like he'd just eaten hot peppers. It made him cough and gag. He wished he had a canteen; he'd have emptied it.

Thorn's spells brought forth from nowhere a translucent dome of crackling green energy that encompassed Thorn, Korrgonn, Jude, and the Orb's trunk.

"Defend us with your lives," said Thorn. "Such is the Lord Azathoth's command." Mason put his back to the small green dome and faced outward, ready to repel any attackers, a great iron hammer in his hand. Mort Zag did the same on the opposite side of the dome. Nord, Thorn's Stowron henchman took a spot between them, a long bone staff in hand.

"If you would defend your friend, priest," said

Mort Zag to Donnelin, "stand with us. You're one of us now, like it as not."

Donnelin took a spot, his back to the dome, Mason to one flank, Mort Zag to the other. Teek stepped up next to him. "I'll never be one of you," muttered Donnelin.

Mort Zag heard him and grinned a toothy grin.

"Can you fight, old man?" said Teek to Donnelin.

"I'm an Eotrus," said Donnelin as if that's all that needed to be said. Donnelin looked the Lugron up and down. "You're as old as me."

"But I'm prettier," said Teek.

Donnelin readied his spells. No doubt, he'd been saving his energy, awaiting another opportunity to escape, but now he'd have to use what strength he'd gathered to stay alive and protect his ward. He'd failed Jude's father. He'd not fail the son.

Par Rhund and Stev Keevis moved to support Ginalli. Par Keld ran around muttering to himself.

Ginalli's exploding spheres had done terrible damage, killing and maiming fifty or more of the giants, but the rest kept coming.

Why? Jude couldn't understand it. What madness drove them on? Why rush headlong into death? They held no grudge against the League. There was no score to settle. Any sane force would have turned and fled after what the wizards had thrown at them. But the giants didn't flee. They kept coming. Why?

61

THE REGENT'S EXPEDITIONARY FORCE (THE ALDER BRIGADE)

YEAR 1267, 4TH AGE
LAST YEAR OF KING TENZIVEL'S RULE

DIRK ALDER

Riker's Crossroads was a war camp. Barricades had been hastily set up around the village. All the windows and doors were either reinforced or in the process. Lots of horses about, which explained how those men gathered there so quickly. Men were everywhere. Northerners. Eotrus bannermen. Untold hundreds of them.

Boddrick, Pullman, and Dirk led their troop up to the northern barricade.

An elder soldier showed himself over the works. "What say you?" is all the man said in greeting.

"I'm Dirk of Alder. We're on a mission from—"

"The trolls are coming," said Pullman. "We'll stand with you."

With that alone, the defenders opened the barricades and let Dirk and company pass in.

"Best you head over to the inn to see Lord Ogden." Many a bow and crossbow was leveled and pointed their way. The Alders were well known and widely disliked in the North.

***

Lord Ogden was as tall and broad as Pullman, but at least twenty years his senior. He had a big gray head of hair. A beard and mustache to match. A deep booming voice that rattled the windows.

"Who be you?" said Ogden as he looked up from a table, maps laid out atop it, various knights and noblemen gathered around. Behind Ogden was a rookery manned by three men that had trouble keeping up with the flow of birds. Ravens and owls were coming and going, messages rolled up and attached to little pouches affixed to their bodies. When a new message came in, they quickly passed it to Ogden and then laid down his reply.

Several northern knights filed in behind the Alders and closed the door. A hard fight to get clear of there if things went bad.

"I'm Dirk of Alder. These be Bald Boddrick and Gar Pullman," he said pointing to his fellows in turn. Sentry of Allendale was with them, so was Bithel the Piper, though Dirk didn't bother to introduce them.

"Never heard of you, Alder," said Ogden, "but of your House I know a great deal. And your fellows have reputations that precede them. Mercenaries. Head crackers. Leg breakers. Killers. Yet here you stand, tails between your legs, running for your lives while the Eotrus stand and fight."

"We've done our share of troll fighting this last day," said Boddrick.

"No doubt, you have. I'm Thaddeous Ogden, Lord of Westforest, and bannerman to the Eotrus. I command here unless and until a northerner of higher rank happens by, which is unlikely. Stand with us, you said?"

"All differences put aside until this is over," said Boddrick.

Ogden eyed them and nodded.

"Afterwards, the Eotrus will answer for the murder of my uncle," said Dirk.

"I hear the Alders have a thing or two to answer for as well," said Ogden. "That reckoning will come in due course. But best we put aside talk of such matters lest we stumble fast into unfriendliness. The wise move is to stand united against the trolls."

"Agreed," said Boddrick.

"Where are my scouts?" said Pullman.

"Cooling their heels in the icehouse," said Ogden. "All but two that got unfriendly. They're in the ice house too; their heels already cool."

"Let them out, will you?" said Boddrick.

"Vouch for them, will you?" said Ogden.

"Aye," said Boddrick.

"I'll hold you to that," said Ogden. "We can afford no more trouble lest our common foe eat us alive."

62

DOR EOTRUS THE UNDERHALLS

YEAR 1267, 4TH AGE
LAST YEAR OF KING TENZIVEL'S RULE

ECTOR EOTRUS

The moment that the Eotrus dropped that granite slab and trapped the troll troop in the acid corridor, the trolls outside began their attempts to break through. They went at the stone block with sledgehammers. They pounded and pounded away without a moment's respite.

"Five feet of stone won't stop them for long," said Ector. "They don't give up. I don't understand why they want to kill us so badly."

"No matter the reason," said Sarbek, "this can only end one way. When they're all dead. Or we are."

Such was the strength of the trolls, within two hours they had the granite block broken apart. They pushed their way past its remnants.

The Eotrus pulled back around the bend in the corridor. Sarbek, Indigo, Ector, and a few officers stood beside the control panel that Indigo had been working. More steel levers remained to be pulled.

The trolls roared and cursed when they saw

what had become of their fellows. This time, they sent in the common trolls. The wild ones. They bounded around. Hollered. Whooped. More like monkeys than men. Undisciplined. Rabble.

Fodder.

The trolls wouldn't send any more of their elites into a death trap. They'd learned their lessons. The wild trolls had barely enough discipline to form a shield wall and stay behind it, though it mattered not, because the Eotrus archers had withdrawn.

Indigo pulled another lever, and a great iron portcullis quickly lowered from the ceiling on the Eotrus side of the pit; bars two inches thick, banded horizontally every foot.

The trolls muscled the last of the large pieces of the granite block out of the breach. The moment that they did, on they came with their bridge — a great tree trunk, no doubt, the same as they used for a ram earlier, hefted by no fewer than a hundred trolls. They charged into the corridor en masse. This time unopposed, except for the great steel gate. Steel that the trolls could eventually breach.

The trolls stormed down the corridor. With each step they stomped upon the bodies of their fellows shot down by the Eotrus. When they reached the end of the stoney area they'd built up, they heaved the great tree trunk across the remaining twenty feet of the pit. For some moments it looked as if they'd not manage it, as if the front edge of the trunk would drop too low and dip into the acid. But somehow they muscled it across, a score of trolls hopping on the very back end of the trunk to counterbalance it. For all their skill and efforts, a few trolls were pushed forward or stumbled and went into the acid. Their screams were terrible, but brief.

The trunk had been down for but a moment when the trolls thundered across atop it. They crowded the corridor once again. Whatever fear of the Eotrus they'd developed, now gone. Their prey hiding in the dark. They'd rout them out. They'd pick their teeth with Eotrus bones.

The trolls went to work on the iron gate. Twenty of them crowded together to lift it. Strong as they were, they could barely move it. They called back for levers.

"Do it," said Sarbek.

Indigo pulled the last lever in his control panel. Again there was a great clanking of metal. From the acid corridor's ceiling, round pieces of stone, an inch or two in diameter, popped out and fell, pushed by iron pipes from carefully cut cores that they'd been wedged in. The trolls stopped their business and looked up. Moments later, from the bottom of those pipes came a green spray.

Barden's Bane. Deadly acid. The same as filled the pit.

It fell like rain. Sprayed every inch of the corridor.

The trolls howled and screamed as the acid fell upon them and burned their bare flesh and what garments they wore.

They panicked.

Crashed into each other. Into the walls.

Many ran or tumbled into the acid pit in their panic. Only a score or so made it out the entry, though not a one was unscathed. The screams were terrible. The trolls were burned to the bone where any drop of acid kissed their flesh. The acid spray was thick and persistent. Despite that, their deaths were much slower than that of their fellows earlier, for the spray was not as swift a killer as immersion.

Ector turned away and left the hall. He withdrew back to the Eotrus lines, deeper into the Underhalls. He couldn't watch. Even Indigo, battle hardened as he was, turned his head, though he stood by Sarbek's side.

Sarbek watched every moment of it. Until the screaming finally stopped. "Bleed for every foot, you bastards. I'll bleed you all dry."

When the last of the trolls in the corridor was dead and still, Sarbek stepped around the corner and pulled the lever, stopping the flow of acid.

"Will they come again, you think?" said Ector. "After that?"

"Aye," said Indigo. "They have some score to settle. I don't think they'll give up."

"We'll burn another batch," said Sarbek. "And another batch after that. We have enough acid to fill that pit twelve feet deep, but we only filled it eight. Plenty left."

"With this portcullis down, there's no way for them to get through," said Ector. "Not so long as we can drop more acid on them."

"What would you do, if you were them?" said Sarbek.

"I'd come at us a different way," said Indigo.

"They've not found the tunnels yet," said Sarbek. "Mayhap they won't."

Indigo pointed to the ceiling. They all looked up. "If they're as smart as we think, it's only a matter of time."

"We've got to plan on it," said Sarbek. "Evacuate this level, save to leave a squad at the stair. Besides the acid, we've one more trick up our sleeves before we yield this level to them."

"I'll have a few booby traps put into place as gifts for them," said Indigo.

"Make it so," said Sarbek, "but let's not let anyone linger too long. It should take days to get through this stone from above, but the trolls have a way of surprising us."

Within an hour, they heard the pounding of hammers above them. No less than twelve inches of solid stone formed the ceiling of the First Underhall. Several feet of soil atop that. The floor and foundations of the Odinhome and the pavement in portions of the courtyard above that. A tall order, but one could dig through it all, given sufficient time and motivation. And the trolls weren't just digging and hammering in one spot. They attacked the ground in at least a dozen locations, trying to burrow their way down into the first level of the Underhalls. If they accomplished it, and opened a hole in the right place, they could bypass the acid corridor. And if they did, how could the Eotrus ever hope to hold them back?

63

DOR LOMION LOMION CITY

***YEAR 1267, 4TH AGE
1ST YEAR OF KING CARTEGIAN'S RULE
CORONATION / WEDDING DAY***

DUKE HARRINGGOLD

The grand ballroom in Dor Lomion was a cavernous space of wood planked walls whose ceiling rose some thirty feet above its polished granite floor. Square stone columns, adorned with Lomerian and Harringgold colors, shields, and banners, regularly spaced, supported the ceiling above. Great chandeliers hung from silver chains and illumed the place. On a catwalk hidden high in the rafters were the lamp men who deftly used long poles to add and remove shades and covers to adjust the brightness of the chandeliers on cue. The place was warm and smelled both smoky and sweet owing to the several hearths, many a lighted pipe, and the perfumed partygoers.

That hall had not seen a party of such magnitude in many years. One thousand guests in attendance served by two hundred uniformed party staff. Honor guards clad in tourney armor were everywhere about the exits.

The people dressed in their finest silks and cottons. Long ball gowns for the women, some scandalously low cut; high heels, some few, six inches or more in height; and hats that ranged from subdued and tasteful to wildly extravagant, the younger women leaning toward the latter. Long-sleeved shirts of solid color for the men, trousers of contrasting hue, vests of black or brown, swordbelts and steel. Many of the dignitaries or relations also wore long coats with black collars, sharply tailored and tailed.

Harper Harringgold twirled about the dance floor, his beloved daughter, Marissa, in his arms. As a proud father, he wanted to enjoy the moment; to get lost in it; to think of nothing but Marissa and the good things in store for her: to be queen, to be a mother, a wife. But he couldn't do that. Nothing in his life was ever so simple as that, especially not at that time. During that first wedding dance, most fathers had only to worry about trampling their daughter's feet or making fools of themselves in front of their guests by bumbling about the dance floor, both of which were distinct possibilities for Harringgold, but for him, there was a good deal more to worry about. He'd taken every precaution. And so had Cartegian. The boy was sharper than the Duke could have hoped for. They had their men lining the hall, inside and out. A score of dramadeens were there, a dozen more strategically placed just outside the exits. Two full squadrons of Harringgolds were in the hall. Tough men. Fighters. Some of the best the Duke had. Loyal. But his ace in the hole was The Fearless: a squadron of elite professional soldiers that had long served his House. Captain Mace Cuda and his men lurked about the back service hallway —

on standby to rush in if anything untoward happened during the wedding festivities.

In truth, Harringgold wasn't worried about Hand assassins attacking en masse. Never had the black guilds done anything like that in public. He was more concerned about the lone assassin with a knife or a poison dart. They'd be after Cartegian, not Marissa, but he didn't want her hurt in the crossfire.

Poison. That troubled him. Would his enemies be so bold? The duke had two loyalists taste-testing the food and drink served at the royal table. But more than that — Grim Fisher and his Rangers had taken over the kitchens. They were charged with watching over every movement in the kitchens to make certain no food or drink were tampered with. Grim escorted the waiters to the royal table himself.

This was all done as unobtrusively as possible, but anyone paying close attention would have spotted the extra scrutiny on everything; the excessive security lurking about. No one would dare object or blame them. The previous king had only recently been assassinated.

Harringgold would make certain that no one hurt his daughter. The queen.

And no one was going to kill another king on his watch.

The actual ceremonies, the coronation and the wedding, had both gone on without a hitch. The lamp men amazed the crowd when they brightened the lights in step with the wedding party as they made their way down the aisle. Bishop Tobin led the proceedings. Harringgold had decreed that the old fart be kept at arm's length, but Cartegian defied him. Insisted that the bishop be invited to lead the ceremony and afforded every honor his office warranted.

Harringgold wasn't happy about it. Not at all. But with that one action, Cartegian gained his respect. Where Harringgold couldn't put aside his negative feelings about the old codger, Cartegian had no trouble doing so, and so, made the politically smart move. Much like a younger version of his late father, was Cartegian. And that gave Harringgold hope for the future.

Par Gatwind lumbered over to Harringgold, sleepy eyed, crumbs in his beard. He was one of only three wizards amongst the Freedom Council not still in hiding. He extended his glass toward Harringgold's. "To new beginnings," he said as they clinked goblets. Gatwind leaned in close and lowered his voice. "The Vizier wants me on the Council of Lords. Says with Malvegil's death he can push through new appointments."

"He wants men of like mind in power," said Harringgold. "Men that owe him their loyalty and their votes."

"I accepted," said Gatwind.

"Who wouldn't?" said Harringgold. "Every vote will count when the time comes, if it comes. I'm glad to know that you're on our side."

"You can count on me," said Gatwind.

64

ISLE OF JUTENHEIM THE GATORMEN'S LAIR

YEAR 1267, 4TH AGE
LAST YEAR OF KING TENZIVEL'S RULE

OB

"That's crazy talk," said Ob to Theta as the big knight made ready to venture deeper in the lizards' lair. "I'm as angry as anybody about this. About what they did. All the men we lost. But somewhere down there, they've probably got young. Wiping them out to the last, just don't seem right."

"They eat people," said Theta. "They attack whoever they see without warning. Then they eat them. That doesn't sit right with me. Dolan, you're with me." He glanced back. Claradon had already left, helping to carry Tanch to safety, most of his knights with him. Artol was still there. So was Trelman. DeBoors. Blain Alder. The Kalathan Knights.

"I'm with you," said Artol. So too said the others.

Theta turned and without a further word marched down the corridor, shield held close before him.

Ob called after the last of the main group leaving the cavern. "Tell Claradon that we'll catch up. Just mopping up a few things."

Halfway down the corridor, Theta paused and spoke. "They'll use their sleep darts now, if they have any left. Be ready for that."

The tunnel seemed to go on forever. Straight for a hundred yards, then it turned ninety degrees. On for a hundred feet, then it branched off in three directions. Each corridor was short.

"Which way?" said Ob.

Theta picked the center tunnel. It was wider than the other two. Fifty feet down, Ob heard them. The gatormen. But the voices were higher, sharper. Females? Young?

Theta stepped around a corner.

Bamn. They hit him.

Half a dozen darts.

His shield caught five of them.

His helmet the other.

He raised his hammer and barreled forward. Ob heard the thunk and splat of that hammer as it came down again and again. Toward the rear of the group was Ob. By the time he made the corner, the fight was over. The short tunnel was filled with gatormen dead. Six or seven of them. Heads crushed and splattered. Their blood was everywhere. Theta was covered in it. Some of them never picked up their spears. They died with their blowguns still in their hands, or else unarmed entirely. In the narrow confines of that tunnel, despite all their speed and strength, against Theta, they had no chance.

The Kalathans checked the fallen gatormen, and put to the sword one or two who still harbored some spark of life. At the end of the tunnel was a door. A great oaken thing, banded of steel. Barred from within. That's where the high-pitched sounds came from. There was shuffling and crying within.

Theta kicked the door — the whole frame shuddered. Sounds of cracking wood rang out, though the door held fast.

Theta kicked it again, but made no progress. He lifted his great hammer high and crashed it down on the door, somewhere near its mid-height. The door exploded. The wood burst from its frame and went flying into the room beyond.

Theta strode in.

Gatormen, or rather, gatorwomen, charged him. Daggers and spears to hand. Dozens of them. Screaming. Wailing. Spitting curses, or so it sounded, at the men. Theta's hammer worked up and down. DeBoors beside him with an axe. Artol his hammer. The Kalathans all used swords. Those gatorfolk had no skill at arms. But on they came all the same. Murder in their eyes. Desperate to hold back the invaders at any cost.

One came at Ob. A clumsily wielded dagger in hand. He dodged and smashed his axe into her leg. She went down wailing, blood spurting. There was fear in her eyes. Terror. She tried to crawl away. The smart move would've been to kill her without hesitation. But she didn't know how to fight; wasn't really a threat; probably no threat at all any longer. A female. It wasn't right. Against Ob's code. But she wasn't a human. Just some lizard thing. A lizard thing that no doubt would have eaten him given the chance. He didn't have the heart. Didn't move forward to finish her. He couldn't do it. One of the Kalathans did. Nearly stepped on her as he maneuvered; saw she was alive, and slashed his sword across her neck.

Ob turned away. It wasn't right. No others came at him. And he was glad for that. The other men had no reluctance to bring the fight to them. They hacked, slashed, and killed. And still the gatorfolk came on. Scores of them ran at them from this way and that. After a while, they stopped coming, and the last of them went down. The gatorfolk didn't run. Hide. Beg. Plead. They just came on fighting until they were all dead.

None of the Lomerians was injured in this melee. They moved across the chamber. A short corridor led to another cavern. High-pitched wails came from within.

One last figure barred their passage.

It could only have been the gatorfolks' chieftain.

He was a massive beast, far larger than any of his fellows. As tall and as broad as Theta. His head and jaws massive. Teeth to match. Who can read the expression on the face of a man-lizard? Ob knew that he could not. Yet, he swore that the gatorman king looked sad. Broken. Defeated.

The chieftain wore a band of fur of unknown make wrapped diagonally across his body, and metal plates polished to a shine covered his torso and limbs — gatorman armor, the best they could manage. A tortoiseshell helmet adorned with glinty stones sat atop his head. He looked battered and scorched. He barely escaped Tanch's fire blast. He held a gold-colored sword in one hand. A matching dagger in the other.

He growled something in his guttural tongue. What words they were, if words at all, no man amongst them could say.

"Come forth and meet your doom," said Theta.

65

PLAIN OF ENGELROTH JUTENHEIM

YEAR 1267, 4TH AGE
LAST YEAR OF KING TENZIVEL'S RULE

JUDE EOTRUS

Ezerhauten's men, supported by the few remaining Lugron mercenaries and Thorn's Stowron lackeys, launched every missile that they had at the Juten Lugron and the giants that assaulted them. Floundering as they were on Brackta's ice field, the Juten Lugron were easy targets. Owing to their size alone, the giants too were easy to hit.

Stev Keevis's sorcery tore open a great rift in the earth some twenty yards from the Sithian line. A hundred feet long was that pit, thirty feet wide, and Odin knows how deep. Once the spell began, the earth fell away in but an instant and with nary a sound. Keevis timed his wizardry perfectly, just as had Brackta with the ice. The chasm opened up at the giants' feet. The behemoths sailed over the edge like lemmings. Row after row, unable to halt, pushed forward by their fellows that charged up behind and knew not the danger. One hundred at least dropped into that abyss, arms and legs flailing as they fell out of sight, roaring in shock, anger, and fear. How far they fell, no man could say, save that there was no escape from that crevasse.

Par Rhund spat his eldritch words like a cobra spits its venom. At his behest, a noxious cloud of green vapor manifested on the giants' side of the pit. It grew larger by the moment. After but a handful of heartbeats it was as broad, then broader still than the rift. Every giant within that cloud's expanse suffered its effects. They coughed uncontrollably. Gagged. Choked. Doubled over. In their pain and confusion, some fled forward, stumbled into the pit and were lost. Most turned tail and ran away. Hacking. Vomiting. Stumbling and falling. Those beyond the fog's reach maneuvered around it, and around the chasm. The giants weren't done yet.

The Juten Lugron hurled spears at Par Weldon's conjured saber cats. They fired arrows at them. Shot rocks from slings. They even threw daggers. Some of them were skilled. Their missiles accurate. Deadly. Three cats went down. Two others pincushioned with arrows. The two wounded cats and then all the rest launched themselves across the ice. They had as much trouble maneuvering on the unnaturally slick surface as did the Lugron, but they persisted, their razored claws aiding them on their way. They suffered under a hail of missiles. But the closer they drew, the more the Lugron faltered as they scrambled back from the big cats. None of the Lugron wanted to go toe to toe with those beasts.

Only four of the saber cats reached the Lugron line. The rest lay dead, of arrow and spear, broken and bloodied on the frigid ice. And the four that made it across were all wounded. But, oh, did they fight. They ripped. They tore. They leaped at one Lugron and then another. Intent on holding back the Lugron advance. They clawed at throats. Slashed open midsections. Crushed skulls betwixt their great jaws. But the Lugron did not panic. They did not rout. Their numbers were so great they could not be turned.

Four saber cats, regardless of their size and ferocity, had no hope to hold them back. No hope to survive them.

The Lugron went at them with spears of wood. Hammers of stone. Bare fist and leather-booted foot. Primitive weapons, yet they sufficed. The Lugron pounded and pounded away. Until finally, the last of the cats was dead.

As the way cleared before them, the Lugron stumbled and pulled themselves across the ice.

Brackta's hands and arms spun another spell; several Sithians guarded her closely with their shields, safeguarding her from Lugron missile fire. Shafts flew all about. Many men were hit, but good Lomerian armor turned aside nearly every blow.

Brackta threw more of her sorcery. A great wall of ice was born at the near edge of her ice field. The water that formed it spurted out of the very ground and froze in a heartbeat as Brackta's hands gestured vigorously, her face stiff with concentration. Two feet high was that wall of ice, four feet thick, and a hundred feet long it became in but an instant.

Then three feet high.
Four.
Eight.

Twelve.

Twenty!

Brackta rushed forward to the confusion of her bodyguards and threw herself against the ice, even as her skin reddened and smoke rose from her arms. After but a moment, it was clear enough that she sought the icy coldness to chill the searing heat brought on by her sorcery.

Par Weldon's brow was furled as he tapped the Grand Weave of Magic, even as Brackta's wall was still growing. Weldon pointed to the edge of Brackta's ice wall, and there appeared another of his mystical black rectangles. One moment it wasn't there, and then it burst into existence.

Weldon was summoning something else.

The eldritch shape hung in the air, defying all logic and reason, twisting ever so slightly as if buffeted by the breeze. Just as the last time, the rectangle rapidly grew larger. But this one's growth continued unabated. In but a few heartbeats it was so large that cavalry could ride straight through it. Then it grew larger still. Much larger. Black were its depths. A fastness where no light dared tread.

From out of those black depths charged a raging olyphant, a giant of its kind, all of which were giants. Twenty-five feet tall at the shoulder. White tusks twelve feet long. Gray legs like great gnarled tree trunks. Its circular feet larger around than a Kernian shield. It raised up its great head and roared — a long blast akin to a trumpet's. It charged the nearest Lugron and with a toss of its head, its massive trunk and tusks sent the Lugron flying. The olyphant thundered forward and disappeared behind Brackta's ice wall. The Juten

Lugron howled in fear as the great beast charged and trampled them with nary a notice or care.

Behind that great pachyderm came another of its kind, only slightly smaller. Then another. And another. Weldon turned toward the other end of the ice wall, his jaw clenched, face red, hair smoking. He pointed his hands down that way. Mouthed some words. Another black rectangle appeared. Four more olyphants thundered through it, twins to the first bunch. They raged and they roared. Their trumpet blasts competing with those of their fellows.

The second herd charged the Juten Lugron. Swept their great tusks this way and that, and sent Lugron flying. So too did they stomp upon them. So heavy were the olyphants, they could squash a man to pulp with a single step.

And they did.

Over and again.

They didn't just charge through the Lugron ranks like frightened animals seeking escape. They attacked the Lugron. Turned about this way and that to go after them. They tried to kill them. So vicious was their assault that some few Lugron flew overtop the ice wall, thrown by angry tusks, only to crash in bloody heaps at the expedition's feet.

Jude heard a whooshing sound. At first he didn't know what it was. And then he recognized it, just as Donnelin said, "Catapult! Keep your heads down."

66

DOR EOTRUS THE UNDERHALLS

YEAR 1267, 4TH AGE
1ST YEAR OF KING CARTEGIAN'S RULE

ECTOR EOTRUS

The second day of the siege. Midmorning. Ector picked his way through the Second Underhall's corridors. Oil lamps flickered in their wall sconces. The stone walls, dry and gray, and in good repair. Well kept, like all of Dor Eotrus.

A faint burning odor and the stink of too many people assailed Ector's senses. It was noisy and crowded. Weary citizens hurried past Ector toward the stair that led down to the Third Underhall. They carried supplies: boxes of who-knows-what, foodstuffs, weapons, and what personal items they'd had time to save — nothing large, mind you, just baubles, mementos, and coin purses. Mostly, the civilians moved the supplies. A few soldiers supervised. The work went on all night. It had too, for they anticipated yielding the Second Underhall to the troll that day. Everything left behind would be lost. Ector hated the thought of it. But they had to give ground. Stay hunkered down behind their defenses as best they could for as long as they could — for open melee with the troll would be the end of the Eotrus; that much was clear.

They had to hold out.

Protect as many folk as possible until help arrived.

If help arrived.

The people greeted Ector respectfully as he passed; perked up at the very sight of him. As if him being with them gave them hope. Hope that they'd survive this. And comfort that they weren't in it alone.

Ector wore a serious look, but flashed a pleasant smile to those folk that made eye contact or that offered more than a passing word.

It's what his father would have done.

He paused for a moment, here and there, but made certain not to be drawn into extended conversation. He had no time for that. He had to keep focused.

He walked straight and tall, chest out, chin high. Confident. Strong. That's what his father would have expected of him. He was an Eotrus after all. It was his duty.

Lead by example, his father always said.

He was doing his best. He wished that his father were there. His brothers. Ob. Sir Gabriel.

But they were all gone. Jude might still be alive. Ector held out hope in his heart. But his head told him differently. With no ransom demand, why would anyone hold his brother for so long? He had no enemies to speak of.

And what of Claradon and Ob? They'd been gone a long time searching for Jude.

Too long.

No doubt they'd run afoul of the same villains that had waylaid Jude. Or some others. If they were ever coming back, they'd have returned already.

Ector didn't want to face those thoughts. They kept popping into his head, most every day. Sometimes, many times a day. And when they did, he pushed them from his mind, pretended that they weren't true. That any day now, Claradon, Jude, and Ob would ride through the gates of the Dor all safe and sound. It was easy to pretend that, if he didn't think too much on it.

But Ector was no fool. He knew the truth. He knew that they'd probably never return. That he was lord of the Dor now. Master of the House, whether he liked it or not. And at the moment, he didn't like it. For he was the acting Lord of Dor Eotrus on the day its walls were breached. On the day that its people went into hiding in the Underhalls.

His father would have found a way to hold the trolls back. To have kept them out of the keep. But he didn't. Not even with Sarbek's help. But thank Odin for Sarbek. Without him, Ector knew that he'd be lost.

Lost because he wasn't ready to lead. Wasn't ready to be in command. That wasn't supposed to be his position. Not now. Not ever. He was the third son. And his father was strong and healthy. The mantle of the House would never fall to him. He'd known that all his life. And where other men might feel envy or resentment, he took comfort.

He didn't want to lead.

It wasn't his nature.

He didn't want to be responsible for the lives of every person at the Dor. The burden of that crushed him. Suffocated him. Scared him more than fighting the trolls did.

But he had no choice in it. He was an Eotrus.

His family ruled these lands for hundreds of years. He had his duty. His honor.

He could not and would not relinquish command to any other.

He would not disgrace himself and his family. Never.

He'd do his best. No matter how hard it was.

As he walked the Underhall's corridors, Ector saw that the people were frightened out of their wits. He wondered if he looked as frightened to them as they did to him. He hardened his face. Tried to look confident. Strong.

Some of the folk looked so weary from their labors that they might drop. Ector felt much the same but made certain not to show it.

Up the steps from the Second Underhall to the First he went. The archers and pikemen who gathered there greeted him solemnly and moved aside to let him pass. An iron portcullis at the top of the stair stood as the only barrier that barred passage from the First Underhall to the stair that led to the Second Underhall below.

Sarbek and Indigo had their noses to that portcullis.

Of course they did.

Ector wondered whether either of them had slept. Had they stood there all night listening to the trolls digging and pounding at the stone slabs of the First Underhall's ceiling?

"They're in," said Sarbek as he glanced briefly at Ector. "I told you to sleep."

"I tried," said Ector. "My mind wouldn't shut off. I kept thinking that they'd burst in at any moment. How many?"

"A scouting party," said Indigo. "They learned their lesson yesterday. No more rushing headlong."

"What do we do?" said Ector.

"We wait," said Sarbek. "And then we kill some more."

"Another of Donnelin's tricks," said Indigo as he pointed to a lever set within a small alcove in the stair wall. "To think we made fun of him for years for spending so much time on these traps."

"And money," said Sarbek. "I never understood why Lord Aradon indulged him as much as he did. Now I'm starting to get it. Your father always liked to be prepared. Had to be. Darned lucky for us or we'd be troll poop by now. Indigo's traps are hounding them too. Every room they breech, they pay for in blood."

They stood quietly for a time. Watching. Listening. An oily haze from the acid trap hung in the air, though happily, little of it ventured down into the lower levels. Ector felt numb. They'd lost the Dor. Dor Eotrus, fallen. Ector's home. His land. Swept away in a matter of hours by creatures he thought were myth and legend only days before. All that was left to them, the Underhalls: a half-dozen basement levels that stretched beneath the Odinhome and beyond. He ventured to every corner of those Underhalls as a child, playing hide-and-seek with his brothers. He knew every room. The choice hiding places were his old friends. Still, he knew that there were secret rooms, passages, and such down there that the Eotrus boys had never discovered. He knew because they had found a dozen concealed doors and hatches that led to secret rooms. But if there were any truth to his father's stories, there was a lot more down there that they had never found. Ob knew every nook and cranny of the place. Donnelin every crack and crevice. Hell, every cobweb. If anyone alive knew those secret ways, it was them. But they weren't there. Probably no one left in the Dor knew more than Ector. He wondered if he'd have to retreat to one of those rooms before it was over. Problem was, collectively, the secret rooms he knew of couldn't hide a fraction of the people hold up in the Underhalls.

"They're coming," said Indigo.

"Archers, move up," said Sarbek. He, Indigo, and Ector stepped to the side. Indigo stood close to the wall panel with the lever. "Pikemen, move forward if they reach the portcullis. Go for the heads."

A soldier ran up from behind. "Castellan," he said. "They've found one of our exit holes. They're in."

"Oh shit," said Sarbek.

67

DOR LOMION
LOMION CITY

YEAR 1267, 4TH AGE
1ST YEAR OF KING CARTEGIAN'S RULE
EARLY MORNING, DAY AFTER THE ROYAL WEDDING

MARISSA HARRINGGOLD

Marissa sat in the corner of Brithhilda's chamber, sobbing. The curtains were drawn, but it was dark, the first glow of dawn appearing on the horizon. Guards stood in the doorway. Two others hovered over Grim Fisher the gnome as he examined Brithhilda's body, which they just pulled from her closet, buried beneath a mound of clothes.

"Grim," said Marissa through her sobs. "What happened to her? What happened?"

"She was strangled," said Grim. "Leren Trak may be able to tell us more. I'm sorry."

"Promise me you will find out who did this," said Marissa.

"I will begin a full investigation, my queen," said Grim. "We will suffer no murderers under House Harringgold's roof. As a precaution, I will double the guard on both you and the king until this matter is sorted out. But tell me, how is it that no one went looking for her until now?

Wasn't it odd that she'd disappeared?"

"Disappeared?" said Marissa. "What do you mean?"

"She's been dead no less than two days," said Grim. "I'd mark it three, but the Leren may know better. She attends you closely, I know. Why didn't you report her missing?"

Marissa shook her head. "No. No. That can't be. You are wrong. I saw her for hours yesterday. She helped me get ready for the wedding."

Grim's brow furrowed. "As you say. I must be wrong."

A guard ran down the hall and entered.

"Leren Trak?" said Grim.

"The duke has taken ill," said the guard. "Down in the kitchens. Leren Trak is with him."

68

ISLE OF JUTENHEIM THE GATORMEN'S LAIR

YEAR 1267, 4TH AGE

OB

Theta moved forward toward the lizard chieftain.

The gatorman launched himself at the great knight.

Ob and all the men watched.

And then came the swordplay. Theta's first strike crashed against the chieftain's sword. Bent it nearly in half. The lizard parried the second strike, but the falchion sheared his sword in two, and kept going. It blasted into the metal plates around the chieftain's chest. But they held. The lizard sprang at Theta, its speed uncanny for its bulk.

Theta sidestepped.

Tripped the beast as it went by.

It fell sprawling. But then bounced up in the blink of an eye.

Theta's sword met its dagger as it lunged. The lizard's blade went tumbling away.

Theta sheathed his sword.

Threw down his shield.

He'd meet the chieftain unarmed. Hand to hand. Or hand to claw.

The chieftain roared. Barreled forward. Claws

poised to strike. What speed he had. A blur of movement. And the strength behind those claws — strength to drop a bull.

Theta's punch was the faster. A jab to the jaw stunned the beast. Stopped it in its tracks. More shocked than hurt. No doubt, it barely saw the punch coming.

Then another jab.

A third.

A fourth.

The chieftain backpedaled. Tried to block the blows. But it didn't know how. It was accustomed to fighting its own kind. And they didn't box. Their techniques were different.

Theta's jabs knocked down its defenses. Five or six blindingly fast strikes did he throw. All to the creature's face, near its eyes.

Patient for the right opening.

And when it came, Theta let fly his left fist. Smashed the chieftain's jaw. Shattered it. But the beast was solid. Strong. It stepped back a single step. Did not go down. Or falter. Or cry out.

Theta stepped forward. Punched with his right hand. Slammed the other side of its jaw. Punched again with his left.

The chieftain's claws raked against Theta's breastplate. But could do no harm. Sharp and strong as they were, those claws failed to even leave a scrape in the ancient metal.

Theta pressed forward. Pummeled the chieftain left and right, left and right, against its jaws. Its teeth splintered. Broke. Crumbled. Blood spurted from its mouth. Its jaw dislodged. Crooked. Its face swelled and bruised. Eyes swelled shut. And still Theta pummeled it. And still the chieftain did not go down.

And then Theta stopped.

The lizard chieftain swayed side to side. Stumbled back against the wall. Barely able to stand, but stand he did.

"Your time has come and gone," said Theta. "Get thee now to the nether realms." And Theta's left fist lashed out one final time. Faster by far than all the other strikes was that blow. Faster than the eye could follow. And when it struck, the chieftain's head cracked like a melon struck with a club. Its corpse crumbled to the ground.

The others stood there, mouths agape.

"The bastard had it coming," said Blain. He spit on the creature's corpse.

Two Kalathans stepped back into the room. They'd scouted ahead.

"It's a nursery of sorts," said one knight. "Little lizards, babes to half grown. Nothing else. A dead end."

The men moved forward, weapons poised.

"Hold on," said Ob as they ventured into the room. It was as the knight said. The lizards' young. Most, completely defenseless. "You can't kill them. They're babes."

"If you cut open their bellies," said DeBoors, "you'll probably find some bits of our dead men."

"They're babes," said Ob. "Maybe the last of their kind."

"And good riddance," said Blain. "If we kill them, then the world is free of them for good."

"We cannot lose our moral compass," said Ob. "Forget who we are. We cannot become beasts ourselves."

"They killed my son," spat Blain. "They killed

my brother. I'll see them dead. Every one of them. And this place brought down."

Theta turned toward the men. "I will do what needs be done," he said. "We've had our victory and our vengeance. I will finish things here. Go now. All of you." He drew his sword and turned toward the nursery. "I will do this alone. The stain of this will be on me and me alone. Now go."

Some of the men were happy to be off. Others were reluctant. But in the end, they all went.

69

PLAIN OF ENGELROTH JUTENHEIM

YEAR 1267, 4TH AGE

JUDE EOTRUS

A great catapult stone, several hundred pounds in weight, smashed into Brackta's ice wall with a terrific report. The rock sunk some feet into the wall and hung there, embedded.

Then came ballistae fire. A battery of them. They shot great arrows, larger than a whaling harpoon or a knight's lance. The first caught a Sithian knight in the chest. It went straight through him; nearly cut him in two. Its head embedded itself in the ground behind the knight, the shaft through his chest. He hung there in death, suspended on his feet.

More great shafts shot down, but each hit the ground ineffectually.

Jude stood up, risking Thorn's wrath. He needed a better view. Had to know what was happening. He saw the line of catapults. A dozen of them readying to fire. The first had been but a test shot, to gauge the range. Skilled or lucky was their crew, since they were dead on from the first.

And they launched. All at once. All directed toward the heart of the expedition's force. Right where Jude was.

Dead gods, this was the end. Jude heard the release as the Juten Lugron let fly their stones. Heard the great whoosh in the air. Saw the stones flying, closer and closer. In that moment, he knew he was a dead man.

And then a flash of light intercepted one of the stones. Then another. Then all the rest.

And instantly the stones reflected back in the direction that they had come.

The catapult crews had a few moments to scatter. Not much time, but enough.

But they didn't scatter. Nearly all of them stood there gaping as their own stones flew back at them. They didn't understand what they were looking at. What was happening. The stones plunged down and each one smashed into the catapult that had launched it, and blasted them to bits. Shrapnel of wood and stone flying; the crews torn and battered by it. Moments later, the ballistae battery suffered the same fate.

Ginalli's work.

Jude heard the priest yell. Saw him throw himself to the ground and roll in the dirt, one arm aflame. He'd thrown too much magic, too soon. *Wizard's Toll* they called it; the burning that wizards felt when they overused their powers. Jude had always thought it a myth. Another fable to make the common folk fear magic and shun it. But he'd seen the *toll* several times of late. His whole world felt turned upside down. Fantasy became reality. And reality tumbled toward madness.

Stev Keevis was conjuring again, his lithe movements sleek and quick, precise and sharp, so different from that of the other wizards, though each one had his own unique style.

A few of the giants sought to leap across Keevis's pit. Gods, they could jump. Twenty feet or more. The strength they had to launch such bulk so far was impressive. But those few that dared it, soon regretted it. For each fell howling into the crevasse. Others were patient enough to simply maneuver around the rift. No need to throw away their lives to try to jump across. The problem for them was, Keevis was ready for them. He opened a second pit nearly as large as the first, and connected the two. The second pit sprang into being just as suddenly as the first. A score of giants tumbled in. Some dropped away as the ground upon which they tread fell away to form the rift. Others stumbled over the edge, unable to halt their charge in time. The second pit grew larger and larger, arcing around until it reached the very edge of Brackta's ice wall. Keevis pivoted, gestured, and spoke his words. A few heartbeats later and a third pit opened up, connected at the far end of the original. It too grew larger and larger by the moment, arcing around toward the other end of Brackta's ice wall. But it didn't make it. Keevis had exhausted whatever reserves of power he maintained. He fell to one knee, his chin dropped to his chest, and he tumbled over. Unconscious. Maybe dead. The edge of his pit was perhaps fifty feet from Brackta's wall. That stretch of ground was now the only direct opening between the expedition and the Lugron and giant armies. For the Jutens to attack them, they now had either to come through that narrow gap, come overtop the ice wall, or somehow cross the pit.

Ezerhauten barked his orders.

"To the gap! Plug it! Everyone, move your butts, to the gap."

The Juten Lugron reached the gap and started to stream in a few at a time. A rabble. The Sithians cut them down with sword and arrow. Then they came on en masse. The expedition spread out across the gap, shoulder to shoulder. The gap was too wide. They didn't have enough men. In most spots, the defensive line was but one man deep, wizards behind.

Thorn and Korrgonn didn't move. That meant Jude had to stay put too. So did the five that guarded them.

The first Lugron troop that poured through the gap ran into Par Rhund's magic. Streaks of light shot from Rhund's fingertips, each with a *pop*, *pop*, *pop* sound, so loud it hurt the ears. Each Lugron hit by the light reacted as if shot with an arrow. Blood spattered. Lugron went down. Howled in pain and surprise. Rhund's magic went on and on. Rapidly firing at the Lugron. A hundred shots? Two hundred? Too fast and too many to count. The Lugron dead piled about the gap. Meanwhile, any missile directed at Rhund bounced off a mystical translucent shield that enveloped him, and clattered to the ground.

Ginalli called down boulders from the sky to stop the next wave of Lugron. Hundreds of rocks, some that topped a thousand pounds dropped from on-high at great velocity and pounded the Lugron line.

Par Keld dragged Ginalli back when he collapsed from the effort.

Then the giants reached the gap. That's when

the chaos truly began.

The giant army crashed against the Lugron. Though they'd made the expedition a common enemy, they had not forgotten their ancient hatreds. They tore into each other like rabid animals. The giants' great clubs blasted Lugron, launching them into the air, crushing and breaking them. The Lugron spears impaled giant after giant. The melee spilled through the gap. Many of the combatants turned toward the expedition and charged, howling their war cries. They trampled their own dead as they went.

"Err, look hear, my lord," said Thorn quietly. "We cannot hold the gap. Can you call forth the holy power of the Orb?"

Jude figured no one but he and Korrgonn could have heard Thorn's words.

Korrgonn made no reply. He gave no indication that he had even heard.

"Err, it may well be our only chance," said Thorn.

Korrgonn opened his eyes and put them on Thorn. "I have been preparing the ritual. But I am loath to use it."

"Surely, Azathoth's power can smite these petty creatures," said Thorn.

"The power of the Orb has waned over the long years," said Korrgonn. "At most, I can call forth its power once and still leave enough energy within it to open the portal to the holy realm."

A volley of spears crashed about them, blocked by Mason, Mort Zag, and the magical dome.

"Call it forth, my lord," said Thorn. "Or all may be lost."

"Your wizardlings have some power left," said Korrgonn.

"The last of it wanes," said Thorn.

"That is a disappointment," said Korrgonn. "My father thought better of you."

70

THE REGENT'S EXPEDITIONARY FORCE (THE ALDER BRIGADE)

YEAR 1267, 4TH AGE

DIRK ALDER

Dirk Alder watched men filter into Riker's Crossroads all day long. They came from the east, the west, and some few from the south. Not many came down from the north. Nearly all the men came in on horse, except for some locals that walked it. There were groups of men from the local farms — lots of brothers, fathers, and such — outfitted with stout leather armor, steel blades and hammers. There were fancy men from the northern manors, shadowed by their guards and workers. Huntsmen came in. Trappers. Mountain men. A ragtag bunch. But they were all northerners. Tall, broad, proud, and surly. Accustomed to hard weather. Hard Life. And nasty beasties. They knew how to fight. And there wasn't much that they feared. Several troops of cavalry came in from the outlying towns and the grand manors that dotted the northlands. Other than locals, only mounted men that moved on the roads got there so quickly. More would come on foot. A lot more, for the northmen had heard their liege's call to arms. And they would heed it, even if it meant rushing headlong to their deaths. The gathering of all their strength would take time. Time that they didn't have.

In late afternoon, the officers gathered in the inn.

Lord Ogden pointed to a large map as he spoke, Dor Eotrus situated at its center. "Three hours before dawn tomorrow, we'll ride out with all our horse straight up the North Road to the Dor, outriders to expose any ambush they've laid for us. When we're in position, we'll launch a coordinated three-pronged attack on the troll. Ravens and owls to carry the messages between our troops."

"Lord Lester will come in from the west with twelve hundred horse. Lord Cadbury will ride in from the east with two thousand horse. We from here with fifteen hundred horse, plus however many more arrive between now and then. With that force, at worst, we'll break the troll siege and relieve the Dor until our footmen can advance and more aid comes up from Doriath and parts south. If the luck of the Vanyar is with us, we'll crush the troll underfoot and disrupt their lines enough that Sarbek can sally forth with his horse. Then we'll be done with this business in a day. But mark my words, even if victory be swift, it will be costly. The trolls are fearsome beasts, and smart. This will be a fight."

"Remember the gorge," spoke several of the older men around the room.

"Yes, remember the gorge," said Ogden. "Someday, mayhap, men will speak of this battle with reverence, the way we speak of Karthune

Gorge. That is, if the stinking troll doesn't kill us all."

The inn's door opened when it shouldn't have. No one but the gathered officers were permitted entry. Everyone turned to look.

Old Lord Nickel shuffled in, the impressive arc of his chest and belly bursting with medals. Master Yallzen, legendary battle mage, gray, pale, and bespectacled, at his side.

Greetings and handshakes all around as Lord Nickel made his way to the map table. Long past his prime, Nickel was a legend on the battlefield. He'd served with Lord Aradon and his father, Lord Nardon, on every major campaign over the last sixty years.

Ogden and Nickel shook hands, but their greetings were not warm. "Whatever you're planning," said Nickel, "it'll need to change."

Ogden's face scrunched up. He wasn't pleased. "Why?"

"The Dor has fallen," said Nickel.

Gasps from around the room.

"The troll have overrun the Outer Dor and breached the citadel," said Master Yallzen.

"How do you know that?" said Boddrick.

"He's an archwizard," said Ogden, as if that was all that need be said.

"The Eotrus have taken refuge in the Underhalls," said Yallzen. "The trolls are sieging the Odinhome. Best I can tell, they haven't yet breached the Underhalls."

"It's only a matter of time," said Nickel. "If we're to save them, we must make all possible speed."

"How is it possible that they got through the

wall so fast?" said Ogden. "A traitor? Did someone open the gates?" His eyes shifted toward the Alders.

"The walls proved no barrier to them," said Yallzen. "I saw some climbing the central tower. They move up and down the stone with the skill of spiders."

"If they freely climbed the Dor's walls," said Ogden, "then no keep in the kingdom is safe. Even Lomion City is at risk."

"Aye," said Nickel. "We need to stop them here. We must leave at once, even if not at our best strength. I've fifty horse with me. Three hundred more will follow in two days, two hundred footmen behind them."

"A fraction of your forces," said Ogden.

"All I can spare," said Nickel, whose fortress was the northernmost of the gathered men.

71

DOR EOTRUS THE UNDERHALLS

YEAR 1267, 4TH AGE

ECTOR EOTRUS

The trolls charged howling toward the portcullis.

Eotrus arrows flew. Peppered their bodies with shafts. Several trolls went down. A half dozen well-placed arrows would stop a troll in its tracks, but only for a short time, unless you caught them in the head, through the brain.

A final fusillade took down four more.

Then they were at the iron.

Crashed headlong into it.

Stout as it was, the gate shuddered. But the bars did not yield.

Eotrus pikemen lunged forward. Thrust their halberds between the bars. Stab and thrust. Over and again. Troll claws had no hope to reach the men, so they attacked the pikes wherever they could. Tightly pressed against the bars were the trolls. No space to maneuver. No way to protect themselves.

The Eotrus skewered them.

The trolls were beat. But there had only been a dozen of them. Probing. Testing the defenses.

They'd sacrificed their own in their search for weaknesses. That proved their smarts once again. And their ruthlessness.

Sarbek turned away from the portcullis and spoke to the soldier who had reported that the trolls had found one of the Eotrus escape tunnels. "Have they breached the Underhalls? Are they inside?"

"No," said the soldier. "They only found the eastern exit cave. They're inside the cave, but they haven't found the hidden door to the Underhalls. Not yet, anyways."

Sarbek ordered Indigo to that eastern tunnel. "Get two companies lined up to repel them if they get inside," said Sarbek. "I'll take your station."

The troll scouts that still lived limped back down the tunnel. Sarbek showed them no mercy. Pelted them with arrows until they were out of sight. The trolls left five dead in the passage. Two brought down by arrows. The killing shots went to the head. Three others died at the portcullis. Some of those that got away had a dozen arrows in them. Some, nearly eviscerated by the pikemen.

Not one Eotrus man suffered so much as a scratch.

"They'll come again in force," said Sarbek. "Ector — set up another squadron of archers and a full company of pike at the foot of the stair. And get a man on the lever; I don't want to be glued to this thing."

Moments later, the trolls came again. This time they filled the passage. Arrows flew like mad mosquitoes. Sarbek didn't want that mob to smash into the portcullis. He feared that they'd tear it down.

He pulled the lever.

At first nothing happened.

Then he pulled again. That did it.

A large panel in the ceiling slid open — on the troll side of the portcullis.

A great rumbling sound.

The trolls came on oblivious.

The trap sprang too slow.

The trolls hit the gate.

Mortar cracked.

Crumbled.

Fell from the ceiling.

The bolts at the gate's base sheared in two.

The gate bent inward, the metal groaning.

The trolls would be through in moments, the whole mass of them.

But then, the five-ton boulder dropped through the open hatch in the ceiling.

A great round ball of stone it was. Carved smooth. It rocketed out of that ceiling shoot faster than a horse's gallop.

Crushed those at the portcullis to pulp. Then continued down the passage. There was no way for the trolls, massed as they were, to turn and flee fast enough.

The massive stone rolled over them.

Crushed them.

Burst them like a horse stepping on apples.

There was no escape for the trolls — the stone, carefully sized to fill the entire width of the passage.

The boulder slowed as it went, but managed the turn in the passage and barreled out of sight.

No less than fifty trolls lay crushed in its wake.

The Eotrus cheered.

"Dead gods," said Ector. "Some of them are

still alive. Still moving. How in Odin's name could anything survive that weight? That impact?"

"Archers," said Sarbek. "Aim for the heads only."

The men let loose their shafts on the wounded trolls. Wave after wave of arrows. After a minute or two, only a few troll arms or legs still quivered. Sarbek called the archers off. Healing powers or no, those fifty were out of the fight. No sense wasting ammunition.

"There's no way to secure the gate," said Ector. It was bent inward more than two feet at its base. A little more and the trolls could squeeze under.

"One more trick we have here," said Sarbek. He used it when the trolls came again a few hours later. Another twist of the lever and more stones dropped down the chute. Not round that time. Just large boulders. Many of them. They piled higher and higher.

The dust and shards drove the Eotrus back from the portcullis and down the steps. When the dust settled, the stones had piled to the top of the gate. The passage was completely blocked. It would take the troll hours to move that debris, and still they'd have to get past the portcullis.

"Delaying tactics," said Sarbek. "That's what this is about. We can't win here, but we can hold them off. Give us a chance for help to come. Or bleed them bad enough that they turn tail and give up."

"What else have we got?" said Ector.

"Another portcullis at the bottom of the stair. And more at top and bottom of the stair to level three. Same at levels four, five, and six. Donnelin wanted more traps like the rolling rock, but the work, the logistics, were too much. Aradon would only take on such a project once every couple of years. Level two is as far as we got, save for the iron."

"And they can crash through the gates," said Ector.

"We'll bolster them," said Sarbek. "Make it as difficult as possible. Slow them at every opportunity."

Indigo returned from his rounds. "They found three of our escape routes, including the one farthest south. But we've been lucky. They only found the antechambers. They either didn't think to check for concealed doors, or else couldn't spy them out."

"Did they set up camp in the exit chambers?" said Sarbek.

"They raided the places," said Indigo, "upending everything, taking whatever supplies they fancied, destroying the rest. But then they left. They thought the caves were only supply caches, not entrances to our tunnel system. It may be that those routes are safer now than the ones that they haven't found. They may not be looking in those areas any longer."

"Or they may have them staked out, figuring that our people would stop there to resupply or hide out," said Sarbek.

"How many could they spare to guard a hidden supply cache?" said Indigo.

"Depends on how many troops they've got," said Sarbek.

"There are secret rooms down here," said Ector.

There was a pause as Sarbek and Indigo turned toward him.

"I know," said Sarbek. "I think it's time we start putting folks in them. Trouble is, some of the hidey holes are on each level. As we retreat down, we'll be leaving folks behind. But if we don't, we'll not have space for them down below anyway."

"The trolls will sniff them out," said Indigo.

"Maybe, maybe not," said Sarbek. "It's a risk."

"It's either that, or else we run for it, through the escape tunnels," said Ector. "Standing here and fighting will get us all killed."

"I'd rather die facing them than getting stabbed in the back running away," said Indigo.

"Me too," said Ector. "But what of the children? The old folk? The women? We can't just worry about the surest path to Valhalla for us."

"If we stand fast," said Sarbek, "they'll slaughter us all for certain unless a major force comes to relieve us in time. That would take most all the bannermen coming in together. And doing it smart. Or else a whole corps up from Lomion City. The bannermen might organize and get here in time. The army won't. If we blast out of one of the tunnels, they'll hunt us down and kill us all the easier. Coming out of several tunnels at once gives us a chance of at least one or two groups getting away. Hiding in the secret rooms gives some folks a chance too. Big risks all around."

"The common element is that if we fight them, we lose," said Ector.

"Pains me to say it," said Sarbek, "but there be the truth."

"Then our best option is to avoid fighting them," said Ector.

"That's what we've been doing skulking down here," said Indigo.

Sarbek smiled a knowing smile and nodded. "Young Master Ector has a head on him, he does. We do it all. We put folk in the secret rooms, hoping the trolls don't scope them out. Them folks should be the slowest and the weakest amongst us: the folk that can't help in a fight and can't run for it. We hold out here in the Underhalls as long as we can, waiting for relief. If it doesn't come, we send all the noncombatants out through the tunnels."

"How many groups?" said Indigo.

"One for every tunnel we've got," said Sarbek. "One squadron will go with each group to urge them along and deal with any troll scouts. But the bulk of our fighting force will stay here and fight them to the end. We don't send folk through the tunnels until the trolls hit us on level six and see that we're going to fight. That will put all their focus on us. All their manpower will be coming down here. Once that happens, we send the folk out the tunnels in six directions at the same time. That's the best chance for some to make it through. And still there will be the folk hidden in these halls. Some Eotrus folk will survive this however it plays out."

"Unless the trolls have a whole troop guarding each one of our escape routes," said Ector. "Then it will be a slaughter out there, and the troll will come in behind us."

"There will still be the hidden folk," said Sarbek.

"It's a good plan," said Ector.

"I make plans to win battles," said Sarbek.

"I'm out of my zone here."
"Let's do it," said Indigo.

72

DOR LOMION LOMION CITY

YEAR 1267, 4TH AGE
1ST YEAR OF KING CARTEGIAN'S RULE
WEDDING NIGHT

DUKE HARRINGGOLD

Harringgold's stomach felt afire. He couldn't sleep due to the pressure and shooting pains. Too much exotic food at the wedding. And too much wine. Now he was paying the price. Ten years prior he could eat anything, and nothing bothered him. Age was coming on apace. And he didn't care for that one bit. He needed to put something bland in his belly, some bread perhaps, and he had no interest in waiting for a servant to be roused from slumber. Down to the kitchens he would go. Two of the three guardsmen that stood outside his door went with him. Old friends they were. Men of the Fearless squadron. Jak the Blademan and Blue Ben. They left the hulking long-hair called the Rage to guard the empty chambers. The Fearless didn't normally stand the guard. They were fighting men. Called out for combat and special operations. But that night, they stood as guards without complaint. No one was going to threaten the family the night of Marissa's wedding. And if they did, they'd get dead.

Harringgold figured that the walk down to the kitchens would do him good. Aches and pains and such were always worse when lying in bed. This time he was wrong. By the time he reached the kitchens, his stomach pained so much he couldn't stand straight.

"You catch a bad bit of fish?" said Jak.

"Fetch Leren Trak," said Harringgold. A moment later, he felt as if he were falling. Then everything went black.

73

ISLE OF JUTENHEIM THE GATORMEN'S LAIR

YEAR 1267, 4TH AGE

OB

Ob wanted to follow Theta. He needed to see for himself what Theta was going to do. Would he really murder those lizard young? Could he do such a thing? Or was this his way of saving them? For Blain Alder would have killed them all himself, if Theta hadn't sent him away. That man was angry. Who could blame him? His eldest son, dead.

Bastard or no, it was his son, for Odin's sake.

And his brother, dead too. Who could blame him for his anger? For his need for revenge?

Who could blame any of them?

But this time, Ob didn't follow Theta. He couldn't.

He was afraid to.

If Theta did that black deed, then he wasn't the man that Ob hoped that he was.

If he killed those young ones, then mayhap he was the brute from all those old stories. The harbinger of doom. His evil reputation well deserved after all.

Ob didn't want to know that.

He couldn't know that.

How could he follow him any longer if that's the kind of man that he truly was?

How could he let Claradon?

And so Ob followed after the others. But his gnomish ears strained to hear any sounds behind him. The squeal, the cries, of those little lizards as Theta killed them.

He didn't want to hear that. But he couldn't help himself from trying to listen. He even stopped twice along the way and went quiet.

But he didn't hear any killing.

He didn't hear any screaming.

Mayhap Theta didn't go through with it. Perhaps he had second thoughts? Perhaps he never planned to do it at all.

Outside, the Eotrus expedition regrouped and licked their wounds. Their losses were staggering. Nearly two hundred men dead. Of all those who were captured. Only six made it out of the lizard caverns alive. And every one of them battered and bruised. But to a man, they had shown their quality. They had fought their way out against unimaginable odds. Barehanded and then only with the primitive weapons of the gatormen, and still groggy and weak from the poison darts that had taken them down, they fought their way clear.

Outside the lair, there were no more gatormen to be found.

The Lomerians bandaged their wounds. More than a few needed field stitching. Ob, Artol, and Slaayde went to work on that; they each had some skill at it. They drank water. Ate food from their packs. And caught their breath. At Ob's orders, they sat in a wide circle, backs to each other. There was no way they'd allow anything to sneak up on them again.

Then they waited.

After a time, not very long, Theta emerged from the cavern. Most all the men glanced over, turned their attention toward him. He was in one piece though blood covered his armor from head to toe. That was no different from how Ob had seen him before he fought the chieftain. Whether there was any more blood on him, newer blood, was impossible to say.

Theta grabbed up a discarded piece of cloth and carefully ran it up and down along his sword, cleaning the blood from it and discarding the rag back on the ground.

Then he joined the others

"All of them?" said Blain Alder to Theta.

"It's done," said Theta.

"And good riddance," said Blain.

"We need to find a place to camp," said DeBoors. "And this isn't it."

"I agree," said Claradon. "I'm all turned around. I'm not even certain which way we should go."

"We've lost our guide," said Ob. "Rikenguard was in there with us. Fought like a demon. But in the end they must have taken him down. What of his sons?"

"I saw them both," said Trelman. "They were in there with us too. In the caverns. They didn't make it out."

"Then we're on our own," said Claradon. "With only Lord Theta's ankh to guide us."

"And our own good sense," said Ob.

"South is that way," said Slaayde pointing. "So

if we want to keep heading south as we were before, that's the way we should go."

"Let's try to find some dry ground," said Theta. "We should rest until morning."

The men formed a column, three rows wide. Headed off south. Ob lingered to the side. And then he made his way over to the cave mouth. Dolan walked behind him. Stealthy like, so that Ob didn't even notice.

Ob bent down and picked up that strip of cloth. The one Theta had used to clean off his sword. He held it up and looked it over carefully. It was stained. It was dirty. But there was no blood to speak of on it. Nary a drop.

Dolan stepped up beside Ob.

"Best you not tell the others about this," said Dolan. "Some of them might want to come back."

"Why didn't he?" said Ob. "Why did he let them live?"

"Lord Angle would never take an innocent life," said Dolan. "He tricked the others so that those innocents might have a chance at life. However slim without their clan."

Ob raised an eyebrow. "You don't think he did the right thing, do you?"

"It was the right thing," said Dolan. "It's just that sometimes the right thing comes back to haunt you."

***

Three days of difficult hiking saw them to the swamp's southern edge. Each day, the men ate more of the nuts and herbs that Rikenguard had given them, to stave off whatever fevers the swamp bugs carried. Whether it worked or not, who could say? But not a man amongst them fell to a fever.

They skirted around great stretches of swampy water, sticking to the driest and firmest ground they could find. But they made certain that they continued south. South. Ever south.

They avoided alligators, steered clear of snakes, and heeled and toed it away from hippos. Most of all, they kept out of the deep water. Anything higher than the ankle held a higher chance of biting fish and deadly predators. That caution cost them a day at least. But they made it through with no more deaths, no serious injuries. When they stepped from that swamp, Theta stood at the van. Artol at his right hand, Claradon at his left. Behind them were Ob, Dolan, and Par Tanch. Of the Eotrus men, Sir Glimador, Kelbor, Trelman, the Bull, Sergeant Vid, Sergeant Lant, and six troopers were all that were left. Slaayde was there. So was Little Tug and N'Paag. The handful of other seamen that had ventured inland with them were all dead. DeBoors was there. So was his henchman Kaladon of the Gray Waste. A dozen Kalathen Knights stood with them. Three Malvegillian archers still lived. So did a dozen Harringgold men led by Sir Seran. Of the Alders, Blain stood in command of but six marines. About sixty men all told, of nearly two hundred and fifty that set out with them from Jutenheim Town. The interior of Jutenheim had proved every bit as dangerous as Rikenguard had warned. And they hadn't even reached their goal yet. Ob wondered if they ever would.

74

JUTENHEIM

YEAR 1267, 4TH AGE

FREM SORLONS

The Black Elves came howling up the stair. Those in the lead tossed handfuls of powder that burst into flame and smoke when they hit the ground. A pyrotechnic show to send the Sithians fleeing.

Perhaps such humbug worked on the local Lugron. The Sithians weren't impressed. They knew it wasn't real magic — just trickery. Even if it were magic, well, it didn't matter. They'd stand their ground anyway. They'd fight to the end. That's what the Sithians were trained to do. Old Ma-Grak Stowron, who stood up front, seemed inclined to do the same.

The Black Elves were hard to read. Their features, small and slight. Their expressions, subtle, muted. Their skin, taught. All the same, Frem swore that they looked surprised when they rounded the last turn in the stair and came face to face with the Sithians and Ma-Grak. They didn't expect to see a bunch of Volsungs and a Stowron facing them down. Perhaps they thought it was the local Lugron that had invaded their city, since by the carnage in the cave above, it was clear enough that the Elfs and the Lugron held no friendship.

And these Elfs did not appear to be stragglers

from the city below. They were fresh and well-equipped. Each one clad in Black Elven armor and equipped with daggers or spear. This was a military unit, or a group of them. Well-girded for war. Much like the Elfs that had ambushed them in the tunnels soon after they entered those underground ways. How long ago was that ambush? Was it a dozen hours? A full day? Two days? Frem didn't know. He'd lost all sense of time while trapped in that place, fighting and running for his life nearly every minute he was there.

Frem figured that these Elfs had come from far afield. They'd been informed of the battle somehow and came in to help their fellows. Maybe these were the guardsmen that patrolled their borders, gathered together into a fighting force. Or perhaps they were the soldiery from another nearby Black Elf town or city.

Another city? Could that even be possible? Who knows? Who knows how far those tunnels stretched? What secrets, wonders, and horrors dwelled within? Frem didn't want to know. He didn't care. He just wanted to get himself and his men out of there. Back into the light. The surface world. That's where his kind belonged.

But first they had to defeat the Elfs. If luck was with them this time, they'd only have to give the Elfs what for, and that would send them scurrying away. But if these Elfs were anything like those they fought earlier, they'd keep coming, to the death. Every one of them.

Just before the lead Elfs crashed into the Sithian line, Par Sevare let fly his sorcery. A swarm of tiny fiery balls launched from his fingertips. Yellow, bright, crackling, a slight fiery tail trailing behind each. No smoke or heat came off them.

One and only one missile hit each Elf at the front line. The other missiles arced around and sought additional targets. The Elfs stopped in their tracks. Clutched at where the missiles hit. Some sank to their knees. Others fell straight forward or straight back — felled like trees. Their line crumbled. Two dozen Elfs went down.

Dead.

The rest halted their advance.

Sevare groaned at Frem's side.

The wizard sank to his knees.

His arms, smoking.

Then they burst into flame!

Sevare yelped and slapped his hands to his forearms to douse the flames. His face was twisted in agony.

"Charge," Frem shouted. This was their chance. If they could set the Elfs to flight, rout them, then, the Sithians would have their victory. They'd survive the day.

His men roared down the stairs. Frem helped Sevare to douse the flames on his arms. In but a moment they went out. The wizard dropped to his rump, moaning, his eyes wet.

The Black Elves didn't flee.

Mayhap they were in shock from what they'd seen — so many of their own going down without a fight.

Mayhap they were stubborn.

Or stupid.

Or brave.

Frem didn't know. And in truth, he didn't care.

Ma-Grak Stowron blasted into the lead Elfs. Trooper Drift was but a step behind him.

Ma-Grak fought like a berserker. Wild, powerful attacks, so fast that the eye could barely follow.

The Elfs held their ground.

Ma-Grak kept advancing. He sliced the head from one Elf. Took an arm from another. But he pressed on too quickly. Elfs got around him. Got behind him.

Drift was on them.

So was Sir Lex. And Torak Lugron. And Sergeant Grainer. The Sithians fought close together. Coordinating their attacks. Coordinating their defenses. Ma-Grak fought alone. As if the others didn't exist. He should have gone down in the first seconds of the clash. But he was so fast. Faster even than the Elfs. And the Elfs didn't try for his back. Those that passed him, went after the Sithians before them, trusting to their fellows behind to deal with the Stowron.

The fighting went on and on. The narrow confines of the stair kept the Elfs from taking advantage of their far greater numbers. The Sithian armor repelled nearly all their attacks.

And then came up the Svart champion. Perhaps even their prince. Frem knew him at once. He wore golden armor, of plate and chain, stitched together with unknown fibers — the leathery hide of some creature of Midgaard's deeps. Frem pushed through the Sithian ranks. That champion was someone he should face.

75

DOR EOTRUS THE UNDERHALLS

YEAR 1267, 4TH AGE

The Sixth Underhall's last gate fell on the morning of the fifth day of the siege. The moment that the trolls brought it crashing down, the Eotrus soldiers sounded their horns, signaling the squadron of soldiers that guarded each escape tunnel to open the hatches and usher the people out.

One-sixth of Dor Eotrus's population poured out each of the six escape tunnels. No doubt, to some, it was a relief. To be out of those cramped halls. Back into the open air. The northern sky above their heads. The fresh, crisp air on their faces. The sun shining down on them. They'd been crammed into the Sixth Underhall for three days. So overcrowded was the space that they were forced to stay lined up in the escape tunnels, night and day, waiting for the order to come. The order to abandon their home. Their land. Their lives. Everything that they knew. They were a simple people, the northerners. Many of them had never set foot beyond Eotrus demesne. Some of them feared doing so half as much as they feared the trolls. But they had to flee. They had no choice. It was their only chance to live. For when that last gate came down, there was no winning. No holding out any longer. There was only escape or death.

The trolls poured past the battered gate and entered the last subbasement far below the Dor's Odinhome. They were angrier than ever, the trolls. They'd lost many hundreds of their brethren to the Eotrus. Most by trap and trickery. The rest, by spear and arrow. Sarbek had done exactly what he'd promised. He bled them for every inch of ground that he ceded them.

But now they were through.

The Eotrus dropped their bows.

They met the trolls with spear, axe, hammer, mace, and muscle. Some few soldiers bore heavy blades, but their use was a challenge in the close confines.

The battle raged.

The most heavily armored knights were up front.

The trolls were out for blood. Vengeance. Or whatever evil purpose. It didn't matter anymore.

The Eotrus fought to protect their people, to cover their escape. Those good folk made up nearly the entire population of Dor Eotrus and its immediate surrounds. Bakers, farmers, shepherds, shopkeepers. Women, children, old folk. Grandparents, mothers, fathers, babies. The soldiers of Dor Eotrus were all that stood between the troll and those innocent folk. Their families. Their friends. Loved ones. Everyone, everything that was precious.

That's what the Eotrus fought for. To protect them. Safeguard their flight. Every moment that they held the troll there gave the folk that much time to get farther away. Increasing their chances that they might make it to safety. That they might live.

The Eotrus soldiers fought with all the skill and bravery that they were famous for. The troll siege of Dor Eotrus, as it came to be known, would be remembered as a last stand of desperate men.

Of heroes.

As that last gate bent and buckled, the Eotrus soldiers spoke the warriors' prayer.

"*Look unto the north and behold the Bifrost and beyond—ancient Asgard, shining and bright, though hard and cold as the stone, the ice, and the sea*," said the officers in unison.

"*To the north lies Asgard*," said the men.

"*Now look unto the east and behold thy brothers, thy sons, and thy comrades,*" said the officers. "*Now look unto the west and behold thy sisters, thy wives, thy mothers, and thy daughters.*"

"*Around us are our kinsmen, always,*" said the men.

"*Now think not again of them until we march on the homeward road.*"

"*Not until the homeward road,*" said the men.

"*Now look unto the south and behold thy father, and thy father's father, and all thy line afore thee, back unto the beginning.*"

"*Unto the beginning,*" said the men.

"*Now look forward and behold thy fate. Before thee . . .*"

And the gate came down.

The trolls charged.

"Tonight, we drink in Odin's hall!" shouted one

man.

"In Odin's hall," shouted the men as the trolls came on.

76

TAMMANIAN HALL LOMION CITY

YEAR 1267, 4TH AGE
1ST YEAR OF KING CARTEGIAN'S RULE
MORNING AFTER THE ROYAL WEDDING

BARUSA ALDER

Chancellor Barusa concentrated on keeping his breathing steady and acting nonchalant while he awaited the new king's arrival in the High Council chamber. His heart didn't cooperate. It pounded in his chest. The blood pulsed at his temples and neck. He sipped from the mug of mead he'd carried in. He watered it down too much. It wasn't working.

Most of the regulars were taking their seats: Bishop Tobin, that addle-pated old fart; Marshal Balfor, blustering buffoon; Slyman, the boorish guildmaster of gluttony; that wretched bastard Harkus Jhensezil; the ice queen, Lady Aramere of Dyvers; Lady Dahlia of Kern; and the Vizier — decrepit black wizard from Helheim. Some of that pathetic bunch were a bit green about the gills from swimming too deep in the wedding spirits the previous night. Embarrassing, but of little consequence. Harringgold was conspicuously absent. Probably drunker than a skunk and still in his drawers, though, in truth, he didn't know

Harringgold to be much of a drinker. They weren't accustomed to socializing together.

He hated them all. The councilors.

Corrupt. Liars. Thieves. Hawks. And more than a few, unabashed defenders of the rich at the expense of the common folk. He tolerated them, some more than others, only because he had to. Because Lomion's current political system demanded it. All too often he needed their cooperation. Their votes. Though if it were in his power, he'd banish them all from the council and appoint a new group devoid of their failings. Patriots. Men and women willing to reform the laws however needed to protect and defend the government and to help the needy.

If he could find such folk.

Even those on the council that were loyal to him, made him sick. Balfor was a toady who gave him his loyalty only because Barusa was the most powerful member of the council. He'd throw his hat in with another if someone else came to power. Slyman thought who the heck he was. Thought he was better than everyone else. Even lorded over Barusa whenever he saw an opening. Barusa knew the truth. The bastard was a fishmonger. A fishmonger! For a dozen years at least. He must have tired of the stench after a time because then he went into politics. Joined the guilds and rose up through the ranks. A self-made man. Barusa respected that. But he suspected Slyman got where he was through lies and corruption, much more so than through merit. And Barusa couldn't suffer that.

Barusa took a long swig from his mug and repeatedly tapped his foot to the floor.

New king or no, Barusa had expected that council meeting to be no different than the others of late. He'd remain in de facto control until he was officially appointed regent of the realm. He'd try to push through the scheduling of that, so that within a few weeks he'd be named. That's when he'd finally have a freer, if not free, hand to begin to change things. Change the face of Lomion. He had but a couple of weeks to think things through and plan out his approach.

But those plans derailed when he spoke to Cartegian during the wedding feast.

The new king insisted on attending the council meeting, despite it occurring the very morning after his wedding. An odd thing, but if he chose to do that rather that frolic with his new bride, so be it. The man's mind was so muddied, perhaps his plumbing was as well. Barusa never expected him to make sense. He barely paid attention to Cartegian's ramblings until the king brought up his regency. When he did, for a moment, Barusa's heart nearly stopped. He thought Cartegian was going to renege on his promise and maintain his position. But that's not what happened. Instead, Cartegian said he planned to ascend Barusa to regent of the realm immediately. That it made no sense to wait a single day. That Lomion needed his leadership. And then he muttered something about needing more time to devote to his troll and to his cat.

Barusa made him repeat the regency remarks twice, to be certain that he'd heard correctly. It was more than Barusa could ever have hoped for.

Cartegian capered in to the High Council chamber, steaming coffee mug in hand, and took his seat at the center of the councilors' mezzanine, disheveled and drooling. His face was unusually pale and sweaty. Barusa felt sorry for the Harringgold girl — to be married to that thing.

"My troll is not feeling well and needed to sleep in, making me quite late for which I apologize." Through a bout of coughing, Cartegian groped about in his pockets and pulled out a scroll, which he unfurled. "Today, I'm issuing my first edicts."

Barusa braced himself, his heart ready to burst from his chest in anticipation.

Cartegian spoke in a shrill voice, very unlike his normal. "At high noon on the morrow, in the center of Lomion Square," he said, paused, and looked around to make certain everyone was paying attention. They were. "The following citizens will be executed."

A hush came over the councilors.

"Did he say, *executed*?" said Bishop Tobin as he leaned toward Marshal Balfor.

Cartegian cleared his throat loudly and emptied his mug before continuing. "For the crimes of Regicide most foul, and high treason against the Realm," he said, "my cat must die. So must my lizard, his evil coconspirator." Cartegian looked around, his face grave. "Let no one dare challenge this decree or else suffer their same fate."

No one spoke for some moments.

"As you will, my king," said Barusa. "Appropriate arrangements will be made to carry out your commands."

Cartegian stood up, a hand on his belly, and coughed again and again. A pathetic sight.

Cartegian looked to Barusa. "Get me a Leren. Now." The king's hand came away from his face dripping red.

Blood.

"Dead gods," said Jhensezil as he rose to his feet. The others did much the same. "Get Leren Banyard," shouted someone. Guardsmen did so.

Jhensezil, Barusa, and Lady Aramere rushed to the king's side. Even Bishop Tobin shuffled over.

Cartegian dropped to his knees. A loud cough sent blood flying across the mezzanine, spraying Aramere's dress and Barusa's trousers.

"What's wrong with him?" said Slyman. "A bad piece of meat?"

"Poison," spat Jhensezil. "Get some water."

Barusa wanted to implore Cartegian to name him as regent while he still could. If not, it might be too late. But how could he? How unseemly that would be. The man was badly ill. Probably dying. To act in so self-serving a manner, at a time like that — how could he? But Mother Alder would wring his neck if he didn't. *Seize the opportunity, firstborn*, she often said.

Leren Banyard arrived a few minutes later and set to work. Cartegian had been coughing and wheezing all the while, each cough weaker but more wet sounding than the last.

After some minutes of frantic attempts to aid the king, the Leren looked up and turned toward the councilors. "He stopped breathing," he said. "His lungs are filled of blood. I've not seen anything like this before."

"Can you save him?" said Barusa.

"Only Odin himself could do that," said Leren

Banyard as he turned toward the gathered councilors. "He's gone. The king is dead."

77

PLAIN OF ENGELROTH JUTENHEIM

YEAR 1267, 4TH AGE

JUDE EOTRUS

Master Thorn's jaw clenched. He pulled himself to his feet. "Err, look here," shouted Thorn. "Headmen, by Azathoth's command, hold no magic back. Crush these heathen scum or I'll put you all on the floor."

Par Weldon stepped through the Sithian line, chanting in a loud voice. His words held power, terrible power. Jude's throat and chest vibrated with each syllable that Weldin spoke, and his hair stood on end. How his words carried at all over the din of battle, Jude could not fathom. Jude didn't know what monster Weldon was conjuring up, but he knew in his bones that it was something terrible. Something far more dangerous, far more powerful than saber cats or a herd of olyphants.

Then an arrow struck Weldon's shoulder. The breath caught in his throat. His casting interrupted. Sparks erupted all about Weldin as the magic fizzled out.

Even as Weldin turned his head to stair wide eyed at the shaft embedded in his shoulder, a second shaft struck him not two inches from the first. Weldon twisted and staggered back two steps.

Lugron charged the line. The Sithians called to him to drop back, but they didn't break their formation to step out and get him. Smart. For a shield wall to work, every man had to keep his place. The Lugron charge crashed against the Sithians.

Jude expected Weldin to get bowled over, trampled, or cut down in the first moments of the melee. Wizards were no fighters. Once you got past their magic, they were nothing.

Well, that notion was wrong. At least in Weldin's case.

He didn't go down. To the contrary, his staff spun and swung. With skill. How he did that with two arrows in his shoulder was another mystery. Jude stood tall. Tried to see as best he could over the Sithian line. Luckily he stood atop a very small rise that gave him a view — no doubt, chosen purposely by Thorn or Korrgonn.

Weldin pummeled the Lugron that came up. His staff staved the head in of one Lugron and then another. Bashed another about the jaw. Knocked the legs out from another. A quick thrust to the chest knocked one Lugron through the air, only to barrel into his fellows, taking two more down with him. Yet Weldin stood alone.

Meanwhile, the bulk of the onrushing Lugron slammed into the Sithian line. Spears and swords, axes and hammers, the fighting was thick and fierce. The Sithians held their line; kept their shield wall in place. The Lugron dead piled before them.

Jude still heard the trumpeting of the olyphants behind the ice wall, though the sounds were less. Some of them had surely fallen to Lugron or giant attacks.

In the narrow gap between Brackta's ice wall and Keevis's pit, now appeared more of the giants. The fighting thick and close with the Lugron. A troop of giants streamed through the gap battling the Lugron as they went. When they saw the expedition, most of the troop turned aside from the Lugron and rushed the Lomerians. The giants battered aside the Lugron that fought against Weldin. Each mighty stroke of a giant's club crushed a Lugron beneath it. As the wild melee swirled about, Weldin still couldn't reach the relative safety of the Sithian line. He was on his own.

Weldin smashed his staff into one giant's legs, knocking him from his feet. Next he battered aside a giant's club — the staff and the club crashing into one another. The staff should've snapped. The club's swing should have carried on and blasted Weldin across the field. But it didn't. It was the giant's club that broke. And it was the giant's head that was staved in when Weldin's next strike hit his forehead. Then some giant's club hit Weldin's shoulder and spun him around. Another club crashed across his back. Sent him flying through the air. Crashed to his knees. The giants closed in around him. To finish him.

Magic ripped into the giants and Lugron from one side and then another. Luminous missiles hit them. Stones pummeled them. Some were battered by unseen enemies. All the wizards threw what magic they had left at their attackers.

Weldin was on his back. Knees in the air. Staff gripped above him in both hands. How many strikes he'd weathered Jude couldn't say. The giants shoved each other. Jockeyed into position to pummel him to death with their clubs.

By this time, the Sithian line had fallen back. Ezerhauten barked orders. His deep powerful voice audible even amongst the chaos. The Sithians arced their line back to avoid being flanked. If they kept on with their maneuvers, they'd soon form a circle. They'd be fighting back to back again.

Stragglers reached Jude's position. Some Lugron. Some giants. They came on a few at a time. Mason and Mort Zag were there. Donnelin, Teek, and Nord didn't have to do anything. The two behemoths made short work of their enemies. Mort Zag's club killed the first two giants that stormed at him, a single strike dropped each. The third came in too quick and grabbed Mort Zag's arms. Sought to grapple with him. Throw him down. That giant was nearly as large as old Big Red. Mort Zag headbutted him. And then somehow tore the giant's arm off with a single tug. Blood washed over Mort Zag and sprayed against the dome, temporarily obscuring Jude's view. That blood sizzled and burned off in seconds. The dome wasn't hot. Not to Jude's touch anyway. So why that happened didn't make sense. Nothing did anymore.

Jude looked for Weldin. Tried to spot him through the melee. He couldn't see him. But giants still flocked about the spot that he'd been. Attacking something on the ground. No doubt, smashing whatever was left of Weldon to mush.

Then Jude heard a thunderous snapping sound, as if an enormous tree broke in two under a hurricane wind. Then all at once, there was a flash of light. Fire. Heat. A blast of air. And everything went dark.

78

THE REGENT'S EXPEDITIONARY FORCE (THE ALDER BRIGADE)

YEAR 1267, 4TH AGE

Gar Pullman and his troop, supported by Boddrick, Dirk, and their bunch, were on point, out in front of the Eotrus bannermen. They made their way on horseback toward the edge of the tree line on the southern approach to Dor Eotrus. From there, they'd get a look at the surrounds.

The wood was quiet.

The Dor was quieter.

An outrider made his report. Said the Dor was dead — as far as he could see from the tree line. No sign of anyone or anything moving.

Pullman and the others rode on, stopped at the edge of the tree line. Wary. It didn't feel right.

The great open fields around the Dor lay empty, save for trampled tents, abandoned wagons, and broken weapons strewn about where the Alder brigade had camped. The road, deserted. No mounds of dead were heaped in the fields or about the campsite. No wandering or fallen mounts. No dead at all. Someone had taken all the bodies. There should have been hundreds.

The walls of the Outer Dor were intact. Smoke wafted in gray tendrils from several spots in the Outer Dor and from the citadel, but no fires raged. The place stood quiet, save for the calls of birds that circled the fortress and flitted about roofs. Hundreds of them. Maybe a thousand. Crows mostly. Vultures too.

The wind turned.

Then they smelled it.

Death.

All too familiar to men like Pullman and Boddrick.

"The south gates to the Outer Dor are closed," said Dirk. "They look intact."

"Must have climbed it, as the old wizard said," said Boddrick. "The stinking sneaky bastards. Maybe they finished off the Eotrus and headed home."

"Maybe," said Pullman.

***

"Get that gate open," said Lord Ogden, "and scout about. I'll not stumble our army into a trap. We need to know what's going on in there."

"We're not under your command," said Dirk. "We're Alders. These men work for me."

"Not anymore," said Ogden. "I've conscripted Pullman and his band. And you too. We're in wartime now, son. Different rules. Get in line and do as you're told. If you don't, I will make an example of you. Do you understand?"

Dirk went pale as milk. His mouth opened, no words dropped out. He managed a nod. Barely.

"I'll get the gate opened," said Pullman. "Just don't leave me hanging over there."

***

Bithel the Piper climbed the Outer Dor's wall before anyone could set a grappling hook over it. How he managed it, no man could say, even though he did it in plain sight. Pullman figured the fellow had a bit of magic in him. But maybe he just had the skill. Some men had all sorts of special talents.

Bithel dropped low behind the parapet and skulked. A few minutes later, he bounced up and signaled the all clear. He dropped some ropes and more men scurried up the wall. They had the gate opened in less than ten minutes. It only took that long because they couldn't figure out how to operate the mechanism. The northerners built differently than folks from the city and parts south.

The streets were deserted.

Word was sent back that the gate was open and clear. Ogden sent up an order to reconnoiter the Outer Dor.

"He's not bringing his troops up until he knows what's what," said Bald Boddrick. "Stinking northerners think they can use us as fodder."

"I'd have done the same in his position," said Pullman.

"So what do we do?" said Dirk. "If the trolls are still here, eventually, we'll find them. Then we're dead."

"I expect that's what old Lord Graybeard has in mind," said Pullman.

"We can't clear the town building to building," said Boddrick. "We don't have enough men. If we blunder forward, they could encircle us. This is the shit."

"We'll stand half our force here," said Pullman. "We'll search all the nearby buildings while we send scouts down each main road; the scouts to meet up at the citadel gates."

"That's suicide for the scouts," said Boddrick.

"Not if they're quick enough," said Pullman. "Or tough enough. You got the stones for the duty, Boddrick?"

Boddrick's face darkened. "Second time this week someone's questioned my courage. I didn't take it from Rom Alder. I'll not take it from you."

"You'll go then?" said Pullman.

"I'll go."

The building to building search turned up nothing but a lot of wreckage. The trolls had rampaged through every shop, every home, every room. The place was battered. But not very bloody. No bodies. No sign of life or death — save a lingering stink of the trolls inside the buildings. And a more potent death scent in the outside air. The scouts went unmolested to the citadel walls. That's where they found the trolls' handiwork. And the troll dead.

The base of the citadel wall smoked and smoldered. A hundred troll corpses, most burned crispy, others pincushioned with arrows, littered the area. The trolls had taken their losses getting over the walls. But they'd done their damage. They had people's heads mounted on pikes. Dozens of them. The area before the main gate was still soaked with blood. Volsung blood. Broken, headless bodies lay strewn there. The bones broken, limbs torn off. A wicked sight of butchery. Savagery. Evil.

Bithel did his climb again. This time it was harder, the wall taller. He had to slink down twice and restart at another spot before he found a path up that he could manage. It took time.

While he made the climb, Pullman's men were still going through the buildings, having checked only a fraction of the Outer Dor. They tried their best to sniff out the trolls, but found not a one. Pullman became convinced that if they weren't all hold up in one spot for some reason, that there weren't any trolls left in the Outer Dor.

As he reached the top of the Citadel's wall, Bithel popped his head over the crenel, then jerked back down in a panic. A half second later, a hand came over the wall and grabbed Bithel by the collar. Lifted him up. A troll.

Bithel's dirk was out in a flash. As the thing pulled him over, he stabbed it through the chest. The troll lunged, pulled Bithel to its jaws, and sank its teeth into his neck. Even as it did so, Sentry of Allendale put an arrow through the troll's forehead. Blood sprayed from Bithel's neck. The troll dropped him and fell out of sight. Bithel's arms flailed as he tried to grab hold of the crenel. He didn't manage it. Fell straight down to the base of the wall. Sixty feet. Landed flat on his back with a sickening crunch. He lay there quivering and gurgling. Blood coming from every orifice. Then a dozen trolls appeared along the battlements. A second later, there were fifty of them.

79

DOR EOTRUS THE UNDERHALLS

YEAR 1267, 4TH AGE

SARBEK DU MARTEGRAN

Ector held a large hand axe in one hand, a big battle shield that reached from chin to toe in the other. He wore his full plate armor, chainmail underneath, helmet, boots, cape, the works. His father had that armor made for him the previous winter. It was forged from stout Lomerian metal, worked by the Dor's own smiths. Emblazoned on his tabard was the Eotrus sigil; on his shield, the sigil of the Tyrian Knights, his patron order.

Sarbek was clad much the same, though his armor was even heavier owing to the style of the Odion Order of knights to which he belonged. Similarly clad were all the knights of the Dor. Even Captain Pellan, though her armor was ill fitting since it was not custom made for her, but rather, pieced together out of spare bits from the armory.

When the trolls burst through to the Sixth Underhall, the Eotrus knights met them with spears to stab them, and nets to trip them up and slow them. Sarbek saw the fall of that last gate coming and made certain to pull Ector far back. He didn't want him anywhere near the front line. Not that it mattered. They'd die no matter where they were. He knew that. But Sarbek wanted to delay the inevitable. He held out hope of some deliverance not destined to come. He told Ector to stick close to him, if he could. They both knew that in the chaos of battle that would be difficult. Only the close confines of the Underhall made it possible at all.

***

ECTOR EOTRUS

Though two hundred men, battle hardened, and packed shoulder to shoulder, stood between Ector and the rampaging trolls, it was not more than one minute after the battle began before the first troll reached him.

The things bounded over one another in their eagerness to get at the Eotrus. So too did they bound over and past many of the Eotrus soldiers. They lunged headlong, oblivious of the weapons that gouged them. If they had a purpose in that tactic, it was to break the Eotrus line. To break their discipline. To send them into a rout. And then take them down one by one from behind. That was troll tactics.

The Eotrus knew better.

They'd not fought on the trolls' terms yet, and they'd not start now. They kept their formations. They fought as a unit. Their opponents had a fraction of their martial skill, but far superior strength, speed, and energy. The Eotrus gear and tactics were defensive. Not so focused on killing the trolls were they, but rather on preventing being killed by them.

The trolls pounded the Eotrus shields. Tore at their armor. For all the trolls' strength, the Eotrus men were well protected. But the trolls never gave up and there seemed no end to them. Ector didn't even have time to take a swing at the first troll that bounded by him, crashing past the men that stood at his side. A few moments later, another troll appeared. This time it was closer. And Ector was ready. He slammed his axe's blade against the back of the troll's neck as it barreled past. The thing faltered, stumbled, and dropped to one knee as blood gushed from its wound. Two spearmen skewered it. Then Pellan crushed its skull with her hammer. Ector was happy to have the beardless dwarf fighting next to him. She was as tough as anyone he'd ever known.

More trolls came on. They pushed through the Eotrus lines. Ector saw Sarbek block one's path.

Sarbek bashed it. Again and again.

The troll lunged for the castellan's throat.

Sarbek grabbed it. Hoisted it up. Slammed it down on its back. The thing was stunned. The wind knocked out of it.

Ector marveled at Sarbek's strength.

Sarbek dropped his knee to the trolls' chest. Shoved his dagger up under its throat. Sank it to the hilt. Three other men stuck their spears in it.

Ector watched more and more of the knights up front falter. When it was several Eotrus soldiers against each troll, the men won. But one on one, not many of the soldiers could stand against the troll.

And so, one by one, they died.

And the trolls pushed their way through.

During a brief respite, Ector caught his breath. His heart pounded in his chest. Veins pumping. Thumping. Threatening to burst at this throat. He struggled to keep his breathing steady. Struggled not to puke. He wanted to run. To get out of there. Find some hole to hide in. One of those secret rooms that he and his brothers had snooped out. But he held his ground. Did his duty. Just as his father would've wanted. Sarbek was near him. So was Pellan. Many others. He wasn't alone. He wouldn't die alone.

He stood fast.

Some few knights from the front lines staggered toward him. Wounded. Bleeding. To no one in particular, they pleaded for help; tried to get clear of the action.

Some few others turned tail and ran for it.

And then the trolls were everywhere. In front of Ector. On his flanks. Behind. There was fighting on all sides.

Ector slammed his axe into a troll's neck — the one who was fighting Sarbek.

Then he did the same to one who fought against Pellan.

Then one came at him. A big one. Well, bigger than most.

Raked his shield with its claws, it did.

Once.

Twice.

A third time.

The fourth strike sent its razored claws through the shield. The elaborate crossguard spared his arm.

He brought his axe down on the troll's

forehead. It sunk deep. Stuck. And the troll kept fighting. Ector let go the axe. He tried to bash the troll with his shield, but the troll was too strong. The shield too heavy. He fumbled for the second short axe at his belt. Thank Sarbek that he had it. The old man insisted he carry two axes, a hand hammer, and a long dagger. *To Helheim with the extra weight*, he'd said. "*We're not going hiking, boy, we're headed for a knife fight.*"

The troll battered his shield to the side.

Its claws laid into his shoulder armor. Nearly tore it off.

Ector stumbled but recovered. He slashed the axe from right to left. Aimed at the troll's throat.

Its arm blocked the blow. The impact so powerful, Ector's arm went partly numb. He barely kept hold of the axe. Backpedaled into the wall. Got the shield between him and the troll.

Its claws raked. Tore chunks out of the shield.

Ector dropped the axe. Pulled his dagger. Gripped it as tightly as he could. Lunged. Stabbed the troll through the neck.

Its claws caught his breastplate. Metal rent. The thing lifted him effortlessly. Ector flew through the air. Slammed into the wall. The impact rattled him, but did little harm. The claws had to have gone through his armor. Only the chainmail shirt and padding below had spared him.

The troll pawed at the dagger embedded in its throat. It was a long wide blade. It went all the way through. Half severed the troll's head.

Ector pulled his hammer from his belt. Down to his last weapon and the battle had just started. It raged around him. Men and trolls were dying on all sides. For that brief moment, no other troll was too close. So Ector stepped forward. Bashed the troll in the face with this shield.

He stepped forward again. Bashed it atop the head with his hammer.

The troll didn't seem to notice. It was still worried about the dagger in its neck.

Ector hit it again.

And again.

At the fourth blow, its skull shattered. Blood and brains ran free.

Somehow Ector managed to grab the dagger from the troll's throat as it fell. His hammer dangled from its wrist strap.

Then another troll came at Ector.

Sarbek cut its head off with a broad swing of his sword. He'd lost his axe as well.

Bodies heaped on all sides.

Men screamed.

Trolls cursed, or so it sounded.

The floor was slick with blood and gore. The stench of innards filled the corridor.

Pellan held a short two-handed pole arm with a long narrow blade on each end. She whipped it from side to side. Up and down. The trolls fell back from her, limbs dangling, torsos torn open.

Another wave of trolls vaulted toward Ector. He was in the middle of a corridor. Far from where he'd started. How exactly he'd got there, he didn't know. A dozen trolls came toward him. No one to stop them.

Then something grabbed him. Dragged him to the side. A grip too powerful to resist. He twisted. Made ready to thrust his dagger. But it was Sarbek. He pulled him through a doorway. Pellan jumped through a step behind him. Two other knights already inside slammed the door closed and threw a deadbolt into place. Other men rolled a barrel in front of the door.

Ector looked around. Besides, he, Sarbek, and Pellan, there were four knights in the room — a storage room of moderate size, filled with boxes — and four men-at-arms. A couple of the men were badly battered, but the rest seemed intact, if exhausted. Every one of them was bloody. Sarbek more than the others, save for Pellan who was covered in red, head to toe. Those two had done far more than their share of damage to the troll.

The door shuddered and buckled.

There was nothing more they could block the door with. Two barrels. All the other crates were too flimsy to be of use. Ector looked around. Hoped that this was a room with a secret chamber. But it wasn't. Just a random supply closet. There was no way out save for the way they'd come in.

"Ready yourselves," said Pellan. "They'll be on us in a moment. Fight back to back. Stand close."

"You hurt, boy?" said Sarbek as he looked him up and down. He barely got the words out, so winded was he, nearly doubled over.

"I'm fine," said Ector.

"Good lad," said Sarbek. "Good lad. Your father would be proud. You've showed the gods your quality today. We all have." He raised his voice so that all the soldiers with him could hear. "Rejoice, my laddies, for we've earned our places. Tonight we drink in Odin's halls with Lord Aradon and our forefathers."

And then the trolls burst in.

80

DOR LOMION
LOMION CITY

YEAR 1267, 4TH AGE
1ST YEAR OF KING CARTEGIAN'S RULE
MORNING OF THE WEDDING DAY

MARISSA HARRINGGOLD

"This is supposed to be the happiest day of my life," said Marissa. She watched a tear roll down her cheek as she sat before the mirror in her chambers, the room filled of silk and lace, fluffy pillows, all pinks and whites.

Brithhilda, her withered servant, listened attentively, nodding, her face filled of sympathy as she brushed Marissa's hair.

"My wedding day. Every girl's dream is to marry a prince. For me it's a nightmare. He's a beast. Out of his mind. Disgusting. He drools over himself. All his shirts are stained of it. Did you notice that?"

"One can hardly miss it," said Brithhilda.

"And the stench," said Marissa. "I don't think he bathes. And now I have to have him near me. Touching me. The same bed. I don't care what my father says, I don't want to endure this. I don't deserve it. You're being too rough with the brush."

"Sorry, the tangles are terrible today," said

Brithhilda. "Dearest, I pray for your happiness and safety above all things, but as the Arch-Duke's daughter you have a duty to the realm. A duty that must take precedence over all else."

"You sound like father."

"The common folk don't understand how hard it is to be a noblewoman of high station," said Brithhilda. "So much harder still to be queen."

"It's all going to be for naught," said Marissa. "Father says Cartegian will name Chancellor Barusa the regent of the realm. Cartegian will only be a figurehead. And me less than that. So what am I sacrificing my happiness for? My future? Father says the chancellor's policies are destroying Lomion. Bankrupting the realm. Stealing our freedoms. I don't know a fraction as much about politics and government as do the High Councilors, but I could do better for Lomion than the chancellor."

"Can you convince Cartegian not to name Barusa regent?"

"I've barely spoken to him. I don't know how he'll react if I tried."

"I know well the Alders' reputation," said Brithhilda. "Once they grab power they don't let go. Ever."

"But when I have a child and she comes of age. . ."

Brithhilda shook her head. "Mother Alder will never yield back that power. If the child resists her influence, the Alders will have her killed."

"Never," said Marissa, her eyes wide, face in a panic. "Chancellor Barusa would not dare. A child!"

"The Alders have done worse, my dear," said

Brithhilda. "Your father has shielded you in this tower from much of the evil of the world. People are capable of terrible deeds in their pursuit of wealth and power."

"Then I am lost," said Marissa. "And Lomion is lost."

Brithhilda struggled to pull the brush through a particularly stubborn knot.

"If only you could rule as queen," she said, "that would change everything."

"How could that happen?" said Marissa.

"Oh, dearest, it's of no matter; it could never happen."

"Tell me," said Marissa.

"One way would be if Cartegian named you regent instead of the chancellor. The other. . . "

"What other way? Tell me."

"It can't happen," said Brithhilda. "He's too young and seemingly healthy — of body at least."

"You mean if he were dead?"

Brithhilda lowered her voice to a whisper. "If Cartegian no longer walked Midgaard, you would be queen. You would be safe, you would rule, and the realm would be spared from his madness and Barusa's treachery. It's a terrible thing to speak of, but if it happened, imagine the good that you could do?"

"I must try to convince him to not name Barusa to be regent," said Marissa.

"Yes, I agree. You must."

"But if I fail, then what?"

"Then, as you said, Lomion is lost."

"And me? And my future children?"

They were quiet for some moments, Brithhilda continuing to brush, though all the knots were long since out.

"I'm going to have to kill him, aren't I? To save the realm. To save myself and my children. That's the only solution. That's what you're telling me, isn't it?"

"I would never suggest such a thing," said Brithhilda. "We were merely making idle talk, my dear."

"Will you help me?" said Marissa, more tears in her eyes. "With more idle talk?"

"Always, dearest."

"The Black Hand? Is that how I would do this, if I was going to?"

"If you were to contemplate such a course of action, there must be no chance it could ever be traced back to you. An assassin would leave a trail."

"Then how?"

"There is a potion. An elixir from the far east that has no effects for many hours, then kills very quickly after the onset of symptoms. Mixed with wine or mead it is tasteless."

"So if he drank it with me, but then was fine for many hours—"

"Then no one would know it was you that gave it to him," said Brithhilda.

"Buying such a potion would leave a trail," said Marissa. "I can't believe we're even talking about such things."

"Have you forgotten, I am an herbalist?" said Brithhilda. "I have treated your hurts and ills since your birth, have I not? I can brew the potion, if it is your will."

Marissa paused for some moments, thinking. "You must. Yes. Brew it. But I will only consider using it if all else fails. I can't believe that I'm doing this. I've never harmed anyone in my life. And now this? To murder him? The king? My husband? How could I?"

"If you must do it, you do it for the realm. To save Lomion. A queen often carries a weighty burden. This one is yours. But you are not alone. I will help you in this. In all things."

81

PLAIN OF ENGELROTH JUTENHEIM

YEAR 1267, 4TH AGE

JUDE EOTRUS

Teek Lugron spit blood from his mouth. More blood trickled from his nose and his ear. "Wake up, Judy boy," he said.

Jude felt a weight upon him, someone shaking him. Opened his eyes. Thorn was atop him. Scrambling to get off and up.

"Err, violation here," said Thorn. "This is not acceptable."

Teek pulled Jude away from Thorn.

The green dome was down.

Everyone was down. Except for Korrgonn. He stood just behind Jude. Mort Zag was just in front of Jude and blocked most of his view. The red giant convulsed, shaking from head to toe and with a grunt bounced up to a sitting position.

Jude looked around in amazement.

"That's right," said Teek as Jude took in the scene about them. "We're into it now, Judy boy. Piled high and deep." Devastation all around. Every member of the expedition was down. All the Lugron and the giants within the circle formed by the pits and the ice wall — down. Dead. Torn to pieces. Burning. Ashes. Smoke. But the expedition's men were not burned. Not torn up. Just battered. Knocked down. Many unconscious. The rest groggy. But not dead.

The closest giants just across the pit were down too. Dead. Those farther away were injured, singed, burned, but alive. Those farther back still were growling and howling and making their way toward the gap. Brackta's ice wall was deeply pitted, cracked. Great chunks were broken. Sections of it were melting into pools of water. Badly gutted was it, but the ice wall still stood. A small breach or two here and there, but it still stood. Still there too, the trumpeting of a single olyphant that still battled the Lugron horde.

Jude wasn't hurt. His eyes were clear and focused. All his limbs responded. No great pain anywhere. He didn't know why he'd blacked out. His head didn't hurt. He reached up. Touched his black hair, the back of his neck. No blood. No bump. No tender spots. He was okay.

He saw Ezerhauten pull himself to his feet. The man looked unsteady. Dazed. Battered. But where the others still lay sprawled, Ezerhauten was up and getting ready to fight.

Jude realized then that it was Thorn's green dome of magic that had protected him and those few around him from the brunt of whatever had happened.

Even Mason was bowled over by whatever hit them. After the giant man of stone stood up, Nord was revealed beneath. Crushed to pulp when Mason fell upon him.

"Err, you great lumbering simpleton," spat Thorn at Mason. "I'll put you right on the floor."

The pasty-faced wizard advanced on Mason and punched him in the gut. No jab was that. A hard punch. All the old wizard's strength behind it. Mason's gut, same as the rest of him, was solid stone. The blow should have injured Thorn's hand. Maybe broken it. Given Mason's enormous mass, he should have been unmoved by the punch, regardless of the power behind it.

But oh, did he move!

Mason doubled over in the air as he flew backward some dozen feet. Hit the ground hard.

"You killed him, you moron," said Thorn. "My loyal servant. Nord. You killed him. Stinking elven creation. We never should have taken you into our service."

Par Keld appeared. His lip split and bloodied. Face covered in dust and grime. "I told you not to trust the elf and his creature. I warned you. No one listens to me. But now you see, don't you?"

"Master Jude," said Donnelin. "Are you hurt?"

Donnelin's face was bloodied and pale.

"Are you?" said Jude.

"The dome blocked most of it," said Donnelin.

"What happened?" said Jude.

"Retributive strike," said Donnelin. "An archwizard's parting shot. They break their staff or whatever the foci of their magic is. It releases all their energy at once. It kills them but takes out whoever was about to do them in—"

Jude started and turned about.

"It wasn't her," said Donnelin. "It was Weldin."

Jude started toward the fallen Sithian line. He was going to find Brackta. Help her.

Mort Zag grabbed him about the collar. "Don't move, manling. Remain next to Lord Korrgonn as you were bidden."

Jude thought to make a run for it. He couldn't outfight Big Red, but he might be able to outrun him. Problem was, there was nowhere to run to. They were entrapped between ice wall and bottomless pit. The only exit soon to be filled with more Lugron or giants or both. There was no escape. Not for him. Not for any of them.

Ezerhauten was shouting and cursing. "Get up if you want to live," he said as he pulled one of his men to his feet. "Get the wizards up. They're still coming. This isn't over."

By the time the Lugron charged anew into the breach, Ezerhauten had more than half his company on their feet and in fighting position. Though more than a few looked unsteady on their feet. Jude saw Brackta. She seemed unharmed, just dazed. She looked for him. Made eye contact and gifted him with the slightest of nods, no more than that, and even that was too much. Too many others to notice.

Ginalli was praying aloud. Some invocation of Azathoth's power and blessing. Thorn still hovered over Nord, glaring at Mason, as if he had forgotten where they were, what was going on.

Korrgonn stood stoic, staring in the direction of the gap. The orb's chest still lay at his feet. Just as he had been so often lately, the son of Azathoth was distant. Vacant. As if in a trance.

"They're coming over the ice walls," shouted Donnelin. The Lugron. Some decided not to wait in line to run through the gap and into the meat grinder that Ezerhauten and the League wizards had assembled. They scaled the ice wall: ropes and pick axes.

"They'll be all around us in a few minutes," said Donnelin.

Then to Jude's surprise, Ezerhauten and his men charged!

They ran straight for the wide breach betwixt ice wall and rift. Fifty feet wide was that gap. Might as well have been a mile.

"He doesn't have enough men," said Jude.

"He's got guts," said Donnelin. "Your father would have done the same."

"No he wouldn't," said Jude. "They can't hold the gap with so few. It's suicide."

"He's not trying to hold," said Donnelin. "He's trying to rout them. Put the fear in them at last. And off they'll go. Probably our best chance."

Jude watched as more of Ezerhauten's men dragged themselves to their feet and staggered after their fellows.

"Brave men," muttered Jude. "Damn brave men."

Par Brackta, Par Rhund, and Stev Keevis stood together amongst the heaped dead where the skirmish line had been. A few Lomerian Lugron stood with him — no doubt, they had no interest to stand with the Sithians in the breach.

"Look here, now," said Thorn. "Everyone up," although everyone around him that wasn't dead was already up. "We're moving. Make speed for that gap and support the mercenaries."

Thorn took off, striding along in his strange fashion — as if he floated rather than walked. Ginalli was at his side. Par Keld followed behind muttering to himself. Korrgonn came next flanked by Mason and Mort Zag. This time, Korrgonn carried the Orb's chest himself. And Mort Zag kept one eye on Jude and Donnelin. Teek kept both eyes on them.

As they reached the skirmish line, Jude saw Weldin. What was left of him. He looked as if he'd turned to ash. His features were still there, recognizable. Even his clothes. But instead of flesh and bone, he was on nothing but a heap of gray-black ash in the shape of a man.

"Dead gods," said Jude.

"That my boy," said Donnelin, "is the *Wizards Toll*."

82

DOR EOTRUS THE UNDERHALLS

YEAR 1267, 4TH AGE

ECTOR EOTRUS

Ector, Sarbek, Pellan, and their small band fought like madmen. They let the berserker rage of the Northmen take them.

All hope was gone.

All chance of victory.

Any chance of survival.

The only unknown was the moment of their deaths.

Their only endeavor, to take as many trolls with them as they could.

Ector's shield was torn from his arm soon after the trolls burst in. His armor kept him alive long enough to pull his dagger. He worked hammer in one hand, dagger in the other. His arms were numb and on fire, both at once. The strength of his blows diminished with every strike, his arms more weary than they had ever been. All he knew then was that he had to keep fighting, striving his hardest against the enemy for every moment until they struck him down.

He had to die fighting.

He could not yield. Not give up. Not collapse in fatigue. Not drop his arms and wait for the fatal blow to be struck. He had to fight to the last. Only that way could he guarantee his place in Odin's hall, and once again sit at his father's side. And so he fought. Blind with sweat, blood, tears, he fought. The trolls pounded and pummeled him. But for the heavy plate and chain, he'd have been dead a hundred times over. But the armor held. He knew we was hurt. Bleeding from any number of wounds, but nothing had hit any vitals. Nothing had yet disabled him.

He knew that some of the others fought on around him. He heard them. Saw the blur of motion as they did their dance of death with the trolls, but he could not take his eyes from his opponents for even a moment to assess the situation.

It didn't matter.

Nothing mattered.

His life was over.

All that mattered now was achieving a warrior's death.

And then the trolls had him up against the wall.

They tore at him.

Tried to bite his throat.

One hand was pinned. The other, stabbed wildly with his dagger.

A great roar. "Not on my watch!" shouted Sarbek. He swung his Odion blade back and forth.

Slashed one troll.

Sliced the next.

They pounced on him.

Pulled him down.

Ector lunged. Stabbed with his dagger. Stabbed again.

Again.
Again.
Again.
Something came down on the back of Ector's head.
His world went dark.
Valhalla beckoned.

83

DOR LOMION LOMION CITY

YEAR 1267, 4TH AGE
1ST YEAR OF KING CARTEGIAN'S RULE
THE DAY AFTER THE WEDDING,
AFTERNOON

MARISSA HARRINGGOLD

Marissa stared at her face in the mirror as she sat at her makeup table. Her cheeks were red, but the tears had stopped. She figured that there wasn't any more water left in there, though she felt like crying more all the same. She didn't understand what had happened, though she felt much of it was her fault. Her fault.

Cartegian was dead. That's what she wanted. It worked out just as she had planned. No, to call it a plan was to make too little of it. To minimize her crime. She'd carried it out. She killed him. Laced his drink with the poison that Brithhilda had brewed up. She gave it to him. He drank it without a thought. Why wouldn't he? And the next morning — the very morning after their wedding day, he took sick, and in but a few short minutes, fell dead. She had murdered him just as surely as if she'd plunged a blade through his heart. She was a murderer. A killer. A cold-blooded killer.

She had done it in self defense. And in defense of the realm. Not for anything that Cartegian had done — but for all that she knew or feared that he would do.

Lomion could not have a madman on the throne. Nor could it afford an Alder as a regent. Brithhilda had convinced her that if Chancellor Barusa were regent, he and his House would not relinquish power when any child she had birthed came of age. And that the Alders may well kill her child to maintain their position. That they'd done as bad or worse in the past.

She couldn't bear the thought of that — her child in danger. Couldn't allow for that possibility. That's what she told herself a hundred times. But she knew that that wasn't the whole truth. It wasn't the main reason for her crime. The main was that she didn't want to be married to a disgusting madman. Didn't want his hands on her. Didn't want him doing things to her. The thought of that made her want to vomit. Made her angry enough and frightened enough to kill.

Marissa recalled the fear she felt when the wedding feast was over and she and Cartegian retired to her chambers in Dor Lomion for the night. Her legs shook as she walked beside him. She was sweating, but her mouth went dry and she held back nausea. She didn't know what he'd do to her. How bad it would be. But she knew it would be bad. Terrible. He might even kill her.

Except that he didn't kill her. Didn't harm her at all. As soon as they were alone, locked within her chambers, he was so different. Like a different person. His eyes were clear, his words made sense. His voice was normal, not the nasally wail that was his usual. He acted like a normal man. Intelligent. Thoughtful. Kind. It was a surprise to her. A shock. He was more concerned for her feelings than anything else.

She tried to make sense of it. She'd heard that there were brief episodes when he was lucid. When his affliction fled. But that the madness always soon returned. She figured that she was lucky. That for their first night together, he was sane. He'd not harm her. But she feared it wouldn't even last the night. That he'd suddenly revert to his lunatic ways. That he'd beat her. Take her against her will. Abuse her.

Except that he didn't. In fact, he told her —he promised her — that he would never harm her. That he'd protect her with his life.

Could that be? Or would the promise last only minutes or hours until the madness was upon him once again?

He didn't force himself upon her. He could have. She would have allowed him to if he'd been gentle enough about it. But he told her that he hoped that in time they'd grow to care deeply for each other. That he hoped that in the end, this would be much more than a marriage of convenience. One of love. He said that he intended to take things slowly. As slowly as they both wanted. He would never pressure her, or force himself upon her. He wouldn't even so much as touch her, unless she gave him leave. Marissa was in such shock at hearing those words coming from him, she couldn't believe it. She would have cried just hearing that. The relief that she should have felt — overwhelming.

But instead, all she felt was guilt.

She'd already poisoned him.

There was no undoing it.

Brithhilda had made it clear that there was no cure for that poison.

She murdered him.

Her husband.

Her king.

For nothing.

Nothing.

And as they spoke, or rather, as he spoke, since she was so torn inside she could get no words out, she found herself wishing that his madness would return. That his eyes would go wild and unfocused. That he'd start capering about the way he did. She even hoped that he'd grow angry. Abusive. That he'd hit her. Hurt her. She'd bear it. She'd bear it knowing that she'd done the right thing with the poison. That she'd done what she had to do. And that he deserved it.

Except that he didn't. He didn't revert. He stayed calm and lucid and thoughtful throughout the evening. He told her many things. Small talk mostly. Things he liked. Food. Music. Art. Shops. History.

He tried to find common ground with her. But she was so torn with guilt and fear she only half listened to his words. Hardly responded at all. She remembered the main topics he'd brought up, but few of the details. And it was clear enough to her that Cartegian had sensed her fear, her trepidation. He must have thought that she was terrified of him. Of his madness. He kept reassuring her that she was safe. That he wouldn't harm her.

At last, he gave up.

He said that there were many things about himself, about his father, about the realm, that he wanted to explain to her, to confide in her about, but that it would wait until she was comfortable with him. Until she was ready to listen. Until she trusted him.

Now that would never happen. Whatever secrets or ideas that he had, he took to his grave with him.

The thought came to her that maybe, just maybe, he wasn't a madman at all. That it was all an act. An act that he put on for some purpose of his own. She tried her best to banish that thought from her mind. That couldn't be the truth. It couldn't be. For if it were, that would make her crime all the more horrible.

And now, after all that, her beloved father lies sick, perhaps dying. No, he couldn't be dying. He couldn't be. She wouldn't accept that as a possibility. He'd be up and around in a day or two, back to his normal self. He had to be.

But Brithhilda was dead. There was no denying that.

Murdered.

Stuffed into her own closet.

Brithhilda had been more than a chambermaid. She'd been a close friend. Confidant. Teacher. Adviser. She loved Brithhilda. And Brithhilda loved her.

And Brithhilda was dead.

All that happening at once could not be mere coincidence.

She felt certain that her father had been poisoned. She didn't want to think about it, but she had to. She had to think it through. Find answers. Put her fears and her guilt aside.

He was poisoned by the same foul potion that she had slipped Cartegian. That was the truth of it. It wasn't certain. But she believed it. By luck or some such, her father must have received a smaller dosage, or else he had some natural resistance to the poison's effects.

Was she responsible for her father being poisoned too? If it were the same brew, then yes, it was her fault. She'd had Brithhilda brew it. If she hadn't told her to, the poison wouldn't have existed. But who could have given it to him? Surely it wasn't Brithhilda. She loved him. She was devoted to them both. To the House.

Marissa concluded that one way or another, it was all her own fault. How could she live with herself if her father died?

She had to tell someone.

Her guilt. How could she bear it?

How could Grim and the guards catch the person who poisoned her father and killed Brithhilda if she withheld information? By doing so, wasn't she making things worse? Compounding her crime?

She had to confess. Or to confide. But to whom? Grim or someone else? It would mean the end of her.

Regicide. Punishable by death.

Then the realm would be without a queen. And again, that would put the Alders in power; half of what she wanted to avoid.

What to do?

Dead gods, what to do?

Then came a knock on her door. It was Grim.

She tried to send him away but he said he had news about her father so she gave him leave to enter. The guards were still outside. Several of them. All men of The Fearless: Balkind the Bowman; Jak the blademan; Blue Ben; the Rage.

Leren Trak was with Grim. There was no smile on his face. *No!*

They'd come to tell her that father was dead!

The world grew dark and she felt herself falling.

84

SVARTLEHEIM CAVERNS JUTENHEIM

YEAR 1267, 4TH AGE

FREM SORLONS

Ma-Grak Stowron went straight at the Black Elven champion long before Frem could reach him. Ma-Grak's sword slashed by at blazing speed. A blur it was. The Elf's blade, just as fast. A black blade was the Elf's, dark as midnight, and nearly as long as Ma-Grak's. The elfin prince fought wildly, but with skill.

A match to the Stowron captain.

The other Elfs pulled back to let the titans battle. The Sithians did the same. Frem moved down the steps. If Ma-Grak fell, he'd be there to take his place.

A full minute they dueled. Stab and strike, slash and whirl. Jump and dodge. Parry and duck. Around and around they fought, up the stair and down.

Then of a sudden, the Black Elven prince stepped back. Clutched at his throat. Blood sprayed from betwixt his fingers. The elfin horde gasped. The prince raised his sword one last time. Ma-Grak brushed it aside; then kicked him in the midsection. The Elf doubled over. Ma-Grak's blade came down hard. Took the top four inches off the

Elf's head. He collapsed face forward to the steps.

A great groan went up amongst the elfin ranks. A sound that spoke of shock and sadness.

As quickly as they came, the Elfs melted back down the stairs. This time, silent, save for the muted sounds of their scurrying feet.

Frem guessed, a hundred dead elfs polluted that stair, including those that Sevare's sorcery had brought down.

How many fled? Frem couldn't say. Hundreds certainly. Their horde stretched down the stair for as far as Frem could see.

Trooper Drift was down. Bleeding out from slashes to his thigh and upper arms. The Pointmen applied pressure. Tried to bind his wounds. He'd lost too much blood.

Frem knelt down beside him.

"Will I drink in Odin's hall tonight, Captain?" said Drift, his voice weak and raspy.

"You've earned your place," said Frem. "You gave them what for, you did."

"I did, didn't I," said Drift managing a smile. And with that, Drift closed his eyes. Didn't open them again.

"You think they'll come again, Captain?" said Putnam.

"No," said Frem. "Their champion is dead. Their wizards. They don't stand a chance against us, their numbers be damned. Not on this stair. Not with us holding fast the high ground. They know that now. I think we've seen the last of them."

That's when the drums started. The booming sound of many drums in the deep. They heard the howling. A chorus of voices. Dark Elven voices.

The last of Svartleheim. How many of them, no man could say. Save that there were far more than before. The sounds came from different directions down below. As if more troops of Elfs were arriving from different passages. The whole horde of the Black Elven nation was converging on the base of the great stair. All to seek their bloody revenge on Frem and his small band.

"Them buggers got more fight left in them, it seems," said Putnam.

"Why don't they give up?" said Frem. "They started this. They came at us. Jumped us. Murdered our men. We were just passing through these darned tunnels."

Frem looked up the steps at his men. Some at the back were still fresh, considering. Many of them had not gotten into the last fight, given the tight confines of the stair. But most of the men were breathing heavily, dripping with sweat. Most of their energy spent. Most were on their rumps, taking what little ease they could, while they could.

They were in no good condition for another skirmish. Especially not another where they were heavily outnumbered.

Then the very stair shook. They heard a rumbling. A stony sound from far below.

"Lex, Torak," shouted Frem to the men near the front line, "what do you see?"

Both men peered over the edge of the stair, straining this way and that. Ma-Grak did the same.

"Hundreds of Elfs," said Lex.

"They got more of them rock monster thingies," said Torak. "Them bigguns what don't go down."

"That means wizards," said Putnam. "This is getting deep, Captain."

"We're done here," said Frem as he turned and started up the stair. "We'll barricade the cave entrance. Try and keep them down here."

"And if we can't?" said Putnam.

"Then we'll take our chances with the giants. If the luck of the Vanyar is with us, the Lugron and giants will have killed each other off by then. And we'll make a run for it."

"You heard the captain," said Putnam. "Up the stairs and out. We're done with Svartleheim."

"And good riddance," said Royce.

The men raced up the stairs toward the secret door that led to the cave, the outside world beyond. They'd not gone more than fifty feet up the steps, when Wikkle crashed out the cave door. Slammed it shut behind him. He turned and looked down the steps, his eyes searching for Frem. "Captain — them giants. They done heard the fight. They're in the cave. Coming for us!"

"Oh shit," said Frem.

"Oh shit," said Putnam.

85

THE REGENT'S EXPEDITIONARY FORCE (THE ALDER BRIGADE)

YEAR 1267, 4TH AGE

As the trolls came over Dor Eotrus's walls, Bald Boddrick shouted the retreat. Sentry of Allendale blew his horn like a madman as he and his raced through the Outer Dor, away from the citadel's walls, pushing their mounts to the limits.

Gar Pullman saw what was coming and turned his men out the Outer Dor's gate. They charged across the grassy plain. Their horses needed little urging. Some 325 men entered the Outer Dor with Pullman. Barely three hundred came out. The lost were from the men searching the Outer Dor. They either didn't make it to their mounts in time. Or else, the trolls caught them as they fled.

A hundred trolls followed Pullman's company beyond the Outer Dor. Racing, doubled over, on four limbs as much as two. Even on open ground they were nearly as fast as the horses. And they were determined to kill more men. As Pullman's troop approached the tree line, a hail of arrows erupted from the woods. Hundreds of shafts flew. Seconds later, hundreds more. Trolls dropped all across the field, though few stayed down for more than moments.

The wizard Yallzen stepped from the trees; his

mouth formed words seldom heard in an age. Old words. Northern magic from a forgotten time when Midgaard was young. His arms and hands moved in elaborate gestures, his robes flowing around him. Gray and pale was the old wizard, long past his prime, but still brimming with power. From his fingertips roared blasts of lightning. One branched off from another, multiplying themselves over and over as they raced through the air toward the oncoming trolls.

The lightning crashed into them and threw them back as if they'd run headlong into a solid wall. A single sparking tendril of electricity struck each troll in the troop.

Every single one of them went down.

Lord Ogden shouted for the charge. Five hundred heavy horse launched across the field from the east toward the troll, lances and spears.

The trolls were not dead. Not a one of them. But they were dazed and disoriented. Some few collected themselves in time to attack the horsemen, some others, bounded to get out of the way, but most were rooted in place, some prostrate, others kneeling, or just making their feet. The cavalry crashed into them. Javelins flew. Lances crashed, split, and broke. Hooves stomped. The charge carried the horsemen through the troll troop and toward the wood to the west.

And then another five hundred horse charged from the west wood, swords, bows, maces, and hammers. Few trolls were up, though there was motion across the field. Trolls pulled lances from their chests. They struggled to rise. And then the cavalry was among them, hacking and slashing and stomping. Pausing only moments to make measured attacks, then bounded on, across the field. The only fighting that lasted was at the front and rear edges of the battle, where some few trolls had escaped serious injury from archers or horsemen. Those, squadrons of cavalry circled and swarmed.

Gar Pullman pulled his horse up beside Lord Ogden's and Lord Nickel's.

"How many more of them are hold up in the Dor?" said Ogden.

"I can't say," said Pullman. "Maybe only a few dozen, maybe a lot more. We didn't see."

"Get your men back out there and finish them off," said Ogden.

"Bring us a prisoner," said Master Yallzen, his voice faltering, two soldiers supporting him. His white face now red and blistered, his arms shaking, the flesh, raw. "One not on death's door."

"We need information," said Nickel.

Pullman signaled the charge to his men, now formed up behind him again.

It was bloody work. Even abused as they were, the trolls were tough to kill. Ogden had to send five hundred more men, dismounted, to support Pullman in finishing off the trolls.

Even after the slaughter, some of the trolls' bodies began to stir. One even sat up — a lance clear through its body, one arm cut off, an arrow through its skull.

"Burn them," said Yallzen. "By the old legends, that and cutting off their heads. It's the only way to keep them down."

Men poured oil over the trolls, and tossed kindling atop them, then set them to blaze. The fire wasn't quick to take, but with shepherding and time, they burned. The men dragged two badly battered trolls before the northern leaders, their arms and legs tied and trussed, gags in their mouths.

"They're animals," said Pullman. "What do you hope to get from them?"

Yallzen flashed him a disappointed look. "They're no more animals than you, mercenary. Or me. They have their language. Their culture. We need only find a way to understand them."

"Anyone that speaks troll, step right up," said Ogden. "We waste our time."

Yallzen put his hand to the forehead of one of the trolls. The soldiers had to hold the troll steady. Yallzen mouthed some words, closed his eyes, concentrated.

After a few moments, Yallzen spoke again. "There are hundreds more trolls in the keep. Delving deep in the Underhalls. Routing out the men who hide there. Tricksy men, he calls them. They set evil traps that killed many of his kind. Where is your leader? Tell me?" Yallzen's brow scrunched up and he fell backward in a faint. They roused him with water to the face, and whiskey at his lips.

"Did you learn anything else, old friend?" said Lord Nickel.

"Their leader went south," said Yallzen. "South with the horde. The horde. What is here is but a small fraction of their strength. They make for Lomion City. They aim to destroy her. To feast upon its souls."

"Oh shit," said Ogden.

A soldier ran up to the leaders. "My lords, we

found people in the wood. The Eotrus. Fled from some hole."

86

DOR EOTRUS THE UNDERHALLS

YEAR 1267, 4TH AGE

ECTOR EOTRUS

Ector jerked awake, head throbbing. Something was on top of him. Around him.

Where was he? Valhalla? It couldn't be. The darkness.

Bodies. Dead bodies were all around.

The stench: death, blood, entrails.

Had he been judged unworthy? Banished to the Nether Realms? Dear gods, don't let it be so.

"Don't move," whispered a voice close to him, so quiet that he barely heard. "Don't make a sound." It was Captain Pellan. She was right next to him, though he couldn't see her.

A troll, apparently dead, was on top of him. Others were piled about. A heap of corpses.

He was alive. And still in the supply room, though now it was dark. One of the two wall sconces was out. The other, nearly as dim as a single candle. The sconces in the hall were out too. There was no sound in the room, save Pellan's breathing — and he could only hear that because she was within a foot of him — apparently buried within the corpse heap herself.

Then he heard trolls stalking down the

passageway outside. By the sound of it, two or three came into the room and skulked about for several moments. Ector held his breath. He dare not breathe. Move. Make a sound. He feared they'd hear his heart pounding in his chest.

Moments later, he realized his mistake. If the trolls lingered longer than he could hold his breath, he may well give himself away when at last he was forced so suck in some air. He closed his eyes. Counted the seconds in his head.

Ten.

Twenty.

Thirty.

The pounding in his head grew worse by the moment.

The trolls checked the bodies. He heard them. Felt the weight of one as it stepped on the corpse next to him.

Then the checker wailed.

Ector shuddered. Prayed it hadn't noticed him move.

The troll dragged one of the bodies across the room, wailing as it did. That attracted other trolls. How many piled into the room, Ector couldn't say. But he heard their footsteps. Their breathing. Their jabbering in a language wholly unintelligible to Ector. They grieved over one of the dead trolls they found. The things felt kinship to each other. Emotions. Strong. More like a man than a wild beast. Ector hadn't suspected that. But it made sense.

They were not animals.

Then they were gone. The chamber grew quiet again. The sounds of battle grew more distant. He heard Pellan breathing again. Had she held her breath the whole time? Or just gone terribly quiet? Or maybe he just didn't notice, all his attention on the trolls.

It seemed that they lay there in silence forever. After a time, Ector couldn't take it anymore. His head felt like it was going to explode. "What do we do?" he whispered.

"Keep still and keep silent until I say otherwise," whispered Pellan. Another ten minutes passed. Mayhap twenty. Ector couldn't track the time. Only the faintest sounds of battle came to his ears.

"Let's move," said Pellan. She heaved bodies off her, then helped Ector pull himself free. Ector felt dizzy and stiff, but his limbs responded. He was able to stand. When he looked around, he saw Sarbek across the room.

On his knees.

Leaning on a sword.

Dead gods!

Sarbek's throat was torn open.

His eyes were open but glassy.

Lifeless.

Dead.

Sarbek was dead.

A dozen troll corpses lay around him. Heads sliced off or staved in, chests sliced open. By Odin, he'd showed them his quality before he met his end.

"Saved your life, he did," said Pellan. She was covered in blood and gore. Half her armor torn off. She still had her double bladed poleaxe.

Ector found an axe, not his own, and picked it up. It was Sarbek's, his sigil etched in the side of the blade. "What do we do?" said Ector. "Mayhap we should stay here? Play dead as we were until they move off?"

"They eat the dead," said Pellan.

Ector's mouth dropped open. He nodded. Looked about for more weapons, and a shield that he could make use of.

They picked their way through to the Fifth Underhall. Made it there unmolested. There were hundreds of corpses along the way. Mostly Eotrus men, but a fair number of trolls too. No one was alive in those passageways. No one cried out.

"They went through and killed the wounded," said Pellan. "Stinking, no good trolls."

"How did you survive back there?" said Ector. "They knocked me out and must have thought that I was dead. But what happened with you?"

"I killed them all," said Pellan.

"What?"

"There were about eight or ten left when you went down. Sarbek took out a couple more of them before he breathed his last. I did the rest. This axe proved a good choice against them. When it was done, I checked and found you alive. There were more of them coming, so I lay down beside you and tossed a couple of troll bodies overtop us. It worked. But we were lucky. If the overall battle had been over, they'd have checked more thoroughly and we'd have been found. That's why we have to get out of here."

They ducked under the remains of the portcullis at the fifth level and heard movement from up ahead. Many feet. They dodged into a doorway. Searched for somewhere to hide.

Then they heard men's voices.

Lord Ogden's men.

Relief had arrived.

Ogden's men poured through the Underhalls en masse, spear and halbard, sword, hammer, and axe. The trolls were trapped between them and the surviving Eotrus men that still fought them in the escape tunnels. The northmen ground them down. The battle went on for hours, though Ector saw no more action that day. He'd done his part.

87

DOR LOMION
LOMION CITY

YEAR 1267, 4TH AGE
1ST YEAR OF KING CARTEGIAN'S RULE
THE DAY AFTER THE WEDDING,
AFTERNOON

MARISSA HARRINGGOLD

Marissa awoke in her bed. Leren Trak stood over her, holding smelling salts to her nose. Grim was there too. Marissa coughed, gagged, and pushed his hand away.

"There, there, young lady," said the Leren. "You gave us a fright."

"Is he dead? Tell me true."

Trak shook his head. "Your father is very much alive. Out of danger, as best I can tell, and on the mend."

"Thank the gods," said Marissa. She took a deep breath. Sat up. She had to make certain that this was real — that she was awake. That she wasn't dreaming or imagining that her father was okay.

"Thank the gods, indeed," said Trak. "I awoke last night with a bad case of indigestion. I may have indulged just a bit too much at the feast. So I made my way to the kitchens to mix some medicinals with milk. When I did, I encountered your father. I walked in just as he fell to the floor. The guards related to me his symptoms. It could have been many things that struck him down. But I had a hunch that it was poison. We'd suspected that The Black Hand or some other unsavory group of criminals might try something like that at the wedding, so I was ready for it. I had every treatment I'd ever heard of for poisons stuffed into my bag, all organized and ready to deploy at a moment's notice. And I had the bag with me to treat my own ailment. I set to work immediately giving the duke a broad spectrum of poison curatives. One or more of them worked, thank the gods."

"The hand of the gods was in this," said Grim. "If Trak hadn't been right there at that moment with poison cures at the ready. . ."

"My father would be dead," said Marissa shaking her head. She leaned over, grabbed Trak, and pulled him close in a warm hug. "Thank you."

"No need to thank me, my dear," said Trak. "Thank the gods. It's they who saved him. I was merely their instrument. And it was my honor and privilege to be so."

Marissa's mind raced. She was filled with joy that her father was going to be alright. But still, that didn't absolve her of her crime. And they still didn't know how her father had been poisoned. If it were Brithhilda's brew, telling Grim the whole story might help him find out who was behind the crime. For no doubt, whoever poisoned her father, was the same person who had killed Brithhilda. She wanted to bring them to justice. To make them pay for those crimes. But then, shouldn't she pay for hers?

"Trak also has news about Brithhilda," said Grim.

"I examined her carefully," said Trak. "There is no doubt in my mind that she has been dead no less than two full days; probably closer to three." Before Marissa could protest, Trak raised his hand to quiet her. "I know, I know," he said. "You spent the day with her yesterday. I believe you. I saw her as well when you two walked down to the main hall together, though no one remembers seeing her during the ceremony or the feast."

"I've spoken to several of the servants and guards," said Grim. "Many folk saw her yesterday, before the wedding, though several report she acted oddly. Did you notice anything out of the ordinary in her behavior? Something in the way she spoke, her mannerisms, her mood? Any lapses in her memory?"

"She seemed fine to me," said Marissa. "Except when she brushed my hair. She's always so gentle. She knows just how to grip it so that it doesn't hurt when she brushes out the knots. But yesterday, it hurt terribly. I just thought she was distracted. And she couldn't find my usual hairbrush, so we used the old one. But none of that can possibly mean anything. Can it?"

"You're one hundred percent certain that she's been dead at least two days?" said Grim to Trak.

"I am," said Trak.

"Then whoever helped ready you yesterday wasn't Brithhilda," said Grim. "It was some impostor. A wizard, no doubt. Used some glamour to take on Brithhilda's aspect, her voice, and such."

"No, no, that cannot be," said Marissa. "I've known Brithhilda all my life. That was her. Not someone in disguise. I'd have noted a trickster immediately. She acted normally. She spoke the right way. She had the right expressions on her face. She knew things that someone else wouldn't."

"But not everything," said Trak. "The missing brush."

"Where do you keep that brush?" said Grim. She told him. Grim retrieved it from right where it belonged. "Have you used it since?"

"I haven't," said Marissa, a surprised look on her face. "That's the first place Brithhilda should have looked. We've kept brushes in that drawer since I was a child. Instead she took the old one from the basket in the corner, next to where I keep my powders and creams."

"She didn't know where that brush lived because she wasn't Brithhilda," said Grim.

"But she knew so much else," said Marissa.

"Magic is not science," said Grim. "It lacks precision. The wizard got nearly all the details right, but not every one. His magic was good enough to fool you, which means it was good enough to fool anybody. No common wizard could do that. It must have been a master of the mystic arts. An archwizard of the highest order."

"So she fooled me?" said Marissa.

"It's not your fault," said Trak. "We were all fooled by her. Anyone would have been."

"The wizard took Brithilda's form to be around you," said Grim. "That got her close to your father and to the king without raising any suspicions. It was the impostor Brithhilda that poisoned the both of them. Of this, I now have little doubt. The real Brithhilda was part of the family. My men wouldn't be any more suspicious of her, than of any of us. An assassin wearing her face would have had free run of all Dor Lomion."

"I can't believe this," said Marissa. "I mean, I don't doubt what you're saying. But how could it have happened? How could anyone do that?"

"For money, more than likely," said Grim. "Probably a very well paid assassin. At least now we have something to go on. Some crumbs to follow. And follow them, I will. I will find that wizard and wring his stinking neck until he gives up his patron. There will be a reckoning for this. A terrible reckoning. Don't you worry, my queen, we will bring the king's killer to justice."

And Marissa knew that he would. Grim was stubborn as a mule. Not a man to ever give up on anything. And he had the Orphans Guild at his command. They could find anybody or anything anywhere in Lomion City. So too could he call The Fearless in to action when the wizard was found. They'd track the wizard down eventually. They'd bring him to heel. And when they did, he'd give her up. He'd tell them that it was she that had poisoned Cartegian. That she'd done it willingly. That it was her idea. And that would mark the end of her brief and tearful reign as queen of the Land of Lomion.

88

THE PLAIN OF ENGELROTH JUTENHEIM

YEAR 1267, 4TH AGE

JUDE EOTRUS

Ezerhauten and his men reached the gap between Par Brackta's ice wall and Stev Keevis's pits. A few Juten Lugron charged them, but the mercenaries swiftly cut them down. The other Lugron turned and fled. Routed. Just as was the plan.

Before the expedition had a moment to celebrate, the giants came on anew. Roaring and cursing.

They crashed into the Sithian line. Some few giants barreled forward, charging in like bulls. It seemed to Jude that they sacrificed themselves, if such primitives were capable of such noble notions, in order to scatter the Lomerians. The Sithians' primary advantages were their formations, their discipline, and their ability to fight as a unit. Those enabled them to stand against far larger forces and survive. Even prevail. Did the giants grasp that? Is that why they charged the way they did? Heroes of their people? Sacrificing themselves so that their fellows might overcome the dread Volsungs?

Or were they merely mindless brutes? Rushing in because they had no self-control. No judgment. Acting on animalistic instincts to attack one's prey? Jude didn't know. At the moment, it didn't matter.

Several giants crashed through the Sithian line, bowling over the men. The Sithians pounced on them. Spear and dagger. Hammer and sword. More giants came on. Hundreds more. No chance to stand against so many.

That's when the sorcery started flying again. Missiles of glowing energy hit some of the giants. Tore into them with a *pop*, *pop*, *pop*. Took down several. Wounded many more.

Several more pits, far smaller than the others, opened here and there in the giants' path. More than a few of the brutes fell in. Dropped to their deaths.

Angular shards of metal appeared from nowhere and flew through the air. Sliced into the giants like a volley of thrown swords.

A whole troop of giants stumbled and got bogged down when the very earth beneath their feet suddenly transformed into deep, clinging mud.

Despite all that, some of the giants got past the Sithian line.

And with the giant's advance, back came the Lugron howling their war cries.

Mason clubbed them with hammer and fist. Mort Zag weighed into them with a great sword.

Teek handed Jude a sword. Jude bent down and picked up a fallen shield just as a giant came at him. Mort Zag intercepted it. The two brutes went at it.

Donnelin fought a Lugron. His staff spun and poked.

Then another giant advanced on Jude. He sidestepped its hammer blow. Spun. Sliced at the tendons on the back of its legs. The giant roared in pain and anger.

Before Jude could turn to finish it, a Lugron ran at him, snarling. Then another. And another. Teek was there. Fighting. Far more skilled at arms was Teek than the locals. Far more skilled than Jude had expected and he was thankful for that.

Donnelin made a sweeping motion with his staff. Barked some wizard words as he did so.

In response, the charging Lugron went flying through the air out of Jude's sight. A half dozen of them. Screaming.

That's when Jude knew that old Brother Donnelin was the real deal. A wizard of skill. Perhaps on par with the Leaguers.

More Lugron charged. More giants.

Donnelin's staff swept this way and that. When it did, it was as if invisible tendrils stretched out from it and battered aside the Lugron. More often than not, the invisible strikes launched the Lugron into the air only to crash into the ground dozens of yards away.

What few Lugron got past those attacks were battered by Mason or Mort Zag. More and more of them came on. Soon they'd be overwhelmed by sheer numbers; that was clear enough to Jude. The problem was, there was no way out. No way to win. Nowhere to hide. Nowhere to run to. They were boxed in.

"My lord," shouted Thorn, loud enough that

Jude heard him over the din of battle. "It is time. You must use the holy Orb, or all will be lost."

Jude wondered if Korrgonn would respond. Was he even paying attention? Did he know what was happening? He seemed to have tuned out the whole world, retreated into himself.

To Jude's surprise, Korrgonn spoke some words in a language Jude had never heard before. Sharp, harsh words that cut through the air and vibrated Jude's whole body. Some kind of chant was it, no doubt an incantation of Nifleheim. Korrgonn spread his arms out, hands upraised as he spoke. His head was back. His eyes were closed. The air around him pulsed with electricity.

Then a giant's club came crashing down toward Jude's head. Lugron were all around. Everyone was fighting now. Desperate and close.

Jude dodged and ducked the giant. Then buried his sword in its gut. For all their size and strength, the giants' fighting skills paled in comparison to a Lomerian knight's.

The giant doubled over.

With all his strength, Jude bashed his fist against the back of the creature's neck. Heard the snap of bone.

The beast went limp. Collapsed.

A Lugron sword thrust toward Jude. It hit his shield. Luck alone saved him. Or else the Lugron's bad aim. Jude stepped forward and bashed the shield into the Lugron's face. Again, he heard the crunch of bones. The Lugron crashed onto his back, felled like a tree. Even as he fought a huge giant, Mort Zag stomped his foot on the fallen Lugron, and that was the end of him — his skull crushed.

Jude picked up the Lugron's fallen sword, his own, lost beneath the giant he'd killed — no time to turn him over and recover it. On came another Lugron. Then another. Then he fought two. Three. Four. Teek was still fighting beside him. So was Donnelin, though he threw no more magic as far as Jude could tell. His staff used now for its more pedestrian purpose. How those two had the skill to withstand the onslaught of the Lugron and the giants, Jude didn't understand. If not for his armor, he'd not have withstood it. Battered two or three times at least to the torso — blows hard enough to have taken him down but for breastplate and chain. No more time to think. Jude was tiring. His arms felt too heavy to lift. He pulled his shield in close. Tried to keep maneuvering. Turning. Dodging. Not letting them have a stationary target. He knew if he did that, he'd be dead. His feet weren't the problem. They had energy a plenty. But his sword felt like it weighed fifty pounds. He fell back on his training. The grueling training that his father, and Sir Gabriel, Ob, and Sarbek had subjected him to year after year from the time he was a small boy. *Never give up* they told him. *Never yield except to an honorable foe when all is lost. Keep fighting until the very moment the Valkyries scoop you up and carry you up to Odin's Halls.* The echoes of his father's voice repeated in his head over and over. The look on Sir Gabriel's face as they sparred — he never tired, always kept going. It spurred Jude on. He kept fighting. Kept swinging his blade.

Until his sword snapped in half.

In the moment during which he glanced about

in search of another weapon, a giant clubbed him in the shoulder. He felt his feet leave the ground. Landed on his back. Vision blurry. He tried to pull his shield to his chin to block any more blows.

A great gold being was a few feet in front of him — safeguarded behind a shimmering translucent green wall of energy. More of Thorn's handiwork. Somehow, Jude didn't know how, he knew that that being was Korrgonn, son of Azathoth. No longer did he wear Sir Gabriel's face or trappings. Now he appeared as a heavenly being of deep golden skin, with great wings of white and gold attached to his back. Taller now even than Gabriel, medium thickness of build, but all rippling muscle. His features stoic and noble, high cheekboned and chiseled. Beautiful. Majestic. Regal. Godlike. Looking at him, Jude had the unmistakable sense of near limitless power, of great age, and of peace. Peace. Comfort. Love. It radiated from Korrgonn like heat from a campfire. Dead gods, was that Korrgonn's true aspect? His true nature? If so, he surely was the son of a god, if not a god himself. Was Jude wrong about him this entire time? Were Korrgonn and the Leaguers the "good guys"? Jude's world turned upside down.

Then Jude realized that Korrgonn floated in the air, his feet pointed down, but hovered several inches above the ground.

The trunk that housed the Orb of Wisdom, whatever that thing was — Jude had never been permitted to see it — floated in the air before Korrgonn. His hand was outstretched, reaching for the trunk. In that instant that Jude looked up and saw this, blows rained down on his shield from several Lugron that stood over him, and Korrgonn's hand grasped the trunk's latch. Flipped open the top. Jude heard a sizzling sound, like bacon frying in a pan, but a thousand times louder. Then the world went black and Jude Eotrus saw no more.

89

DOR EOTRUS
THE CENTRAL TOWER

YEAR 1267, 4TH AGE

ECTOR EOTRUS

Ector and Captain Pellan marched down the once regal corridor toward Dor Eotrus's audience hall, in the heart of the citadel, blood still dripping off them, the stink of battle clinging to them. Tapestries torn down from the walls lay shredded and defiled. Vases and statuary smashed. Paintings vandalized. Long smears of blood on the floor told of bodies dragged. The slaughter had touched every part of the Dor.

Lord Nickel sat alone in the hallway, on a bench not far from the audience hall.

Ector heard Lord Ogden's booming voice coming from within the hall. He'd already started the briefing. Ogden shouldn't have done that. It wasn't his place.

Lord Nickel waved Ector over and grasped his hand. His grip, surprisingly strong. "It's good to see you, lad," said Nickel, wheezing. "When we found the walls overrun, we feared we were too late."

"Thank you for coming to our aid, Lord Nickel. A friend in time of need, is a true friend indeed."

"No need to thank me. I consider the Eotrus,

family. Always have." He lowered his voice to a whisper so that the door guards and perhaps Pellan couldn't hear him. But Pellan didn't step away and no doubt overheard the entire exchange.

"But thank them others, in there," he said, gesturing toward the audience hall. "They're loyal men, but many have egos a mile wide. Show them respect and they'll love you. But don't show them deference. Mark me well. Never show them deference. You're the acting Lord of the North. They're your vassals. Don't let them forget that. Especially, Ogden. A decent man, but he'll roll over you if you let him. So don't let him. Now pull me up. These old bones are tired."

Ector helped the gray lord to his feet. Nickel pulled Ector close and stared him in the eye. "You're an Eotrus, Master Ector. Make your father proud with what you say in there, just as you did in battle these past days. You understand me?"

Ector nodded.

"Good lad," said Nickel. "You'll have my support. And that of others too. But you'll have to make a stand. A strong one. Don't let them bully you. Now get in there. Speak loud and bold. Loud and bold, boy. And look them straight in the eyes when you speak. You can do it."

Lord Ogden stood up front on the dais, in the place reserved for the Dor Lord, his tabard bloody. The side of his face, cut and bruised. He had already begun to recount the outcome of the battle and did not miss a beat on account of Ector's arrival. Lord Nickel hobbled in behind Ector looking ancient and tired. He plopped himself down in a chair next to Master Yallzen and looked as if he couldn't rise. Yallzen's hands and arms were bandaged and shaky. He looked half dead. Gar Pullman sat in the corner of the room. Dirk Alder and Bald Boddrick beside him. Rom Alder and Black Grint, lately freed from captivity sat next to them. Lord Lester was there. So was Lord Cadbury, Lord Brian, and two score other northmen — House patriarchs or war marshals all.

"The Alders are there," whispered Pellan as she gave Ector a light shove to the small of the back.

Ector walked toward the dais. "Lord Ogden, those men are my prisoners," he said pointing to the Alders.

"Tact," whispered Pellan.

"They stood with us against the troll," said Ogden as Ector stepped up beside him extending his hand. They shook. Ector turned toward the gathered lords. His voice slightly shaky and not as loud as he would have liked.

"In a time of desperate need, House Eotrus called for aid," said Ector. "And each of you answered our call. Owing to your speed, many of our folk were saved. Your loyalty and sacrifice will long be remembered by my House. By all the North."

"You honor us with your words," said Lord Nickel. "And by your deeds in battle. You are worthy of the Eotrus name, Sir Ector. You will wear the mantle of Lord of the North with as much honor as did your father and his before him."

"I walked the Underhalls," said Lord Lester,

tall, broad, and blond, as he rose to his feet. "The Eotrus put down hundreds of trolls using every trap and tactic imaginable. And they fought to the last. Heroes I name them."

"Here, here," shouted the men, pounding the tables.

"Thank you, my lords," said Ector. "But unlike you, the Alders were not invited here. They came bearing a writ penned by their own kinsman, Chancellor Barusa, authorizing them to take control of the Dor and arrest every member of my family. Death if we failed to comply."

"You murdered my uncle, Brock Alder," shouted Dirk. "The lawfully appointed regent. There will be a reckoning."

Lord Ogden raised an eyebrow.

"It was Sarbek du Montegran that killed the Alder," said Pellan. "He acted of his own accord, under no orders from Sir Ector. And Sarbek is dead. Fallen as a hero against the troll. The matter is resolved."

"By Helheim it is," spat Dirk.

Pellan stepped toward the Alders. "If you care to press a claim against us, you can do so by the old code. A trial by combat. You for the Alders and I for the Eotrus."

"Who are you to speak for the Eotrus, Dwarf?" said Boddrick as he rose to his feet and stepped up to the Captain.

"She is my Guard Captain, and has a voice here, same as any other," said Ector.

"Then perhaps she'd like to duel *me*?" said Boddrick as he towered above her.

"Let's not be hasty," said Ogden. "We have a common foe to fight. Not each other."

"An alliance," said Rom Alder. "Our forces have aided you thus far in your battle against the troll. We will continue that aid, gladly. In times such as these, all Lomerians must band together. Put our own squabbles aside for the good of the realm. A truce I call for. And an alliance. Until this matter with the trolls is concluded."

"Well said," said Ector. "Let's forget that you came here to murder my family and steal our lands. Let's put that aside. Let's set you free to help us fight the troll. And when it's done, you'll come at us again, more murder in your eyes. That's the way of southerners. Of city folk. Of House Alder. Not here. Not in the north," shouted Ector, no hint of fear or hesitation remained in his voice.

Black Grint pulled a throwing dagger from where it lay hidden up his sleeve. He fingered it, adjusting his grip.

And then he rose up unnaturally into the air. His eyes wide in shock. He had no idea what was happening. Then he crashed against the wall, his arms pinned to his sides. The dagger fell with a clang to the floor.

Boddrick's hand went to his sword hilt.

Pellan was there. Her leg swept behind Boddrick. She pushed and the big man crashed to the floor on his back.

Gar Pullman was up, sword out, and then he too rose up into the air, and crashed against the wall, Dirk Alder beside him.

Master Yallzen's fingers gestured. It was his magic that held the Alders at bay.

"Take their weapons," said Ector. "And throw them in the dungeon. We still have a dungeon, don't we?"

Pellan shrugged.

"There will yet be a reckoning," said Rom Alder, "for crimes present, and crimes long past."

He stood but did not go for his weapons.

With a flick of a finger, Yallzen's magic assaulted him, but it failed to lift him like it did the others.

Rom waved his hand from side to side. Somehow, brushed off the magic.

Pellan pointed her axe at his neck. The blade was but an inch from his flesh. "Drop your swordbelt or die where you stand."

Rom stared at the Dwarf. His eyes narrowed. It was some moments before he yielded.

As the Alders were being tied up, hands behind their backs, Ector spoke privately to Ogden.

"You shouldn't have freed them. And you certainly shouldn't have given them their weapons and invited them to this council."

"They proved effective against the trolls," said Ogden. "For every troll they kill, it's one less that *we* need kill. For every casualty that they sustain, that's one less that we have to bear."

"It was not your place to make that decision," said Ector. "House Eotrus rules here, not House Ogden."

Ogden paused a moment, then smiled and nodded. "You are truly Aradon's son, and a worthy lord I think, should your brothers not return. My apologies. House Ogden stands with you, my lord."

90

DARENDOR
THE DALLASSIAN HILLS

YEAR 1267, 4TH AGE

BORNYTH TROLLSBANE

"I don't have time for this," said Bornyth Trollsbane, Dwarven High King of Clan Darendon. Bornyth stood in a small circular chamber, a stone plinth at its center, atop which sat a seer stone — a true seeing stone, not some glass bauble bought at the bazaar. "Can she contact Malvegil or not? She is a she, isn't she? Hard for me to tell; none of you people have beards."

A Svart Seer, long necked and thin as a rail like most of her kind, hovered over the stone, her long, four-knuckled fingers, caressing it as colors erupted in waves from within its depths, washing across the inside face of the stone like multi-colored fog. Without taking her eyes from the stone, the seer exchanged words in Svartish with the Orator, the official spokesman for the Svart High King. Like Bornyth, the Orator stood behind the railing that encircled the plinth and assured that onlookers kept a safe distance from the Stone to avoid its debilitating effects.

"Cardakeen rack Mortha, she senses," said the Orator, "but contact, it is weak. Separated from the Sventeran Stone she may be. Patience we must have."

"Dallassian Dwarves are not known for our patience," said Bornyth. "Especially not when enemies have come knocking."

An image appeared within the depths of the seer stone. Bornyth stepped closer and leaned against the railing to get a better look. The moment his head passed beyond the railing's edge, his stomach churned. A blurry image of a woman appeared within the stone. A Volsung. He didn't recognize her. They all looked mostly the same anyways. Not so much as the Svarts, but close enough to cause him no end of confusion.

The svart seer was surprised and flustered by the contact.

"The Sventeran Stone that be," said the Orator, "but operates it, a Volsung seer does."

"Well, find out who and why," barked Bornyth. "Is your girl on vacation? Did Malvegil stick her on a spit?"

"Who be you?" said the Orator, pressing as close to the stone as he dared, for he was no more immune to its effects than was anyone else.

"You contacted me," said the woman —who was in fact Mother Alder, though none in the room knew her. She sat before the seer stone that she had appropriated from the Grandmistress of the Black Hand, who in turn took it from Torbin Malvegil upon his "assassination". "Who are you? What are you?" said Mother Alder.

"Possess you the Sventeran Stone, why?" said the Orator. "Where be Cardakeen rack Mortha?"

"The stone is mine now," said the woman. "What are you?"

"First Orator of Thoonbarrow be I," said the

Orator.

"Thoonbarrow?" said Mother Alder. "You're a Svart. A real Svart?"

"And who is that with you?" said Mother Alder.

"Bornyth Trollsbane, Lord of Darendor," said Bornyth. "No need to bow."

"Where be Cardakeen rack Mortha?" said the Orator.

"Who cares where stinking what's-her-name is?" shouted Bornyth. "Who are you woman and where are you? I need Torbin Malvegil. Is he there, or not?"

"Torbin Malvegil is dead," said Mother Alder. "Killed along with King Tenzivel several days past."

Bornyth drew back. Paused. That news was most unexpected. "Who killed them?"

"The Black Hand says the wind," said Mother Alder.

"Assassins killed the king of Lomion?" said Bornyth. "And who in Helheim are you, woman?"

"She who controls this seer stone, Dwarf. That is all that I will say."

"Are you in Lomion City? Dor Malvegil? Elsewhere?" said Bornyth.

"Why does it matter?"

"I need to get a message to the High Council, assuming that no one has killed them off too," said Bornyth. "Have they? It can't wait."

"What is your message?" said Mother Alder.

"The Draugar are coming," said Bornyth.

"The what?"

"Draugar. The dead that walk."

"You're not making any sense," said Mother Alder.

"Draugar destroyed Thoonbarrow of late. Now they march on Darendor. We've seen them in the hills these past several days. Now we've found them in our caverns. They're coming up out of the deeps. And they're heading north. A plague of them. A plague that may swallow all Midgaard if left unchecked."

"This story is hard to believe," said Mother Alder. "What proof?"

"The Svarts. You think we'd ally with them but for grave need?"

"I care little for the ways of Dwarves or Svarts. And even less for Draugar and assorted bogeymen."

"Have you a means to convey my message or not?" said Bornyth.

"I do and I will, though it will not be believed."

"Can you get somebody in authority on your end?" said Bornyth. "It's your kingdom that's on the line here, woman. I'm trying to help you people."

"I'll see what I can do," said Mother Alder. "Contact me again at sundown."

"Agreed."

91

ISLE OF JUTENHEIM THE PLAIN OF ENGELROTH

YEAR 1267, 4TH AGE

OB

"**D**ead gods," said Ob as they walked through the battlefield on the Plain of Engelroth where the Leaguers had fought the Juten Lugron and the Ettin. "In all my days, I've never seen anything quite like this."

As far as they could tell, nothing lived across that plain's expanse. Stev Keevis's pits were still there, yawning chasms ready to suck down anyone who ventured too close. Brackta's ice wall was gone, melted, and dried up — so they knew not that it had ever existed. There were bodies everywhere. Thousands of them. Most covered in ash, head to toe, not the least bit of flesh showing.

"I've seen something like this before," said Dolan. "After Mount Rhatick exploded. Spewed fire and smoke for weeks. I had business in the nearest town. The place was covered in ash a foot deep. The people were covered too. Died where they stood. Maybe burned, maybe from bad air. I don't know. But they looked like these. A terrible thing."

"Spread out and see what you can find," said Theta.

"What are we looking for?" said Ob.

"You'll know it when you find it," said Theta.

Ob gently brushed his foot against an ashen corpse that lay on the ground. "A Lugron," said Ob.

Ob's foot met little resistance. He pressed harder and the ash collapsed beneath his foot. The body was burned through and through.

"Nothing left of the flesh but ash," said Ob.

"Why didn't they fall over?" said Artol. "If some blast of fire or magic hit them, wouldn't they get knocked over? Wouldn't they dive to the ground to escape it? Most of them are still standing."

"A lot of them got their arms up covering their faces," said Dolan. "Others are ducking down. Saw something coming, they did. Not enough time to do anything else."

"Like it hit them quick," said Ob "Sorcery for certain."

Ob and Dolan approached one standing corpse. Ob pulled out his dagger and poked its point into it. The blade's tip sank into the ash with no resistance. Ob pushed it in harder. The entire corpse collapsed into a formless ashen pile. "Dead gods, there is nothing left of any of them. What could do that to a man? To so many?"

"Could be an archwizard's last sorcery," said Par Tanch. "It's the way a wizard kills those that have done him in. Sorcerers call it a retributive strike."

Ob looked over the edge of one of Keevis's

pits. "Dark and deep as death down there," he said. "You see any bottom?"

"Nothing but the black," said Dolan.

Ob found a stone, picked it up, dropped it into the pit. Cocked his head to the side, listening.

After several seconds, Ob said, "I got nothing. You hear it hit bottom?"

"Nope," said Dolan shaking his head.

"Stinking wizards mucked the place up good," said Ob. "People and critters will be falling down that hole for the next thousand years."

"It's here," said Glimador. He and Theta stood farther into the killing field. Two of the corpses there weren't burned to ash like the rest.

Theta knelt down beside them. One was Lugron. The other, a red armored knight.

"The Lugron is no local," said Ob. "He's from up our way by the look of his face and gear. A mercenary I'd bet. The other fellow is a mystery to me. I don't know no knightly order what wears red plate armor, head to toe. Anybody else recognize this armor or his sigil?" he said as he looked around to the others.

Theta bent down and studied the knight's body. So did Dolan; he went through the knight's pockets and gear.

"Why didn't these burn like the rest?" said Artol.

"They died after the magic was thrown," said Theta. "They both bled out from their wounds."

"I don't follow," said Ob. "You mean, these fellows came by later and killed each other, or somebody else killed them?"

"That is possible," said Theta, "but I don't think so. Someone set off the magic that burned all these. I believe that magic only affected the wizard's enemies, and the corpses of the already dead. These two were on the wizard's side, and they were still alive, so they escaped the burning."

"And what happened to the wizard and his cronies?" said Ob.

"The blast killed all his enemies," said Theta. "So he walked off with whatever allies of his were still alive. They left these two behind, probably because they were on death's door."

"A bunch of the corpses around here are of armored knights and men; probably more of those mercs. If you're right, Theta, then these would have been dead before the blast, so they got burned crispy. The armor is turned to ash too. That makes no sense to me. Should've melted. Crazy wizard magic."

"We should get moving," said Claradon. "Continue south."

As they renewed their march, DeBoors came up to Theta and spoke in quiet voice.

"I recognize that dead knight's sigil," said DeBoors.

"I thought you might," said Theta.

92

DOR EOTRUS THE CENTRAL TOWER

YEAR 1267, 4TH AGE

ECTOR EOTRUS

"**D**id we get them all?" said Lord Nickel through a bout of coughing and wheezing. All the men in the audience hall quieted down when he spoke.

"The bulk," said Lord Ogden. "The trolls flooded through the Sixth Underhall and attacked the defenders of all six escape tunnels. They overcame the Eotrus at two of the tunnels. Those ones fled through the exits and out into the wild when they saw us coming. In the other four tunnels, we crushed the trolls between us and the Eotrus. Save for a few prisoners we took, we wiped them out. Cut their heads off, just to be certain. We're going to burn the bodies. We'll take no chances with them. We've seen these things get up from incredible wounds. They heal up faster than any natural creature. Demon spawn or some such they must be."

"Hogwash," said Nickel. "Primitive folk of some ancient line otherwise long dead is all they are."

"Believe as you will," said Ogden. "As will I."

"How many trolls escaped through those two tunnels?" said Ector.

"We don't know," said Ogden. "Our horse took out another twenty or so in the wood. No doubt others escaped. Maybe only a few. Maybe a lot."

"The civilians?" said Nickel. "Did they get clear?"

"The civilians that fled from the four tunnels that held out were untouched," said Ogden. "Not a single casualty as far as we know. Our horse are still rounding them up. Most of them stayed together, but a few small groups split off and went their own ways. We haven't found all of them yet. In the two tunnels that broke, the trolls caught a few folk. But only a few. A squad of soldiers stayed behind at each exit to cover their escape. They fought to the death. Stopped many of the trolls right there. That gave the civilians the chance they needed to escape. But for their sacrifice, it could have been a lot worse." Ogden turned his gaze to Ector. "A miracle you folks held out as long as you did."

"It was good planning what did that," said Indigo as he walked into the room. Malcolm was with him. Baret too. "And a bit of northern engineering."

Ector bolted to his feet and ran to his brother. They embraced. "I thought you dead," said Ector.

"I almost was," said Malcolm. "It was a close thing."

"Good," said Ogden. "Both Eotrus heirs are still with us. Your people will need you both."

"Is it over?" said Malcolm.

"It's only just begun," said Ogden. "The bulk of the troll horde moved south after your folk took refuge in the tower and the Underhalls. The force we defeated was a smaller group that they left behind."

"Then by bringing all our folk back to the Dor, aren't we just putting them in grave danger again?" said Malcolm. "If the horde turns back this way, they'll overrun the walls again, just as they did before."

"Another thousand bannermen rode in this afternoon," said Lord Nickel. "Some under my own flag. Thousands more are on the way. We're ready for them now. A much tougher fight they'll have if they head back this way."

"When they head back," said Ogden. "They came down from the mountains, didn't they? Win or lose, eventually they'll head home."

"Are we going after them?" said Malcolm.

All eyes turned to Ector.

"When House Eotrus called for aid, the north answered us," said Ector. "Did Lomion City?"

"I received a message," said Ogden.

"I did as well," said Nickel.

"They asked me if there was verification of the "*outlandish*" reports of trolls active in the north lands," said Ogden.

"And they asked me to investigate the reports on their behalf, as if House Nickel was beholden to the Council rather than the Eotrus. We were about to leave for here when that message came in."

"So Lomion City is doing nothing," said Ector.

"If we ride out with all our horse, we can support Lomion," said Ogden. "Perhaps crush the troll between our forces and the city's."

"If the city is ready for the fight, our presence will make little difference," said Ector. "But if they're caught unprepared, we'll take the brunt of the fighting. Our forces will be decimated even if we ultimately win the battle."

"Let's send the ravens," said Nickel. "Ogden's, mine, yours, Lester's, Brian's, and Cadbury's. All warning about the horde. About their marching on the south. About the climbing of the walls. Resistance to injury. Everything. If they believe us, they'll be prepared. They have a huge standing force that they can put in the field."

"We can't abandon Lomion City entirely," said Malcolm. "The Eotrus are the wardens of the north. It's our responsibility to hold back the wild or die trying."

"We did hold them back," said Ogden.

"We need to send the Alders back," said Ector.

"What can three hundred men do?" said Ogden.

"They can be our scouts," said Ector. "As condition to their release, they must report back via raven everything happening in the south. We'll keep them abreast of what's happening here — at least as far as what we want them to know."

"Can they be trusted?" said Indigo.

"Mayhap in this," said Ector. "But it will get them out of our hair either way."

"Keep Rom," said Nickel. "As a hostage until this legal matter is resolved."

"Agreed," said Ector.

"Then what do you propose we do?" said Ogden. "Fortify? Hunker down?"

"The troll attacked our homes," said Ector. "They did their best to wipe us out — man, woman, and child. I aim to return the favor. We're going to take the battle to *their* lands. We're going north. To the mountains. We track them back to their lair."

Surprised looks filled the men's faces. Deep breaths all around.

"We might be better off chasing after the horde," said Ogden. "The deep mountains are treacherous."

"Where is Sir Sarbek?" said Malcolm. "I would hear his council on this."

93

HIGH COUNCIL CHAMBER TAMMANIAN HALL LOMION CITY

YEAR 1267, 4TH AGE
FOUR DAYS AFTER KING CARTEGIAN'S ASSASSINATION

BARUSA ALDER

Barusa pounded his gavel to get the councilors' attention. They'd been arguing for four days and four nights with little break. Arguing about the succession. Cartegian was dead. Tenzivel had no other surviving children. By tradition and long-standing law, Cartegian's wife was heir to the throne. Period.

Except that she'd been his wife for less than twenty-four hours.

Was that long enough for the marriage to be considered legitimate? Valid? Incontestable?

And what of Cartegian's mental afflictions? Did that invalidate the marriage? Especially in light of its short duration?

And what of the delicate question of whether the marriage had been consummated? If it had not been, was it null-and-void — at least as far as the succession goes?

Did any of those questions have merit? Or was

Marissa Lomion's new monarch, and that was that?

The councilors could not agree.

But if not Marissa, then who is the lawful ruler of the Kingdom of Lomion? Does the rule fall to the king's closest kin or to Barusa as Chancellor?

Closest kin said the laws.

But Lomion's annals told a different story. Disputes about the succession were not uncommon. Regents had been named more than once. Royal Houses changed more than once — more than a few times, truth be told.

There were arguments for both sides.

The king's paternal uncle was the Archduke of Kern, the kingdom's second largest city. A man well equipped to rule. But he hadn't lived in Lomion City for decades. Despite his pedigree, that made him an outsider. Some of the councilors would not accept an outsider.

The debates had grown loud. Personal. And bordered on violent at several times over the previous days. Law scholars had been brought in to issue opinions to inform the councilors' judgments. So had historians.

No consensus had yet been reached.

"My friends and colleagues," said Barusa after the meeting was called to order on the fifth day of deliberations, "these difficult times grow more difficult by the moment. We must gather our strength and put aside our grief over the death of King Cartegian, and face a new threat."

A loud huff came from the Vizier. "You will not bore us with another tale of fancy, will you? If I hear another report of monsters creeping out of the northern woods, I'll puke."

"With all due respect, I must agree," said Guildmaster Slyman. "Such creatures, if even they exist, are the domain of the marcher lords, not the concerns of this council. Let the Eotrus handle the creatures of the northern wilds. Or the Regent duly appointed by this council. Such petty matters are not for us to get involved in."

"The magnitude of the threat is far more than what we assumed," said Barusa. "We have it now from several sources. Dor Eotrus fell to the troll some seven days ago."

Gasps all around.

"Their garrison?" said Marshal Balfour.

"We don't know the details, save that there were heavy losses to our citizens."

"What of your brother, Regent Brock?" said Bishop Tobin.

"Dead," said Barusa. "Along with nearly his entire brigade."

"Dead gods," said Bishop Tobin. "My sympathies to you and all House Alder, Chancellor. It boggles the mind how such a thing could be true. Creatures out of fairy tales defeating armies of well-trained Lomerian men? Can we trust these reports?"

"All but one is from northmen," said Barusa. "Men loyal to the Eotrus. One is from Dirk Alder, my nephew, and Gar Pullman — his name you may know, a mercenary of some repute. They corroborate the northmen's claims."

"Could they be under duress?" said Bishop Tobin. "Prisoners, perhaps, their hands forced to write such accounts?"

"There remains that possibility," said Barusa. "The reports claim that the Eotrus called in all their bannermen, and the combined might of the northmen expelled the troll, but at great cost."

"Expelled them or destroyed them?" said Lord Jhensezil.

"The northmen claim to have destroyed a small force of trolls that remained in occupation of Dor Eotrus after its fall," said Barusa. "But the main force, which they characterize as a *horde*, is marching south."

"Dead gods!" said Bishop Tobin.

"Toward us or toward Kern?" said Slyman

"Toward us," said Barusa.

"By all that's holy, this cannot be," said Tobin.

"Let them come," said Balfor. "Our army will crush them. We have the largest standing force in all Midgaard, well trained and well equipped. Just because some border fortress fell to these creatures doesn't mean they'll prove any threat to us."

"Again, you underestimate our northern cousins," said Jhensezil. "Dor Eotrus is like an armed camp. Walls high and thick. Ballistae, catapult, trebuchet. Cavalry and archers by the hundreds. If they were overcome, I assure you that Lomion City herself is under grave threat. I suggest that the good marshal prepare his forces."

"The patrols will give us fair warning of the approach of this so-called horde," said Balfour. "No doubt, a vigorous cavalry charge will set them to rights, and we'll be done with this business."

A commotion could be heard in the antechamber. Voices grew loud. The council chamber guards went to investigate.

The doors burst open. It was Lord Sluug and a group of his rangers.

"What is the meaning of this?" said Barusa.

"Lord Sluug, this is most irregular," said Tobin.

"An army of creatures are approaching Lomion City," said Sluug. "They swept through the outskirts of Doriath and overran multiple villages along the way. Chased some of my rangers all the way from northern Doriath. Faster than horses over long distance are these things."

"Creatures, you say?" said Barusa. "What are they?"

"I don't know for certain," said Sluug. "I've never seen their like. But the old folk. They name them trolls."

"So it's true," said Barusa. "How many?"

"Thousands," said Sluug.

Balfour stood and took his leave, sweating and flustered. "I'll assemble a force. Meet them on the field. Then we'll see their quality."

"You don't have much time," said Sluug. "Their scouts are within a mile of the walls by now. Their main force no more than a couple of hours behind."

"These things, trolls or whatever they are," said Tobin, "can't possibly be a threat to Lomion City. The walls. The gates—"

"May do us little good," said Barusa. "The ravens claim the troll climbed Dor Eotrus's walls with little effort. Overran the whole of the Dor within hours of their arrival."

"Dead gods," said Tobin. "What sins did we commit against the gods to bring on such torment?" The old fart hadn't shown so much energy in twenty years.

"Perhaps what the seers have been whispering is true," said Lady Aramere.

"No, no, I can't accept that," said Bishop Tobin. "Idle gossip. Pure speculation. Nothing more."

"What say you?" said Barusa.

"Rumors have been spreading far and wide for months now," said Lady Aramere, "claiming that seers are foretelling the coming of the end times. That we teeter on the brink of ruin. That the end of all Midgaard is at hand."

"Oh, joy," said Barusa.

94

HOUSE ALDER LOMION CITY

YEAR 1267, 4TH AGE

BARUSA ALDER

"**H**ow do you even know it was Bornyth Trollsbane that contacted you?" said Barusa.

"I don't," said Mother Alder. "But he was quite convincing. A credit to his reputation as a callous blowhard, though that can be applied to most men of power."

"How likely is it that we could be attacked by two armies made up of mythical creatures at the same time?" said Barusa. "These reports have to be false."

"Trolls are not mythical beings," said Mother Alder. "They're as real as you and I. They're just not a lot of them left. Withdrawn to the deep mountains several decades ago. And apparently now they're back. Come back for a reckoning, I suppose. Why do you think they disappeared into the high mountains? For fun? For love of snow and ice and barren waste? They went there because our kind drove them there. Hunted them nearly to extinction."

"They eat people, if the accounts are true," said Barusa.

"There is that," said Mother Alder.

"Trolls I can buy," said Barusa, "though I doubt the numbers ascribed to them, and the physical feats reported. Exaggeration and imagination at work, I suspect."

"Underestimate them at your peril, firstborn. Trolls are not like Dwarves or Elves or Smallfolk. They are not men. Not men at all. They're of a different breed entirely."

"And Draugar?" said Barusa.

"I don't know," said Mother Alder. "The stories have them as either animated corpses or ghouls."

"Corpses don't walk," said Barusa. "Not unless some necromancer's magic is at work. And ghouls? I know them only from fireside tales."

"Another breed left over from olden times," said Mother Alder. "Like the trolls, they are not men. They're something else. Creatures with an affinity for the dirt, for graveyards, and for all things dead."

"I disbelieve," said Barusa.

"Let's get him on the stone and we'll see what's what."

95

SVARTLEHEIM JUTENHEIM

YEAR 1267, 4TH AGE

FREM SORLONS

A huge weight crashed against the stone door to the cave as the Pointmen on the spiral stair looked on in shock. The door shuddered. Dust flew. Wikkle Lugron stepped back from the door, axe to hand.

"Put your shoulder to it," shouted Putnam from the stairs below. "Keep the buggers out."

Wikkle did.

Another great impact hit the door. Stone cracked and crumbled. Wikkle was knocked back for a moment, then retook his place.

"Captain," shouted Wikkle, "it's not going to hold!"

Frem looked back at Sevare. The wizard had no business running up the stair the way he was, even helped by Maddix and Grainer. He ought to be on his back for a week. He wouldn't be of much help. A spell. Maybe two. And nothing big. Even so, the magic might kill him.

"How are we going to get our butts out of here?" said Putnam to Frem.

Frem looked around; shook his head.

"Looks like there's no escape for us this time,"

said Torak.

"Let's give them what for," shouted Putnam.

"Odin!" shouted Frem.

"Odin," shouted the men, the traditional warrior's call to alert the gods to make ready their places, for they'd soon be joining them in Valhalla.

Several of the men braced themselves against the door to the cave, bolstering it.

Frem moved quickly to Sevare's side.

The wizard was dazed. He reeked of smoke and burned flesh. Wisps of smoke trailed from his arms, through the strips of cloth that bound them.

"Sevare, are you with me?" said Frem.

"I hear you, Captain," said the wizard, though his eyes were glazed over and gazed off into the distance.

"We need to either block off the stair below us or else seal the door above us," said Frem.

"Which?" said the wizard.

"Either."

Sevare paused before responding. "I can't think straight," he said. "The pain. My head is spinning. Tell me which."

"Block the stairs," said Frem.

Sevare paused again, thinking.

The Elfs roared as they bounded up the spiral stair. The entire structure shuddered with their passage, in large part due to the massive weight of the rock elementals that were the Elfs' minions. The door to the cave shuddered and cracked more under repeated impacts. The giants would be through within a minute or two. The Svarts weren't far behind. Trapped between two forces, each too numerous to possibly defeat. But by magic or stroke of luck, they could neither win the day, nor survive it.

"Sevare," said Frem. The wizard's eyes were closed. He swayed to the side and started to fall. Maddix and Grainer caught him; held him up.

"He's out on his feet," said Grainer. "His magic is spent."

"Putnam, your smelling salts," said Frem. "Quickly."

Putnam dashed over, hands rummaging in his belt pouch. "He's out of the fight, Frem. We're down to knife work."

"Bring him around," said Frem. "I've an idea."

"There's no time," said Putnam. "We've got to be up there when that door goes."

"We've got a mission," said Frem. "We need to make it out of here to accomplish it. We need Sevare in the game to do that."

Putnam put the smelling salts under Sevare's nose. He coughed and shuddered, but his eyes opened.

"Sevare — that time in Droginsville. You made Putnam and the boys go invisible. Those watchmen passed them by. Remember?"

The wizard nodded.

"I need you to do that again," said Frem. "To the whole squadron. We'll bunch together. Can you do it? Do you have the strength left?"

"How long to hold the spell?" said Sevare.

"A minute or two," said Frem. "No longer. Can you do it?"

"I think so," said Sevare. "But I won't be able to hold it for long."

"We're all dead if you don't," said Frem.

"Put me where I need to be," said Sevare. "My legs aren't working right now."

Frem scooped up the wizard, no small man, turned, and rushed up the rest of the steps, the others following. At the top of the step, the landing was wide. There was enough room for all Frem's remaining men to huddle close together and be out of the direct path between the door and the spiral stair. He directed the men into position, all but a handful that remained to bolster the door, which was crumbling under the giants' onslaught.

"How long to cast your magic once you start?" said Frem.

"Ten seconds, or thereabouts," said Sevare. "If I can do it at all."

"You can do it," said Frem. "We're counting on you. Don't forget to cloak yourself too. We all need to be hidden for this to work."

The Elfs still thundered up the stairs, but they were yet several levels down, not in direct sight.

Frem took position with the men holding fast the stone door. He threw all his weight and strength against it. Sevare stood before the huddled men some feet away.

"On my mark, we run to the others so the spell will cloak us too," said Frem.

"Sevare, start your casting."

He did.

"On five, we run to the others," said Frem. He counted out loud. "Now!"

As one, the six men let go the door and dashed to their fellows on the other side of the landing.

Just as they slid into position, two things

happened. Sevare's arms stretched out before him, fingers spread. A white beam of light came from his fingertips. Bathed all the Pointmen with its light. And the stone door was blasted inward, crumbling to pieces, a giant fallen atop the rubble. A cloud of thick dust filled the doorway.

One and all, the Pointmen began to fade from sight. Three heartbeats later, they were gone. One of the giants barreled through the opening, pushing through the dust, stepping on and over his fellow as he did, huge war club in hand. He looked around. It seemed to Frem that the giant's eyes fell directly upon him, yet he did not react. The giant didn't see him. The spell had worked. The men however were all visible to each other and could see the giants freely. It was clear enough to the giants, a battle force was pounding up the stairs. The giant decided to charge. His fellows followed.

A few moments later, giants poured through the sundered portal and roared as they clumsily charged down the spiral stair, their feet too large for the treads. More and more came.

With wild war cries and terrible clash of arms, the giants crashed into the Black Elves and their stone minions. The entire stair shook and shuddered.

Sevare shook too. His body vibrated. His skin darkened. Blackened. As if he'd been thrown into a fire. His jaw was clenched. Straining. All his remaining strength brought to bear to hold that spell.

"Keep holding it," said Frem, no louder than he had to for the wizard to hear.

"Dead gods, how many of them are there?"

said Putnam after three score giants had roared through the door and down the steps. More kept coming. A breeze blowing into the cavern through the doorway.

Flakes of ash began to blow off Sevare's body. From his head, his arms, his clothes. The moments ticked by, the men huddled close as the thundering horde of giants passed within arm's length of them.

Frem stared into Sevare's eyes. They were alert now, though the whites were going gray. The wizard shook from head to toe.

"A little longer," said Frem. "Hold a little longer."

The flakes of ash blew from Sevare's body like a gray and black snowfall. More and more came off him. Still the giants thundered through the doorway and down the stairs. A hundred passed. A hundred and fifty. Two hundred.

Sevare started to come apart. Frem could see through holes in his arm and shoulders. The wizard's eyes were locked on Frem.

"Keep holding," said Frem, though he barely got those words out.

And finally, the last of the giants roared by. The doorway and landing stood empty save for the rubble and the concealed Pointmen.

"Thank you," said Frem to Sevare. "You've earned your place in Odin's Halls."

And with that, Sevare came apart and blew away in a stream of ash.

The Pointmen gasped in shock.

"Dead gods," said Royce. "What happened to him?"

"The Wizard's Toll," said Putnam, his voice

solemn. "The weighty price a wizard must pay when they throw too much magic."

"Let's get out of here while we can," said Frem. "We've deeds yet to do before we sleep."

96

DOR EOTRUS THE ODINHOME

YEAR 1267, 4TH AGE

ECTOR EOTRUS

Sarbek's body lay on an oaken board atop a pyre in the great hearth at the Odinhome's center. He was clad in his battle armor, equipped with helmet, shield, and a full array of weapons — all cleaned and polished to a shine.

Save for the blue tint to his skin, he could have been sleeping.

All the surviving knights of the House and most of the men-at-arms were there. So were some of the Eotrus bannermen: lords, officers, and regulars that had served with Sarbek over the years. In one section of the hall stood the veterans of Karthune Gorge, gathered together as was their tradition when one of their brethren passed. Sarbek's family would have been there too, but he had none. His parents and brothers were long passed. His soldier's life never left time for a wife or children. That was a sad thing, thought Ector. He vowed not to make the same mistake.

All the soldiers stood at attention and in full battle gear. The Eotrus brothers stood side by side. Beside and around them were Sir Indigo,

Lord Ogden, Lord Nickel, and Master Yallzen.

"Forty years did Sir Sarbek du Montegran faithfully serve House Eotrus," said Brother Merils of House Ogden, the ranking priest on hand, as he stood beside the pyre in his priestly garb. "An Odion Knight was he. A castellan. A weapons master. A scholar, a teacher, a confidant, a taskmaster, a friend. We are weaker without him. The north is weaker without him. But let his memory inspire us to greatness. He died as he lived. A hero. A warrior. Protecting the borderlands. Protecting his Dor. Protecting House Eotrus. In his last moments, he bravely defended Sir Ector against the troll, as was his solemn duty, and once again, proved to all his quality. Even now he looks down upon us from Valhalla where he sits in Odin's great hall. Aspire to join him there we all do, when the gods decree, but not a moment before. Valhalla awaits us."

"Join me now in the warrior's prayer," said Brother Merils.

"Look close unto the stark north lands and behold the Bifrost Bridge and the heavenly realms beyond — ancient Asgard, shining and bright, though hard and cold as the stone, the ice, and the northern sea," said Brother Merils.

"To the north lies Asgard," said the men in unison.

"Now look unto the east, mysterious and bright, and behold thy brothers, thy sons, and thy comrades."

"Now look unto the new lands to the west and behold thy sisters, thy wives, thy mothers, and thy daughters."

"Around us are our kinsmen, always," said the

men.

"Now think not again of them until we march on the homeward road."

"Not until the homeward road," said the men.

"Now look unto the proud south and behold thy father, and thy father's father, and all thy line afore thee, back unto the beginning."

"Unto the beginning," said the men.

"Now look forward and behold thy fate. Before thee, the paths of victory and glory, the paths of defeat and disgrace. Betwixt them, the roads to Valhalla and to eternal darkness."

"Beware the dark road," said the men.

"Now look above thee and behold the all-father in all his wisdom and glory. He beckons us forth to meet our fate. The all-father tells us that the path we choose is of our own making."

"Our path is our own," said the men.

"Now my northern brothers, vow thy path."

"To victory and tomorrow if we can, to victory and Valhalla if we must," said the men. "This we vow."

"Along with all the Eotrus, Sarbek spoke this ancient prayer for the last time just before the final battle with the troll," said Brother Merils. "It is fitting that those words were some of the last that he heard. Some of the last that he spoke. For he had spoken this prayer before battle more than two hundred times down through his long years. A warrior to be remembered. To be honored. We are all the better men for having known him. May each of us face our end as bravely as he did. This we vow."

"This we vow," said the men.

"Rise now my brothers," said Brother Merils,

"and go to thy fate with Odin's blessing."

Ector stepped up beside Brother Merils, a lit torch in his hand. He looked down at Sarbek for a moment before he spoke. "Until we meet again in Valhalla," said Ector. And then he lit the pyre.

The next morning the Alder expedition was sent packing south. Gar Pullman agreed to maintain contact via raven, though he did so over Dirk Alder's objections.

Not long after noon that day, the Eotrus rode north. By then, their horse corps was eight thousand strong. A long supply chain, guarded by some three thousand footmen followed. All the remaining strength of the north gathered at Dor Eotrus and secured it against further troll incursions. Malcolm assumed command of the Dor at his brother's order. Baret was appointed his official bodyguard. Lord Nickel and Master Yalzen remained with Malcolm as advisers for they were too old to make the journey into the deep mountains. Rom Alder remained locked in the dungeon.

With Ector went all the Eotrus knights, including Sir Indigo. With them rode the combined cavalry forces of the Eotrus bannermen, including Lords Ogden, Lester, Brian, Cadbury, and those of Lord Nickel. The north had not fielded such a force in more than a dozen years. Woe to the trolls for they had drawn the ire of the northerners. And the north was taking the fight to them. There would be a reckoning.

97

HOUSE ALDER LOMION CITY

YEAR 1267, 4TH AGE

BARUSA ALDER

"They're in my tunnels," said Bornyth Trollsbane, his voice strained. Out of breath. He stood as near as he dared to his seer stone. "Every Dwarf they kill rises up as one of them. As a stinking Draugar. I don't know if we can hold them. They're coming from multiple directions. Their numbers without end."

"Have you tried to negotiate?" said Barusa speaking through the Malvegil Stone that Mother Alder operated. "To understand what they want?"

Bornyth spoke his next sentence very slowly, as if he were speaking to a backward child. "They want to kill us and make us into Draugar, you moron. Best we can tell, they're coming up from the south, mostly. If they pass us, and carry straight on, they'll start to hit your towns and villages soon enough."

Wild howling sounded in the distance. A high-pitched croaking sound. Bornyth jerked around, a great axe in his hand.

Dwarves rushed into the chamber encased in silver plate armor, head-to-toe.

"My lord, we've got to get you out," said one

soldier. "They're coming."

"Take the stone and the svart," said Bornyth.

Then the croaking sounded again. This time much louder. Much nearer. Then a flurry of movement. Shouting. The moment before contact broke, a figure appeared behind Bornyth, in the chamber's doorway. Its head lolled to the side, neck obviously broken, but it lunged for the Dwarves, croaking and gibbering.

"Shit," said Bornyth.

"Shit," said Barusa.

98
ISLE OF JUTENHEIM ANGLOTOR

YEAR 1267, 4TH AGE

OB

Theta's ankh guided the Eotrus expedition ever south. They trudged across a plain of high grass where a large pride of lions shadowed them for three days, but didn't chance an attack on so large a group of men. The expedition suffered under the heat of the day, especially given the heavy gear they hauled, and burned quickly through the water they carried with them. A dozen men stood the watch through the night, torches aplenty. That kept them safe. They chased off the boldest of the lions more than once. But never did the men rest easy. The memory of the gatormen was too close. Too terrible. And hungry lions too near.

Beyond the grassy plains, the expedition ventured through a large forest of tall trees and sunlit glades, troubled twice by biting ants that came in the night by the thousands. Chaos, searing pain that persisted for hours, and lost sleep was what the ants brought. The men weathered it, though it drew further down their reserves of strength — the physical and the psychological. Under the forest canopy, the nights grew cold and chilled them to the bone when not near enough to a campfire.

Soon after entering the forest, their primary supplies ran out, forcing them to forage and hunt for food and water. The shortage of supplies would have been demoralizing given their ordeal, except that the forest was bountiful and many of the expedition were skilled hunters and fishermen. Game and fish teemed in the wood and the streams; fruits and berries of many types were abundant. They managed well, the worst being vomiting for some few men that sampled unfamiliar fruit. The trouble was, foraging and hunting took time. A lot of time. It slowed them down tremendously. Yet they had to do it. They needed food to keep up their strength. Not only to go on, but to have the strength to face the League when at last they caught them.

The days stretched into a week, then two since they passed over the rock and entered Jutenheim's interior.

At last they cleared the forest and entered a rocky hill country. The breeze came up from the south and was cool on their faces. Its scent hinted at the sea. After a time, they trudged up a rocky slope, and at the top, came upon a slender watchtower of stone. A man hung unmoving partway out a window. The center of his back looked charred, though it was hard to tell given the distance.

As they drew nearer and got to a better vantage point, they saw that the tower was the scene of a battle. The League had been there. They'd killed the occupants of the tower, and moved on.

The occupants were curious indeed. Soldiers clad in gold and white uniforms over finely wrought chainmail. Most were men — of the same form and size as the folk of Jutenheim. But some few among them were Black Elves. At least two were Dwarves. The soldiers' tabards bore a striking sigil. A golden lion swallowing a black winged serpent.

"You know this sigil?" said Ob to Theta.

"The crest of Uriel the Bold," said Theta.

"Friend of yours from the way back?" said Ob.

"The bodies are not long dead," said Dolan. "One day, no longer. They were abandoning the tower when they got hit."

"What say you?" said Ob as he turned and took a closer look at the dead.

"Those wagons are loaded with supplies," said Dolan pointing to three large carts along the side of the rocky track that ran past the place. "They were making a run for it when the League showed up."

"Dolan is right," said Artol. He'd just exited the tower. "The place is cleaned out. They had forewarning and were hightailing it. Two men inside, tied to chairs. Officers. They worked them over but good."

"Dead?" said Theta.

"Better part of a day at least," said Artol.

"There's a barn in back," said Glimador. "Stalls for twenty horses; all empty."

"We must fly," said Theta. "The League is close, but so is the temple. With horses, they'll move the faster."

And with that, Theta was off. Dolan behind him.

When they passed over the next hill they saw it.

A castle.

A grand work of stone that stood high on a rocky escarpment that overlooked the sea. Its walls thick and tall. Its towers and turrets impressive. No doubt the top of the watch tower they passed had a clear view of the castle and all the surrounding hills.

A wisp of smoke rose from the castle's central tower — the remnant of a fire that still smoldered. The gatehouse was a ruin that spewed black smoke. Several outbuildings were also smoking wrecks.

"That's no ancient temple," said Ob. "It's a fortress. Bigger than the Dor."

"We're too late," said Kayla.

"The League has sacked it," said Claradon.

"We're not too late unless they've got a portal opened," said Tanch. "I see no evidence of that."

"How many men could they have to take down a fortress like that?" said Kayla. "It's large enough to house an army?"

"It may have been sparsely defended," said Ob. "Had to be since we didn't pass any towns or villages. And for all we know, the League may have lost. They may be hanging from the walls even now."

Theta stepped atop a boulder and turned to address the expedition. "That place is the fortress of Uriel the Bold, long ago an ally of mine. If luck is with us, he still is. The temple of power that the League seeks lies at the heart of that fortress. Uriel and whatever forces he commands will defend it against the League unto the death. We must lend Uriel our aid. That is why we are here. The end of our quest is at hand. We must stop the League. Keep them from opening that gateway. Or close it if they've already opened it. There will be no retreating from here. No surrender. No withdrawal. We win or we die. I will make all haste to the castle. Follow me as best you can. Uriel and his men will not know you. They may think you're with the League. Tell them you've come with Thetan the Lightbringer to aid them. Tell them that."

Dolan pulled a roll of cloth from his pack. Unfurled it. There were three squares of cotton, each the size of a book. Theta's sigil emblazoned on each. "Show them those," said Theta. "Good luck."

"But we're all coming with you," said Ob.

Theta sprang from the boulder and sprinted up the trail faster than any armored man should be able to move. Dolan a few strides behind him.

"Let's move," shouted Ob.

They were some two or three miles from the fortress. With the armor and gear they carried, if they ran full out, they'd be spent by the time they reached it. Instead, they jogged along, making the best pace they could without exhausting what little remained of their energy. Only DeBoors and Kaladon raced after Theta, quickly outdistancing the rest of the group.

Ob figured that DeBoors was one of Theta's lot, whatever they were, so it made sense he was of similar constitution. Kaladon was a Pict. Wore no armor to speak of. Carried almost nothing. Made sense that he could move like the wind.

Artol looked over at Ob as they jogged along.

"I heard somewhere that Gnomes are dangerous over short distances; not such good runners over the long."

"You're thinking of Dwarves, Too Tall," said Ob. "Gnomes only run if something too nasty to fight is chasing us. This here is a big exception that I'm making."

"You think we'll beat them?" said Artol. "The League?"

"Have to," said Ob. "All Midgaard depends upon it."

END

GLOSSARY

PLACES

THE REALMS
Asgard: legendary home of the gods
—**Bifrost**: mystical bridge between Asgard and Midgaard
—**Valhalla**: a realm of the gods where great warriors go after death
Helheim: one of the nine worlds; the realm of the dead
Midgaard: the world of man
—**Lomion**: a great kingdom of Midgaard
Nether Realms: realms of demons and devils
Nine Worlds, The: the nine worlds of creation
Nifleheim: the realm of the Lords of Nifleheim / Chaos Lords
Vaeden: paradise, lost
Yggdrasill: sacred tree that supports and/or connects the Nine Worlds

Places Within The Kingdom Of Lomion
Dallassian Hills: large area of rocky hills; home to a large enclave of Dwarves
Dor Caladrill:
Dor Eotrus: see Eotrus Demesne below
Dor Linden: fortress and lands ruled by House Mirtise, in the Linden Forest, southeast of Lomion City
Dor Lomion: fortress within Lomion City ruled by House Harringgold
Dor Malvegil: fortress and lands ruled by House Malvegil, southeast of Lomion City on the west bank of the Grand Hudsar River
Dor Valadon: fortress outside the City of Dover
Doriath Forest: woodland north of Lomion City

Dover, City of: large city situated at Lomion's southeastern border
Dyvers, City of: Lomerian city known for its quality metalworking
Farthing Heights: town ruled by House Farthing.
Grommel: a town known for southern gnomes
Hollow, The: a town;
— **Ancestor Hill:** cemetary
— **Azrael's Manor, known as Virent Hall**
— **The Constabulary:** sheriff's office
— **House Falstad Manor**
— **The Odinhome**
Kern, City of: Lomerian city to the northeast of Lomion City.
Kronar Mountains: a vast mountain range that marks the northern border of the Kingdom of **Lomion**
Lindenwood: a forest to the south of Lomion City, within which live the Lindonaire Elves
Lomion City: see below
Portland Vale: a town known for southern gnomes that are particularly skilled bridge building masons
Tarrows Hold: known for Dwarves

EOTRUS DEMESNE

Dor Eotrus: fortress and lands ruled by House Eotrus, north of Lomion City
— **Citadel, The**: a generic name for the main part of Dor Eotrus — the castle itself. It is also often used to specifically refer to the castle's central tower.
— **Courtyard, The**: open area between the

main citadel walls and the central tower and other buildings.
— **Keep, The**: synonymous with Citadel
— **Odinhome, The**: temple to Odin located in Dor Eotrus; also used as a generic terms for temple/church of Odin.
—**Outer Dor, The**: the town surrounding the fortress of Dor Eotrus. Also used generically as the name for any town surrounding a fortress.
— **Underhalls, The**: the extensive basement levels beneath the citadel.
Berrill's Bridge: a large bridge over the Ottowhile River, northeast of Dor Eotrus, on the West Road
Eastern Hills: in the northeast section of Eotrus demesne
Hollow, The: town where Azrael lives
Markett: a village east of Dor Eotrus, within Eotrus demesne
Mindletown: a town of 400 hundred folk, a few days northeast of Dor Eotrus, in Eotrus demesne. Recently wiped out by trolls.
Ottowhile River: a large river northeast of Dor Eotrus, passable only via bridges for much of the year.
Rhentford: small village on the road between Dor Eotrus and Mindletown. Recently sacked by trolls.
Riker's Crossroads: village at the southern border of Eotrus lands, at the crossroads that leads to Lomion City and Kern.
Roosa: a town
Stebin Pass: a pass through the foothills of the Kronar Mountains, northwest of Dor Eotrus.
Trikan Point Village: village east-northeast of

Mindletown, in Eotrus demesne
Vermion Forest: foreboding wood west of Dor Eotrus
Temple of Guymaog: where the gateway was opened in the Vermion Forest
Westforest: the heavily forested area, beyond the Vermion, to the west of Dor Eotrus
West Rock: at the northwest edge of Eotrus demesne, at the foothills of the Kronar Mountains.
Wortsford: a northern town within Eotrus demesne

LOMION CITY (aka Lomion): capital city of the Kingdom of Lomion
— **Baylock's Rest**: an inn.
— **Bizaar, The**: outdoor and indoor mercantile area
— **Black Hall**: the home base of the Black Hand.
— **Blackron's Tavern:** fancy eatery in the High District
— **Dor Lomion**: fortress within Lomion City ruled by House Harringgold
— **Channel, The**: moat around Lomion City, 150 ft. wide by 30 ft. deep; connected to Grand Hudsar Bay
—**Fister Mansion**: a fancy old hotel in Lomion City
—**Grand Hudsar Bay**: the portion of the Grand Hudsar River that meets Lomion City's south and east borders.
—**Great Meadow, The**: picturesque swath of grassland outside the city gates

—**Tammanian Hall:** high seat of government in Lomion; home of the High Council and the Council of Lords
—**Tower of the Arcane**: high seat of wizardom in all Midgaard; in Lomion City
—**The Heights**: seedy section of Lomion City
—**Southeast**: dangerous section of Lomion City

PARTS FOREIGN

Anglotor: the temple of power in Jutenheim; also the name of Uriel's fortress
– The Olden Dome: strange mystical room at Anglotor
Azure Sea: vast ocean to the south of the Lomerian continent
Black Rock Tower: Glus Thorn's stronghold
Bourntown:
Churthick: a land well east of Lomion
Darendor: dwarven realm of Clan Darendon
Dwarkendeep: a renowned dwarven stronghold
Dead Fens, The: mix of fen, bog, and swampland on the east bank of the Hudsar River, south of Dor Malvegil
Evermere, The Isle of: an island in the Azure Sea, far to the south of the Lomerian continent.
— **The Dancing Turtle**: Evermere's finest inn
Grand Hudsar River: south of Lomion City, it marks the eastern border of the kingdom
Emerald River: large river that branches off from the Hudsar at Dover
Ferd: Far-off city known for its fine goods
Gothmagorn: city of trolls, deep in the Kronar

Mountain range, within Mount Troglestyre
Jutenheim: island far to the south of the Lomerian continent (see below for more details).
– **Jutenheim Town**: only large town in Jutenheim
– "**Over the Rock**": anywhere within the interior of Jutenheim, beyond the cliffs south of Jutenheim Town.
– **Plain of Engelroth**: a great plain in the center of Jutenheim
Karthune Gorge: site of a famed battle involving the Eotrus
Kirth: Par Keld is from there
Kronar Mountains: foreboding mountain range that marks the northern border of the Kingdom of Lomion.
Lent
Lothmargen Plains: site of a famous battle during the Age of Heroes
Minoc-by-the-Sea: coastal city
Mount Troglestyre: mountain within the Kronar Range; home of mountain troll kingdom of Gothmagorn
Ratick, Mount: volcano erupted there, Dolan was there
R'lyeh: a bastion for evil creatures; Sir Gabriel and Theta fought a great battle there in times past.
Saridden, City of:
Shandelon: famed gnomish city
Southron Isles: islands in the Azure Sea
—**Hargone Bay:**
Starkbarrow: underground Svart city on Isle of Jutenheim.
Thoonbarrow: capital city of the Svarts;

underground
Trachen Marches: Theta and Dolan fought the Vhen there.
Tragoss Krell: city ruled by Thothian Monks, on the coast of the Azure Sea.
Tragoss Mor: large city far to the south of Lomion, at the mouth of the Hudsar River where it meets the Azure Sea. Ruled by Thothian Monks.
Trollheim: the land of the trolls

JUTENHEIM
It's an island continent in the far south of Midgaard's southern hemisphere. It's also the name of the primary human settlement (a large town with a significant port) on the continent.

Anglotor: Svart name for the temple of power where Korrgonn seeks to open a gateway to Nifleheim.
Eye of Gladden, The: stone arch within the tunnels of Svartleheim (Starkbarrow)
Grasping Grond, The: an inn
Monastery of Ivald: populated by the monks of Ivald.
Starkbarrow: underground city of the Black Elves;
Svartleheim: tunnels within and below the cliffs separating Jutenheim Town from the interior of the Isle of Jutenheim.

PEOPLE

PEOPLES OF MIDGAARD
Emerald elves
Lindonaire Elves (from Linden Forest)
Doriath Elves ('dor-i`-ath') (from Doriath Forest)
Dallassian Dwarves (doll-ass`-ian) (from the Dallassian Hills). Typically four feet tall, plus or minus one foot.
Elves: generic name for various peoples known to be long-lived, with pointed ears, and sharp features. The females tend to be very curvy while the males tend to be slender.
Elfs: generic term for various non-Volsung or non-human peoples. Often used in reference to Svarts, Stowron, and others. Sometimes Picts are incorrectly labeled "Elfs".
Ettins: hairy, primitve giants
Gnomes (northern and southern), typically three feet tall, plus or minus one foot.
Humans/Men: generic term for people. (In usage, usually includes Gnomes, Dwarves, and Elves)
Juten Lugron: the variety of Lugron that live on the Island of Jutenheim
Lugron (usually pronounced 'lou-gron'; sometimes, 'lug`-ron'): a barbaric people from the northern mountains, on average, shorter and stockier than Volsungs, and with higher voices.
Mistkelstrans: an extinct race
Picts: a barbarian people
Stowron (usually pronounced 'stow`-ron'): pale, stooped people of feeble vision who've

dwell in lightless caverns beneath the Kronar Mountains
Svarts: gray skin, large eyes, spindly limbs, three feet tall or so. Often called "Black Elves" or "Elfs", though they are unrelated to true Elves.
Trolls: primitive; they heal rapidly; faster than horses over long distance; incredible agility and great strength
Vanyar Elves: legendary elven people
Vhen, The: cousins of the Lugron; dwell in northernmost mountains; sometimes eat people.
Volsungs: a generic term for the primary people/tribes populating the Kingdom of Lomion
Zorns: an extinct race.

HIGH COUNCIL OF LOMION
Selrach Rothtonn Tenzivel III: His Royal Majesty: King of Lomion
Aldros, Lord: Councilor
Aramere, Lady: Councilor representing the City of Dyvers
Balfor, Field Marshal: Councilor representing the Lomerian armed forces; Commander of the Lomerian army
Barusa of Alder, Lord: Chancellor of Lomion; eldest son of Mother Alder
Cartegian Tenzivel, Prince: Selrach's son, insane; Councilor representing the Royal House.
Dahlia, Lady: Councilor representing the City of Kern
Glenfinnen, Lord: Councilor representing the City of Dover
Harper Harringgold, Lord: Councilor representing Lomion City; Arch-Duke of Lomion

City
Jhensezil, Lord Garet: Councilor representing the Churchmen; Preceptor of the Odion Knights
Morfin, Baron: Councilor
Slyman, Guildmaster: Councilor representing the guilds; Master of Guilds
Tobin Carthigast, Bishop: Councilor representing the Churchmen
Vizier, The (Grandmaster Rabrack Philistine): The Royal Wizard; Grandmaster and Councilor representing the Tower of the Arcane
— **Leren Banyard**: physician to the High Council

NOBLE HOUSES

<u>**House Alder**</u> (Pronounced All-der)
A leading, noble family of Lomion City. Their principal manor house is within the city's borders
Batholomew Alder: youngest son of Mother Alder
Bartol Alder: younger brother of Barusa, Myrdonian Knight
Barusa Alder, Lord: Chancellor of Lomion, eldest son of Mother Alder.
Blain Alder: younger brother of Barusa
Brock Alder: 6th son of Mother Alder (deceased)
Dirk Alder: eldest son of Bartol Alder
Edith Alder: der of Blain; a child
Edwin Alder: son of Blain
Mother Alder: matriarch of the House; an Archseer of the Orchallian Order

Rom Alder: brother of Mother Alder
Sirnick Butler: House butler
Zilda Alder: 1st daughter of Bartol

<u>**House Eotrus**</u> (pronounced Eee-oh-tro`-sss) The Eotrus rule the fortress of Dor Eotrus, the Outer Dor (a town outside the fortress walls) and the surrounding lands for many leagues.
Aradon Eotrus, Lord: Patriarch of the House (presumed dead)
Adolphus: a servant
Claradon Eotrus, Brother: (Clara-don) eldest son of Aradon, Caradonian Knight; Patriarch of the House; Lord of Dor Eotrus
Donnelin, Brother: House Cleric for the Eotrus (presumed dead)
Ector Eotrus, Sir: Third son of Aradon
Eleanor Malvegil Eotrus: (deceased) Wife of Aradon Eotrus; sister of Torbin Malvegil.
Gabriel Garn, Sir: House Weapons Master (presumed dead, body possessed by Korrgonn)
Humphrey (Humph): Claradon's manservant
Jude Eotrus, Sir: Second son of Aradon (prisoner of the Shadow League)
Nardon, Lord: Aradon Eotrus's father (deceased)
Pontly, Castellan: House Castellan prior to Ob.
<u>Knights & Soldiers of the House</u>:
— **Sergeant Artol**: 7 foot tall veteran warrior.
— **Sir Paldor Cragsmere**: a young knight; formerly, Sir Gabriel's squire
— **Sir Glimador Malvegil**: son of Lord Torbin Malvegil; can throw spells
— **Sir Indigo Eldswroth**: handsome, heavily muscled, and exceptionally tall knight

— **Sir Kelbor**
— **Sir Ganton**: called "the bull" or "bull"
— **Sir Trelman**
— **Sir Marzdan** (captain of the gate, deceased)
— **Sir Sarbek du Martegran** (acting Castellan of Dor Eotrus), a knight captain of the Odion Knights
— **Sir Wyndham the Bold of Weeping Hollow**: knight captain (deceased)
— **Lieutenant, The**: veteran cavalry officer (deceased)
— **Sergeant Vid**
— **Sergeant Lant**
— **Sergeant Baret**
— **Trooper Graham**
— **Trooper Bront; Trooper Krint; Trooper Dross; Lieutenant Krander; Captain Haden of the archer corps;**
— Trooper Harsnip (deceased), Sergeant Balfin (deceased), Sir Miden (deceased), Sergeant Jerem (deceased), Sir Conrad (deceased), Sir Martin (deceased), Sir Bilson (deceased), Sir Glimron (deceased), Sir Talbot (deceased), Sir Dalken (deceased)
Malcolm Eotrus: Fourth son of Aradon
Nardon, Eotrus, Lord: Aradon's father
Ob A. Faz III: (Ahb A. Fahzz) Castellan and Master Scout of Dor Eotrus; a gnome
Pellan, Captain (aka, the beardless dwarf)
Pontly: former Castellan of the House prior to Ob being appointed to that position
Sirear Eotrus, Lady: daughter of August Eotrus (deceased)
Stern of Doriath: Master Ranger for the Eotrus (presumed dead)

Talbon of Montrose, Par: Former House Wizard for the Eotrus (presumed dead), son of Grandmaster (Par) Mardack
Tanch Trinagal, Par: (Trin-ah-ghaal) of the Blue Tower; Son of Sinch; House Wizard for the Eotrus. Aliases: Par Sinch; Par Sinch Malaban.
Sverdes, Leren: House physician and alchemist

Eotrus Bannermen
Brian, Lord: patriarch of House Brian
Cadbury, Lord: patriarch of House Cadbury
Lester, Lord: patriarch of House Lester
Old Lord Nickel: patriarch of House Nickel
– **Master Yallzen:** an archwizard in service to House Nickel
Thaddeous Ogden, Lord: Lord of Westforest: patriarch of House Ogden

House Harringgold
Harper Harringgold, Lord: Archduke of Lomion City; Lord of Dor Lomion, Patriarch of the House. He has a brother in Kern.
Brithhilda: Marissa's servant
Fearless, The: elite Troops
— **Captain Cuda**: commander of The Fearless
— **Balkind the Bowman**
— **Blue Ben**
— **Jak the Blademan**
— **The Rage**
Grim Fischer: agent of Harper, a gnome
Leren Trak: House physician
Marissa Harringgold: daughter of Harper, former love interest of Claradon Eotrus.
Seran Harringgold, Sir: nephew of Harper

House Malvegil
Words: *"Honor and vigilance always"*
Torbin Malvegil, Lord: Patriarch of the House; Lord of Dor Malvegil, Lord of the Eastern Marches.
Landolyn, Lady: of House Adonael; Torbin's consort. Of part elven blood.
Clan MacRondal: ruled the Eastern Marches prior to the Malvegils. MacRondal warcry: "*You've no idea what we're made of*"
Eleanor Malvegil Eotrus: (deceased) Wife of Aradon Eotrus; sister of Torbin Malvegil.
Gedrun, Captain: a knight commander in service to Lord Malvegil
Glimador Malvegil, Sir: son of Torbin and Landolyn; working in the service of House Eotrus.
Gorlick the Bold, Master: House Weapons Master – 29th Weapons Master to the Malvegils; son of Thraydin and Bernda
Gravemare, Hubert: Castellan of Dor Malvegil
Hogart: harbormaster of Dor Malvegil's port.
Karktan of Rivenwood, Master: Weapons Master for the Malvegils
Leren Tage: House Physician, circa 1242.
Mordel: Castellan of Dor Malvegil circa year 1,212 - 1,24x.
Ronald, Brother: House Cleric
Rorbit, Par: House Wizard to the Malvegils
Stoub of Rivenwood: Lord Malvegil's chief bodyguard; brother of Karktan (deceased)
Tage, Leren: House physician
Torgrist, Brother: Dor Malvegil's high cleric.
Troopers: Bern, Brant, Conger: Malvegillian soldiers

Tybor, Red: House Master Scout; a Pict

House Morfin
Baron Morfin: Patriarch of the House; a member of the High Council
Gallick Morfin: eldest son of the Baron.

House Tenzivel (the Royal House)
King Selrach Rothtonn Tenzivel III: (deceased) His Royal Majesty: King of Lomion
Cartegian Tenzivel, Prince: Selrach's son; insane.
Dramadeens: royal bodyguards for House Tenzivel
— **Korvalan of Courwood, Captain**: (deceased) Commander of the Dramadeens.
— **Mavron**: second-in-command of the Dramadeens; a hulking brute

OTHER NOBLE HOUSES OF LOMION
House Tavermain; House Grondeer; House Dantrel;
House Forndin
A minor House loyal to and located within Eotrus lands. Their major holding is known as Forndin Manor.
Alana Forndin, Lady: matriarch of the House
Sir Erendin of Forndin Manor: eldest son of the House (deceased)
Sir Miden of Forndin Manor: younger brother of Erendin (deceased)
Sir Talbot of Forndin Manor: younger brother of Erendin (deceased)

House Hanok
A minor House loyal to and located within Eotrus lands. Their major holding is known as Hanok Keep.
Sir Bareddal of Hanok Keep: in service to the Eotrus (deceased)

House Mirtise
The Mirtises rule over the area surrounding the fortress of Dor Linden, which lies south of Malvegil lands on the west side of the Grand Hudsar River.
Lady Mirtise: matriarch of the House
Leren Jrack: House Physician

OTHER HOUSES AND GROUPS

Clan Darendon of Darendor
Royal clan from the Dwarven kingdom
Bornyth Trollsbane, High King of Clan Darendon.
Galibar the Great: the prince of Darendor, first son to Bornyth and heir to Clan Darendon
Jarn Yarspitter: councilor to Bornyth

The Black Hand
A brotherhood of Assassins
Black Hall: the home base of the Black Hand in Lomion City
Brethren, The: term the assassins use for fellow members of The Hand.
Coburn: a Hand leader
Grandmistress, The: the leader of The Hand
– **Mila**: one of the grandmistress's favorites
Mallick Fern: an assassin; The Hand's second

ranking agent (deceased)
Rat, The: a Hand leader
Rifkin: a Hand assassin
Weater the Mouse: a Hand leader

Brood tet Montu of Svartleheim
The royal house of the svarts
Diresvarts: svart wizard-priests
Guyphoon Garumptuss tet Montu: high king of Thoonbarrow, Patriarch of Brood tet Montu, Master of the Seven Stratems, and Lord of all Svartleheim, offspring of Guyphoon Pintalia of the Windy Ways, Traymoor Garumptuss the Bold, and Trantmain lin Backus tet Montu, great king of the undermountains
Cardakeen rack Mortha: a svart seer
Orator, The: the spokesman for the svart king

Black Elves (Svarts) of Starkbarrow
Diresvarts: Svart wizard-priests
Karaka niln Bertel: The Seer of Starkbarrow
Ramluk the Diresvart: High Magus of Starkbarrow
Rock Elementals: giant, fire-breathing minions of the Starkbarrow Svarts.
Throonbilg biln Mac-Murth: high king of Starkbarrow

The Lords of Nifleheim and Their Minions
Azathoth: god worshipped by the Lords of Nifleheim and The Shadow League/The League of Light; his followers call him the "one true god".
Arioch: a Lord of Nifleheim

Bhaal: a Lord of Nifleheim; came through the gateway in the Vermion but was banished back by Angle Theta
Hecate: a Lord of Nifleheim.
Korrgonn, Lord Gallis: son of Azathoth
Mortach: (aka Mikel): a Lord of Nifleheim; killed by Angle Theta
— **Reskalan**: demonic foot soldiers in service to the Lords of Nifleheim
— **Zymog**: a reskalan
— **Brigandir**: supernatural warrior(s) of Nifleheim
— **Einheriar**: supernatural warriors of Nifleheim

The Asgardian Gods
Odin (the All-father) (aka Wotan): king of the gods
Thor (aka Donar): son of Odin
Tyr (aka Cyo):
Heimdall (aka Vindler):
Loki:
Baldr:
—**Valkyries**: sword maidens of the gods. They choose worthy heroes slain in battle and conduct them to Valhalla.

Other Gods
Armagarg: troll god
Dagon of the Deep: appears as a giant lizard; lives in caverns beneath an uncharted island deep in the Azure Sea.
— **Dwellers of the Deep**: very large, bipedal sea creatures that worship Dagon.
Thoth:
Donar: worshipped by the Jutens; akin to Thor;

son of Wotan.
Wotan: worshipped by the Jutens; akin to Odin

Great Beasts, Monsters, Creatures, Animals

Barrow Wight
Borkoth Garaktok, the Lord of Shadows; Duke of the Nether Marches**:**
Blood Lord: legendary fiends that drink blood and eat humans.
Dire Wolves: extremely large breed of wolves
Duergar: mythical undead creatures
Draugar: undead creatures that feast on the living
Dwellers of the Deep: worshippers of Dagon; huge, bipedal fishlike creatures
Ettins: giants of Jutenheim
– **Koobtak**: chieftain of the Ettins
Fire Wyrm or "**Wyrms**": dragons
Giant (aka Jotun, pl. Jotnar):
Grond: a type of large monkey or ape native to Jutenheim
Gronsel: they smell bad
Holyphant: a mammoth
Jotnar: giants (plural of Jotun)
Jotun: a giant
Ogres:
Olyphant: a mammoth
Leviathan: a huge sea creature
Red Demons of Fozramgar: Mort Zag is one.
Saber-cat: saber-toothed tiger
Shadow Demon: a monstrous dragon of the Nether Realms, perhaps, undead, or else immortal.

Shamblers: undead; zombies.
Throan Gron Sek Nifleheem: Thrice Horned Demons of the Nether Realms
Tranteers: the lithe, speedy horses bred in Dover
Trolls, Mountain: mythical creatures of the high mountains; many live within Mount Troglestyre
— **Armagarg**: troll god
— **Gotrak of Gothmagorn, son of Tirb the Bold**: troll chieftain; his son has the same name
— **Shevtak**: friend of the troll king
— **Tarmain**: High Magus of all Trollheim
— **Terna:** wife of Gotrak
Wendigo: monster of legend that eats people.

The Crew of *The Black Falcon*
Slaayde, Dylan: Captain of *The Black Falcon*
Bertha Smallbutt: ship's quartermaster and Slaayde's consort (deceased)
Bire Cabinboy: ship's cabin boy — was in league with Darg Tran
Chert: a young seaman
Darg Tran, son of Karn, of old House Elowine: ship's navigator; secret wizard & traitor (deceased)
Eolge: a crewman (deceased)
Fizdar Firstbar "the corsair": former first mate (presumed dead)
Gurt, Seaman: (aka Gurt the Knife) a crewman; known for knife fighting skills (deceased)
Guj: boatswain. A half-Lugron. (deceased)
N'Paag: First Mate
Old Mock: a crewman (deceased)

Ravel: ship's trader and medic (deceased)
Tug, Little: Near 7 foot tall part-Lugron seaman; Old Fogey — Tug's battle hammer

The Passengers of *The Black Falcon*

Sergeant Artol: 7-foot-tall veteran warrior.
Claradon Eotrus, Brother: (Clara-don) eldest son of Aradon, Caradonian Knight; Patriarch of the House; Lord of Dor Eotrus
Dolan Silk: Theta's manservant
Ganton, Sir (the Bull): a knight of House Eotrus
Kayla Kazeran: part Lindonaire elf, rescued from slavery in Tragoss Mor; love interest of Claradon
Kelbor, Sir: a knight of House Eotrus
Lant, Sergeant: a soldier of House Eotrus
Lomerian Soldiers: a squadron of soldiers of House Harringgold, assigned to assist House Eotrus. Under the command of Seran Harringgold.
Malvegil, Sir Glimador: first cousin to Claradon; son of Lord Torbin Malvegil and Lady Landolyn
Malvegillian Archers: a squad of soldiers assigned to assist House Eotrus by Lord Malvegil
Ob A. Faz III: (Ahb A. Fahzz) Castellan and Master Scout of Dor Eotrus; a gnome
Paldor Cragsmere, Sir: a young knight of House Eotrus, formerly, Sir Gabriel's squire
Seran Harringgold, Sir: nephew of Arch-Duke Harper Harringgold — assigned to assist House Eotrus
Tanch Trinagal, Par: (Trin-ah-ghaal) of the

Blue Tower; Son of Sinch; House Wizard for the Eotrus. Aliases: Par Sinch; Par Sinch Malaban.
Theta, Lord Angle (aka Thetan): a knight-errant from a far-off land across the sea. Sometimes called the Harbinger of Doom
Thothian Monk, a: an elderly fellow; taken prisoner during the incident with Prior Finch at Tragoss Mor
Trelman, Sir: a knight of House Eotrus
Vid, Sergeant: a soldier of House Eotrus

The Crew/Passengers of *The Gray Talon*
Alder Marines: squadrons of soldiers from House Alder; Finnias of Alder
Azura du Marnian, the Seer: Seer based in Tragoss Mor.
Bartol Alder: younger brother of Barusa; a Myrdonian Knight
Blain Alder: younger brother of Barusa
DeBoors, Milton: (The Duelist of Dyvers). A mercenary
Edwin Alder: son of Blain
Kaledon of the Gray Waste: a Pict mercenary
Kleig: Captain of *The Grey Talon*
Knights of Kalathen: elite mercenaries that work for DeBoors
Myrdonian Knights: squadron of knights assigned to House Alder

The Crew/Passengers of *The White Rose*
Brackta Finbal, Par: female archmage of The League of Light
du Mace, Varak: Captain of *The White Rose*
Ezerhauten, Lord: Commander of Sithian Mercenary Company

Frem Sorlons: captain of the Sithians Pointmen Squadron
Ginalli, Father: High Priest of Azathoth, Arkon of The League of Light.
Hablock, Par: an archmage of the League of Light (deceased)
Keld, Par of Kerth: a middle-aged wizard of the League of Light, short, stocky, balding, and nervous.
Landru, Par: a wizard (deceased); has several brothers
Lugron: a barbaric people from the northern mountains, on average, shorter and stockier than Volsungs.
Mason: a stone golem created by The Keeper of Tragoss Mor; companion to Stev Keevis.
Miles de Gant: a sithian soldier (deceased). Son of **Count de Gant**
Morsmun, Par: an archmage of the League of Light (deceased)
Mort Zag: a red-hued giant
Oris, Par: an elderly wizard of the League of Light; former mentor of Par Keld.
Ot, Par: an archmage of the League of Light (deceased)
Pointmen, The: an elite squadron of the Sithian Mercenary Company
Rascelon, Captain Rastinfan: former captain of *The White Rose* (deceased)
Rhund, Par: a wizard of the League of Light
Sevare Zendrack, Par: Squadron wizard for the Pointmen
Sithians: mercenaries under the command of Ezerhauten; some are soldiers, some are knights

Stev Keevis Arkguardt: an elven archwizard from the Emerald Forest allied with The League of Light; former apprentice of The Keeper
Teek Lugron: Lugron guard/jailor
Tremont of Wyndum: a sithian knight (deceased)
Weldin, Par: a wizard of the League of Light
Thorn, Par (Master) Glus: an archwizard of the League of Light; a sorcerer
—**Lasifer, Par**: Glus Thorn's gnome assistant/apprentice.
—**Nord**: a stowron in Thorn's employ
Tribik: Lugron guard/jailor (deceased)

Sithian Mercenary Company
Ezerhauten, Lord: Commander
Frem Sorlons: Captain, Pointmen Squadron
Bradik, Leutenant: 4th Squadron
Cotter the Dandy: company wizard (deceased)
Grainer, Sergeant: 2nd Squadron
Landru, Par: a squadron wizard (deceased)
Markus, Captain: 2nd Squadron's captain
Miles de Gant: a knight; son of Count de Gant (deceased)
Rewes of Ravenhollow, Sir: a knight (deceased)
Stanik Lugron: 4th Squadron
Tremont of Wyndum: a knight captain (deceased)

The Pointmen (an elite squadron of the Sithian Mercenary Company)

Frem Sorlons: captain, Pointmen Squadron
Sevare Zendrack, Par: squadron wizard for

the Pointmen
Putnam, Sergeant: Pointmen,1st Squad
Boatman: Pointmen (deceased)
Borrel Lugron: Pointmen
Bryton: Pointmen (deceased)
Carroll, Sir: Pointmen; a knight
Clard: Pointmen; a Lugron
Drift, Trooper: Pointmen
Dirnel: Pointmen; a Lugron (deceased)
Held: Pointmen (deceased)
Jorna: Pointmen (deceased)
Lex, Sir: Pointmen
Little Storrl: Pointmen,1st Squad; a young Lugron
Maddix, Trooper: Pointmen
Ma-Grak Stowron
Maldin, Sergeant: Pointmen,2nd Squad, (Badly wounded, spear through chest)
Moag Lugron: Pointmen,1st squad; Master Scout
Roard, Sir: Pointmen,1st Squad; a knight (deceased)
Royce, Sir: Pointmen; a knight
Torak Lugron: Pointmen
Ward, Sir: Pointmen
Wikkle Lugron: Pointmen

The Dead Fens Expedition (Year 1242 of the 4th Age of Midgaard)

The Bellowing Banshee: one of three ships that went missing; its disappearance precipitated the expedition.

The Malvegils:
1. Lord Torbin Malvegil: the Great Lord of the Malvegils
2. McDuff the Mighty: friend of Torbin; a dwarf
3. Master Gorlick the Bold: House Weapons Master (deceased)
4. Par Rorbit: House Wizard (deceased)
5. Red Tybor: Master Scout (deceased)
6. Karktan of Rivenwood: Gorlick's Lieutenant

The Eotrus
1. Lord Aradon Eotrus: the Great Lord of the Eotrus (deceased)
2. Ob: Master Scout
3. Sir Gabriel Garn: House Weapons Master (deceased)
4. Par Talbon of Montrose: House Wizard (deceased)
5. Brother Donnelin: House Cleric
6. Artol: a young warrior of the House

Bonebreakers, The

Famed Lugron mercenary company
Brontack: former leader of the Bonebreakers (deceased)
Gorgorath the Bonebreaker: Captain of the Bonebreakers (deceased)

Grontor: son of Gorgorath
Hartick: former leader of the Bonebreakers (deceased)
Mog, Old: the Bonebreaker's battle mage (deceased)
Mordo: 500 lb Lugron soldier (deceased)
Morgorlain: a Vhen; chieftain of the Stikdar Vhen, son of Gartak, slayer of Domis Darackti, and Lord of the Torg Peaks. (deceased)
Mort of Bemil's Vane: founder of the Bonebreakers (deceased)
Radsol: a Lugron soldier
Teek: a Lugron soldier
Trench, Old: the Bonebreaker's cook (deceased)
Tribek: a Lugron soldier (deceased)
Wolfrick: the leader of rival Lugron mercenary company

The Regent's Expeditionary Force
Alder, Brock (aka The Regent): 6th son of Mother Alder (deceased)
Alder, Dirk: eldest son of Bartol Alder
Alder, Rom: brother of Mother Alder
Bald Boddrick: (aka 'The Backbreaker')
Bithel the Piper: well-known mercenary
Black Grint: infamous killer
Gar Pullman: famed mercenary
Kralan, Captain: a Myrdonian Knight in command of the Myrdonian cavalry squadron (deceased)
Martrin, Captain: the Lomerian guard captain in command of the regulars (deceased)
Sentry of Allendale: well-known mercenary

Militant and Mystic Orders
Caradonian Knights: priestly order; patron—Odin
Churchmen: a generic term for the diverse group of priests and knights of various orders.
Freedom Guardsmen: soldiery of Tragoss Mor
Grontor's Bonebreakers: a mercenary company. The Lugron, Teek and Tribik belonged to it.
Halsbad's Freeswords: a mercenary company that Pellan once worked for.
Kalathen, Knights of: mercenary knights that work for Milton DeBoors
Myrdonians: Royal Lomerian Knights
Odions, The: patron—Odin; Preceptor—Lord Jhensezil; Chapterhouse: in Lomion City
Orchallian Order, The: an Order of Seers; Mother Alder is one of them.
Order of the Arcane: the wizard members of the Tower of the Arcane
Rangers Guild, The: Chapterhouse — Doriath Hall in Lomion City; Preceptor: Sir Samwise Sluug; loyal to House Harringgold.
— **Drydan, Captain**: a guard captain
Sithian Knights, The: Preceptor—Lord Ezerhauten
Sundarian Knights: patron: Thor; Preceptor: Sir Hithron du Maris; Chapterhouse: hidden in Tragoss Mor
Tyr, Knights of (aka Tyrians): patron—Tyr

The Evermerians
Ebert Cook: (deceased)
Duchess Morgovia of House Falstad: ruler of Evermere (deceased)

Moby and Toby: brothers; the "beloveds" of Penny. (deceased)
Penny: a tiny wisp of a girl (deceased)
Rasker: he guards the Duchess's warehouse (deceased)
Rendon, Lord: a noble of Evermere
Slint: aka the "scarecrow"; the Duchess's henchman (deceased)
Trern: he guards the Duchess's warehouse (deceased)

People of Anglotor
Uriel the Bold
Brithlinda: a consort of Uriel's
Girthmagen: a consort of Uriel's
Kapte: an apprentice/consort of Uriel's
Malth'Urn: Uriel's Seer
Mysinious: an apprentice/consort of Uriel's
Trilda: a consort of Uriel's

People of The Hollow
Azrael: alchemist/tinker/wizard/Eternal (deceased)
Bron Mason: a member of the hunters
Brother Jarkin: town cleric for The Hollow
Constable, The: chief lawman of The Hollow; the marshals report to him.
Ebert Cook: a cook (deceased)
Falstad, Lady Dahlia: sister of Cassandra Farthing (deceased)
Duke Baltan of **Farthing Heights** (deceased); late husband of Lady Cassandra
Farthing, Lady (Duchess) Cassandra Falstad (deceased)
Farthing, Miss Pennebray: daughter of Lady

Cassandra (deceased)
Hunters, the: men organized by Azrael.
Jaros Tull: famed mercenary captain; one of Azrael's hunters.
Marple Butler: Azrael's butler / lead servant
Mashals, The: lawmen of The Hollow (deceased)
Mayor Barnton: mayor of The Hollow (deceased)
Mikel Potter: a skilled potter. (deceased)
Pennebray (aka Penny): daughter of Lady Cassandra (deceased)
Refisal: Azrael's elderly gnome assistant
Rintle Blacksmith: a member of the hunters; brother of Triber
Rit Bowman: a member of the hunters
Triber Blacksmith: a member of the hunters; brother of Rintle
Widow Lothborg: enemy of Lady Cassandra Farthing

People of Mindletown
A town of several hundred folks within Eotrus demesne. The Odinhall is their most secure building. All listed are missing, dead, or presumed dead, except for Pellan.
Alchemist, the: town council member of Mindletown (deceased)
Baker, The and sons: townsfolk of Mindletown
Butcher, the: town council member of Mindletown
Cobbler: townsman of Mindletown; lives across the street from the alchemist
Constable Granger: constable of Mindletown

Farmer Smythe: a townsman of Mindletown (deceased)
Iceman: an ice merchant that sells his ice to Mindletown; hails from the northwest.
Innman: an innkeeper in Mindletown
Mikar Trapper: a trapper that sells his wares in Mindletown
Miller and his sons: townsmen of Mindletown
Old Cern: town elder of Mindletown (deceased)
Old Marvik: a Mindletown merchant that lived across from the alchemist
Pellan: the "beardless dwarf"; a town council member of Mindletown and former Captain in Dor Eotrus''s guard
Tanner, Mileson: a townsman of Mindletown
Thom Prichard: a townsman of Mindletown (deceased)
Wheelwright and his wife: townsfolk of Mindletown (both deceased)

People of Jutenheim
Angel of Death, The: a seer / "woman of the bones" / the crone of Jutenheim. Travels with a large boy and wolf.
Darmod Rikenguard: a guide. Works with his two sons.
Helda: Rothmar's wife; Ragnar's mother.
Kordan: a guide
Juten: generic word for a resident of Jutenheim
Old Fortis: proprietor of The Grasping Grond
Red Demon of Fozramgar, The: its coming was foretold by the Angel of Death.
Ragnar: Rothmar and Helda's son
Rothmar: owns Jutenheim's leading smithery;

husband of Helda; father of Ragnar
Seer's Boy: the grandson of the crone of Jutenheim.

Monastery of Ivald, The
Brother Abraxon: chief monk of the Ivald Monastery (deceased)
Brother Bertold: the monastery's keeper of maps
Brother Rennis: he's a guard post in the seventh underhall
Old Brother Hordin: former keeper of maps (deceased)

Others of Note

Azura du Marnian, the Seer: Seer based in Tragoss Mor. Now travels with the Alders on *The Gray Talon*.
Gorb: Azura's bodyguard (deceased)
Rimel Stark: Azura's bodyguard and famed Freesword
Dirkben: Azura's bodyguard (deceased)
Balthazar: battled with Azrael the Wise in ancient times
Brondel Cragsmere, Sire: father of Sir Paldor of Dor Eotrus
Coriana Sorlons: daughter of Frem Sorlons
Dark Sendarth: famed assassin in league with House Harringgold and House Tenzivel
Du Maris, Sir Hithron: Preceptor of the Sundarian Chapterhouse in Tragoss Mor; from Dor Caladrill
Graybeard, Captain: the captain of the schooner docked at Evermere

Halsbad: a mercenary leader
Harbinger of Doom, The: legendary, perhaps mythical, being that led a rebellion against Azathoth
Jaros, the Blood Lord: foe of Sir Gabriel Garn
Keeper, The: elven "keeper" of the Orb of Wizard beneath Tragoss Mor
Krisona, Demon-Queen: foe of Sir Gabriel Garn
Kroth, Garon: newly appointed High Magister
Marbon, Lady: friend of Mother Alder
Mardack, Grandmaster (Par) of Montrose: famed wizard; father of Par Talbon of Montrose
McDuff the Mighty: (aka "Red Beard"); a dwarf of many talents
Pipkorn, Grandmaster: (aka Rascatlan) former Grand Master of the Tower of the Arcane. A wizard.
Prior Finch: a prior of Thoth in Tragoss Mor (deceased)
Sarq: a Thothian Monk. Known as the Champion of Tragoss Mor
Shadow League, The (aka The League of Shadows; aka The League of Light): alliance of individuals and groups collectively seeking to bring about the return of Azathoth to Midgaard
Sluug, Sir (Lord) Samwise: Preceptor of the Rangers Guild; Master of Doriath Hall
Snor Slipnet: Patriarch of Clan Rumbottle; a gnome
Spanzileers, The: attacked the Eotrus by way of the eastern hills.
Sons of Ivaldi: Beckir and Birkir; Svarts; makers of magical wonders
Talidousen: Former Grand Master of the Tower

of the Arcane; created the fabled Rings of the Magi.
Thothian monks: monks that rule Tragoss Mor and worship Thoth
Throng-Baz : an ancient people that used runic script
Valas Tearn: an assassin said to have slain a thousand men; foe of Sir Gabriel Garn
Valkyries: sword maidens of the gods. They choose worthy heroes slain in battle and conduct them to Valhalla.
Vanyar Elves: legendary elven people

Titles
Archmage / Archwizard: honorific title for a highly skilled wizard
Archseer: honorific title for a highly skilled seer
Arkon: a leader/general in service to certain gods and religious organizations
Battle Mage: a wizard whose skills are combat oriented.
Castellan: the commander of a fortress/Dor; in service to the Dor Lord.
Constable: chief law enforcement officer of a village or town.
Dor Lord: the leader of a fortress; usually a noble, and often the Patriarch/Matriach of a noble House.
Freesword: an independent soldier or mercenary
Grandmaster: honorific title for a senior wizard of the Tower of the Arcane.
Hedge Wizard: a wizard specializing in potions and herbalism, and/or minor magics.

High Cleric: the senior priest of a church/temple, or of a religious order.
High Magister: a member of Lomion's Tribunal.
High Priest: the senior priest of a church/temple, or of a religious order.
House Cleric: the senior priest in service to a noble House
House Wizard: a senior wizard in service to a noble House
Leren: (pronounced Lee-rhen) generic title for a physician
Mage: a practitioner of magic; a wizard.
Magling: a young or inexperienced wizard; also, a derogatory term for a wizard.
Marshal: a law enforcement officer; typically reports to a Constable of village or town.
Master Oracle: a highly skilled seer.
Master Scout: the chief scout/hunter/tracker of a fortress or noble House.
Par: honorific title for a wizard
Seer (sometimes, "Seeress"): women with supernatural powers to see past/present/future events.
Sorcerer: a practitioner of magic; a wizard.
Tower Mage: a wizard that his a member of the Order of the Arcane.
Weapons Master: the senior weapon's instructor/trainer/officer at a fortress.
Wizard: practitioners of magic

Wizards of the Arcane Order
Arcane Order: formal organization of wizards. Their home base is the Tower of the Arcane, also known as, the High Seat of Wizardom in Lomion City.

Gatwind, Par: a wizard originally from the Southron Isles; a member of the Freedom Council.
Pentarkian Order: an order of war wizards within the Arcane Order
Pipkorn, Grandmaster (aka Rascatlan): former Grand Master of the Tower of the Arcane. Aka, "Old Pointy Hat"
Spugnoir, Grandmaster: a grandmaster of the Tower of the Arcane
Trask, Par: a member of the Freedom Council (deceased)
Triman, Par: a member of the Freedom Council
Vizier, The (Rabrack Philistine): aka The Royal Wizard; High Councilor representing the Tower of the Arcane

The Freedom Council
Grandmaster Pipkorn
Grandmaster Mardack
Sir Samwise Sluug
Lord Mirtise
Lord (Duke) Harringgold
Par Trask (deceased)
King Tenzivel (deceased)
Baron Morfin
Gallick Morfin
Grandmaster Spugnoir
Captain Korvalan (deceased)
Par Triman
Par Gatwind
Lord Smirdoon of Lockely Bay
et.al

Arkons of Azathoth
Arioch; Azrael the Wise; Bhaal; Gabriel; Mikel; Mithron: armor and cape black as obsidian Thetan the Lightbringer; Uriel the Bold

Allies of Thetan from Olden Days
Azrael the Wise
Gabriel
Gladsol, Emperor
Hoenir the Swift
Mithron: armor and cape black as obsidian
Magni the Strong
Melkar (King) of Ulek Morn
Modi the Poet
Njord of the Sea
Thetan the Lightbringer
Uriel the Bold
Vali the Avenger
Vidar the Silent

THINGS

Miscellany
Alder Stone, The: a Seer Stone held by House Alder
Amulet of Escandell: a magical device that detects the presence of danger; gifted to Claradon by Pipkorn
Articles of the Republic: the Lomerian constitution
Asgardian Daggers: legendary weapons created in the first age of Midgaard. They can harm creatures of Nifleheim.
Axe of Bigby the Bold: made of Mithril; gifted

to Ob by Pipkorn
Barden's Bane (aka Hellfire Oil): highly concentrated acid; green, murky
Bellowing Banshee, The: one of the ships lost in the Fens
Book of the Nobility: treatise containing the traditional Lomerian laws with respect to the nobility.
Bloodlust, The: name for the affliction affecting people in The Hollow
Chapterhouse: base/manor/fortress of a knightly order
Dargus Dal: Asgardian dagger, previously Gabriel's, now Theta's
Dor: a generic Lomerian word meaning "fortress"
Dulcite: a precious gemstone
du Marnian Stone, The: a Seer Stone held by Azura du Marnian
Dyvers Blades: finely crafted steel swords
Dyvers Thraysk: a short wide sword.
Ether, The: invisible medium that exists everywhere and within which the weave of magic travels/exists.
Ghost Ship Box: calls forth an illusory ship; created by Pipkorn and gifted to Claradon.
Graban: a precious gemstone.
Granite Throne, The: the name of the king's throne in Lomion City. To "sit the granite throne" means to be the king.
Mages and Monsters: a popular, tactical war game that uses miniatures
Mithril: precious metal of great strength and relative lightness
Mjollnir: the legendary hammer of the god Thor

/ Donar.
Orb of Wisdom (aka Portalis Nifleleir): mystical crystal spheres that can be used to open portals between worlds.
Ragnarok: prophesied battle between the Aesir and the Nifleites.
Ranal: a black metal, hard as steel and half as heavy, weapons made of it can affect creatures of chaos
Raspen Brandy:
Rings of the Magi: amplify a wizard's power; twenty created by Talidousen
Seer Stones: magical "crystal balls" that can see far-off events.
Shards of Darkness: the remnants of the destroyed Orb of Wisdom from the Temple of Guymaog.
Spottle: a dice game that uses a live frog
Sventeran Stone, The: a Seer Stone loaned to the Malvegils by the Svarts.
Tribunal: the highest-ranking judiciary body in the Kingdom of Lomion; members of the tribunal are called "High Magisters."
Valusian steel: famed for its quality
Weave of Magic; aka the Magical Weave: the source of magic
Wintersfest: a winter holiday celebrated in Lomion.
Wizard's Toll: the burning that wizards suffer when they throw too much magic
Worfin Dal: "Lord's Dagger," Claradon's Asgardian dagger
Wotan Dal: "Odin's Dagger"; gifted to Theta by Pipkorn.
Yggdrasill: sacred tree that supports and/or

connects the Nine Worlds

Miscellany: Herbs, Medicines, Poisons, Food and Drinks
Arrowroot Leaf: chewable painkiller
Barsen's Reserve: a high quality brandy
Brombottle:
Cavindish Wine: a sweet white wine made in Lomion
Cottonrounds: chewable painkiller
Dwarven Rum:
Essence of Elmwood: can be used to preserve parchment
Essence of Nightshade: a lethal, fast-acting poison; carried by Black Hand agents as suicide pills to thwart capture.
Essence of Tarrow Root: powerful pain killer.
Gnome Mead:
Gnome Whiskey:
Mearn: comes in a jar
Oil of Adarisk: topical burn remedy; smells bad
Raspen Brandy:
Tinger Leaf:
Trackan Brandy:
Treant Leaf Resin: has curative properties, dulls odors when smeared on face.

Sigils and Standards
Standard of the Lomerian Guard: a white tower on a field of green. Soldiers wear red helmets and red and gray tabards with the standard embossed on at the center of their chests
Lomion Colors: red and gray
Myrdonian Knight Colors: emerald greed

armor and weapons

Languages of Midgaard
Lomerian: the common tongue of Lomion and much of the known world
Cleritus Mysterious: ancient mystic language of the priests of the Aesir
Magus Mysterious: olden language of sorcery
Militus Mysterious: olden language of sorcery used by certain orders of knights
Old Negish: an olden language, long dead
Old High Lomerian: an olden dialect of Lomerian
Old Tongue, The: a long-dead language from a previous Age.
Throng Baz: a dead language
Svartish (aka Svartlespeak in gnome): language of the svarts
Trollspeak: language of the mountain trolls

Ages of Midgaard
The Before Time
The Dawn Age: First Age
The Age of Myth and Legend: Second Age
The Age of Heroes: Third Age
– Places from the Age of Heroes: Lothmargen Plains; List; Tyre; Myrr; Dragoth Peaks; The Horn; Drogan Bay; Dingel; Malik-Morn (city of monsters)
– Peoples from the Age of Heroes: Miskelstrans from Dragoth Bay; Wild Men from The Horn
The Age of Enlightenment: Fourth Age

Combat Maneuvers, Techniques, and Styles
Dyvers' thrusting maneuvers
Dwarvish overhand strikes
Cernian technique
Sarnack maneuvers
Lengian cut and thrust style
Valusian thrust

Military Units of Lomion
Squad: a unit of soldiers typically composed of 3 to 8 soldiers, but it can be as few as 2 or as many as 15 soldiers.
Squadron: a unit of soldiers typically composed of two to four squads, totaling about 30 soldiers, including officers.
Cavalry Squadron or Troop: same as "squadron" but often has additional support troops to tend to the horses and supplies.
Company: a military unit composed of 4 squadrons, totaling about 120 - 150 soldiers. Mercenary Companies can be of any size, the word "company" in their title, notwithstanding.
Brigade: a military unit composed of 8 companies, totaling about 1,000 soldiers
Regiment: a military unit composed of 4 brigades, totaling about 4,000 — 5,000 soldiers
Corps or Army: a military unit composed of 4 regiments and support troops, totaling about 20,000 — 25,000 soldiers

Military Ranks of Lomion
(from junior to senior)
Trooper
Corporal
Sergeant

Lieutenant (a knight is considered equivalent in rank to a lieutenant)
Captain
Knight Captain (for units with Knights)
Commander
Knight Commander (for units with Knights)
Lord Commander (if a noble)
General (for Regiment sized units or larger)

ABOUT GLENN G. THATER

For more than twenty-five years, Glenn G. Thater has written works of fiction and historical fiction that focus on the genres of epic fantasy and sword and sorcery. His published works of fiction include the first ten volumes of the *Harbinger of Doom* saga: *Gateway to Nifleheim*; *The Fallen Angle*; *Knight Eternal*; *Dwellers of the Deep*; *Blood, Fire, and Thorn*; *Gods of the Sword*; *The Shambling Dead*; *Master of the Dead*; *Shadow of Doom*; *Wizard's Toll*; the novella, *The Gateway*; and the novelette, *The Hero and the Fiend*.

Mr. Thater holds a Bachelor of Science degree in Physics with concentrations in Astronomy and Religious Studies, and a Master of Science degree in Civil Engineering, specializing in Structural Engineering. He has undertaken advanced graduate study in Classical Physics, Quantum Mechanics, Statistical Mechanics, and Astrophysics, and is a practicing licensed professional engineer specializing in the multidisciplinary alteration and remediation of buildings, and the forensic investigation of building failures and other disasters.

Mr. Thater has investigated failures and collapses of numerous structures around the United States and internationally. Since 1998, he has been a member of the American Society of Civil Engineers' Forensic Engineering Division (FED), is a Past Chairman of that Division's Executive Committee and FED's Committee on Practices to Reduce Failures. Mr. Thater is a LEED (Leadership in Energy and Environmental Design) Accredited Professional and has testified as an expert witness in the field of structural engineering before the Supreme Court of the State of New York.

Mr. Thater is an author of numerous scientific papers, magazine articles, engineering textbook chapters, and countless engineering reports. He has lectured across the United States and internationally on such topics as the World Trade Center collapses, bridge collapses, and on the construction and analysis of the dome of the United States Capitol in Washington D.C.

CONNECT WITH GLENN G. THATER ONLINE

Glenn G. Thater's Website:
http://www.glenngthater.com

To be notified about new book releases and any special offers or discounts regarding Glenn's books, please join his mailing list here: http://eepurl.com/vwubH

BOOKS BY GLENN G. THATER

THE HARBINGER OF DOOM SAGA
GATEWAY TO NIFLEHEIM
THE FALLEN ANGLE
KNIGHT ETERNAL
DWELLERS OF THE DEEP
BLOOD, FIRE, AND THORN
GODS OF THE SWORD
THE SHAMBLING DEAD

MASTER OF THE DEAD
SHADOW OF DOOM
WIZARD'S TOLL
VOLUME 11+ *forthcoming*

THE HERO AND THE FIEND
(A novelette set in the Harbinger of Doom universe)

THE GATEWAY
(A novella length version of *Gateway to Nifleheim*)

HARBINGER OF DOOM
(Combines *Gateway to Nifleheim* and *The Fallen Angle* into a single volume)

THE DEMON KING OF BERGHER
(A short story set in the Harbinger of Doom universe)

Visit Glenn G. Thater's website at http://www.glenngthater.com for the most current list of my published books.

Printed in Great Britain
by Amazon